No Going Back

Lynda Page

headline

First published in 2004
by HEADLINE BOOK PUBLISHING

First published in paperback in 2005
by HEADLINE BOOK PUBLISHING

10 9 8 7 6 5 4 3 2

ISBN 978 0 7553 0879 4

Typeset in Times New Roman by
Letterpart Limited, Reigate, Surrey

Printed and bound in Great Britain by
Clays Ltd, St Ives plc

Headline's policy is to use papers that are natural, renewable and
recyclable products and made from wood grown in sustainable forests.
The logging and manufacturing processes are expected to conform
to the environmental regulations of the country of origin.

HEADLINE BOOK PUBLISHING
A division of Hodder Headline
338 Euston Road
London NW1 3BH

www.headline.co.uk
www.hodderheadline.com

Lynda Page was born and brought up in Leicester. The eldest of four daughters, she left home at seventeen and has had a wide variety of office jobs. She lives in a village near Leicester. Her previous novels are also available from Headline, and have been highly praised:

'You'll be hooked from page one'   *Woman's Realm*

'Cookson/Cox aficionados who've missed her should grab this. Romantic and gripping'
                                        Peterborough Evening Telegraph

'Filled with lively characters and compelling action'
                                        Books

'As always with Page, the text is rich in Leicester dialogue, there's a wealth of well-drawn characters and a happy ending'   *Leicester Mercury*

'A nostalgic background for its mix of colourful characters fronted by the delightfully strong leading lady'
                                        Lincolnshire Echo

'An enjoyable read with lots going on to keep you hooked until the very end'   *Wiltshire Times*

For all abandoned children and
the army of special people who
care for them and show them love.

Chapter One

'You're sacking me!'

Judith Chambers looked sternly at the young woman before her whose pretty face was twisted into an expression of utter astonishment. 'You're well aware of the company rules, Mrs Campbell. You're paid to work from eight-thirty to five-thirty. Apart from your lunch hour, when you can do as you wish, you're expected to stay at your desk, not leave it to rush out of the building whenever you feel like it without asking permission. And even then the situation would have to be a matter of life or death before it was granted.'

'But it was life or death,' Cherry Campbell insisted. 'I got an urgent message that me son had had an accident in the playground at school and needed hospital treatment. I didn't know how bad it was. In fact he'd badly cut his leg, Miss Chambers, needed several stitches. He was ever so upset, poor little soul.'

'Hardly a life or death situation. Surely your nanny was capable of dealing with it?'

'Eh! Nanny?'

'Nanny . . . child-minder . . . whatever you call the

1

person who looks after your children while you're supposed to be working.'

Cherry stared at her, gob-smacked. Was her boss mad? Nanny indeed. Her children, bless their hearts, looked after themselves out of school hours. Though she herself didn't like it she had no other choice, kept busy as she was earning them their scant living which barely included rent and basic necessities, let alone child-minding costs. 'Latch-key kids' her children were labelled, same as thousands of others around Leicester and the Shires whose parents couldn't afford the couple of pounds a week it would cost for someone to look out for their offspring after school or during holidays until their parents arrived home.

Had Judith Chambers any idea what it was like for people like herself, fighting to juggle their time between their families and their work, especially a single-parent family like Cherry's? Her kids no longer had a father because her beloved husband Brian had been killed in an accident on the building site where he had worked long hours to provide for them, the accident more than likely caused because he had been exhausted from the 'foreigners' he undertook on top of his normal working hours, to top up his wage and provide little extras for his family such as a coach trip to the seaside.

Could Judith Chambers imagine how it felt to crawl into bed at night worn out from hard work, even at weekends, after trying to catch up with all she hadn't had time for? Judging by the look on her boss's face, her whole demeanour for that matter, Cherry doubted that the formidable Judith Chambers had a clue how Cherry and her like managed to cope. But then, why would she? She'd obviously been brought up and still lived in a world of accommodating nannies and housekeepers.

But to Cherry the way her boss lived was not of paramount importance at this moment; keeping a roof over her children's heads and food in their bellies was. In truth she hated working at Chambers' and knew that with her skills as a typist she could get another job relatively easily. But it wouldn't be so close to home, and she got on so well with the rest of the workers, several of the other women having become close friends of hers. She didn't like the thought of having to start afresh at another place, not when she was just beginning to find her feet after Brian's traumatic death.

Taking a deep breath, she wrung her hands tightly and implored: 'Please, Miss Chambers, I promise it won't happen again. In the year I've worked for yer, yer've never had cause to complain about me work or conduct before. So please, can't you overlook this?'

Judith walked around her desk, sat down sedately on the well-worn office chair and crossed her shapely legs. She raised her head and stared coolly at Cherry's desperate expression. Judith's personal feelings didn't come into this. Cherry Campbell could beg and plead for her job until she was blue in the face, it wouldn't make an iota of difference. The decision to fire her was not Judith's. Unfortunately for Cherry, Judith's father had noticed her absence and told his daughter in no uncertain terms to deal with it, reporting back to him when she had. He had also harshly berated her for her own lapse in not noticing for herself that one of the staff was absent without permission.

As owner of the firm, Charles Chambers never passed up an opportunity to remind his workforce, including his own daughter, of how he liked his company run. He had set down a strict code of conduct on starting the business forty-four years ago and wouldn't allow the slightest deviation from it. It was his firm opinion that leniency shown to any employee set a dangerous precedent for the rest. It was hopeless trying to change his mind, and fully aware of his uncompromising attitude Judith hadn't put herself in the firing line.

'Your employment with Chambers Leather Goods will be terminated as of Friday evening, Mrs Campbell. Now, if you'll excuse me, I have work to do and so do you.'

'What happened then?' Fay Cross demanded of Cherry when she arrived back at her desk in the general office. 'Give yer a bollocking, did she, for rushing out without asking?'

'A bit more than that, Fay. She sacked me,' Cherry muttered, fighting hard to stem a flood of tears. 'I finish on Friday.'

Never normally lost for words, Fay's mouth hung open in shock.

'She bleddy sacked yer?' Nadine Hands exclaimed loudly from her desk behind them. She turned to face the rest of the six women who made up the general office staff. 'Did yer hear that, gels? That hard-faced cow has sacked Cherry for going with her boy to the hospital. Good Lord, what was yer supposed ter do? Wait until finishing time then go to the hospital to see if he was alive or dead?'

Cherry gave a hollow laugh. 'She said my nanny should have dealt with it. Nanny? Can yer credit it, and me hardly able to afford to buy new shoes for me kids. How does she expect me to employ a nanny? She knows very well what I get paid. I tell yer, gels, our so-called betters wouldn't have a clue how to manage on the paltry pittance they pay us, just expect us ter feel honoured they allow us to work for them.'

The clack of Imperial 66 typewriters came to a sudden halt; the telephonist operating the small plug board flicked a switch to mute her voice over the wires; the office junior stopped licking stamps for the post. A sea of faces stared at Cherry in sympathy and shock.

'We could walk out in support,' Doreen the telephonist suggested.

Cherry shook her head. 'I appreciate the offer, Doreen, but you all need yer jobs as much as I do. Old man Chambers would sack you all without a by your leave, you know he would.'

They all looked at her silently, acknowledging she spoke the truth.

'Well, all I can say is, I hope one of these days that miserable old bugger gets what he's got coming to him – and his daughter an' all 'cos she's just as bad,' Nadine mumbled disgustedly as she whipped off an invoice form from a pad of blanks and proceeded to insert several sheets of carbon paper between the copies. 'Working here is like working for the Gestapo. Yer can't go to the lavvy out of break-time without getting the third degree. I'd like to see what Icy Lil woulda done if she'd have got a message saying one of *her* kids had been rushed off to Casualty.'

5

'Well, that ain't very likely to happen as she ain't got any, has she?' Doreen piped up. 'She ain't married. She's a dried-up old spinster still living at home with her mam and dad. At her age still living with her folks is unnatural, if yer ask me.'

'And is anyone surprised she ain't married?' Nadine snapped back. 'Okay, no one can deny it – she ain't a bad-looking woman. Got a good figure for her age, which I'm envious of I don't mind telling yer, and let's face it she's gotta be forty if she's a day. But she'd frighten any man to death with her cold ways. My old man calls her type Frigid Fridges. Says he wouldn't swap my lumps and bumps keeping him warm in bed for a shapely looker like her that he'd be terrified to touch in case she turned him to stone with one of her glares.' She laughed harshly. "Cos that's what she needs, in my opinion. The likes of a good man to warm her up a bit.' Her voice trailed off and her face screwed up in thought. 'Unless . . .'

They all looked at her expectantly.

'Unless what?' Jill the office junior eagerly asked.

Nadine pursed her lips meaningfully. 'She's . . . well, yer know . . . *queer.*'

Before anyone could respond they all froze as they heard the clack-clack of high heels approaching down the corridor. Next moment the subject of their discussion was standing before them, her face carefully bland.

'Are the invoices for Maynard's ready for my inspection?'

Nadine grabbed a pile from her desk and held them out. 'Yes, Miss Chambers. I was just about to bring 'em through.'

Judith took them and said briskly, 'I hope they're all correct. They need posting tonight and we haven't time to redo them. I don't need to remind you that Mr Chambers will not allow any paperwork to leave the premises that is anything less than perfect.' She then glanced around at them all, arching one dark eyebrow, and asked, 'Is there a good reason why work in this office seems to have come to a halt?'

They all jolted back into action. 'No, Miss,' they muttered.

Back in her office Judith shut the door behind her and slowly made her way around her desk to sit down. Still clutching the batch of invoices, she gave a deep sigh. She was well aware that the workforce didn't like her. They saw her as a hard woman who ruled them all with a rod of iron, demanding perfection in everything they produced – and how could she blame them for seeing her that way? That was exactly how she had to be because she was their boss.

But that overheard description 'queer' reverberated in Judith's mind. As well as everything else, was that how she was viewed? An object of sexual conjecture because she was not married? Did they not stop to think that her spinster status might be of her own choosing? For whatever reason might she not simply have decided to remain unattached? As things stood some dismissed her as a dried-up old spinster, and without a shred of evidence to back up their claim a queer one at that. She gave another deep sigh and shook her head, feeling an overwhelming urge to go and put them all right. A dictat of her father's prevented her. *We are not here to make friends. Our*

7

personal lives are nothing to do with anyone but ourselves. Keep yourself to yourself. Having long ago realised that to question his words was not worth the dire consequences she chose to adhere to them, and was so used to abiding by them now they had become her way of life.

She suddenly realised that time was wearing on and he would be waiting for her to present herself in his office along with the daily paperwork that required his signature before it could be posted. Arriving even a second past the appointed time was to risk incurring grave displeasure. Glancing at the clock on her office wall, it concerned Judith to note that she risked being late if she proof-read the invoices that Nadine had just given her. She had no choice but to hope that the woman had done her job properly and there were no mistakes or it would be Judith herself who took the blame.

Rising, she smoothed down the straight knee-length skirt of her smart blue suit, straightened the collar of her crisp white blouse, ran a comb hurriedly through her thick dark hair. At forty-three she still showed no signs as yet of greying, she was pleased to note. She hastily wiped a small scuff from her two-inch-heeled black patent leather court shoes then, satisfied her appearance was immaculate, picked up the leather-bound folder containing the paperwork for her father's scrutiny and made her way up to his inner sanctum, situated on the top floor of their three-storey Victorian red-brick premises on Braunstone Gate in the West End of Leicester.

Charles Chambers' prim secretary, Maude Greengate, a middle-aged matron unflatteringly dressed in a brown tweed box-pleated suit and matching twinset, heavy legs swathed in thick beige stockings, sparse pepper-and-salt hair cut in a severe bob, momentarily looked up from the letter she was typing and greeted her boss's daughter with a brisk, 'Good afternoon, Miss Chambers. Mr Chambers is busy on the telephone at present. If you'd care to take a seat he will buzz me when he's ready to receive you.' She resumed her task.

Judith sat down on a hard-backed chair by the door. Whether or not her father was occupied on the telephone was questionable. He was good at this, keeping inferiors waiting, his own daughter being no exception. She knew he did it to remind them of their subservience. It made him feel powerful. Well, let him do as he wished. She was used to it.

While she waited Judith glanced around the room. In contrast to the lower levels of the building where the main operations of the company were conducted, which were austere to say the least, the top floor where prospective buyers for Chambers' range of leatherwares were received was positively plush. It was accessed by a lift just inside the entrance doors in the small reception area on the ground floor. Up here thick red carpet covered the floor; heavy red and beige flock wallpaper lined the walls, and the furniture was of good solid wood, unlike the rickety things she and the rest of the office staff used. The well-worn work benches the three men who managed the receiving, packing and despatching of goods had to make do with were the original fixtures installed when the company was first opened.

Highly polished double doors at the back of the top-floor reception room, at this moment closed, led through

9

to a large showroom. Here there were sumptuous displays of the latest goods Chambers' was offering. Entertained with cups of coffee or tea, buyers from shops and stores in Leicester and the Shires would browse then hopefully place substantial orders. Chambers' offered top-quality handmade leather handbags, luggage, a range of professional briefcases and doctor's bags, gloves and belts, all aimed at the higher end of the market. Since the end of the war – a period which had seen the company struggle to survive due to shortages of both leather and staff – some of their goods were now imported from Europe, mainly Italy, due to enhanced customer demand for high-fashion goods.

From what Judith could deduce from the orders she saw placed in the general office, Chambers' was now doing well. Her father kept the financial side of the business very much to himself but there seemed to be the funds to pay the workforce and keep the members of the Chambers family themselves: Judith, Charles, and his wife, Winifred, who all resided in a detached, double-bayed, three-storey Victorian house in Clarendon Park, an affluent area on the outskirts of the city, with a live-in housekeeper to care for the three of them.

Judith had worked for the family business since leaving Wiggiston Girls' School at the age of fifteen. Although a pretty child, she had been a painfully shy and withdrawn adolescent, finding it very difficult to make friends. This was made worse by the fact that she was never given any encouragement by her parents to do so, and consequently her childhood was a solitary one. She spent endless hours alone reading books she had taken out of the library, losing herself in the pages of authors such as Dickens, Stevenson and Defoe. As the time to leave school approached she saw her ideal future as working in a library cocooned amongst the precious literary works that had become her substitute friends, an environment that would suit admirably her reserved character. But her parents, particularly her father, wouldn't entertain the idea and gave her no choice but to join the family firm, starting as the office junior to work her way slowly up through the ranks, any dreams of her own she'd harboured quashed out of hand.

Despite her status as daughter of the owner she was given no extra privileges, her father insisting her treatment be exactly that of all the other staff. While he drove to work and back home in his Daimler, she caught the bus. That continued to this day. Apart from a brief period of several months in her early twenties, her service at Chambers' was unbroken and her climb to her present position of office manager a long time coming. For her labours she was paid a small sum a week, barely enough to keep her in clothes and personal items, and she'd had no choice but to accept this arrangement, assuming that when her father retired she would take over the running of the business which was when she would receive her just rewards.

Her idle glance around the room brought her back to Miss Greengate, still tapping away on her typewriter, plain face wreathed in concentration as she read back her own shorthand. It suddenly struck Judith that Maude Greengate was a spinster. Were the women downstairs as unkind in their description of Maude as they were about

Judith? As she scrutinised her father's secretary it suddenly occurred to Judith that she knew nothing personal at all about this woman who had worked for her father for over thirty years. In fact, she knew nothing personal about any of the other staff either. Her father strongly disapproved of friendships between management and staff; of office parties at Christmas or company outings of any description. His opinion was that the workplace was a place to do just that, not socialise, and he had severely warned his daughter that should he catch her discussing anything other than business with any of his employees, she would be demoted to a position that precluded any such contact.

The loud buzz of the intercom made Judith jump. It wasn't a gentle alerting buzz but a short commanding one. Without pausing in her task, Maude Greengate briskly announced, 'You may go through now, Miss Chambers.'

As she rose she felt the nervousness that was always present when she was in her father's company, whether at work or at home. He was not a man to mince his words and used each one sparingly, as if he was paying for them and therefore trying to save himself money. Her daily visit to his office was the part of the day she dreaded most. Charles Chambers never lost the slightest opportunity to fault her work and she worried that he would find something wrong with the invoices she hadn't had time to check.

He appeared to be engrossed in studying a document when his daughter entered and it was several moments before he condescended to lift his head and acknowledge her presence. He was a wiry, pale-skinned, sharp-featured man, dressed very expensively in a dark grey handmade suit. The high-backed leather chair in which he sat seemed to diminish his small stature to even less than its actual five foot six. 'What have you to report?' His tone was curt. He held out one bony hand and flapped it at her irritatedly.

Judith realised this action was by way of a demand for her to pass over the folder containing the papers for his signature, which she was clutching tightly to her chest as if afraid to part from it. She hurriedly thrust it towards him, holding her breath, closely watching his every move as he opened the file and began to sift first through the invoices, proceeding on through the pile of general correspondence. Her anxiety eased slightly as he signed off the last of the invoices and began on the letters. So far so good, she thought. But her reprieve was short-lived. Pen poised to sign the last letter, he paused, issuing a loud disapproving grunt before scoring a huge cross covering the length and breadth of the letter and sending it skimming across the desk towards her.

'Do you check these?' he barked, annoyance glinting in his eyes.

'Yes, of course I do, Mr Chambers.' Judith was forbidden to address him as Father during working hours. Her brow creased worriedly. She had thoroughly checked those letters and found nothing amiss. She couldn't for the life of her think what her father's keen eye had spotted.

'Pull yourself up, girl. You're allowing standards to slip and you know I won't tolerate shoddy workmanship. The

13

top of the letter "s" is missing from "sincerely".'

She picked up the letter and looked at it. The missing end of the curve at the top of the 's' was so minute it was barely noticeable. 'It's the keys of the typewriter that are at fault. On rare occasions they don't hit the ribbon squarely. The machines are so old . . .'

'A typewriter is a tool and therefore its operator is responsible,' he cut in sharply. 'I want that letter in the post tonight. You do it personally, and make sure you reprimand the typist responsible for such slipshod work.'

She felt his criticism to be totally unwarranted but nothing unusual, and as he hadn't found the slightest error in anything that had come from the general office for the last few days she should have expected he'd find something today. This was just another ploy of his to remind her and everyone else who was boss.

Slapping the leather binder shut, he pushed it across the desk towards her then clasped his hands on the desk. 'I trust you dealt with *the problem* satisfactorily?'

She knew instantly to what he was referring. 'Mrs Campbell leaves on Friday.' She wanted to say that she personally felt they were being harsh in their punishment of Cherry Campbell. After all, the reason for her sudden departure from the premises, albeit without permission and against company rules, was a valid and understandable one. But should she voice this opinion her father would only slap her down for showing personal sympathy for an employee. He'd accuse her of becoming fond of them when in order to do her job properly she should keep herself detached.

He glared at her, astounded. 'Friday! You should have

14

given her instant dismissal.' He paused and looked at her questioningly. 'Not showing sympathy towards the workers, are you? How many times do I need to tell you that sentimentality does not keep a business successful? The workforce are paid to carry out their set duties to my set of rules unquestioningly, and if they don't do that then they can go, make room for someone who will.'

Judith took a deep breath. In an even tone she said, 'Cherry Campbell is our best typist and she'll be hard to replace. We need time to find someone as suitable, so I . . .'

'Nonsense,' he snapped, cutting her short. 'Typists like her are two a penny. Plenty more where she came from. Get on to it immediately.' He eyed Judith meaningfully. 'I'll remind you that office managers are too. Your privileged position within this company is at my discretion. I can demote you at any time if I don't feel you are up to scratch. There's only one irreplaceable person in this company and that's me – and don't you forget it. I built this company from nothing and I'll never let anything or anyone jeopardise its success. Have I made that fact plain enough for you?'

She held his gaze. 'Yes, Mr Chambers.'

'Good. Now you can go.'

Taking a deep breath, she turned and walked out thankfully.

Chapter Two

Winifred Chambers eyed her daughter reproachfully as she entered the dining room that evening and sat down at the table. 'I shouldn't need to remind you that dinner is at eight sharp. I don't appreciate being kept waiting.' She turned and flashed a look at the woman standing patiently by the door that led into the kitchen. 'You may proceed, Miss Betts.'

The fact that Judith was barely thirty seconds past the appointed hour could hardly be classed as late. It was more than likely because the clock in her bedroom was out of sync with the imposing grandfather model standing in the hallway, but no excuse she offered would absolve her so Judith declined to try. She watched silently as Ida Betts their housekeeper placed a dish of potatoes sprinkled with parsley and another containing roast parsnips and boiled carrots beside the salver of sliced lamb on the highly polished mahogany dining table. Judith waited patiently while her father then her mother helped themselves before she filled her own plate.

This meal, the same as any other that was eaten in the Chambers household, was conducted in virtual silence. In fact conversation in general was rare except for customary greetings. Her parents showed no interest in Judith's personal life and discussed none of theirs in front of her; she assumed they were waiting for an occasion when she wasn't around which was often enough. She spent most of her spare time in her room either reading or listening to the radio. After dinner her parents routinely retired to the lounge. While her father read his newspaper, her mother occupied herself with her needlepoint. They sat opposite one another in comfortable armchairs on either side of the fireplace, listening to their own radio. Judith was never invited to join them.

Apart from tradesmen, there were no visitors to the house, they never entertained, and as far as Judith was aware her parents appeared to possess no friends between them. She had long ago concluded that they mutually fulfilled their own needs, not requiring the companionship of others. As for relatives – as a child Judith was bluntly informed they were all dead, Winifred refusing to speak of them, telling her daughter that there was no point in her knowing about people who were no longer alive to affect her life.

Judith neither liked nor disliked her parents. In truth she knew so little about them personally she could hardly make such a judgement. She always felt anxious when in their company, constantly waiting for a look, sign or verbal comment that she had done or said something they didn't approve of, and strove hard to keep her own counsel so as not to incur their displeasure. Indeed most of the time she felt like an intruder instead of part of the family. Judith could never remember receiving so much as a hug from either of them, but then neither did they show any affection towards each other that she had ever witnessed and she had long ago accepted that this was just the way they were.

As she laid down her knife and fork on her now empty plate, she glanced at her parents from under her lashes. She couldn't blame the women in the general office for thinking her odd because she still lived with them. But what they couldn't know was that she had moved out once.

She jumped as she realised her mother was addressing her.

'Judith, Miss Betts has asked twice if you require pudding?'

'Oh, I'm sorry. Just a little, please.'

As usual as soon as her father stood up, signalling that the meal was over, Judith escaped to the sanctuary of her bedroom.

Having washed and dressed herself more comfortably in her nightdress and dressing gown, she switched on the radio and settled back in her chair by the window to listen to a story before she retired to bed. Tonight it centred around a Jewish mother in search of the child she had been parted from during the war. As the heart-wrenching tale unfolded, despite fighting as hard as she could, Judith could not stop her thoughts drifting back to a time in her own past when she herself had lost a child . . .

Her eyes drooped shut and a vision of her child's father flashed before her as vividly as the first time she had ever clapped eyes on him, smiling charmingly at her across the reception counter. He had been incredibly handsome, so smart in his suit and crisp white shirt and several years older than herself. As her eyes met his she almost lost her breath. She had been nineteen at the time and inexperienced in all matters to do with the opposite sex, the scant information she had gleaned drawn from her books and from a very short and uncomfortable interview with her mother when she had reached puberty.

'So what's a pretty girl like you doing hiding in a place like this when you should be on display to the world, modelling clothes or acting in films?'

Judith had turned the colour of beetroot at his flirtatiousness and he had grinned at her obvious discomfiture. Handing her his business card, he announced, 'Clive Lewis. I've an appointment with Charles Chambers to view the new stock you have in.'

With great difficulty she had found her voice and was mortally embarrassed when it came out sounding like a high-pitched squeak. 'If you'd like to sign in then go up in the lift to the top floor, I'll inform Mr Chambers' secretary that you're on your way.'

After signing the book he made his way over to the lift but not before giving her a long lingering look, and once inside the lift he kept his eyes fixed on her as he pulled the doors shut in front of him.

She sat transfixed for an age, staring at the closed lift doors. No man had ever looked at her like that before and his attentions had awoken strange feelings within her. Her skin had prickled all over, she had felt giddy, and for a moment she had wondered what it would feel like for him to sweep her into her arms and kiss her, like all the dark handsome men did to the heroines in the romantic stories she read. Then she realised she was being silly. Such a handsome man, so much older than herself, would never look at a young girl like her in any other way but a friendly one. That was it, Clive Lewis was just being friendly.

It was over an hour later that she heard the lift descending and presently the doors opened. Clive Lewis walked out and came straight over to her. He leaned on the counter, staring intently at her. 'So what does a pretty girl like you do with herself on an evening?'

She stared back at him tongue-tied, very conscious of his deep brown eyes boring into her, sending waves of shivers down her spine. It was very apparent he wasn't going anywhere until she had answered him. Swallowing hard, she falteringly replied, 'Er . . . well . . . nothing much. Read my books or listen to the radio.'

'Oh, come, come,' he said, still looking at her intently. 'Surely you can think of more interesting things to do? Like meeting me this evening for a drink?'

She gawped at him. 'A drink? Oh! I . . . but I don't drink.'

'You don't? Well, you have to start sometime. All right, what about a walk in the park?' His voice was soft, persuasive, and he was looking at her so closely. 'Just a walk and a talk. No harm in that, is there?'

A walk in the park? It sounded so romantic. She couldn't believe he was actually asking her to spend time with him. Before she knew what she was saying she had agreed to meet him at the entrance to Victoria Park at eight-thirty that night.

She had been extremely anxious during dinner that evening, worried she wouldn't be able to converse with him, or she'd not be suitably dressed, or his invitation had simply been a joke and he wouldn't be there. But regardless she knew she had to go, some invisible force pushing her on. Slipping out had been easy. She told her parents the truth, that she was going out for a walk, and neither of them showed the slightest interest.

He was waiting for her when she arrived and any nervousness Judith was feeling was quickly dispelled at the obvious delight in his eyes and the way he took hold of her arm and hooked it through his. It was immediately apparent to Judith that he was glad she had come.

Silently they strolled through the entrance to the park together and down a long winding path. Presently they arrived by a small clearing in the trees and shrubs. He pulled Judith into the clearing and took her in his arms. 'Well, here we are,' he whispered as he began kissing her neck. Before she realised what was happening, he had lowered her to the ground and was on top of her, lifting up her dress and pulling down her knickers.

Her mind raced frantically. Despite her limited knowledge she knew this was not right, that he should not be touching her in this way. She opened her mouth and shrieked: 'No . . .'

He clamped one hand over her mouth and next she felt a sharp pain as he pushed something hard inside her. He was pumping up and down frantically against her, his breath coming fast then released in a guttural groan. He lay still, then moments later jumped up from her and was straightening his clothes.

He looked down at her, smiled briefly, and jauntily strode off down the path.

She lay frozen in shock, her thoughts racing wildly. Clive Lewis had violated her, she wasn't so naïve as not to know that. It had all happened too quickly for her to try and stop him. She had believed he wanted to walk and talk with her when all he'd wanted her for was a quick release of his lust. He'd said hardly a word to her, hadn't even asked her name. But had she encouraged him somehow, given him the impression she had been willing for him to do that to her? Had her agreeing to take a walk given him the go ahead? Regardless she felt so dirty, so humiliated. The tears came then, great choking sobs racking her body.

She suddenly became aware of the predicament she was in. For anyone to discover her like this didn't bear thinking about. No one must find out about this, not ever. Snatching up her knickers, she pulled them hurriedly back on, rose awkwardly and rushed home as fast as she could, her head hanging down.

Her parents were closeted in the lounge when she slipped in at the front door. She went straight upstairs and ran herself a bath, scrubbing every inch of herself red raw. Over the next few days, if anyone did happen to notice that she was even more quiet than normal then they never commented. No one took much notice of her anyway and for once she was glad of it.

Memories of that awful night plagued her thoughts for weeks until gradually they began to fade. She worked hard to lock them away in the back of her mind, forcing herself to believe it had never happened. One cruel lesson she had learned was that she would never wittingly put herself in a position like that again. If a man did ask her out and she felt it safe to accept, she would make sure they went to a very public place until she was absolutely sure about being alone with him.

She'd felt funny for a while after that, nothing she could put her finger on just not her usual self. She was putting on a little weight too. She couldn't understand why as she wasn't eating any more than she usually did. It was one of the girls at work who alerted her to what was going on inside her.

She was in the toilet washing her hands when Mavis Dobbs had come in. Judith didn't like Mavis Dobbs. She was cocksure and cheeky and had taken umbrage against Judith when she learned about her relationship to the owner of the company. She passed snide comments whenever she got the opportunity. She'd been in Chambers' employ for just over a fortnight as a clerical assistant and was terrible at her job. Judith knew it wouldn't be much longer before she was given the sack, and she herself would be at the top of the list of those glad to see the back of Mavis.

The girl glanced the boss's daughter up and down scathingly as she entered. 'Oh, daddy's little girl getting a fat belly?' she had sneered mockingly. 'If I didn't know better I'd 'a' said you'd a bun in the oven . . . yer know, pregnant. But then, what man's gonna want to stick his privates into a little mouse like you? It must be all that posh food you eat. I'd cut down if I was you before you burst.'

Laughing loudly, she had disappeared into one of the cubicles.

Judith looked down at her own stomach, ran her hands

24

over it and felt the mound that was forming. Her face paled in alarm as the significance of it dawned on her. Pregnant meant you were expecting a baby . . . No, she couldn't be! She had read in her books that men and women got married and that night they got into bed together. Babies followed but how they were made remained a mystery to her. Was what Clive had done to her how babies were made? Oh, God, no, no! She'd read in her books of fallen women who had been shunned by their family, thrown out on the street with nowhere to go. Oh, God, if she was pregnant then she had no doubt that was what her own parents would do to her. But she couldn't be, she'd had her period. Admittedly the last couple had been very light and neither had lasted as long as usual, but she'd had them all the same. She couldn't be pregnant. She must be eating too much.

For the next couple of weeks she hardly ate anything but she lost no weight. In fact, she seemed to be getting bigger. She could hardly button her skirts now. Then her worst fears were confirmed. Her next period failed to appear. She was out of her mind with worry by now and how she managed to present to the world her usual staid exterior was a mystery to her. She knew she had no choice about what to do. She had to find Clive and tell him her news. He was bound to be shocked at first but she felt sure he'd do right by her and their baby, as any honourable man would. Then a problem struck her. She couldn't remember where he worked and if she asked questions about him at Chambers' then questions would be asked of her as to why she wanted to know. Then she remembered. He had given her his business card. Had she still got it?

Frantically she searched through the items on the shelf under the reception counter and couldn't believe her luck when she found his card under the pile of old signing-in books where it must have slipped. Clive's business card stated he worked as chief buyer for the leather goods department of Lewis's department store.

That night after her parents had retired to bed and she was positive Miss Betts had too, Judith packed her case and slipped out of the house. She had tried numerous times to write them a letter of explanation for her sudden departure but just could not find the right words. Eventually she had given up, convincing herself that it would be better to tell them face to face once Clive was by her side, supporting her. She spent the rest of the night, frightened and extremely cold, huddled on a park bench and come morning knew she looked a dreadful sight. Nine o'clock found her wandering around the leather goods department in search of Clive. She wasn't looking forward to their meeting but felt positive that by tonight she would be with him and together they would be planning a future for themselves and their expected baby.

A middle-aged assistant, looking at her suspiciously, came across. 'Can I help you, Miss?' she asked tartly, glancing Judith up and down critically.

She gulped. 'I . . . er . . . I'm looking for Clive Lewis.'

'And what would you want with Mr Lewis?'

'That's my business,' Judith replied. 'Would you please fetch him?'

'Huh,' the woman grunted. 'And who shall I say wants him?'

'Judith Chambers.'

'Wait there. I'll see if he's available.'

She disappeared through a door at the back of the department and it was a while before she returned. 'He doesn't know a Judith Chambers.'

Oh, of course, she thought, he wouldn't know her by name. 'I can assure you he does know me. It's urgent I speak to him so please can you fetch him?'

The woman flashed her a look of disdain before she strode off towards the door again. It was several minutes before Judith saw Clive emerge. He looked around, spotted her and came over.

He stared at her blankly. 'I'm very busy, what is it you want?'

She stared back at him, horrified. He didn't know her! 'You don't remember me, do you?' she uttered, deeply distressed.

He gave a nonchalant shrug. 'Should I?'

'After what you did to me, yes, you should. You took advantage of me and now I'm pregnant with your child.'

He stared at her for a moment, stunned, then his face darkened thunderously. Grabbing her arm, he pulled her across to a pile of suitcases so they were hidden from view from the shop assistants' counter where several people were gathered, watching the proceedings with great interest.

Clive pushed his face close to hers. His voice low and menacing, he said, 'Now listen here, you little tart, I never touched you! It's your word against mine and you can't prove anything.' He flashed a scathing look at her stomach before bringing up his eyes to bore into hers. 'That bastard could be anyone's. No use trying to pin it on me.'

He noticed her suitcase, a thought occurred to him and he smirked at her knowingly. 'Oh, I see, you thought as my name was Lewis I must be connected to the family who owns this store. I'd take you home to mummy and daddy and we'd all live in a huge great house in luxury. Well, I'm not related to the Lewises who own this store, I only work here, so your little scheme to grab yourself a comfortable future was a waste of time.'

She felt sick. She hadn't known what to expect of Clive when she broke her news but she hadn't for a moment anticipated anything like this. She wanted to turn and run from him, get away from his sneering face, but she couldn't. It was his fault that she was in this terrible position and he had a duty to help her. She took several deep breaths and said with conviction, 'This baby I am carrying is yours. You talked me into going for a walk with you and then you did what you did to me. It's your moral duty to help me.'

'Morals?' He looked at her scathingly. 'You've got a nerve saying I've a moral duty when you've obviously got none – landing yourself in the situation you're in. Now get out of here before I have you thrown out!' He thrust his hand into the small of her back and pushed her forcefully in the direction of the stairway, then picked up her case and slid it across the floor towards her. 'Go on, I said. Skedaddle – and take your bastard with you.'

Dazed, she looked back at him and heard him say loudly to the assistant who had first approached her, 'That woman is making a nuisance of herself. I've never seen her before in my life. If she doesn't leave voluntarily, have her removed forcibly.'

28

They were all looking at her. Judith stared back at them mortified as a wave of utter desolation swept over her. She saw the middle-aged assistant make to approach her. Hurriedly she grabbed up her case, dashed across to the stairs and down them, dodging through customers and out into the street where she didn't stop until she had reached the Town Hall Square.

Sweating profusely and gasping for breath, she sank down on to a bench where her whole body started to shake in sheer terror of her dire predicament. She had no idea what to do. She couldn't bear to go home just for her parents to throw her out; had no other family or friends to turn to for help or advice. She had never felt so alone in all her life. She might as well kill herself.

Tears of wretchedness slid down her face and she began to sob hysterically.

She felt a hand on her arm. 'You all right, lovey?'

She lifted her head and through tear-blurred eyes looked up into the face of a policeman.

'I'm fine, thank you.'

'And I'd have to be blind to see that you're not. Want to tell me and I might be able to help you?'

'No one can help me,' she sobbed.

The seasoned policeman noticed her suitcase and looked at her thoughtfully. He'd seen girls this distressed before and the cause was all down to the same thing. 'Let me guess. You're pregnant, boyfriend dumped you and your family have disowned you?'

His assumption wasn't quite true but she knew that if she went home she would be disowned.

'Yes,' she agreed.

'You must have a relative who will help you?'

'I've no one.'

He took her arm. 'Come with me,' he urged.

'Where to?' she asked warily.

'A place that helps girls in your situation.'

At the bottom of a long winding drive, the four-storey house loomed menacingly. High brick walls edged the garden's boundary. As the policeman guided her through the entrance gates, Judith felt as if she was entering a prison.

She stopped short and looked at him questioningly. 'What is this place?'

'Somewhere where you'll be looked after while you have your baby. You'll be safe here. It's run by a charitable organisation which was specifically set up to help girls like you.'

His face was kindly so she trusted his word. She had to, there was no other choice.

They were met at the door by a tall severe-faced woman in her early thirties, dressed very dourly in black.

'Constable Main, how nice to see you. Brought us another, have you?'

'Found her in the Town Hall Square.'

She took Judith's case. 'Leave her to us now.'

He placed his hand on Judith's arm. 'Best of luck,' he said sincerely.

'Thank you,' she faltered.

The woman led Judith into a large entrance hall and on into a room which was furnished like an office. She indicated a chair before a desk and told Judith to sit down. Searching through a drawer, she pulled out a printed form and looked hard at Judith, who quivered under her scrutiny.

'I'm Miss Brewster. The rest of the staff will introduce themselves as and when you meet them. Consider yourself very lucky, young lady, that we have a vacancy. Name?'

'Judith Chambers,' she whispered tremulously.

'I can't hear you?'

'Judith Chambers,' she repeated more loudly.

'Address?'

She couldn't give out her address for fear they would report her to her parents. 'I haven't got one,' she replied.

'You must have lived somewhere at some time? If you're concerned we will alert your family to where you are, don't be. What is the point as you wouldn't be here if you were welcome at home. We just need it for our records.'

She gave her address.

Tutting disdainfully, Miss Brewster shook her head. 'I'd have thought, coming from such an address, you'd have had more sense than to land up like you are. But when it boils down to it you're all the same, wherever you come from. A man shows some interest and you give him your all without a thought for the consequences. Date of birth?'

She gave it.

'When's the baby due?'

Judith looked at Miss Brewster helplessly. 'I don't know.'

'Have you seen a doctor at all?'

She shook her head.

Miss Brewster studied her condescendingly. 'You girls

have no thought for your babies' welfare. I shall arrange for a doctor to see you as soon as possible. Now we have rules here which we expect all our expectant mothers to observe. Let me assure you, this is no hotel. You will do your share of the housework right up until the birth unless you are suffering from medical complications. Daily exercise will be taken within the grounds, leaving them is not permitted. You are in our care now and we need to know where you are at all times in case of emergencies. Any questions?'

Judith shook her head.

The woman rose and walked across to a large cupboard at the side of the office. She opened it and, having selected several garments, handed them to Judith. 'Your maternity wear. Your own clothes you will leave with us as you won't be needing them until you leave. Shoe size?'

Judith gulped. She really was in prison. 'Six,' she muttered.

The woman handed Judith a pair of heavy-looking plain black lace-up shoes which had obviously been worn before. She then shut the cupboard and walked across to the door. 'Come along,' she ordered. 'I will show you to your room.'

Carrying her clothing, Judith silently followed her back out into the main entrance hall and up two wide flights of stairs and then a steep narrow set to the top of the house. Two doors led off a short landing. Miss Brewster opened one and ushered Judith inside. 'You are once again very fortunate, you have a room to yourself. I will leave you to get settled. Bring your own clothes back down with you when you hear the gong for dinner. The clothes will be laundered and packed away in your case, ready for your departure after your baby is born.'

With that she shut the door, leaving Judith on her own.

She stared around her. It was a tiny room, walls painted a dull beige. It held a single bed, washstand and small chest of drawers. The floor was bare-boarded save for a small knitted rug by the side of the bed. On the wall at the side of the attic window was a framed print of Jesus crucified on the cross. The dismal room, though, was nowhere near as desolate as Judith felt.

She laid her clothes down and went across to the window where standing on tiptoes she tried to see out. All she could see was a small patch of cloudy sky. Going back to the bed she sank down on it. The mattress was hard and unyielding. Judith buried her face in her hands. Her landing up in this prison-like place wasn't fair. She had made the mistake of trusting a man and now her whole life lay in ruins. Her parents had no idea where she was as she hadn't left a note, but they would know she had left home when they discovered her clothes had gone. Would they care? She had no idea. Her father would probably miss her only for the work she did at Chambers'. She knew he'd be cross because now he would have to pay someone the full going rate.

She jumped as a tap sounded on the door. It opened and straight away a girl of about her own age came in. Her limp mousy hair was tied at the back of her neck and her face was covered in big spots. She seemed to be very pregnant.

'You the newy?' she asked directly. 'I'm Beryl Winters. What's your name and when's yer baby due? Father dump yer, did he, and family threw yer out? Well, yer not on yer own. It's happened to all of us in here. This is my second visit.' She gave a laugh. 'They reckon if they see my face again after this they won't let me in. Like a prison, it is. The staff are awful, treat us all like dirt. Some charity! They ain't soft-hearted, that's fer sure. Keep us at it all day, making sure this place is spotless. I can't wait for this little blighter to come out then I can leave. Better dossing under the arches than in here. Not that I have ever dossed under the arches, I ain't that low, just that I have a habit of falling for smooth-talking men that scarper at the first hint of trouble. Don't say much, do yer? Got any money?'

Judith shook her head.

'Oh,' said Beryl, pulling a disappointed face. 'If yer had I was gonna sneak out and get some fags. Gasping, I am.' She scanned Judith. 'You look like a posh bird ter me. I bet you've lied and yer have got some money.'

She made a grab for Judith's handbag but she held on to it tight. She had lied, she had a few shillings in her purse, but that was all she had in the world and this woman certainly wasn't having it for her cigarettes.

'I told you, I haven't,' snapped Judith, annoyed.

She wanted desperately to be on her own. She was still trying to make sense of what had happened to bring her here and didn't appreciate Beryl's uninvited intrusion into her privacy or her trying to take what little money Judith had off her. 'If you don't mind,' she said, 'I'd like to be on my own.'

Beryl looked at her as though Judith had just committed a mortal sin. 'Oh, like that, are yer? Yer snotty cow!

Well, don't pay ter mek enemies in here and you just made the biggest.'

Judith stared at her, astonished. All she had done was request to be on her own. The girl must surely understand that having just arrived here she was traumatised and needed a bit of time to herself. 'But I . . .'

'Save it,' spat Beryl. 'You wanna be on yer own, gel, then you got it. No one tells me to leave. You're gonna be sorry you chucked me out.'

With that she stormed out and slammed the door shut behind her.

Judith stared at it and gave a little groan of despair but there was too much going on in her mind for her to dwell on Beryl and her tantrum.

Putting her clothes on the floor, she lay down on the bed and closed her eyes. The next thing she knew a woman in her late twenties dressed in a uniform similar to that of a nurse was looming over her, her plain face set hard. 'Chambers, did you not hear the gong for dinner? And why haven't you changed yet? Get up and get a move on.'

Still fuddled with sleep, Judith sat bolt upright, not quite sure where she was. Then it hit her: she was in a home for fallen women. Not quite like the dire places she had read about in Dickens's novels but bad enough from her own short experience. 'I'm sorry, really I am, but I fell asleep.'

'Just get a move on,' the other woman ordered before turning and walking out.

By the time Judith had changed into the baggy brown mid-calf dress, beige woollen stockings and the biggest, loosest pair of knickers she had ever seen in her life and which she was having a hard job keeping up, deposited her own clothes on the office desk then found her way to the dining room, twenty minutes had passed.

As she entered the room the hard-faced woman who had come into her bedroom approached her. 'I'm Miss Hales. Don't make a habit of this, Chambers. Expectant mothers need good nourishing food and it's no use to them if it's cold.' She guided Judith over to a table on which stood several metal containers holding what looked like some sort of stew, carrots and mashed potatoes. 'Get a plate and help yourself. Then go and sit down at the table with the rest.'

Judith glanced over to a long table where over a dozen women in varying stages of pregnancy sat chatting over their dinner. Sitting in the middle of them and facing her was Beryl. She looked across at Judith with a look of pure malice. Her heart sank. It didn't seem that Beryl was the forgiving sort.

She'd no appetite now but knew Miss Hales was watching her. Feeling she'd got into enough trouble for one day, she put a small portion from each container on her plate, picked up a knife and fork and went across to join the others. There was a vacant seat at one end. She pulled out a chair and sat down. As she did so all the others picked up their plates, stood up and walked across to the table with the containers on and stacked the plates on it. As the others left the room, two of the women stayed behind and began collecting the used crockery and containers then headed off with them through a swing door at the back of the dining room, to what Judith assumed was the kitchen.

Beryl, who had loitered by the table until the others had left, sauntered across to her, leaned over and whispered in Judith's ear, 'See, I told yer you'd made a big mistake, chucking me out. I'm the chief here, see. The other gels all follow my lead, 'cos they know what's good for 'em. Don't blame me, it's all yer own fault. You wanted ter be on yer own . . . well, yer will be, 'cos no one will speak ter yer the whole time yer here. Yeah, I'll be gone in a couple of months but I'll mek sure my successor carries this on. No one likes snotty cows, see.' She straightened up and gave Judith a mocking grin. ''Bye, 'bye, Snotty Cow.'

She felt like weeping at this ignorant woman's cruel treatment of her, as if she wasn't suffering enough already, but her practised self-restraint played its part and she did no more than pick up her knife and fork and begin eating. The food was cold and very bland. Judith had to force it down. It was a great relief when she'd finished her meal and could escape to her room, but as she made to ascend the stairs in the entrance hall, Miss Hales waylaid her.

'Chambers, one minute, please. In the office.'

Wondering what Miss Hales could want with her, Judith followed her through.

Inside Miss Hales turned to her, her face severe. 'I didn't want to say anything before you'd eaten your meal as you were late as it was and I couldn't hold it up any longer, but you've been with us barely a few hours, Chambers, and it appears you've already caused Beryl Winters to become upset. She was most distressed when she came to see me earlier. I had quite a job to calm her down. Getting in a state like that is not good for her baby. Paying her back for the kind gesture of calling on you to welcome you here by throwing her out of your room so forcibly that she nearly toppled down the stairs is an act of violence in my book, and your being pregnant is no excuse for such behaviour. It will not be tolerated. Neither will trying to prise money out of her for cigarettes, which I assume you were hoping to sneak out and buy. You haven't done yourself any favours, Chambers. It's obvious you're a trouble-maker with no regard for the rules. I will nip such behaviour in the bud here and now.

'I shall recommend to Miss Brewster tomorrow morning that you be kept away from the other girls. You'll be found duties that don't involve contact with them. A table will be set for your meals away from the others. I've met your type before. You think because you've had a more privileged upbringing than most you're somehow superior. Well, let me tell you, in here you are just another silly girl who has got herself into trouble. Take a bit of advice, Chambers. Keep your head down for the rest of your stay or you might find yourself out on the street, and then where will you be? Report to Miss Brewster's office at nine tomorrow. Now I suggest you go to your room and think hard about what I've said. Off you go then.'

Feeling the weight of the world on her shoulders, Judith turned and walked out. Accustomed to spending most of her spare time on her own, and not having been allowed to mix socially with her work colleagues on her father's instructions, being ostracised from the others here did not pose as much of a problem for her as it would have done for someone else. What did upset her greatly though was the fact that Beryl had lied so blatantly about her, and Miss Hales had accepted this version of events without giving Judith the opportunity to explain her side. Judith wanted no trouble, had enough to contend with as it was. She would follow Miss Hales' advice and keep herself to herself, she decided.

As she made her way upstairs to her room she could hear all the women chatting and laughing together in the room next to the dining room, which she assumed was the common room.

For the next four and a half months, Judith was thankful to experience no further mishaps. The other pregnant women avoided her and she avoided them. The staff kept their distance from her too. She carried out her solitary duties, ate her meals alone, went out on her walks around the grounds by herself, and spent her free time in her room reading books from the library. She was deeply worried about the actual birth, not having a clue what to expect, and supposed she should ask what happened after her baby's birth as she hadn't a clue about that either, but was so afraid of being seen to overstep the mark after how they'd treated her over Beryl's lies that she kept quiet. She assumed that the staff here would help her find a place to live and some sort of funding until she could manage for herself. She saw the doctor once a month. After taking her blood pressure, he'd place a silver trumpet-like instrument against her swelling belly and ask her if she had any problems. When she said she had none she was sent on her way until the next check up came around.

The regimented days ran into one another and, as her baby grew, strangely Judith found she was experiencing a kind of peace within herself that she'd never felt before and wondered if this was due to not living under her parents' critical eyes any more. She knew people watched her here but not in quite the same manner as her parents had done. She did feel a certain sense of guilt towards them, sorry for having gone off without a word, and worried that they had looked for her and been concerned when she hadn't been found. Facing up to them was something she wasn't looking forward to, but she couldn't hide her baby. It was something that would have to be done in due course, but whether they'd want anything to do with her afterwards remained to be seen. Maybe they would surprise her and welcome daughter and grandchild home once they got over the shock.

As she lay in bed, her uncomfortable bulk making it difficult to sleep, Judith would try to guess what the baby would be. A boy would be nice but she'd love a girl just as much. Names . . . She'd pondered for hours over them and finally settled on Samantha for a girl and Samuel for a boy. One thing she knew was that this baby, unlike herself, would be shown love, lots of it, be hugged and kissed and never, ever looked at with critical eyes. She hoped it would understand why it hadn't a father. She would tell him or her that their father had been an orphan who had died traumatically in an accident. Better that than knowing the truth. She would be a good mother, that she promised her unborn child.

Eight days before her official due date she was in the large walk-in airing cupboard on the first landing when she felt a gush of liquid flow from between her legs. Horrified, she thought she had wet herself. She found a rag to mop the floor with then heaved her heavy bulk up to her room, to wash herself down and change her clothes. That done she hurried as fast as she could back to her chore before it was discovered she was missing and she was accused of shirking. The pains across her stomach began as more of a niggle at first and she wasn't sure what they were. It was while she was having the afternoon rest that the staff insisted those over eight months due took each day that the niggles turned into a pain so severe Judith cried out in agony. The woman in the next room, someone who'd never said a word to her in all the four months Judith had been at the home and whose baby was due just after hers, burst through the door.

Wild-eyed, she looked at Judith writhing on her bed. 'Good God, I thought by that yelp yer'd bin murdered! Oh, yer've started. Stay there, I'll get help.'

Getting Judith down the steep attic stairs was not easy, especially as she kept having to stop as a pain took hold. Finally they made it to the labour room and she was helped on to the table by Miss Hales, her unflattering brown smock awkwardly replaced by a white gown and her knees bent up, feet placed in stirrups. She was told by Miss Hales to breathe deeply when a pain came, that she would be back shortly. Miss Hales then walked briskly out leaving the terrified girl on her own.

It seemed ages to Judith before she returned accompanied by the doctor. Without acknowledging Judith in any way, he sat down on a stool at the foot of the bed and examined her internally. Judith, not knowing what to expect, was mortified at having a man, albeit a doctor, peering and poking so intimately but that feeling soon passed as she was gripped by a pain so severe she thought she would burst open. Then she couldn't give a damn who was looking at her or where, she just wanted this baby out and the pain to go away.

It took six long hours of what felt like hell to Judith before she screamed out that she felt a great urge to push and strained down so hard she thought she was pushing her insides out. Finally she gave one last heave and felt something big slithering out from inside her.

'The baby's born, Chambers,' said Miss Hales matter-of-factly. 'You can relax now.'

She heaved a great sigh as she sank back against the bed. 'Is my baby all right?'

'It's fine,' Miss Hales said brusquely.

Judith gave a sigh of relief then struggled to sit up. 'What is it? A little boy or a girl?'

She saw the doctor drying his hands and Miss Hales holding a swaddled bundle in her arms. She was heading for the door. 'Where are you going?' Judith cried. 'Where are you taking my baby?'

The woman turned back, looked across at her and in a warning tone, said, 'Now, Chambers, don't cause a scene. I'll be back in a minute.' She disappeared out of the door.

'A straightforward birth, Miss Chambers. After a good rest you'll feel fine,' said the doctor. 'Must get off.'

He picked up his bag and left.

Several minutes later Miss Hales returned. 'Now, let's get you cleaned up and then I'll fetch you a cup of tea. As soon as you feel able we'll get you back up to your room where you can have a sleep. Couple of days, all being well, you'll be able to leave here.'

She stared frantically at Miss Hales. 'My baby? Where's my baby?'

She did not look at Judith. 'With its mother.'

Judith stared at her, mystified. 'What do you mean? I'm its mother.'

The other woman looked at her. 'Don't be silly, Chambers, you're in no position to raise a child. If you had had the means to do so yourself, or the father's or your family's support, you wouldn't have landed up here in the first place. It's gone to a good home with a mother and father who can provide for it.'

'No . . . NO!' she wailed. 'You can't do this . . .'

'It's done,' she snapped harshly. 'All the babies that are born in here are adopted.'

Judith's eyes were wild. 'I was never told that.'

'Well, it was assumed you knew. Now be a good girl, be glad your baby has gone to a good home. Not all babies are as fortunate. You can resume your own life. Just take my advice, think twice before you let a man have his way with you again. You know the consequences, don't you? Now sit up while I get this gown off you.'

Judith was frozen in shock. She couldn't believe her baby had been taken from her. She hadn't even seen it, held it. They couldn't do this! She struggled to get off the bed but Miss Hales held her down. 'I said, no nonsense, Chambers. If you continue to cause me problems I will get Miss Brewster in here and she won't stand for it, let me assure you.'

Judith knew by her tone that there was nothing she

could do. Her shoulders sagged despairingly and in a choking whisper she asked, 'What was it? At least tell me that?'

Miss Hales responded firmly, 'Best you don't know. It's over, done with, so forget it.'

Something happened to Judith then. A part of her died. Later, as she lay recovering in her room, numb with grief for the loss of her child, she made a solemn vow to herself. Never again would she suffer as much pain as she was doing now; she couldn't, it would kill her. To avoid anything like this ever happening again, under no circumstances was she going to let a man near her in an intimate way. Forging a steel cage around her heart, she mentally locked the door of it and threw away the key.

Four days later she was pronounced fit enough to leave: breasts bound tightly to stop her milk coming in, dressed ready for the off. Miss Brewster handed her back her case. 'I hope I don't see you again, Chambers,' were her parting words.

You won't, thought Judith as she walked out.

She knew she had no choice but to go home. What she would face there she did not know but she had nowhere else to go and no money apart from the few shillings in her purse she had arrived with. Even being back with her parents under their austere roof seemed preferable to Judith than staying among the type of people she had just spent the last few months with. Her parents were saints compared to their callous ways. One thing she knew was that whatever excuse she devised to cover her four-and-a-half-month absence it would not include telling the truth. Her secret would remain untold until the day she died.

Steeling herself for what faced her back home, she idled the day away wandering around town. By the time she'd plucked up enough courage to confront her parents it was approaching eight o'clock.

The door was opened to her by Miss Betts who stared at her in amazement before she eventually stood aside to allow Judith through. She heard her mother call out, 'Who is it, Betts?'

Before Miss Betts could respond Winifred came out of the dining room. When she saw who the caller was her face set hard and she said, 'You could have called at a more convenient time, we were just sitting down for dinner. What is it you want?'

Judith took a deep breath and replied, 'I live here, Mother.'

Winifred reared back her head and said stonily, 'You haven't for the last four and a half months so wherever you've come from, I suggest you go back there.'

'I can't,' said Judith softly.

'Huh! Thought you'd make your own way in the world and found you can't, so now you come crawling back with your tail between your legs. Well, it doesn't work like that. You decided to leave. As far as I am concerned you've left.'

Her father appeared then. He stared at Judith coldly. 'So, the prodigal daughter returns. I hope you realise what a predicament you left me in by deserting your post?'

'I'm sorry about that, Father.'

'Sorry isn't good enough. I've had the inconvenience of employing several girls to cover your work, and all of them have proved useless. Now this kind of thing must

45

not happen again. It was unforgivably selfish, Judith. I'll expect you at work at eight-thirty sharp tomorrow morning. And be warned, you have a lot of catching up to do. Now go to your room.' He turned to his wife, his voice cold and demanding. 'Winifred, we were about to have our dinner.'

She shot her daughter a look of disparagement before abruptly turning her back and following her husband into the dining room.

Upstairs in her room, which was exactly as she had left it, Judith put down her case and walked across to the window to stare out into the night. Her parents' reaction had in fact been far easier than she'd dared hope for, if not exactly a heartfelt welcome. She turned and stared around her room. A feeling of familiarity enveloped her. She might never have left it. The last few months seemed like a story she'd read in a book. Only the pain she had experienced and the harsh realities she had faced reminded her otherwise . . .

Music filtered through Judith's subconscious and her eyes flickered open. She realised that her drift back into the past had lasted the duration of the play. Now the theme tune was announcing the end. Taking a deep breath, she mentally scolded herself. Giving way to her memories had served no useful purpose, only reminded her of a deeply distressing and painful time. As Miss Hales had said to her after she had taken Judith's baby away: 'It's over, done with, so forget it.' Her life since then might have been uneventful, loveless, for the most part solitary and constantly a struggle to appease her parents, but at least she'd never had to deal with such physical and

46

emotional trauma again, and for that alone she was thankful.

Rising, she switched off the radio, took off her dressing gown and got into bed.

Chapter Three

The next morning she arrived promptly in the dining room at seven o'clock to have her breakfast before rushing off to catch the bus for work. Surprised her parents were not already present, and finding herself unable to remember the last time, if ever, she had arrived for breakfast before them, Judith helped herself from several silver chafing dishes set out on a warming tray on the large walnut buffet, sat down at the table and tucked into scrambled eggs accompanied by a slice of crispy bacon and a couple of devilled kidneys.

She had nearly finished her meal when her mother came in. After a stilted greeting she filled a plate with the same choice of food as Judith and sat down in her usual place opposite her. Winifred poured herself a cup of tea, adding a slice of lemon, and as she picked up her knife and fork to begin eating, said matter-of-factly, 'Charles won't be at the office today. I trust you are able to oversee the smooth running of the business in his absence.'

Fork poised in mid-air, holding the last piece of devilled kidney, Judith stared at her, surprised. She couldn't remember the last time her father had taken a day off work, not even for a holiday. 'Yes, of course. Is Father ill?' she asked in concern.

'He's dead.'

The fork dropped from Judith's hand to clatter down on her plate. Her face wreathed in confusion, positive she had misheard her mother, she stuttered, 'Pardon?'

'You heard me correctly. And please close your mouth. You're reminding me of a fish.'

She shook her head, stupefied. 'Dead! Father's dead? But he wasn't ill. How . . . ?'

'He's died in his sleep. The doctor has been and diagnosed a heart attack. I hope I don't need to remind you that this is a family matter and I want it kept that way. The funeral will be a private affair. I'll advise you of the arrangements when I've spoken to the undertakers.'

'But . . . but what about everyone at the firm, Mother? I'll need to tell them, surely? Also the business people that Father associated with, some over many years. They'll want to pay . . .'

Her mother glared at her. 'Did you not hear what I said, Judith? This is a private matter. Now I wish to finish my breakfast and you need to get to the office.'

With that she began to eat.

Judith stared at her mother. The shock of this news had stunned her senseless, but more so her mother's attitude. She had just lost her husband yet was showing no outward emotion whatsoever, just carrying on with her morning ritual as if nothing was amiss. And why was she so adamant that no one was to be informed of Charles Chambers' death, at least allowing those who wished to pay their last respects?

And what about Judith herself? She had just been informed that her father was dead, was far too numb with the suddenness of it to have gauged how the news was going to affect her, but her mother was expecting her to go to work as normal and, worse still, keep the terrible news to herself. She couldn't do it.

'Mother, I . . .'

The look her mother gave her was enough to set Judith on her feet and heading for the door.

Maude Greengate stared at her, astounded. 'Mr Chambers won't be in today? Oh!' She shook her head, bemused. 'He never has a day off. Is he ill, Miss Chambers?'

Judith couldn't bring herself to lie blatantly to the woman, but neither could she disobey her mother's orders. For a moment she stared at her father's secretary, dumbstruck. She decided it would be best to dismiss the question. 'Had Mr Chambers any appointments today?'

'No, and nothing for the rest of the week. He has several for next week but he'll be back by then, won't he?'

Judith ignored this question too and said, 'I trust you have enough to keep you busy for today at least?'

'Er . . . Oh, yes. Mr Chambers' absence will give me a chance to catch up on some mundane tasks that have been piling up.'

'Good, then I'll leave you to it.'

She turned and hurried towards the door, thankful to be making her escape from further probing questions she was under instructions not to answer. She had just pulled it open when she heard Maude Greengate call to her.

'Miss Chambers, what about anything that needs sign-ing? Will you be taking responsibility in Mr Chambers' absence?'

She turned back and immediately knew by the smug look on the woman's face that she was fully aware that Judith herself had no such authority. Should she endorse anything it would not be legally binding. The reason for Maude's taunt was apparent. She deemed herself Mr Chambers' right hand and therefore felt peeved that she hadn't been given all the details of her boss's uncharacter-istic absence.

Judith's mind whirled as she tried to find an answer to give the woman. Her father had never confided in her about anything to do with the business other than what she needed to know to do her own job. Now he was dead she had no idea who could act with proper authority when it came to the business. As his next-of-kin, she supposed that task fell to her mother. 'Put what needs signing into a binder and I will take it home with me tonight.'

'But what about the urgent items, Miss Chambers? Mr Chambers is a stickler for doing everything promptly. I've several letters he dictated last thing yesterday and I know he means for them to be in this lunchtime's post.'

Judith fixed her eyes on Maude's and said firmly, 'As I said, Miss Greengate, put everything in a binder and I will take it home with me.'

She saw the woman's face tighten. 'As you wish, Miss Chambers.'

Back in her office, Judith sank down on her chair and heaved a deep sigh. All the relevant people had been informed her father would not be present today – what she would tell them tomorrow was another matter – and they had all shown the same shock as Maude Greengate though luckily no one else had probed further. She leaned back in her chair and raised her eyes to the ceiling. It was strange but as yet she had experienced no emotion whatsoever for the loss of her father. No great sadness; no anger for his sudden demise. Surely she should feel something? But then, she thought, how could she mourn for the loss of a man she'd hardly known; who in reality had shown his daughter no parental warmth whatsoever?

She sat and pondered and it was with a great sense of shock that she realised she did feel something: relief. As if a great weight had been lifted from her shoulders – a sense of freedom at not having to look ever again at that critical glint in his eyes. Now she only had her mother to contend with. Only half a battle instead of a full one. Then another thought suddenly struck her. Could it be that Winifred was the way she was because of her husband's controlling influence? Hope rose in Judith. Now he was no longer around, her mother might mellow a little. Maybe they might even get to know one other. Judith found she liked the thought of finding out more about the woman who had given birth to her.

She turned then to Chambers Leather Goods. As her father's only child, the running of the family business would automatically fall to her. She hoped she was up to the job. Of course she was, she scolded herself. She knew the business inside out, far better than her father had ever given her credit for, and what she didn't understand of the financial side or anything else he had kept strictly to himself, she could quickly learn. She visualised herself sitting in his office, dealing with the day-to-day running of the company but also with the buyers from the numerous shops they supplied, coaxing them into taking new lines, something she had always longed to be involved in but had never been allowed.

Often she had wished she could approach her father with her ideas for modernisation, such as expanding their lines to include more affordable items for the modern miss. Young women these days were embracing the throwaway society due to the quick changes in fashion trends and Judith felt positive there were good profits to be had there which they were not taking advantage of. Now she could do that. A surge of excitement shot through her at the prospect, followed very quickly by a surge of guilt. It was unthinkable to be planning such things and her father not yet buried. Plenty of time for thoughts of expansion within the business when his funeral was over.

The rest of the day was hard for Judith to get through but passed without mishap. She arrived home to find her mother waiting for her in the wide entrance hall. She explained what the binder contained. Her mother retrieved it from her and said, 'I'll deal with these and give them to you in the morning. I trust there were no problems today?'

'None. Everything ran smoothly. What do I tell those who need to be told about Father's absence tomorrow?'

'The same as you did today, and again the day after. The funeral is on Friday at eleven o'clock. We will be leaving here at ten-thirty to travel to the church. I have instructed the Vicar just to say a few words over the coffin and then we proceed immediately to Welford Road Cemetery. It should take about half an hour all told.'

Judith stared at her, taken aback. 'No proper service, Mother? What about hymns and prayers?'

'Did you not listen to me, Judith?' Winifred barked. 'I have just outlined my instructions and don't appreciate having to repeat myself.'

Judith looked at her, stunned. 'But what about you, Mother?'

'What about me?'

'Well . . .' She gazed at her mother searchingly. 'A service helps the bereaved come to terms with a loved one's death. Aids the grieving process.'

Winifred smiled at her mockingly. 'Oh, and you're the expert all of a sudden, are you? How I choose to grieve for my husband is my business. If I wanted your opinion I would have asked for it. Now I'm expecting a dinner guest tonight so you'll be having your meal in your room. Miss Betts will bring it up to you.'

A dinner guest! This news took Judith completely by surprise. They'd never received a dinner guest before to her knowledge, and now of all times. Who was this guest? Also she felt very hurt that she wasn't being asked to join them. Then she realised the guest was obviously the family solicitor and it was business that was being discussed. But then she was family, and as she was going to be running the company surely she should be included? But why her mother had broken the habit of a lifetime to invite him to dinner at such a time as this when she never invited anyone even in normal times was very confusing. 'Mother, shouldn't I . . .'

Cold eyes rested on Judith. 'Shouldn't you what?'

She shifted her feet uncomfortably. 'Well . . . I know I've never been allowed to be involved in business decisions before but it's different now, isn't it? And if it's business matters that are being discussed then I should be present, shouldn't I, as I'll be running the business from now on?'

Winifred looked at her sardonically. 'You assume such a lot, Judith.' With that she turned and walked down the hall to the lounge, shutting the door behind her.

Judith stared after her. What had her mother meant by that remark? That Judith was wrong to assume the dinner guest had been invited to discuss the business, or that Winifred herself would be in charge of it now? Just who was this mystery guest? Her curiosity rose. She wondered if there was any way she could catch a glimpse of whoever it was, but as her room was at the back of the house, overlooking the garden, there was no possibility of seeing anyone arriving. The only vantage point was from the two bay-fronted rooms her parents occupied at the front of the house. She'd never been invited inside either of them, being aware from an early age that these rooms were her parents' private sanctums and out of bounds for her. It was against her upbringing even now to disobey them. It appeared her curiosity was not going to be satisfied. Just then she saw Ida Betts emerge from the door that led to the kitchen and head towards her.

Arriving next to Judith she clasped her hands in front of her and said in her usual stiff manner, 'Mrs Chambers has informed me you will be taking your meal in your room tonight, Miss Chambers. As I'll be serving Mrs

Chambers and her guest at eight, would eight-thirty be suitable for you while I'm between courses?'

'Yes, yes, that will be fine. Er . . .' She wanted to ask Ida Betts if she'd any idea who this guest was but thought better of it because it just might get back to her mother that she was acting familiarly with an employee and Winifred would definitely not be pleased. 'Thank you, Miss Betts.'

She made her way up to her room, taking off her working attire and settling down in her chair by the window to read a book while she waited for Miss Betts to bring up her dinner tray.

Chapter Four

Friday morning dawned bright and clear. Judith, dressed smartly in a dignified knee-length black shift dress and fur-collared wool coat that she had bought especially for the occasion, using up most of her savings, waited in the hall for her mother to appear. It was twenty-five past ten. The hearse holding Father's coffin had drawn up outside several minutes previously and the funeral director, along with the driver of the black Daimler that was to ferry Judith and her mother there and back, waited patiently outside. Judith felt it was sad that only she and her mother were in attendance, feeling positive that should her mother have relented and publicly announced the death, then if no one else certainly some members of staff and long-standing customers would have wished to have paid their last respects.

Judith turned to see her mother arriving at the bottom of the stairs.

'Come along,' she commanded peremptorily.

Driving to the cemetery, Judith stole a sideways glance at Winifred sitting ramrod straight beside her, clasping her handbag on her knees. Her mother had not uttered a

word since they had got into the car, just sat staring
stonily ahead.

Despite her own feelings towards her father, Judith
nevertheless felt that this rushed and impersonal send off
was a shabby way to say goodbye to any human being.
The minister, a sombre-looking man with a droning voice,
seemed mortally uncomfortable to find himself saying the
few short words marking the birth, life and unlamented
death of Charles Chambers. Immediately following the
ceremony the funeral parlour's hired pallbearers walked
slowly out of the church with the coffin which was loaded
back on to the hearse for its short journey to the cemetery. By the newly dug grave in a central plot Judith and
Winifred watched in silence as the coffin was lowered in.
Winifred, her face a blank mask, bent to pick up a
handful of earth which she sprinkled on top. Then, still
without a word, she made for the waiting Daimler. After
giving the Vicar a hurried thank you, Judith rushed after
her.

The journey home was conducted in the same frigid
silence. As the car drew up outside their house, Winifred
turned to Judith and said matter-of-factly, 'You'll need to
get a move on and change and get to work. Tell Miss
Greengate to clear your father's office and box up any
personal items. You can bring them home with you
tonight.'

In readiness for Judith herself to take over the office,
she assumed. 'Yes, Mother. What explanation do I give
her?'

Winifred looked at her irritatedly. 'No explanation is
necessary. Miss Greengate is an employee. She'll do as

she's told. She, the same as all the others, will find out soon enough what's happening.'

Within an hour of Judith's asking Maude Greengate to clear her father's office, rumours ran like wildfire around the company. Charles Chambers had been forced to retire through a sudden debilitating illness and his daughter was taking over. As Judith approached the general office early that afternoon she heard Nadine say, 'Maybe things might be better here now the old man's retired. Hey up, Cherry, Icy Lil might let yer keep yer job if yer ask her.'

Cherry snorted. 'And if yer think that yer in cuckoo-land! She's as bad as him – like father like daughter. And have yer thought, now she's in charge things might get worse, if that's possible. I'm glad to be getting out of here. I can't wait to work for a boss that ain't breathing down me neck all the time and picking fault with me work just for the sake of it. I was upset when I first got the sack because better the devil yer know, but the agency have got some temp work lined up for me from Monday. They said that with my skills I can pick and choose among the permanent jobs, there's plenty going. I shall miss you lot but we'll keep in touch, won't we?'

Judith walked in then and they all abruptly stopped their chatting and pretended to be immersed in their work. She walked up to Nadine's desk and said, 'Are all the despatch notes completed? Mr Evans is waiting for them so he can finish parcelling up today's despatches.'

'Just a couple more to do, Miss Chambers.'

Judith looked at her sternly. 'And if you hadn't all been wasting time chatting those would have been finished when they were supposed to have been. Your delay has kept the parcel man waiting, and he has a schedule to keep to.' She gave them all a sweeping glance. 'I don't want to have to remind you again after this to conduct personal conversations in your own time, not when you're being paid to work.' She stepped across to stand beside Doreen Fisher, the telephonist. 'Miss Fisher, I have had a complaint from Mr Gilbert in the sales office that it took you over five minutes to respond to his request for an outside call this morning.'

'Yeah, well, the board was particularly busy this morning with incoming calls, and I was also dealing with other requests for outside calls I received before his. Mr Gilbert seems to think I should drop everything when he wants something. Besides, the company he wanted was engaged and it took me several attempts to get through, then I had to wait while I was connected to the person Mr Gilbert wanted to speak to. He doesn't appreciate how difficult my job can be. Maybe he should come and sit with me for a morning, then he might understand what being a telephonist is all about.'

Judith frowned severely at her. 'I don't appreciate backchat, Miss Fisher. Neither will I tolerate you speaking out of turn about a more senior member of staff. I'll see about getting someone in from the GPO to watch you at work. They can instruct you where you're going wrong and suggest improvements. If that doesn't appear to have effect on your efficiency then we'll need to reconsider your position with Chambers.' She turned to Nadine. 'I'll expect you to bring those completed despatch notes to my office in five minutes.'

Leaving Doreen staring after her and Nadine typing furiously, Judith made her way back to her own office.

The fact that she had caught them all slacking brought to mind her father's diktat that if she didn't watch her workers like a hawk, constantly checking up on them, then they would carry on as they pleased and the business would suffer. He had been right all along, she conceded, as wasn't that just what had happened today? The women hadn't realised she was back on the premises after her time off this morning to attend her father's funeral – not that they were aware of that as yet – and she had caught them red-handed, idly chatting when they should have been working. If her father had witnessed the way Doreen Fisher had spoken to her, he would have sacked her on the spot and afterwards severely reprimanded Judith herself for allowing a lowly employee to speak to her in such a way. She wondered if Doreen truly appreciated the fact that she had chosen to ignore her insubordination, instead offering her a way to keep her job by enhancing her skills. Her father was right: employees were not to be trusted and must be constantly monitored. When Judith was officially put in charge she would have to make sure she employed a likeminded office manager to preside over them.

Never having experienced any other working environment than the one her father had created, Judith had no yardstick by which to measure the atmosphere at Chambers and truly believed that every company was run in the same strict paternalistic way.

On the bus journey home that evening, Judith carried a box containing her father's Parker fountain pen, matching propelling pencil and silver letter opener. She stared out of the window, deep in thought. The dry bright morning had given way to a dismal afternoon and a light rain was falling. She watched trancelike as drops ran down the panes. It had been a strange day. This morning she had stood alongside her mother as they had buried her father, Judith inwardly racked by guilt because she felt no sadness or loss for his sudden demise. She couldn't mourn a man she wouldn't in truth miss. Surely this wasn't the reaction of a dutiful daughter?

That afternoon she had carried on her normal working routine, constantly worried that a member of staff would ask awkward questions that she was under strict instructions not to answer truthfully while still trying to come to terms herself with the fact that her all-seeing, all-powerful father was no longer there to correct her. The trouble was her father had been such a strong influence on her, she wondered if she would ever stop sensing his presence still controlling her.

Her thoughts turned to her mother. After all their years of being together Winifred must be missing her husband dreadfully and Judith wondered what she could do to let her know she was there to help her through this painful time, if Winifred would allow her to. Somehow she had to find a way to get beneath her mother's steely exterior, make her aware that Judith was very eager for them to get to know each other better, maybe even forge a closer bond if that was possible. She pondered her problem for quite a while before a way to begin to break down the barrier struck her and she smiled to herself. It was worth a try.

Her mother did not appear to be at home when Judith arrived. After stripping off her coat and hanging it on the hall closet, she made her way upstairs to her room, still carrying the box. As she passed her parents' room she heard noises coming from one of them and realised her mother must be inside.

She tentatively knocked. 'Mother, it's Judith. I've brought Father's things home with me from work as you asked me to do.'

There was a period of silence before the door finally opened enough for Winifred to step through, pulling it closed behind her. She took the box from Judith without so much as a thank you.

'I've left the binder of today's correspondence downstairs, Mother. Would you like me to bring it up for you?'

'No, I'll deal with it later. I won't be down for dinner so you'd better inform Miss Betts whether you wish to eat in the dining room or have a tray brought to your room.'

Judith's hopes of making friendly overtures as soon as possible were quashed. 'Oh! Er . . . yes, I will.' She saw Winifred make to return inside her room. 'Er . . . Mother?'

Winifred turned and looked blankly at her. 'Well, what is it?'

She took a deep breath, looking at her mother anxiously. 'It's just that the staff have assumed that Father has retired. Should we not tell them the truth? They deserve to know.'

'Deserve! They get their pay, they deserve nothing more. The staff will be made aware of what's going on in due course. Is that it?'

65

'Oh . . . er . . . well, what about me?'

'What about you?'

'My situation at work is very difficult. I'm overseeing the business yet not officially in charge. I can't make decisions affecting the company, and neither do I legally have the right to sign company correspondence. It's demeaning for me in front of the staff.'

'Maybe you think too highly of yourself, Judith. And just what decisions have you needed to make since, as you put it, you've been *overseeing* the business?'

'Well, nothing yet but . . .'

'And what has needed to be signed that couldn't wait until I did it?'

'Well, I . . .'

'So what is all this urgency? Now, anything else?'

For the life of her, now that her father was buried and her mother had fulfilled her wish for a private funeral, Judith couldn't see the point of waiting any longer to announce his death and officially put her in charge of the business. She was the only offspring of the family so it was not likely there was anyone else in the running for the position. Then a thought struck her. As next-of-kin, Winifred was now legally head of the company. Did she plan to step in and head it up herself? But as far as Judith was aware Winifred had never even visited the building, had no idea of how to run a business so was in no way equipped to take over the reins. Then another thought struck her. Was it that her mother was playing devil's advocate and enjoying keeping her daughter waiting? If so it was very capricious of her. But whatever the reason for her mother's seeming unwillingness to formalise this matter, she herself had no choice but to wait patiently.

'No, Mother, there's nothing else. Er . . . yes, there is.' She took a deep breath. 'I wondered if you'd like me to sit with you in the lounge tonight and listen to the radio? I'd like that, Mother. Or we could talk . . .'

'I'm busy sorting through your father's things so I won't be sitting in the lounge tonight.'

'Oh, well, maybe another night then.' She asked tentatively, 'Would you like me to give you a hand?'

Her mother's response was abrupt. 'No, thank you.'

'Oh, well . . . if you change your mind, please call on me. I'd be happy to help you.'

What her mother said next shocked Judith speechless.

'*You're* the last person I'd accept help from.'

With Judith struck dumb with astonishment, Winifred slammed the door on her.

Afterwards, sitting on her bed, hands clasped tightly in her lap, staring into space, Judith tried to fathom her mother's sudden hostility towards her and the only conclusion she could arrive at was that she couldn't possibly have meant those things, that she was still so deep in shock at Father's sudden death she was unaware of what she was saying.

For the rest of the weekend Judith saw nothing of her mother, who was having her meals delivered on a tray to her room. How she was spending her time, Judith had no idea. She worried over this state of affairs, concerned that in her grief her mother was shutting herself completely away. Judith didn't think this was good for her. There was nothing she could do, however, but wait until her mother was ready to face the world again.

The weekend passed normally for Judith, except for the fact that she didn't join her parents in the dining room at mealtimes. On Saturday, after shopping for some toiletry requirements and pairs of stockings from the local shops on Allendale Road, she spent her time in her own room, reading or listening to the radio, and on Sunday did likewise. Used to her own company, this state of affairs did not cause her any problems. Apart from feeling concerned about her mother's state of mind and her unwillingness to allow her daughter to help her with the grieving process, Judith just got on with what she normally did.

Chapter Five

Judith arrived for work promptly at eight-thirty on Monday morning, looking her usual smart, efficient self in a dark grey suit and crisp pale blue blouse, her dark chin-length hair brushed and shining. After doing her rounds of the office staff, checking they were present and had plenty to keep them occupied, and then the same with the storeman, his assistant and the despatcher, she decided to pay a visit upstairs to have a discussion with Maude Greengate. Now work was not being generated by Charles Chambers, she needed to keep the secretary occupied until her mother saw fit to appoint Judith officially as the new head of the company. Judith knew she would need a secretary but was not sure that Maude would be her preferred choice. Still, that was not the issue at the moment, keeping Maude occupied was, and she had a suspicion that the woman wasn't going to take kindly to what she was about to suggest. But then, she was an employee, Judith her superior, and she had no real choice in the matter.

Judith found her sitting at her desk thumbing through a magazine. She hurriedly thrust it in her drawer and busied herself sorting through a pile of paperwork when she realised Judith had entered.

'Can I help you, Miss Chambers?' she asked briskly.

Arriving at her desk, Judith said equally briskly, 'We need to discuss your workload.'

Maude gave a defensive toss of her head. 'Well, I'm managing to keep myself busy rearranging the filing system which I've been wanting to do for ages and never had the time because of how busy Mr Chambers always kept me. And I've telephone calls to deal with in his absence. As soon as Mr Chambers is back I shall be inundated again. You will give him my best wishes, Miss Chambers, won't you, and hopes for his speedy recovery? What is it – 'flu? Terrible thing is 'flu. My mother had it last year and she was ill for weeks . . .'

Her father had always warned her not to engage in familiar chit-chat with the staff. Familiarity breeds contempt, he always told Judith. Never leave them in any doubt who's boss or before you know it they'll be walking all over you. With his instruction ringing in her ears she said, 'With the departure of Mrs Campbell we're short-staffed in the general office so until further notice I want you to go and give a hand in the typing pool.'

Maude looked at her, astonished. She had paid her own way through secretarial college on leaving school at fourteen by working the evening shift in the local factory so she could give her hard-up mother her keep while she studied, and had worked damned hard to get a pass certificate so she could get herself a decently paid job. Over the years she had honed her skills to perfection. She was a first-class secretary and even the formidable Mr

Chambers had hardly ever found reason to complain about her work in all the years she had been his personal assistant, which was an accomplishment in itself considering how pernickety he was. His daughter was showing no respect for Maude's status at all. She was quite willing to help out other departments when necessary, but not to be asked if she minded or given a please or thank you, just to be told that she would, did not sit well with her.

Face tight, she said, 'You want *me* to work in the general office? But I'm a highly trained secretary.' She sounded mortally wounded.

Judith looked her in the eye. 'Then your skills will come in very useful in helping to stem the backlog of typing until we can find a suitable replacement for Mrs Campbell. Please report there immediately.'

Judith made to turn and leave but was stopped short when the ante-room door opened and a tall, handsome, very smartly dressed man strode purposefully through. He seemed to be aged around the mid-thirties, and was carrying a heavy-looking briefcase which Judith immediately recognised as being handmade from calf and that didn't come cheap.

Flashing Maude and Judith the relieved look of someone who had just escaped imminent death, he proclaimed, 'Goodness me, that lift needs attention! It's a bit juddery, isn't it? I suspect it needs a good service or even replacing as it's rather ancient. We'd better put that on the list of things to be done. Can't have any of the staff risking their lives, can we?' He gave a sudden engaging grin. 'How rude of me, I do apologise. Matthew Burbridge. Unfortunately my father's been called away on very urgent business that

71

he couldn't get out of. He sends his apologies and will be in around lunchtime. In the meantime there's a lot of groundwork I can be getting on with. Right, I think first things first. I'd like to be shown around and introduce myself to all the staff. Which one of you ladies is going to do the honours?' He was smiling at them both.

Judith looked at him, taken aback. Why on earth would a customer want to introduce himself to the staff? 'Have you an appointment, Mr Burbridge?' She flashed a quick look of annoyance at Maude for not informing her of this beforehand so she could at least have acted as though she was expecting him, and made a mental note to ask Miss Roberts, the young girl down on the reception desk, why she had allowed this man to come up unannounced. Or was it that she hadn't been at her post? Either way it would be addressed.

He looked puzzled. 'No, should I have?'

'It's usual practice,' Judith said tartly. Unless, she thought, this was a special customer of her father's with whom there was an arrangement he could call in whenever he wanted, but if that was the case she was most surprised considering how strictly regimented her father had been in his approach to everything. She planted a welcoming smile on her face. 'Would you like to come through to the viewing room? Mr Chambers is . . . indisposed at the moment, so I'll take you through our current lines. We have some new styles not long in. I'm sure you'll like them.'

He eyed her strangely. 'Mr Chambers being "indisposed" is putting it mildly, in my opinion. Look, viewing the stock can wait for now. I'd sooner meet the staff first and introduce myself.' He smiled at her. 'You haven't given me the pleasure of informing me who you are yet?'

'Judith Chambers.'

His face filled with genuine delight. 'Oh, how nice to meet you. In the circumstances I didn't expect welcoming on board by a member of the family. If you don't mind, I'd like to take advantage of your kind gesture as there's a lot you can fill me in on with the finer details of the business.' He looked at Maude. 'And Mrs . . . er . . .'

A baffled Maude, who couldn't decide whether this man was a genuine customer, was in the wrong company or was not right in the head, automatically responded importantly, 'Miss Maude Greengate. I'm Mr Chambers' personal assistant.'

'I'm very pleased to meet you, Maude. I'm sure you and I are going to get along fine.' He held out his hand to her which she automatically shook, inwardly shocked at the impertinent way he had addressed her by her Christian name. 'Would you kindly make us some tea, please? I take two sugars. I trust you already know what Judith likes.' He turned and headed off towards the office. 'Want to come through, Judith.'

Her face tightened in indignation, anger mounting at the rudeness of this man, not only to be addressing her by her Christian name, and Maude Greengate too, but also issuing instructions and, most annoying of all, acting as though he owned the place. But before she could say anything he had disappeared into what until last week had been her father's private domain. Judith shot after him and was just about to launch into an attack on his conduct when she stopped short, shocked to see he had made himself at home in her father's chair.

'This is really comfy,' he said, relaxing into it. 'I can see me having a fight with my father over who's going to have this. Nice desk too. Better than the one I've just left back at our other office. Please sit down, Judith. We're not standing on ceremony here.'

This man really was taking liberties and she was beginning to suspect he wasn't completely compos mentis. 'Excuse me, Mr Burbridge, I have no idea what your game is but I won't stand for any more of it. I'll ask you to leave now, and if you don't I'll call the police and have you escorted off the premises.'

He looked at her, bemused. 'And why would you want to call the police?'

'Why! I have no idea who you are yet you are ordering my staff around, acting as though you own the place.'

He eyed her, puzzled. 'But I do. Well, my father does to be exact. But I'll be running this business while he concentrates on our other concerns.'

His announcement took the wind from Judith's sails and she stared at him open-mouthed for several long moments before she uttered, 'Pardon? What do you mean, you own the place?'

He looked at her in confusion. 'I thought you introduced yourself as Judith Chambers?'

'That's correct.'

'Charles Chambers' daughter?'

'Correct.'

He rose from the chair and walked around the desk to stand before her. 'Weren't you aware that your mother sold the business to my father?'

74

She stared at him, stupefied. 'But you must be mistaken . . .'

'No, no mistake. It's all been signed and sealed and monies exchanged. We officially took over from eight this morning.'

A sickening bile rose in her stomach. Her mother had sold the business, their livelihood, that she herself had been expecting to take over. Had handled all the formalities of the sale and not breathed a word to Judith, despite having ample opportunity to do so. She was bound to have known what would happen this morning. How could she have knowingly placed her own daughter in such a humiliating situation? Winifred was sick, she had to be. It must be grief that was having such a terrible effect on her. A visit from the doctor was obviously urgently required. But whatever medication he gave her would be administered too late to do anything about this if contracts had been signed and money had changed hands. She desperately fought for a way to salvage a shred of pride, and what she came up with was so lame it was pitiful. 'How stupid of me. I thought my mother said the handover day was tomorrow. I don't know what you must think of me.'

'Well, I expect you've had a lot on your mind recently.' He smiled at her kindly. 'I'm . . . er . . . sorry about your father,' he said sincerely. 'He died suddenly, didn't he? It must have been a terrible shock for you.'

'Yes, it was, and thank you,' she responded stiffly. Her mind was whirling, trying to take in all that was happening.

Matthew had walked back around the desk and resumed his seat in her father's chair. 'We were only too delighted to be given the chance to buy a company like Chambers' as obviously for us it's a natural business progression to complement our shops. We're the owners of Cobbler's Shoes, have ten shops across the Midlands. Maybe you've bought shoes for yourself from our shop on Gallowtree Gate? I never had any dealings directly with Chambers' personally as my father saw to all that side but we've bought our quality leather bags from you for years, so naturally when Mrs Chambers put forward a proposal to sell last week when she invited my father to dinner . . . well, we pulled out all the stops. Your mother was adamant it had to be agreed and executed within days, and we didn't want to lose this opportunity of supplying our own shops and cutting out the middle man, but of course it's been no pleasure for us acquiring it through Charles Chambers' death. Still, in respect of yourself and your mother, we paid a good price so I expect you'll be able to live very comfortably.'

He looked at her in sudden concern, noticing she had steadily grown deathly pale. 'Are you all right?'

'Yes, I'm fine, thank you,' she said stiltedly. All Judith wanted to do was to get away from this awful situation. It was her mother's right to sell the business, but the least she could have done was tell Judith and save her this terrible humiliation. She forced a smile to her face. 'Miss Greengate will show you around and I'm sure she can answer any questions you may have. But you'll find everything in order. We ran a tight ship. I really think it best I leave you to it. I'll clear my desk and be off the premises in less than an hour.'

He smiled, genuinely disappointed that she was leaving

without his having the chance to pick her brains, but said, 'It's been a pleasure meeting you, Judith, and good luck for your future.'

He rose again, walked around the desk and held out his hand to her. Judith walked out in dignified fashion, shutting the door behind her. On the other side she met Maude Greengate about to enter with a tray of tea. She felt she really should warn the woman about the change of ownership but couldn't bring herself to, still reeling from the shock herself. 'Oh, Miss Greengate, I won't be taking tea. Take care of Mr Burbridge. I'm afraid I can't as I have urgent things to do. Goodbye, Miss Greengate.'

At the finality of her tone, Maude looked at her, taken aback. 'Oh, er . . . goodbye, Miss Chambers.'

Judith could not clear her desk quickly enough for fear that news of her father's death and the change of ownership would soon get around and then she would have to face smug looks and possibly snide comments from the staff as she walked out, no longer with any power over them to chastise them for it. At this moment she wasn't mentally able to cope with the inevitable barrage of questions they would fire at her. Let the new owners deal with it. Thanks to her mother, she no longer had any connection with Chambers Leather Goods.

Being the methodical worker her father had shaped her to be, there was not much for Judith to clear and within a matter of minutes she had sorted and labelled everything that was outstanding, instructing whoever took over her position what needed to be done. The only personal items she had kept at work were a silver pen and pencil set she had bought herself years previously from W. H. Smith's which she now slipped into her handbag. Putting on her coat, with head held high, she walked out of the building, mortally relieved that she bumped into none of the staff en route.

Outside on the pavement, she paused and ran her eyes over the building where she had worked for all but a few months of her adult life. Its walls had been like a second home to her. She couldn't believe that never again would she have any right to enter these premises apart from as a visitor, and she couldn't envisage any reason for her ever doing that. By selling the business her mother had made sure there was no going back for Judith. She took a deep shuddering breath before she turned and hurried off in the direction of the bus stop.

Chapter Six

In her haste to get home and hopefully receive some sort of answers from her mother on what she planned for their future, the bus ride seemed to take forever to Judith. As if she hadn't received enough shocks for one day she was not prepared for the sight that greeted her when she turned the corner of the road on which she lived. Parked outside the house was a large removals van and it was being loaded with what looked like their furniture by several brown-coated men.

As she arrived at the back of the van, Judith paused long enough to look inside. It was definitely their furniture.

One of the men tipped his cap at her as he loaded a heavy tea chest inside. 'Mornin', Madam.'

She ignored him and hurried up the front path and into the house where she found her mother supervising the other removals men.

'Goodness me, be careful with the table! If there's any damage at the other end, I shall be seeking compensation. Ah, Miss Betts, a cup of tea is what I need. Make it strong and see to it immediately.'

'What about the men?' the housekeeper asked.

'What about them?'

'Should I make them tea too, Madam?'

'You certainly will not! I'm paying for them to remove my furniture, not lounge around drinking tea.'

With that Winifred made her way into the living room.

Judith followed her through, shutting the door behind her. 'Mother, what's going on?'

Winifred slowly turned around and looked at her daughter, one eyebrow raised. 'You obviously know I've sold the business? Well, I've sold the house too and we're moving. That's quite plainly obvious, I would have thought, from what's going on around here.'

'But, Mother, couldn't you have told me and then at least I would have been prepared? Where are we moving to?'

'I'm off to my villa in Italy.'

'Villa! In Italy!' she exclaimed, totally mystified. 'But . . . you've never even been to Italy so how did you buy a villa there?'

'Have you never heard of property agents, Judith? It's possible to buy anything these days, anywhere in the world, when you have the means to pay someone to represent you. The sale of the business and house and what was already in the bank – a very tidy sum, I was glad to discover – will keep me comfortably for the rest of my days. Miss Betts is coming with me. As for you . . .' She scanned Judith, eyes cold. 'Where you choose to live is your decision. I've had your possessions packed up and the removals company will store them for you until you find yourself somewhere to live. Be warned, though, weekly storage doesn't come cheap.'

Judith was staring at her, flabbergasted. 'Mother, why? Why are you treating me like this?'

Winifred narrowed her eyes, her gaze becoming harsh. 'Because I hate you,' she spat. 'Have done from the minute you were born. Before that, even.'

Judith was horrified by this admission. 'But why, Mother, why do you hate me so much? Whatever have I done to you to make you feel like that towards me?'

'Because *you* were the reason I was tied to your father in the first place,' she hissed.

Judith recoiled at this savageness. 'But . . . but I don't understand? Did you not like Father?'

'*Like!* I *loathed* him. He was a despicable little man. I felt ill just looking at him.'

'But why?' she implored. 'If you didn't like him, why did you marry him?'

'I had no choice!'

Judith looked at her, mystified. 'Why did you have no choice, Mother?'

Winifred stared at her for several long moments. 'I suppose you have a right to know. But be warned – when I have finished you might just regret hearing what I'm about to tell you.' She walked across to the fireplace. Hands clasped in front of her, eyes glazing over, she began: 'I was pretty, had the world at my feet. My family were comfortably off and I wanted for nothing. I had an elder sister and brother. They were both married and I was the only one left at home. My parents doted on me. I knew they secretly hoped I'd fall in love and marry the son of my father's business partner. He was a nice enough man, would make me a good husband, but I was having too much fun to think of settling down for another couple of years at least. My friends were all going off to London for the season but my father wouldn't hear of me going because he felt at nineteen I was too young, even though several of my friends' mothers would be there to chaperone us. He was very protective and old-fashioned in his views was my father. I pleaded with him but he wouldn't change his mind.

'I was furious. The long summer months stretched before me and I had nothing to do and no friends around me. I was soon bored. I met Charles Chambers on a shopping trip into Leicester. He was assistant manager of the leather goods department for Adderly's. I wanted a new vanity case and he served me. I could tell that I had caught his eye, but what I ever saw in him I have no idea now. It's not as if I found him attractive. But with nothing better to do, when he asked me to have lunch with him, I agreed. I lived to rue the day I did that!

'Over lunch he told me that he came from a good family in Northampton who'd had their own business until his father's partner embezzled the accounts and ran off. Both his parents died and at the age of fifteen he came to Leicester to get away from Northampton as it held so many bad memories for him. He got himself a job in Adderly's as a junior in the leather goods department and worked his way up to assistant manager. Working in that department gave him an idea. He said he could see the need for a leather goods agency where owners and buyers of retail outlets could come to view samples of leather goods from all over and place orders for their requirements, Charles then taking his commission from the suppliers. This method of buying in turn cut down on shopowners needing to see travelling salesmen or themselves having to visit individual factories. That's how Charles was going to make his fortune, he said, and he was saving every penny he could towards the day when he was in a position to start it.

'His sad history touched me and I felt sorry for him. When he asked to see me again I hadn't the heart to say no. When my father found out I was meeting a lowly shop assistant he forbade me to see Charles but I was still angry with him for not allowing me to go to London with my friends so I went behind his back, telling him I was visiting the aunt of one of my friends who was sick and was going to spend the evening reading to her. Charles took me to the music hall and the evening passed pleasantly enough. I could tell he liked me and I suppose I was flattered. I thought having an occasional night out with him would be a distraction, something to while a little of the time away until my friends came back. But I also knew it was wrong to continue to let him grow fond of me, that it wasn't fair to him, so I arranged to see him again the following Thursday evening with the intention of finishing our liaison then.

'I sensed he had a suspicion of what I planned as he was subdued all evening. He was walking me to the cab rank when he asked to see me again and I made my excuses. I've never seen such a quick change in a person. Furious, he accused me of teasing him, of leading him on. Said I was a spoiled rich brat, just having fun with a man I felt was beneath me. No doubt it gave me something to laugh over with my friends at his expense. He said he was going to teach me a lesson I'd never forget, that I'd think twice before I ever did anything like this to anyone again. I don't wish to relive all the sickening details but he dragged me down a dark alleyway, overpowered me and had his way with me, leaving me to find my own way home.

'I've never felt so wretchedly degraded. I can't even remember the journey home. I was just glad that I managed to slip inside and get up to my room without anyone seeing me. I scrubbed every inch of my body. I dared not tell my parents what had happened. My father had forbidden me to see Charles. If he discovered I'd gone behind his back, I dreaded to think what my punishment would be, and I knew he'd have murdered Charles for what he'd done to me. I had to keep this quiet.

'When I realised I was pregnant I was beside myself to think that I was carrying that awful man's baby. My best friend was still in London and I wasn't sure when she was due back so I had no one to confide in. I was starting to show and my mother had remarked that I was putting on weight. I knew it wouldn't be long before she guessed the truth. I thought it'd be better if I told my parents before they guessed. I thought that once they'd got over the shock, I would be sent to a relative where I'd have the baby and it would be adopted out and all of it hushed up. Then I could just get on with my life and forget about it.

'I was so wrong to have hoped for that. My mother collapsed with the shock of it and my father flew into the most furious rage. He said I'd brought disgrace on the family, and whether I liked it or not I was going to marry my child's father. I tried to tell them what had happened, that the man had forced himself on me, but they wouldn't listen, said I was trying to make excuses for my own disgusting behaviour. When I finally admitted that Charles Chambers was the father, the very man my own father had forbidden me to see, he hit me across the face. He'd never raised his hand to me before and I knew by his action that I really had done the very worst thing I could ever have done to him. I begged him to forgive me but he wouldn't. He said as if my getting pregnant wasn't bad enough, to be got pregnant by a penniless shop assistant made me beneath contempt.'

Judith was staring at her mother dumbstruck, hardly able to believe how history had practically repeated itself years later. She had never suspected anything like this in her mother's past and it was so shocking to hear.

'My father went to see Charles in his lodgings and demanded he marry me,' Winifred continued. 'Charles laughed in his face, said he wouldn't have me if he was paid to. He told my father that I was a slut who had willingly given myself to him. Every man has his price, though. Your father settled for a thousand pounds. The wedding was arranged for a week later and during that time I was locked in my room and my meals sent up. On the morning of my wedding my father announced to me that he was disowning me, and the rest of the family were instructed not to have anything to do with me either. If anyone were caught associating with me then they would be disowned too. I was put in a cab along with my possessions and sent off to the register office. That was the last time I saw any of my family.

'It became clear from right after the ceremony that Charles had no interest in me. He gloatingly told me that from the first he'd only seen me as a means to making his fortune, which was why he flew into a rage when I tried to finish our liaison. Not because he felt I had used him, but because the chances of him snaring anyone else with a suitable dowry were very remote. He used the money my father paid him to start a business and put a deposit on this house. Charles was consumed by the thought of money. That was all that was important to him. People he had no regard for at all. To him they sought out your weaknesses and used them for their own ends. Well, that was never going to happen to him, he wouldn't end up like his father. The fact that he had used me for his own ends didn't even occur to him.

'He gave me no money of my own. Everything I needed, I had to ask him for the money and give him a receipt. He gave me the barest of housekeeping, allowed me no friends, and when I defied him he humiliated me so badly in front of them I couldn't bear it to happen again. He enjoyed seeing me miserable, it made him feel good, as if somehow he was getting his own back for what others had done to him. He knew I couldn't leave him because I had nowhere to go and no money. I was stuck with him for life and he knew it. Every time he touched me when he needed to vent his passions, I was physically sick afterwards. Thank God it wasn't often, and thank God also I never fell pregnant again. I think I would have killed myself if I'd had to bear and look after another child of his. Looking after you was bad enough. You were a constant reminder of why my life was so terrible.

'You left home once and I was so glad! One of my Nemeses was gone from me and I lived in hope, prayed for the day when the other would too and then I'd be free of it all. I feared that day would never come . . . then *you* came back. If it had been up to me you would not have been allowed back here but you were useful to Charles, because you were cheap labour. What he saved on your wages was a bonus to him. He had no love for you, no feelings at all, so don't think he did. Charles didn't know how to love. He knew you lived in fear of him like I did, and your discomfort gave him the only pleasure he craved.

'When I found him dead in bed beside me, I could have wept for joy. My dream, my prayers, my hopes, had all come true! I was free at last, and all that he'd left was mine now to do with as I wished. I've earned it, too, through my years of misery. I am sixty-two years of age and what days I have left I intend to enjoy to the full. I shall relish spending every penny of the money he left as I see fit, knowing Charles Chambers will be turning in his grave. I gave him the pauper's funeral he deserved. I only hope he was looking up from Hell, witnessing the fact that not one tear was shed over him.'

Winifred reared back her head and fixed Judith with her eyes. 'Now you know why I hate you so much and why I don't ever want to see you again. Where I am going I want no reminders of my forty-four years of Purgatory.' She walked across the room and picked up her handbag. From inside she pulled out a wad of notes. She extracted several, walked back and threw them at Judith. 'Just to show you I'm not completely heartless, there's enough there to get you settled. Now I want you to leave.'

With that she strode out of the room.

Judith stood frozen, numb with shock, her mind a jumble of confused thoughts. She couldn't take in what her mother had told her, it was all so terrible, and the worst thing for her was the discovery that she had been the product of rape, just as her own child had been when Clive Lewis had taken what he wanted from her. No wonder her mother had shown so much hostility towards her; in truth Judith couldn't blame her after what she had suffered. She wanted to run to her mother, tell her how sorry she was that she herself had been the cause of so much misery, but she knew without a doubt that her mother had meant every word when she had told her how much she hated and resented her. Any plea for Winifred to reconsider would be rejected out of hand, and another trauma on top of this was more than Judith could bear.

A small part of her hoped that it was merely a nightmare she was having, that she would wake up to find the morning light filtering through her bedroom curtains and herself refreshed and ready to start another day at Chambers Leather Goods, but that did not happen. Removals men were carrying out their business of emptying the house, moving around her as if she didn't exist, and in the distance she could hear her mother's voice urging them to hurry.

She gave a violent shudder, feeling as if someone had walked over her grave. Blindly, she bent down to scoop up the money her mother had thrown at her and stuffed it in her pocket. Then, with all the will she could muster, she turned and walked out of the house that had never truly been her home.

Chapter Seven

Judith looked searchingly around again before bringing her attention back to the young man hovering impatiently by the door. She noticed he kept glancing at his watch, silently urging her to hurry up and make up her mind. But she would not be hurried. She had a hundred pounds to her name, a small fortune to her, but regardless it needed to stretch a long way to cover the cost of setting up a home for herself plus keeping her in basic necessities until she was earning. Also the place she chose as her home needed to be one she felt at ease in, offering her safe harbour, something she had never felt residing under the same roof as her parents. Only now did she realise the devastating reason why.

She wondered if the young man waiting impatiently for her decision could ever imagine anything so dreadful. It still seemed incredible to her, and despite her forcing it away deep down in the recesses of her mind, it was in danger of surfacing to consume her again.

After leaving the house the previous day she had stood in the street, not knowing which way to turn. It didn't really matter which way she went because she had nowhere to go. After her mother's appalling story she had felt so much guilt for being the cause of such misery she had just wanted to sleep, shut it all out. With that sole thought driving her, she had run into the first hotel she had come across and despite its being early afternoon had taken a room and shut herself in. She had wrenched off her clothes and got into bed, curled herself into a foetal position, pulled the covers over her head and sobbed herself to sleep.

Her dreams had been vivid. Her father had taken on the form of the Devil with protruding horns and cloven feet. Out of his mouth billowed great streams of fire. He had been stabbing a sharp-tongued pitchfork at her mother and Judith herself who were cowering, terrified, on the ground beneath him. But instead of fighting to protect her daughter as a mother should, Winifred had been shouting: 'Kill her! It's her fault!' to the monster looming over them.

Sixteen hours later Judith had woken with a jolt just as the pitchfork was about to pierce her heart. As the truth of her origins flooded back she curled herself up and wept again, heart-wrenching sobs that racked her body. Finally, with no tears left, she perched on the edge of the bed, to stare blindly across the room.

What did the future hold for her now? She knew she could not live the rest of her days blaming herself for her mother's unhappiness. No one had any control over the way they arrived in the world. Somehow she had to lock it away along with the other traumas in her past and build a new future for herself the best way she could. Thankfully she did not find herself completely destitute. In their own

90

ways each of her parents had left her a legacy: her mother's that grudging parting gift of a hundred pounds; her father's the office skills with which to secure a decently paid job and provide for herself.

Twenty minutes later, looking her usual calm efficient self, she had settled her bill and enquired from the helpful young reception clerk where to find a good rentals agency. That was how a while later she had found herself in the offices of J. Jarrom and Sons, Estate Agents, on Peacock Lane. Regrettably, she had been informed, all the senior members of staff were out on business. An eager young assistant out to impress his bosses said he was the only one available to attend to her.

After perusing the list of rented properties they had on their books, she had selected four she hoped would be suitable for her. Immediately she had been whisked off on an inspection tour by the eager young man, the same one who was now showing impatience with her as she took her time to make up her mind. She knew there must be questions a prospective tenant would ask before they decided to rent; indeed, she had some of her own but worried they might sound trivial and she'd make a fool of herself in front of the assistant.

Judith assumed an air of confidence and said to him: 'The rent is eight pounds a week, you say?'

He looked expectantly at her. 'That's correct, Madam, with a month's bond as security. It's an immediate occupancy, as you requested, and you can see the furniture is of good quality. When the landlord converted this building several years ago he aimed at attracting the better class of tenant, if you understand what I mean.'

So she was a better class of tenant, was she? He had taken her for such because she was smartly dressed, spoke articulately, and because the last address she had given for herself was considered to be in an affluent residential area. He had thus shown her properties commensurate with what he assumed her status to be. He had overestimated that status. Unless she got a reasonably paid job the money she had in hand would not enable her to live in this place for much longer than a few months. But then, she felt positive that well-paid work would be offered her once prospective employers realised her expertise.

Judith stared thoughtfully around again. This was the nicest flat she had been shown. The lounge was light and airy with high ornate ceilings, white woodwork and cream walls, giving it a feeling of spaciousness. The suite was pale blue moquette and looked clean and comfortable. There was a bookcase in the alcove by the wooden-surrounded fireplace which had been boarded up and a modern gas fire installed. A low coffee table of light wood sat on a dark blue rug in the middle of the room. Above the fireplace hung a print of The Oriental Lady. At the other end of the room was a G-plan dining table, four chairs and matching sideboard. There was a good-sized kitchen, its long sash window overlooking the large back garden. The kitchen held a table against one wall with two matching chairs; by the sink and wooden draining board stood an electric cooker – not that she had a clue how to use it – several wall shelves for pots and pans, and a hanger for a roller towel screwed to the door of a large walk-in pantry. The landlord had had the thoughtfulness to provide basic tableware and cutlery, two saucepans and a frying pan, so if she took the flat she wouldn't have to buy her own immediately.

There was one good-sized bedroom with a double bed and matching wardrobe, and a much smaller single with a bed and chest of drawers. A small bathroom was adequately fitted out and all the plumbing appeared to be in working order. She'd have the use of the communal large garden to hang out her washing and to sit in should she want to during the summer, for which she was expected to pay a contribution of ten shillings a week towards the upkeep.

She had no idea whether this flat on the first floor of an imposing Victorian red-brick house near her parents' former home was being offered at a fair rent or not, but the other three had not been of the same standard so surely the higher rent was justified?

The young man glanced at his watch again. 'Look, I'm sorry to hurry you, Madam, but I've other appointments to show people around properties, this one included. I've no doubt if you don't want it, it'll be snapped up by the next person I show around. Properties of this standard at such a reasonable rent don't come up that often.'

Judith did not appreciate his trying to blackmail her into making a swift decision. She eyed him sharply. 'Young man, you should be well aware that choosing a place to live is an important decision. Prospective tenants deserve the courtesy of being allowed a little time to consider without being pressurised into committing themselves.' She paused for a moment, watching his face redden, before adding, 'I'll take this flat.' She hoped her decision was the right one but only time would tell.

He breathed a huge sigh of relief. 'Right then, if you'd like to come back to the office we can deal with the formalities, and then you can move in as soon as you like.'

Several hours later Judith inserted the key into the door of her new home. On leaving the estate agents she had gone straight around to the furniture removers and, after paying their dues for the storage of her possessions, arranged delivery to her new address which she had insisted be that afternoon. They had hummed and hawed, saying how busy they were and that it might not be possible, but Judith had stood her ground and got her way. This was the second day she had worn these clothes and she needed to change, and despite not owning much except for her radio and books she needed something familiar around her in her new place of abode so that she did not feel completely alien. It was nearing four now and she hoped they would hurry up. She wanted to get everything put away as she intended concentrating on job hunting tomorrow.

Walking into the kitchen, she deposited three laden brown paper carriers on the table. She took off her coat and walked back into the hall to hang it on the coat rack screwed to the wall just inside the door. In the lounge she walked across to the window to look out. As her gaze fell on the unaccustomed view suddenly the total solitariness of her situation enveloped her, a knot of sheer fear gripping her stomach. She had never had to deal with anything like this before. All her life her every move had been dictated for her and now she had no one to turn to, to ask for help or advice.

She felt tears of desolation prick her eyes which she fought to quash. Right from when she could remember she had been firmly led to believe that to show any sort of emotion revealed your vulnerability, marked you to others as a weak-willed person, one to be used by them for their own ends. Despite there being no one to witness her defencelessness now, nevertheless Judith knew she had to be strong or she'd never get through what she faced on her road to building a new life. She would have to do what others did when they found themselves having to cope: be prepared to make mistakes and learn from them.

Taking a very deep breath, she made her way back into the kitchen and emptied the carriers of the purchases she had made, proceeding to stack the food items away on the shelves in the pantry. The packets of salt, pepper, tea, sugar, butter, cornflakes, tin of Campbell's chicken soup, one of Irish stew and one of Frey Bentos corned beef, bag of potatoes, loaf of Mother's Pride sliced bread, half-dozen eggs, quarter of Leicester Red cheese and quarter-pound of sliced ham, hardly filled half a shelf in the large cupboard but was all she could carry along with the cleaning materials the very congenial Pakistani lady in the corner shop had insisted she'd need when she had finally twigged her customer was moving into a new place of abode and starting from scratch. Judith planned to have the soup tonight and in the morning buy herself a book by way of learning how to cook.

A loud knock on the door alerted her to the fact that thankfully her possessions had arrived and she spent the next hour unpacking them. As she was doing so she realised she possessed very little to show for her years of life. Her totally inadequate wage, hardly more than was paid to an office junior, had meant she had had to save hard for whatever she had wanted over and above her basic weekly necessities of toiletries, hosiery, bus fares and a lunchtime sandwich. She felt stupid now to think that for all those years she had never disputed her wage with her father, secure in the belief that once he retired she would claim her just deserts. Her mother had been right to tell her on several occasions that she should not make assumptions.

A while later she drew the curtains to shut out the night and sat down at the kitchen table to eat her solitary evening meal of soup and a slice of bread and butter. Never having had the need to open a tin previously, she felt proud she had escaped doing herself serious damage in her clumsy efforts which had left sharp metal protrusions. The cooker too proved a mystery and she had stood before it for quite a while, fathoming out which knob to turn. But she had eventually achieved it and was pleased with herself.

Picking up her spoon, she was about to start her soup when suddenly she was plunged into darkness. Judith stifled a scream of shock. She was not unused to power cuts, they were a fact of life, but was unprepared for this one, not having had the foresight to buy any candles. Miss Betts had always seen to that kind of thing. Laying down her spoon, she wondered how long the power would be off for. Sometimes it was only minutes, sometimes hours. She'd have to sit it out, hope it wasn't for long. She rose and tentatively felt her way over to the window to draw back the curtains, hoping the moon was not hidden and the light it afforded would enable her to see her way around and what she was doing until the power was restored.

Unfortunately the moon was masked behind a bank of thick cloud and the drawn-back curtains hardly made any difference to the visibility inside the kitchen. Then she noticed that the lights in the back of the houses opposite were on and as she looked down into the garden below she could tell by the shadows cast across the grass that the flat below hers had lights on too. This was a strange power cut, she thought, as it only appeared to have affected her flat. Then it struck her that it wasn't a power cut at all, but that the electrics in her flat must be faulty. She had no idea what to do now. Her mind raced. In her effort not to appear foolish to the estate agent's assistant she had not asked what the procedure was in emergency situations. She remembered seeing such arrangements outlined on the contract she had signed but she hadn't digested the information and it was too dark for her to read it now. She gave a despondent sigh. As she saw it she had two choices: either she waited until morning or she asked for help from another tenant. She did not relish the latter prospect. Ingratiating herself with others wasn't one of her strong points and meeting new people at the moment seemed a daunting prospect. But she had planned to scour the *Leicester Mercury* Job Vacancies column this evening in preparation for her urgent task of securing employment, which she could not delay. She must have light.

Feeling her way to the front door, Judith went across the landing and steeled herself to knock purposefully on the door opposite. Presently it was opened by a very distinguished-looking, tall, broad man of around Judith's own age who glanced her up and down before snapping brusquely: 'Yes?' Then before she could respond he barked, 'If you're canvassing for something I'm not interested.'

She eyed him stonily. 'I'm not a canvasser. My name is Judith Chambers. If you would just do me the courtesy of hearing me out . . . I've moved into the flat across from you . . .'

'Nice of you to introduce yourself,' he interjected sharply. 'Now, if you'll excuse me?'

She felt herself bristling at this man's unwarranted rudeness towards her. 'If you could just spare me a minute? As I said, I've just moved in across the way and the electrics appear to have stopped working and I wondered . . .'

Before she could finish he said offendedly, 'I'm not an electrician.'

'I didn't assume you were,' she responded tartly. 'But having just moved in, I'm not sure of the procedure for rectifying faults and I was hoping you could inform me.'

'Well, if you'd read your tenancy agreement properly you would not have had any need to disturb me. You contact the agents and they send the appropriate tradesman out, but as it's after hours you'll have to wait until first thing tomorrow.'

Spending the rest of the evening in darkness did not appeal at all but it appeared Judith had no choice. 'I apologise for disturbing you and I'll make sure it never happens again.'

She abruptly turned and stepped back across the landing.

Nathan Banks stared after her annoyed, still smarting from her sardonic remarks, but he was an intelligent man and not oblivious to the fact that she was probably acting in response to his own abrupt manner towards her. Thanks to past events he harboured a deep resentment towards women of all ages, shapes and sizes, avoiding contact with them as much as possible. He had been fully aware that a new tenant was moving in opposite, but what the over-enthusiastic estate agent's assistant had failed to take note of about this particular property was that it had been stipulated it was for male tenants only. By the time his mistake had been noticed a contract had been signed and money paid over and it was too late to withdraw.

When Nathan had tactfully been informed the new tenant was a single woman in her forties of good background he had not been happy, but because of her age and unmarried status had visualised a dowdy, reserved spinster, the sort whose residence in the house would hardly be noticed – definitely nothing like the strikingly smart, formidable woman who'd hardly taken up residence here before she was making her presence felt.

He was aware though that he was sending the newcomer back to spend an evening in the dark and his conscience pricked him. His own aversion to the female sex was not her fault, and whether he liked it or not she was going to be living opposite for at least the year's term of her tenancy. He ought to offer to try and do something for her but would also make her well aware this was a one-off and in future he wanted his privacy respected.

'Look . . . er . . . have you checked your fuses in case one has blown?' he called after her.

Judith turned and looked back at him blankly. 'Fuses?'

He gave a sharp irritated sigh. 'Hold on a minute while I get my torch.'

Minutes later he climbed back down from Judith's kitchen chair. 'Well, nothing is wrong there. All the fuse wires are intact so I can't think what it could be.' He stared at her thoughtfully. 'The wiring can't possibly be faulty as I know this house was fully rewired when it was turned into flats a few years back.' Then a thought struck him. 'I suppose I don't need to ask if you've fed your meter?'

She looked back at him questioningly. 'Fed my meter?' she repeated, puzzled.

'Put money in?'

'Money? But I didn't know I had to,' she exclaimed, then suddenly felt very foolish. 'I've . . . er . . . never had to put money in a meter before.'

He raised his eyebrows. 'That's more than likely your problem, it's run out.' Then as an afterthought he added, 'I'd better show you how to do it and save you disturbing me again. I must advise you that I'm a private man and keep myself to myself.'

Several minutes later, after grudgingly thanking Nathan for what from his attitude was his grudgingly given help to her, she closed the door after him and leaned back against it with a deep sigh. That was one neighbour she would endeavour to avoid in future. She wondered if all the others were as offhand in their manner. Still, that wasn't really a problem for Judith as like him she intended to keep her privacy. One embarrassing lesson she had learned, though, was that in future she should keep both gas and electric meters topped up to avoid this situation ever happening again.

Her soup was now cold and looked most unappetising. She seemed to have lost her appetite anyway. She stacked the dirty crockery and utensils in the sink. After picking up that evening's *Mercury* she went into the lounge, spread it across the table and opened it at the Job Vacancies pages, Biro poised ready to tick the suitable positions. Optimism rose within her as several jobs she felt she would be suitable for caught her eye. Closing the newspaper, she realised she was tired. It had been a long and eventful day. Wanting to be fresh and alert in the morning to tackle the task of finding herself a job, she decided she'd retire to bed.

In the bedroom she switched on the light and with dismay stared at the bare mattress. How stupid of her not to have realised that she had no linen, blankets or pillows, and neither had she any towels. She had no choice though but to make do for tonight. Tomorrow that was another urgent task she'd need to attend to.

Drying herself after her wash using one of her underslips, she lay down on the mattress and curled up, covering herself as best she could with her dressing gown and coat. She dearly hoped she wasn't in for a restless night but at least the mattress was comfortable.

Chapter Eight

The night proved a chilly one and next morning Judith woke aching and fatigued. She had slept only fitfully. As she stiffly rose, pulling her dressing gown around her for protection against the early-morning chill of the room, she wondered what obstacles might present themselves today. But then, despite her humiliating lack of knowledge about feeding meters and providing herself with towels and bedding, on her first day totally alone in the world she had managed to secure herself somewhere to live and she felt she should be proud of herself for achieving that.

After a breakfast of cornflakes and a rather weak cup of tea as she hadn't as yet worked out how many spoonfuls of leaves were required to make it the strength she preferred, she sat down to write several application letters for the jobs she had circled the previous evening in the *Leicester Mercury*. Those in envelopes, she attended to herself, again using an underslip to dry herself on, then dressed ready to go out and post her job applications plus resolve her lack of bedding and towels.

By the time she'd reached the town centre and had

queued for a while in the busy Bishop Street Post Office to post her letters it was lunchtime. After a cup of coffee and a sandwich in Brucciani's coffee shop, she spent the next few hours wandering around the shops, picking herself a basic cookery book and costing out her requirements for bedroom and bathroom, finally settling for a set of good quality bedding in pale peach, a pair of pillows, two pairs of white sheets and pillowcases, plus a set of white towels from British Home Stores, pleased that the full cost of her purchases, although hefty, hadn't made too big a hole in the money she had left.

Laden down now, she was making her way slowly through town on her way to the bus stop when an object in a china shop window display caught her eye. It was a pearlised glass vase in delicate shades of blue and she fell instantly in love. It seemed to be calling out to her to buy it. It would look lovely on the wooden fire surround, and the colours were just the right shades for her room. The price was four pounds seventeen shillings and sixpence – not quite as much as she had paid for her bedding but nevertheless a considerable amount to pay for an ornament. She had never been in a position before where she actually had the money to buy such a frivolous object. She stood for a moment and struggled with her conscience. Common sense told her she should not even be thinking of buying such a thing until she had a regular wage coming in and she knew where she stood moneywise, but the vase would do so much to help her personalise her flat, make it seem more of a home to her, and it would give her so much joy to look at. Without further ado she went in and bought it.

By the time she reached home it was nearing six o'clock and the late-spring evening was drawing in. As she turned into the gate of the house she now lived in, her heart sank. Before her, opening the front door, was her surly neighbour from across the landing. She was tired after her day out spent carrying heavy cumbersome parcels and the last thing she felt like was an altercation with him. As he took his key out of the front door, stepped inside and turned to shut it behind him, he saw her and after a slight hesitation held the door open for her.

'Thank you,' she said briskly as she walked through.

He looked at her parcels. 'Do you want a hand carrying those up the stairs?' he stiffly offered.

She would dearly have liked to have had a hand with her packages but wouldn't lower herself to accept his offer after his attitude the previous evening. 'I can manage, thank you,' she responded, equally woodenly. With great difficulty she negotiated the stairs under the weight and awkward shape of her purchases, but after refusing his offer couldn't bring herself to let him see she was regretting rejecting his help. Outside her own flat door she hurriedly deposited her parcels at her feet in order to free her hands and retrieve her keys from her handbag, conscious that he was now behind her letting himself into his own flat, when suddenly something struck her and before she could stop herself she exclaimed loudly, 'Oh, no!'

He turned and looked at her. 'Something wrong?'

She slowly turned to face him. 'No.' Then she issued a deep sigh of annoyance. 'Yes, there is. I've forgotten my keys.' She could visualise them now, sitting on the kitchen table. She hadn't picked them up on her departure this morning in her haste to accomplish her urgent tasks.

He stared at her patronisingly. 'Misfortune seems to follow you, doesn't it, Miss Chambers?'

She was surprised he had remembered her name but his condescending attitude towards her apparently hadn't softened overnight. 'It's an easy enough mistake to make,' she responded tartly. 'Do you happen to have an out-of-hours number I can call the landlord on?'

'He won't be pleased at being disturbed.'

Just like you, she thought. 'This *is* an emergency.'

'An avoidable one. You should have had yourself a spare key cut. Well, you're in luck, Miss Chambers. The last tenant left a spare with me. If you wait there, I'll get it.'

Oh, so you willingly helped out the last tenant, thought Judith, but you can't extend the same courtesy to me. As he disappeared inside his flat she gave a sigh of relief. It was bad enough being at loggerheads with her opposite neighbour; the last thing she wanted to do was get on the wrong side of the landlord after only taking over the tenancy so recently.

He returned moments later and handed the key to her. Headmaster-like he said, 'I trust you'll be more diligent in future.'

She looked at him stonily. 'I apologise for any inconvenience my *unavoidable* emergencies have caused you.'

With that she spun round to face her door and as fast as she could opened it up, retrieved her parcels and disappeared inside.

Her neighbour's hostility towards her was soon forgotten as she carefully unwrapped her frivolous purchase and placed it on the fireplace. She then stepped back and looked at it. It was perfect. The vase caught the light and seemed to bring the room to life. Pleased with her efforts, she set about making up her bed, looking forward to having a restful night's sleep in it, and then draped the new towels over the rail in the bathroom.

Those tasks finished, she cleared up the debris from the packaging of her purchases by pushing it all into the plastic bin in the kitchen, then got out her cookery book. She had decided on boiled potatoes to accompany the tin of Irish stew for her evening meal. The instructions outlined in the cookery book for boiling potatoes were very easy to follow. Peel potatoes, cut into equal-sized pieces, put in saucepan, adding a half-teaspoon of salt, cover with cold water, bring to the boil and cook for twenty minutes.

Thirty minutes later Judith stared down at the food on her plate. The puce mass masquerading as Irish stew tasted disgusting, the meat in it mostly fat and gristle, nothing like the tender pieces the picture on the tin had shown and nothing like the delicious stews Miss Betts had produced. She wouldn't be buying a tin of that ever again. She poked a fork into one of the potatoes. It was hard. But she had cooked them as instructed by the book. She couldn't think how but somewhere she had obviously gone wrong. Then a thought struck her. Maybe she had cut the chunks too big and they needed boiling for longer. Maybe her mistake was as simple as that. She'd have another go tomorrow. Clearing it all away, she stacked the pots in the sink and made herself a cheese sandwich, something that required no culinary skills and only a complete idiot could mess up.

After eating that she then realised the dirty crockery and pans which had been accumulating since the previous evening needed washing. She really should get used to the fact she had no Miss Betts at her disposal to tackle such jobs. Collecting the bottle of Fairy washing-up liquid from a shelf under the sink, she read the instructions. Squirt a measure into the washing-up bowl, add hot water. That was simple enough. She hadn't as yet a washing-up bowl so the sink would have to suffice. Emptying the sink of the dirty pots, she put in the plug, pointed down the spout of the bottle and squeezed out a generous amount of the thick green liquid, then turned on the geyser tap.

As she waited for the sink to fill with water her eyes fell on the overspilling waste bin by the far wall. That was another job that needed doing. It should be emptied and the rubbish put into the dustbins which she presumed were outside in the back garden. She was beginning to realise how many tasks had been performed by Miss Betts to which she herself had given no thought but had merely taken for granted. Going over to the bin, she took out the discarded brown carriers then proceeded to fill them with the rubbish that had accumulated since she had moved in. She also broke down the cardboard packing case she had left in the hall for easier disposal. She had just finished when the sploshing sound of water reached her ears. She turned and couldn't believe the sight that greeted her. The sink was overflowing on to the kitchen floor and a mountain of soapy bubbles was cascading all over.

She leaped across to the sink and turned off the tap,

then stared in dismay at the huge expanse of soapy water spreading over the grey and white speckled linoleum covering the kitchen floor. It took her nearly an hour to soak up the water and get rid of the bubbles, and not having a mop or any dishcloths she had no choice but to use one of her new towels.

Finally the floor was dry and the washing-up done and all stacked on the draining board. She felt in dire need of a hot bath. But as she turned to leave the kitchen her eyes settled on the overflowing bin, carrier bags of rubbish and flattened container needing to be put out for collection by the dustbin men. She really should do that first then she could enjoy a nice long soak before settling down for the remainder of the evening in her armchair by the fire to listen to the radio while reading a book.

Making sure she had her keys safely in her pocket and armed with her rubbish she made her way down the stairs and along the dimly lit corridor that led she believed towards the garden door. Thankfully she was right. From her position in the doorway she could see a row of metal dustbins standing against the boundary wall at the side of the house. Making her way over she saw each bin had a number painted in white on top and for a moment wondered what the numbers represented. Then it registered. The number represented the flat. She lived in flat three so dustbin number three must be allocated to her. She lifted the lid and as she did so a cat jumped out, issuing a loud yowl as he whizzed past her, so shocking Judith she almost leaped out of her skin. She lost her balance and toppled into the row of dustbins. The loud clanging and crashing they made as they all fell over like a pack of cards, lids rolling, rubbish spilling all over, filled the air.

A window on the second floor at the back of the house shot open, a head poked out and an angry voice boomed, 'What the hell is going on down there?'

Splayed across a bin, Judith looked upwards and her heart sank. It was her neighbour from across the way. 'It's Judith Chambers,' she called back, peeling herself off the dustbin to stand up awkwardly. 'I've had a slight accident and . . . er . . . somehow the dustbins fell over.'

'Well, if you'd put out your rubbish like any sane person would do during daylight hours you wouldn't have been floundering about in the dark and had your . . . *accident*. Please keep the noise down while you're clearing up the mess, I'm trying to concentrate on some work up here.'

Before Judith could respond he had withdrawn his head, yanked down the window and pulled across the curtains. She stared up, feeling a mixture of foolishness at yet again being caught in a humiliating predicament and anger at this man's rudeness towards her. Anyone would think she had caused the commotion on purpose just to disturb him. The arrogance of the man!

Clearing up the mess in darkness was neither a pleasant nor an easy task and although she was reluctant to agree with him, her neighbour had been right to suggest that in future the putting out of the rubbish should be done during daylight hours to avoid anything like this happening again. It was a good while later that Judith returned to her flat reeking of a mixture of foul smells and feeling filthy. As soon as she closed the door behind her, thankful she'd met none of the other tenants en route, she stripped off her clothes and ran herself a hot bath, putting in a liberal amount of bath salts. It was with great relief that she eventually climbed into bed, pulling her new covers cosily around herself. At least no further misfortunes could happen today.

Tomorrow was another matter. She was running out of clean clothes and a visit to the launderette was required.

Chapter Nine

'Morning, ducky. Don't recognise yer. First time here, is it? Number two's free.'

Judith stared nonplussed at the overalled, middle-aged woman, cigarette dangling from the corner of her mouth, pulling out dried laundry from a huge dryer and folding it into a large plastic washing basket.

'Number two,' the woman repeated, nodding her head in the direction of a row of industrial washing machines to the side of Judith.

She went over to the machine and stared at it blankly. She knew she should ask for help but somehow couldn't bring herself to let this woman know that at her mature age she had no idea how to work a washing machine.

Unknown to Judith the woman was watching her and gave a knowing smile. 'Hang on a minute and I'll come and give yer a hand.'

Judith patiently waited and minutes later the woman came over and opened the top of the machine. 'Right, pop yer stuff in there, ducky. Daz or Tide?' she said expectantly, holding out her hand.

Judith looked at her quizzically. 'I beg your pardon?'

113

'Daz or Tide? Soap powder.'

'Oh. Er . . .' She gave a shrug. 'Whatever you think best.'

'I've a penchant for Daz meself. Shilling then?'

'Shilling?'

'To put in the vending machine fer the powder.'

'Oh, of course.' Judith opened her handbag and pulled out her purse, feeling more and more inadequate by the minute. She handed the woman a shilling and, while she went over to the machine on the wall to fetch the powder, Judith emptied two carriers containing her washing into the machine.

The woman sprinkled the powder on top and shut the lid. 'Half a crown,' she said, holding out her hand.

'I beg your pardon?'

'To put in the washer. Yer do want yer washing doing, don't yer, and it ain't free, not in here it ain't.'

She dug in her purse again and watched the woman put the half-crown she had given her into the slot and the machine started up.

'Right, well, it'll tek about three-quarters of an hour so yer might as well park yer bum and have a rest. We women don't get much feet-up time so I'd tek advantage if I was you, gel. Or for a price I'll watch it for yer while you go off to do yer shopping. Be folded up nicely for when yer gets back.'

Judith was conscious that after her frivolous buy of yesterday her money was dwindling and she ought to start being careful until she was earning and knew where she stood. 'I'll wait.' Against the wall opposite was fixed a wooden bench and she went over and sat down on it.

'Just moved around here, have yer?' the woman asked Judith as she opened up the machine next to the one she was using and began unloading it. Without waiting for a response she continued, 'Nice around here – better than where I live on the Highfield Estate. Used ter be nice up there but it's bin going downhill for a while now. Lots of them student types moved in and they're a scruffy bunch, if yer ask me. I've yet ter see one of 'em give their step a scrub or their nets a wash. Hippy types they call 'emselves nowadays, don't they? And drink! That's all they do is smoke and drink. Yer can't get in our local some nights 'cos of all the students. Yet I bet they go home and tell their parents how hard they've bin working at them 'versity places they're supposed to be studying at.

'Got some of them immigrants moved in an' all. Seem a decent enough lot, when yer can understand 'em that is, but they ain't half got some funny ways. There's a family moved in not far from us in a two-up, two-down and at least twenty people live in that house: aunts, uncles, grandma, grandad, and at least ten kids. The old dear cooks in the garden in a big pot over an open fire, and you should smell the stink! I dread ter think what's in that pot.' She gave a shudder. 'Why the hell she don't use the cooker is anyone's guess. It'd be a bleddy sight easier for her than squatting for hours like she does, stirring that great big cauldron. Mind you,' she mused thoughtfully, 'she probably ain't ever seen a cooker where she comes from. Mud huts is all they have, and a cow if they're lucky. Can't blame 'em really, wanting to come over here and mek a better life for 'emselves, can yer?'

She broke off her chatter to attend to several customers

who came in. As soon as they had departed she resumed her one-sided conversation to Judith.

'Your washer broke, is it?' she said, shutting the lid of the emptied machine and moving across to the dryer where she proceeded to load the wet washing inside. 'Only yer don't look ter me like the normal launderette type.' Again without waiting for a response she continued, 'So is it a big house yer've moved in ter? Some lovely houses around here, ain't there? What's yer husband do then? I bet he's got a good job. Oh, that's yer load done. Want a hand with it?'

Judith rose and went across to the machine. 'I can manage, thank you.' She opened the lid and as she had watched the woman doing, pulled out her washing to load it into a basket. As she did so she stared at it dumbfounded. 'Look what the machine has done to my clothes!' she exclaimed.

The woman came over and inspected the washing. ''Tain't the machine what's done that, ducky, it's you.'

Judith looked at her astounded. 'Me?'

'Yeah. Yer've mixed yer whites with yer darks. Yer never sorted 'em, did yer? The dye from yer darks has ran in ter yer whites.'

'But they're ruined!'

'Yeah, they are,' the woman chuckled. 'New underwear for you it looks like unless yer fancy wearing dingy grey. And I don't expect yer bought that towel that colour.' She patted Judith's arm. 'It's an easy mistake ter mek, gel. Show me a woman yet who ain't cocked up the washing at some time in their lives. My friend's husband ended up with pink underpants once – oh, and didn't we have a laugh over it? Mind you, wouldn't have bin funny for him if he'd had an accident and ended up in hospital, now would it? Me, I was over-enthusiastic with a bottle of bleach once and me sheets ended up in great holes 'cos as well as teking the stains out it rotted the material. Sometime in the future this'll happen again ter yer, you'll see.'

It won't, thought Judith, I can't afford to keep making mistakes like this one. She started to fold the washing to put it in the bag to take home and hang out on the washing line. Then a thought struck her. It would need ironing. She hadn't an iron or a board. Another expense on top of the mistake she had just made, and another skill to learn as she had never ironed so much as a tea towel in her life before. What catastrophe was she going to make of that? she thought worriedly, visualising burned clothes. She had a sudden overwhelming feeling of being out of her depth. She couldn't cope, it was all too much. Practically everything she was tackling she was making a mess of. It was one disaster after another. She was useless, utterly so. She then gave herself a mental scolding. She had promised herself yesterday to learn from her mistakes and must look on today's mishaps as just part of the process.

Leaving a sixpenny tip on top of the machine for the launderette woman, she picked up her bag of washing and walked out.

Later that evening she stood back and admired her efforts. Her new underwear, which she was determined not to ruin in any way, had been neatly folded and put away, a new towel to replace the dingy grey mistake of that morning folded neatly on the bath rail, and her

117

clothes, painstakingly pressed – she being very vigilant to ensure the newly purchased iron was not too hot – were hanging up in the wardrobe. Her evening meal that night had consisted of a pork chop, which admittedly had been a little too well done, but the potatoes were edible and the tinned peas, although in the past she had been used to fresh, were heated through perfectly.

A warm glow filled her. Not everything she had tackled had ended in disaster today and she felt a little more optimistic that with time she would become quite competent at taking care of herself. All she needed now was to get herself a job and her future was heading in the right direction.

Chapter Ten

Two days later the plop of the first post landing on the floor by the flat's front door had Judith rushing to collect it. She was dearly hoping for news of her job applications. There were four white envelopes on the mat. Two contained rejection letters, but the other two were requests for her to attend interviews that afternoon. One was for two o'clock and the other four. The timings couldn't be better, she could attend both comfortably. Her heart soared. Hopefully by evening she would have secured herself one of them.

It wasn't until after she was ready to depart for the first of her interviews that nervousness at what she faced started to manifest itself. Suddenly it hit her just what she was in for. During her time at Chambers' she had never been allowed by her father to interview new staff, or even in fact to sit in on the process. All she had been allowed to do was to send through the candidates, for him to decide who would work for Chambers' and who wouldn't. She was now on the other side of the procedure and she suddenly felt daunted by it all, worried she would somehow mess up like she had over simple household tasks.

But then she mentally scolded herself. She needed a job or she would soon be facing a lot more problems than she did merely attending an interview. She must pull herself together and get on with it.

Grabbing up her coat, and after double checking that she had her keys in her handbag, she set off.

Graham Sneddon of Sneddon Electrical Wholesalers Limited nodded, impressed. Judith Chambers had answered all his questions very directly and precisely, it was readily apparent that she was very efficient and it seemed to him there wasn't anything she didn't know about running a general office. What he couldn't understand, though, was why for a woman of her maturity and experience she seemed to be so on edge, sitting as she was stiffly on the chair opposite him, clutching her bag on her knees. She hadn't shown even a flicker of a smile when he had made several humorous comments in an effort to put her at her ease. But then, that could be down to nervousness. He had asked her to tell him her working history and learned that she had so far worked only for the family firm until her father had passed away and the decision had been taken recently to sell the business. Attending interviews was obviously a new experience for her. Why, though, wasn't she sitting back and enjoying the benefits gained by selling off the family firm, instead of choosing to continue to work? She must enjoy working, that was all he could think. She did seem, though, to be exactly what he was looking for and had impressed him more than the other candidates he had seen, several of whom had obviously lied in their application letters and had neither the skills nor the experience to supervise themselves, let alone a busy office.

He smiled at Judith. 'As I explained earlier, very sadly our office manageress Enid Price has left through ill health. It all happened suddenly which means that finding a replacement for her is urgent. Your ability to start immediately would suit us fine. Obviously all firms operate their own individual procedures but the principles are the same. I'm sure it won't take you long to get to grips with ours. We keep things effective but simple here. The staff are a good hardworking bunch even if one or two can be a bit of a handful, but I'm sure they won't pose any problems for you. Would you like to meet them all?'

Her heart raced. Did this mean he was offering her the job? When Mr Sneddon had outlined the basics it sounded ideal for her, what was expected of her being almost identical to her routine at Chambers', apart from one glaring fact that was immediately apparent to Judith: Graham Sneddon hadn't given her the impression he would be breathing down her neck all the time, finding fault where none existed, constantly reaffirming and threatening that things were to be done a certain way, with no deviation whatsoever, or else she'd suffer the consequences. Graham Sneddon's idea of management was the antithesis of Charles Chambers'. He wanted an office manager he could rely on to use her own initiative, only involving him in issues beyond her responsibilities, so that he could concentrate on managing the company. The pay was good too, more than she'd ever received from Charles Chambers' hand: twenty-four pounds a week net of deductions for income tax and social security, but hopefully more than enough to pay her bills, for food, and leave some over for all her other living expenses without having to penny-pinch too much. All in all, she couldn't have hoped for better.

'I'd like very much to meet the staff, Mr Sneddon,' she responded formally.

His smile broadened. 'Good. Follow me.'

From Judith's observations as she was being shown around the staff seemed very relaxed, and it became apparent to her that Mr Sneddon's observation about their needing a firm hand now and again was a gross understatement. As they had entered the general office, albeit the staff had been working away at their various tasks, they had been chatting and laughing between themselves, and two women were even discussing an article in a magazine which they hadn't the grace to try and cover up as their boss entered to introduce the person who could be in charge of them. The staff at this company did not need a firm hand now and again, they needed bringing into line, being made to realise that the workplace was somewhere they could expect to work, not treat as a social opportunity. The last office manager had clearly had very lax rules if she'd allowed this kind of behaviour. Judith herself would soon sort it out, have the place running like clockwork. Mr Sneddon would be very impressed with her, she had no doubt about that.

They parted, having shaken hands on the deal, and arranged that an inwardly elated Judith would start her employment at eight-thirty the following Monday morning.

Out of courtesy she then attended the other interview

which was for an office supervisor for a builder's mer-
chants. The owner who interviewed her had obviously not
been truthful when he had advertised the position. It
wasn't an office supervisor he needed but a general dogs-
body to do everything, ranging from making tea, tackling
all the office work and even rolling up their sleeves to help
out in the yard when required, which was something
Judith was definitely not prepared to do. Besides, putting
all the duties together, it was clearly not humanly possible
for one person to get through all this even working a
continuous twelve-hour day. The pay he was offering was
hardly more than slave-labour rates and the conditions
she'd be expected to work in were dire to say the least.
The old-fashioned equipment and drab facilities on the
lower levels of Chambers' premises had been a palace
compared to this place. The proprietor of the business
seemed genuinely surprised when she declined to accept
it. She shook his hand and departed.

Judith didn't feel for one moment that her last interview was a waste of her time. What it did was confirm to
her that she had been extremely lucky in securing a
position so very much more suitable for her at her first
attempt. Her first day at her new job was three days away
and she was already somewhat daunted at the thought of
finding her way around, getting to grips with the way
Sneddon's operated, and tackling what she saw as her first
priority: regimenting the undisciplined staff.

Tonight, though, she was going to celebrate her good
fortune by treating herself to a piece of good steak with
salad to accompany it, washed down with a decent bottle
of white wine. From what she had gleaned from her

cookery book, steak didn't look difficult to cook – a piece half an inch thick needed three minutes each side in a hot frying pan. All she had to do with the wine was open the bottle and she had seen her father do that enough times over the years. She couldn't go wrong, surely?

So preoccupied was she by the day's events, Judith had already got off the bus when she realised she had alighted a stop too early. Oh, never mind, she thought, the short walk would do her good. She had almost passed the building before she realised what it was: the public library. She'd had no idea that she lived so close to one. She inwardly smiled. Finding a library had made her day perfect. Without further ado she went inside and spent a pleasant half-hour browsing the shelves for a book that interested her which she hadn't read before. She found three. Delighted, she approached the counter to have them stamped.

The pretty dark-haired young woman behind the counter stopped cataloguing a pile of books and came across to Judith, taking her books from her. 'Oh, good choice,' she said, smiling. 'Have you read Steinbeck before? He's very good. *The Grapes of Wrath* is a particular favourite of mine. How people coped with the Depression in the nineteen-thirties amazes me. We don't realise how lucky we are, do we? I should be interested to hear your comments when you bring it back.'

'I'll do that,' Judith responded, handing over her tickets which she had taken out of her handbag.

The woman stamped the books, took out the buff identification card from each which she inserted into Judith's tickets, and just as she was about to file them

Judith said, 'Oh, I should inform you that I have changed my address. My old library was on Welford Road but as I have moved to this area this will be my library from now on.'

The young woman smiled at her, passing her a white piece of printed card. 'Jot your new details on that and I'll have your new tickets ready for you when you return.'

Just then, a staid-looking older woman arrived behind the counter and addressed the younger. 'I'll take over from you, as a gentleman over by the local history section has requested help in searching for the book he's after.'

The young woman smiled politely. 'Yes, of course, Miss Sturgess.' As she departed, she said to Judith, 'Enjoy your books.'

Armed with her precious reading matter, Judith arrived back at the house and was just about to unlock her door when she jumped as a male voice boomed out, 'Well, well, well, so you're the new tenant of number three? Far prettier than the last occupant, I must say.'

Judith stared blankly at the fat, middle-aged, shiny-suited man approaching down the corridor towards her.

He held out one podgy hand. 'Roger Makepiece. He was a man.'

She stared at him blankly, his manner of address not making sense to her. 'I beg your pardon?'

'The last tenant. He was a man.'

'Roger Makepiece?'

'Yes, pleased to meet you,' he said, thrusting his hand nearer to her.

She suddenly twigged what he had meant. 'Oh, *you're*

Roger Makepiece and the last tenant of my flat was a man?'

'Yes, that's what I said.' He withdrew his hand as he realised the attractive new tenant was not going to accept his friendly gesture. 'There's never been a woman tenant since I've been living here. Make a nice change having you around the place. Settling in all right?'

'Yes, thank you,' she said briskly, wishing this man would just go away. 'If you'll excuse me?'

She made to turn and unlock her door but Roger wasn't giving up that easily.

'I live in the attic flat and I'm in medical supplies. Would you like to come up for coffee?'

She definitely would not. 'No, thank you. Now, if you'll please excuse me . . .'

Just then Nathan Banks arrived at the head of the stairs in time to hear Roger say, 'Tomorrow night then? I'll get a Madeira cake special.'

Nathan, who was now standing at his door opposite, gave Judith a look as if to say 'Are you that desperate?' before opening the door and disappearing inside.

She flashed Roger a look of reproof. 'Please excuse me, Mr Makepiece. As I said, I really am busy.' She hurriedly unlocked her own door and as she shut it, heard him call to her, 'What about Sunday night then?'

She gave a sharp sigh as she put her carrier of shopping on the kitchen table and proceeded to strip off her coat. Roger Makepiece really was the limit, not taking the hint that she didn't want anything to do with him. But as for her neighbour from opposite . . . how dare he give her such a reproving look? He had assumed she was making arrangements with Makepiece, and despite his assuming this totally wrongly, so what if she was? What had it to do with him? Awful man.

A while later, Judith laid down her knife and fork and gave a satisfied smile. She couldn't quite believe it but the steak had been most palatable. A little overdone but not enough to spoil it. She would know next time that a piece of steak the size she had bought did not need quite so long a cooking time as her book had said it should. She was beginning to realise that cooking was learned by trial and error and using the cook's own judgement. She suspected she'd have a few more mishaps before she was adept. She had found, though, that she was actually enjoying looking after herself. It was very satisfying to eat a meal she had prepared. Even washing up was proving rewarding. She derived a certain satisfaction from surveying a tidy kitchen, having cleared away the debris after she had made her meal.

Judith suddenly felt she was getting somewhere. Albeit her attempts were still clumsy ones, she was fending for herself and her flat was actually beginning to feel like a home to her, which was something she had never experienced before. Now she had a job and could provide for herself, her future wasn't looking quite so bleak.

Chapter Eleven

In the reception area of Sneddon Electrical Wholesalers, Graham Sneddon warmly shook Judith's hand when she arrived to start her new job promptly at eight-twenty the following Monday morning. To him she still seemed to be showing the slightly stiff manner she had displayed at her interview but again he put it down to tension at starting a new job. There was no doubt though that she was an attractive woman and he couldn't understand why she wasn't married. If he wasn't happily so himself or was the philandering sort, he would have found her hard to resist, if ever a way through that very noticeable invisible barrier she seemed to erect around herself could be found.

'Welcome aboard,' he said sincerely, and jocularly added, 'Wish all my staff showed such eagerness to start.'

The clerical staff will in future, Judith thought. They had all obviously run rings around her predecessor but no more liberties were going to be taken now she was in charge of them.

'Now I really wanted to be on hand to help you settle in this morning,' Graham continued. 'Sit with you for an hour or so to start to familiarise you with our business,

129

but something urgent has come up with one of our major suppliers and I have to go to a meeting with them. I doubt I'll be back until late this evening as I have to travel up to Middlesbrough which is a good five-hour journey. Our briefing will have to wait, I'm afraid. It's a bit unfair considering it's your first day but with me out you're in charge of the office side. I don't envisage you'll encounter any problems, as I said before the girls are a good bunch, but Jeff Vine the warehouse manager will gladly help you out should you need it. Jeff's been with me since day one and knows the business inside out.'

Graham looked at his watch. 'Better get off. I only came in to welcome you on board.' He made to go then stopped to readdress her. 'Oh, your office is the one next to the general office and I asked Karen last Friday . . . she's our office junior, lovely girl, very obliging . . . to make sure it's cleared of Enid's possessions for her husband to collect and equipped for you with new stationery et cetera. The girls do all the day-to-day typing, but for more private correspondence and personal things for me if my secretary happens to be off, I've had a new typewriter bought for you.' He gave a laugh. 'I've been on to Enid for years to part with her old Imperial 66 but she clung on to it like grim death. Said it had been a good friend to her and to part with it would be like parting with a family member. I'm sending it over with her possessions as a reminder of her time with us and of how much we thought of her, along with the gift of a sherry decanter. She loved a drop of sherry, did Enid. Anyway, I hope everything is to your satisfaction but should it not be we can resolve anything when I get back. I want you to

130

be happy working for us, Judith.'

Despite feeling very uncomfortable at being addressed by her Christian name in the working environment, she was also surprised and overwhelmed by her new boss's show of concern for her well-being. She wasn't used to that either. Her father had not shown any concern whatsoever for the welfare of his employees. 'I'm sure everything will be just fine, Mr Sneddon. I hope your trip is successful.'

'So do I or I've the task of finding a new supplier of electrical cabling. Right, now I'd really better get off.'

Judith found her office, where she deposited her coat on the stand just inside the door, and walked around her desk to sit down. The room was light and airy and equipped with decent wooden furniture and a comfortable leather chair for her to sit on. On the far side stood several filing cabinets, which she assumed amongst other things contained all the personnel records. On her desk was a modern Olivetti typewriter, and neatly laid out letterheads and assorted colour copy papers, along with a new box of carbons. There were also new writing pads, pencils, sharpener, paperclips, stapler, and an assortment of coloured Biros. Also provided were a new bottle of ink and a blotting pad, should she prefer to use a fountain pen. On the window ledge stood several well-tended pot plants, something Charles Chambers had never allowed, and Judith had to admit their existence did add a pleasant touch to the office. She heard the women arriving, chatting loudly as they took off their coats, and gave them some moments to settle at their desks before she went through.

131

Just inside the general office doorway she stood and said briskly, 'Good morning.' When she had their attention she announced, 'I'm Miss Chambers, your new office manageress.' She looked at her watch. 'Work begins at eight-thirty. It is now twenty-seven minutes to nine. From now on I will expect you all to be at your desks at eight-thirty sharp and working. In future lateness will not be acceptable without a very valid excuse.'

Her eyes settled on a young girl standing by the Banda machine, staring nervously back at her. She was dressed very fashionably and it suited her but Judith did not approve of the shortness of her skirt, feeling it most unsuitable office wear. 'Your name is?' she asked.

The girl gulped. 'Karen Weatherall,' she faltered.

'Well, Miss Weatherall, what you wear out of office hours is your own business, but during office hours I insist on proper dress code. Please wear something more fitting in future. That goes for all of you. I will be coming to speak to you individually to find out exactly what your duties are so I can judge how efficiently you use your time and if necessary instruct you as to how improvements can be made. Should you need me for the next few minutes I'll be visiting the accounts department to introduce myself, but after that I'll be in my office going through the personnel records to familiarise myself with your backgrounds before I come and sit with you. You may continue.'

As she walked out of the office to make her way across to the accounts department she missed the look they all gave each other.

Muriel Wilks, a woman in her early fifties, looked up

from her work in accounts as Judith entered. 'Oh, hello, you must be Judith – or do you prefer Judy? Muriel Wilks, pleased ter meet yer. I hope yer settling in all right?'

'I'm settling in fine, thank you, Mrs Wilks,' she replied. 'I've come to inform you that I'll require at least an hour of your time during the next couple of days for you to outline to me your duties so I know exactly what you do. If necessary I can implement improvements. And I wish to be addressed as Miss Chambers. Familiarity breeds contempt, doesn't it?'

Muriel looked at her blankly. 'Does it? Oh. Well, *Miss Chambers*, have yer brought me in yer P45?'

'P45?'

Judith's manner was just too formal for Muriel's liking and her instincts told her that none of them were in for an easy ride under the stewardship of their new office manageress. What Graham Sneddon had been thinking of when he took her on to be in charge of them, Muriel couldn't imagine. Nevertheless she was far too long in the tooth to let anyone intimidate her easily, especially this upstart. Let her try and lick them into shape. Enid had never seen the need. Muriel loved working here because it was a happy office, they were all like one big family. She greatly feared the arrival of Judith Chambers was about to upset all that.

Muriel knew she was good at her job. Admittedly she might work a little untidily, but she ran her department competently enough as far as she was concerned and didn't take kindly to the fact that the new office manageress wanted to come and nit-pick over it.

133

She responded with a hint of mockery in her voice, 'I expect I don't need ter tell yer, you being our superior like, that no P45 means me putting yer on Week 1 which means a big deduction from yer wage until the Revenue sort yer tax code out, and *they* can tek ages. I do the payroll Monday and Tuesday so I really need it pronto. If you want some time with me then it'll have to be later on in the week. I'll let yer know when I can spare you some.'

The last thing Judith wanted was a big lump taken out of her wage as she wasn't sure of her weekly outgoings yet or of what she would have left over to play with, even though she knew she would eventually get a tax rebate. But that could take weeks. A visit back to Chambers' did not appeal to her at all. Having the humiliating task of asking for the form would immediately alert them to the fact that despite the sale of the business she herself was still making her own living. They would also now all be aware of how she'd lied to them over Charles Chambers' death, unaware she'd been under strict instructions to do so. The thought of the contemptuous response she would receive was unbearable. Neither had she appreciated Muriel Wilks' attitude towards her. Judith looked her straight in the eye.

'It's in hand and you will receive it as soon as I am in receipt of it myself. Eleven o'clock on Wednesday morning will do for me to review your work. Please make sure you're free then. You may proceed.'

Leaving a fuming Muriel Wilks glaring at her, Judith turned and walked back to her office. Sitting down behind her desk, she pondered the problem of obtaining her P45 with minimum impact on herself. Then an idea struck her. She took a deep breath and picked up the telephone, asked the switchboard operator for an outside line and dialled Chambers' number. She was taken aback but not totally surprised when the telephone was answered at the other end with the name Burbridge's Leather Goods and not Chambers', and heard a catch in the telephonist's voice when she realised who she was speaking to.

As they spoke Judith could hear background voices. It was plain that much camaraderie was taking place. Obviously in her short absence the place was falling into chaos and if the Burbridges did not take better control of their staff their business was going to suffer greatly. But then the success of the Burbridges was not her problem, her responsibilities and loyalties now lay with Sneddon's.

Judith spoke briefly to Mr Mackie, the payroll and accounts manager, and in a brisk, no-nonsense tone asked him to issue her with a P45 urgently and despatch it round via one of the junior staff to her old address in Clarendon Park. Purely out of respect for her previous position and family connection to the company, he did not question this. That part of her plan successfully concluded, she replaced the telephone then made another call to order herself a taxi for one o'clock. She then proceeded to go through the personnel files and familiarise herself with what else the filing cabinets held.

At one o'clock precisely she donned her coat along with the rest of the staff, apart from those who were taking their lunch in the heavily subsidised staff canteen which was run by a sprightly elderly woman who served up large portions of whatever was asked for, usually fried and accompanied by chips, and got into the waiting taxi, instructing the driver to take her to the address she gave him in Clarendon Park.

As they pulled up outside the house she had lived in so long and had been so cruelly forced out of just a short while ago, Judith felt a knot of anxiety niggling away in her stomach. She stared across at it, half-expecting her mother and father to emerge and their cold disapproving eyes to settle on her. Her face tightened as she remembered the awful story behind their marriage. She mentally shook herself. Her father was dead, her mother miles away living the high life on the proceeds of her years of misery. Judith herself was a free agent now, no longer under their control. Her future was in her own hands and she must get on with it.

She asked the driver to wait for her then alighted from the taxi. Making her way up to the front door, she rapped the brass door knocker purposefully.

Presently a flustered young woman answered it, wiping her hands on a tea towel. By her side was a little girl aged around three, her face, clothes and hands covered in a dusting of flour.

'Hello,' the woman addressed Judith, smiling brightly. 'Please excuse the state we're in but we're making cakes for Daddy, aren't we, poppet?' She gave the child at her side a fond look. The child smiled back, nodding vigorously. The woman brought her attention back to Judith. 'What can I do for you?'

She looked at the child and then back at her mother. The love this woman had for her daughter was readily apparent, as was the child's for her mother. That's how it should have been for Judith herself instead of what she had experienced, and suddenly she felt cheated. Memories flooded back of her own child whom she had never even been given the chance to hold in her arms before it had been taken from her. She had not allowed herself even to think much about it since leaving the house where she had given birth, the memory was too painful, but now as she stood witnessing this touching scene she couldn't hold back the emotion and sincerely hoped that her own child had not fared as she had; that it had been raised by decent people like Miss Hales had said it would be after she had whisked it away, and that those parents had nurtured her child like this little girl's obviously did her.

Judith suddenly realised the new occupant of the house was addressing her. 'I beg your pardon?'

'I just enquired if you were all right? You're looking at us rather strangely.'

Judith mentally shook herself. 'I apologise,' she responded briskly. 'My name is Judith Chambers and I believe you've had some correspondence delivered here this morning for me?'

The woman nodded. 'Yes, I have. I'm quite surprised to meet you as I understood the people we bought the house from were moving abroad to live. I was going to forward it on to the agents we bought the house through for them to deal with it. I'll fetch it for you.'

She disappeared inside, leaving the child staring up at Judith. She felt uncomfortable. She had no direct experience of children and didn't know what to say to her. Thankfully seconds later the woman returned with a white envelope which she gave to Judith. 'If you give me your new address then anything else that gets delivered here for you I can forward, save you the trouble of the journey.'

Judith didn't want to belittle herself by informing this woman that the risk of anything else addressed to herself arriving here was a remote possibility as she had no one who would want to correspond with her, friend or business connection, so futile as she felt it was, she gave her address.

As she prepared to depart the woman said to her, 'It must have been so sad for you leaving such a lovely house, but we all have to move on sometimes, don't we? Can I assure you we will take great care of it and I know we'll be happy here, as you must have been because who wouldn't be happy in a house like this?'

Judith flashed her a brief smile before she turned and made her way back to the taxi.

Later that evening she picked up her empty dinner plate and proceeded to fill the sink with water. Having learned her lesson over the amount of washing-up liquid to use, she gave only a small squirt from the bottle. As the sink filled with soapsuds she thought back over her day. Apart from the unexpectedly emotional visit back to the house, which she had locked away at the back of her mind, she felt she had had a very productive day. Despite a strong feeling that she would meet a certain amount of resistance from the staff after the way her predecessor had allowed them to carry on, she knew there were rules she needed to implement to make the office run far more efficiently and felt positive that Graham Sneddon would be pleased with the results on his return.

Chapter Twelve

At eight-thirty the next morning Judith received a telephone call from Mr Sneddon informing her that his car
had developed faults on the journey back from Middlesbrough. The garage as yet had no idea what was wrong
with it which meant he had no idea when he would return
and hoped Judith was coping all right. She told him not
to be concerned, that she was getting on with familiaris-
ing herself with the staff and their duties, and without
going into detail informed him that she'd already started
implementing improvements. He seemed pleased with her
response and having told her he'd be back as soon as was
physically possible, hung up.

As it was the car took three days to fix and Graham
Sneddon did not arrive back in the office until after lunch
on Thursday afternoon. Aware that he had arrived and
feeling pleased with what she had achieved so far, Judith
waited patiently for a summons from his secretary for a
meeting with him so she could outline her progress. Well
over an hour passed before her telephone rang and she
was asked to go to Graham's office.

The secretary told her to go straight in but Judith

knocked politely on the door and respectfully waited for his summons before she entered.

She was surprised to note that he looked quite grave as he told her to sit down and wondered if his business trip hadn't been as successful as he'd hoped it would be.

Looking directly at her, he scraped his fingers through his hair and sighed heavily. 'Judith, these new rules you've implemented, just what are they?'

She was still rather uncomfortable about his informal attitude towards her but, pushing this aside, answered, 'Well, it was very quickly apparent to me that the staff here have more or less been allowed to do what they like and there were many areas where we could become far more effective in how the workload is handled. I've informed the clerical staff that talking will no longer be tolerated during working hours unless it concerns business matters, and they are also well aware that I expect them all to be working at their desks by eight-thirty sharp and lateness will not be tolerated without a valid excuse. Neither do they begin to pack up to go home until five-thirty whereas before they were starting to do that from five-twenty in some cases. The brewing of tea seemed to take place at regular intervals throughout the day so I've had the equipment removed and arranged with Mrs Biddles to bring a trolley around the offices at eleven o'clock in the morning and at three in the afternoon. The staff are allowed a ten-minute break in which to drink it. I have ascertained that this will add at least ten minutes on to the working day of each individual.

'Some of the work produced I felt was very slipshod in so much as letters weren't set out as precisely as they should be, and the boxes on the invoices weren't being filled in exactly the centre, creating a bad impression on our customers. Filing was being left to accumulate, resulting in time wasted searching through uncollated paperwork for particular items if a query arose, so I've insisted that it's done immediately. The staff are now well aware that they need to pay far more attention to their duties and that all work passed to me for checking I will expect to be perfect, in effect eliminating the need for corrections which in turn will up productivity. I've also devised a new procedure for the way paperwork is passed through the departments, saving much time-wasting by staff from the warehouse coming into the general office and disrupting the workflow by chatting to the women. It's a start, Mr Sneddon. I feel I've made good progress towards the ultimate aim of having the office run like clockwork.'

He was staring at her dumbstruck. 'Is this how Chambers' operated?'

'A lot more efficiently, Mr Sneddon, but by the time I've finished revamping the departments under my charge, they will do too,' she said proudly.

He raised his eyebrows at her. 'Really? Was the turnover of staff high at Chambers'?'

She couldn't see the reason for his question but regardless answered him. 'Workers come and go all the time, Mr Sneddon. Obviously I have only ever worked for Chambers' but I expect our turnover of staff was the same as all other companies. People aren't so loyal as they used to be towards their employers. Another few shillings a week is enough to lure them away, but there's always someone willing to take their place.'

141

'You don't think they left because of the way they were treated?'

She looked at him blankly. 'I don't understand?'

He gave a deep sigh. 'Judith, I expect my staff to do a good job, but just because I pay them I don't think that gives me the right to treat them like imbeciles, checking everything they do, owning them body and soul while they are on my premises.'

'But they treat you with contempt if you don't,' she responded with conviction. 'Workers need to be watched like a hawk and constantly reminded who's boss.'

He looked at her sadly. 'I told you at your interview that I like my staff to be happy and enjoy coming here, and in return they give me their absolute loyalty. Those that do take liberties over and above what I consider acceptable, I deal with firmly. I've people still working for me that I took on when I started this company twenty-five years ago and I know they won't leave unless the company goes under or they retire. Just why have you insisted that all the clerical staff address each other by their surnames, yourself included?'

'Well, it's not right they're so familiar with each other, and it's very disrespectful to address their superiors in such a manner.'

'Maybe in Victorian times, Judith, when the workplace was a miserable environment and bosses viewed all their workers as the scum of the earth, but those ways have practically died out now, thank goodness. Just because I'm the boss doesn't mean I'm superior to everyone who works for me. Let me tell you, most of my staff could teach me a thing or two about improving my business methods, and have done, believe me. And I listen to what they have to say and value their opinion. After all, it's them that know best about the work they're doing and how to do it, like I do with my side of things.

'Judith, apart from the junior staff, the rest are very experienced and it's demeaning for them having you check through their work. I like everything that leaves this office to be neatly and tidily presented but the main thing to me is that it goes out on time and is accurate, not if it's typed absolutely perfectly in line. Our customers are more interested in receiving their goods on time and being charged correctly, I doubt very much they take a ruler and measure if the typing is perfectly centred.

'And does it really matter if the staff chat while they're working, or call each other by their Christian name, or make a brew several times a day? Don't you think it helps create a more friendly environment for them? And as for starting work on the dot and finishing on the dot, well, a little flexibility on our part doesn't hurt when the overall output is one hundred per cent, which I know it is. And I know without doubt that if we were faced with a crisis, all my employees would stay behind if necessary until that crisis was over.

'Judith, my idea of an office manageress is someone to guide the staff, make sure they're happy and have all they need, deal with crises. Not treat everyone here like unruly schoolchildren, ruling them with a rod of iron, slapping them down should they dare to speak out of turn.

'I was expecting you to carry on from where Enid left off, and if any changes were necessary see that they improved the staff's lives, not made them miserable.' He

143

ran a hand wearily through his hair. 'Look, I'm sorry, Judith, but it's obvious my idea of running an office and yours are poles apart. I have a mutiny on my hands. The staff refuse to have you in charge of them any longer and say if I don't resolve it they'll walk out. They mean it too. I have no choice but to ask you to leave. I've asked Muriel to make your pay up until the end of the week.' He pushed an envelope towards her. 'I can only recommend that in future you see your charges as your allies not your enemies.'

Judith sat staring at him, stunned. She had entered this office fully expecting to be praised for the changes she had made, not to be told the staff had refused to work with her any longer and be asked to leave. Did Graham Sneddon not realise that by allowing his staff to continue in this way he risked the downfall of his business? But her need to make him see the error of his ways was overridden by a feeling of mortified embarrassment at the situation she was in. She wanted desperately to escape as quickly as she could. Accepting the envelope, she stood up. 'Thank you, Mr Sneddon,' she said hurriedly. 'I shall clear my desk and be off the premises as quickly as I can.'

Without waiting for any response from him, she turned and walked out.

All the way home she was totally confused, quite unable to understand what had happened. On Monday she had started a promising new position. Three and a half days later, after believing herself to be doing a good job, she had been told she had achieved the opposite and had been sacked as a result.

It was not until she was home and nursing a cup of tea

at her kitchen table that the truth of it all hit her full force. She had been very naïve to assume that all offices were run on the strict principles Charles Chambers had advocated, and after his death she had been very wrong to think that at least he had left her with the ability to acquire and keep a managerial job. In Graham Sneddon's opinion her ways of doing things were the sort that alienated people, not kept their loyalty. Her father's legacy to her was no gift, it was a burden.

She gave a deep desolate sigh as a feeling of total incompetence and uselessness swept through her. She saw the bright future she had begun to make for herself disintegrate. She had no idea how to make people's lives happy, only miserable. Oh, God, all those hordes of employees who had come and gone over the years through Chambers', arriving with high hopes of a good job in a friendly atmosphere only to have them quashed, finding themselves rigidly ruled over by Judith and her father. She was not properly equipped to be responsible for the true welfare of staff and could see now why Graham Sneddon had had no choice but to ask her to leave when his own staff had refused to have her manage them any longer.

In future all she could hope to hold down was a job of a subordinate nature on much-reduced pay, which would barely keep a roof over her head, pay for basic food and little else. And how would she cope with such a job? Not having her own office to escape back to, she would be working at a desk alongside others, no doubt finding it difficult to converse with them and to join in with their camaraderie. They wouldn't understand that and she

145

would be ostracised, forced out again because she did not fit in. Her shoulders sagged despairingly. What was going to become of her?

There was a loud knocking on her front door and she slowly rose and walked to the end of the hall. She couldn't answer it, she couldn't face anyone at the moment whoever they were. Another loud rap. Whoever it was, they weren't going away. Taking a deep breath, she walked down the hallway to respond, hoping she could get rid of them quickly.

She stared in surprise at the two scruffy teenage boys facing her, their arms filled with bunches of late-spring flowers. 'Yes?' she said tartly.

'Wanna buy some flowers, Missus? Two bob a bunch. The two blokes in the downstairs flats each bought a bunch off us and one sent us up here. Said a lady lived on the middle floor and she was bound to want some. Ladies love flowers, don't they? So how many bunches do yer want then?'

She looked at them. The flowers were drooping and straggly and she assumed more than likely stolen from people's gardens, judging by the appearance of those selling them. She did love flowers but her mother hadn't allowed her to have any in her bedroom and Judith had known better than to question her reasons. Now she realised it was by way of depriving her of anything that might bring her cheer. Her mother had had no cheer in her own life so why should Judith have any when she had been the cause? Her mother, though, wasn't around any longer to stop her having flowers if she wanted, stop her doing anything that brought her happiness for that matter. As straggly as they were, a bunch on her kitchen windowsill might go a very small way to lift her feeling of wretchedness. 'One. Wait here while I fetch your money.'

Having paid them and received her flowers she made to shut the door and as she did so heard one of them say to the other, 'She's a miserable old bat, ain't she? I bet if she'd 'a' smiled she'd have cracked her face open. I bet she's hard pushed to find a man who'd wanna keep her warm at night.' She heard them both laughing as they made their way to the flat upstairs.

Judith stood in the passageway, staring blankly at the flowers. She had responded to the boys as she felt politely, bought flowers from them, yet they had described her with such hostility. She felt their remarks to be unwarranted and they had cut her deeply.

Walking into the kitchen, she laid the flowers on the draining board then made her way into the bathroom where she stood before the medicine cabinet mirror. She studied the face staring back at her. Those boys were right. She had never scrutinised herself so closely before and it shocked her to see that she did look miserable, the corners of her mouth turned downwards, eyes expressionless. But it was easy to smile when you had something to smile about. Since she could remember she never had and most certainly not now, so smiling to her was something that required a great effort and did not come naturally as it did to others. But just because she hadn't smiled wasn't enough in her opinion to warrant what she had overheard one of the boys say about her.

She heard the muffled sound of voices out in the

passageway outside her flat and realised the boys had come back down from the flat upstairs and were passing her door on their way down to the ground floor. She suddenly desperately needed to know what reason she had given for one of them to speak of her so disparagingly. Without another thought she shot to the front door and pulled it open. The boys were just about to descend the stairs. 'Excuse me,' she called to them.

They stopped and turned to look at her. 'Want another bunch, Missus?' one called back.

She walked across to them. 'No. I overheard what you said about me.'

The boys looked guiltily at each other. 'Oh, now, eh up, Missus, we . . .'

'It's all right,' she interjected. 'I'm not going to get you into trouble over it. I just want to know what I did to make you say it?'

They both looked at her uncomfortably.

'It's important I should know,' she urged.

'Well, Missus,' the older of them began. 'It's just the way you came across to us like.'

'And how did I come across?'

'Well, like yer are now. Nasty.'

She looked at him, stunned. 'Nasty?' she uttered.

'Yeah, sharp like. You ain't a teacher, are yer?'

'No. Why do you ask?'

''Cos I had a teacher like you. She used to scare the shi— the living daylights outta me. She had a way of looking at yer that'd mek yer shake in yer shoes and she spoke like you an' all, abrupt all the time. No one liked her. None of the other teachers did either. Yer could tell

148

'cos they all avoided her like the plague. She warra spinster and me mam said that weren't surprising 'cos what bloke in their right mind 'ud wanna wake up to her face every morning? Me dad liked her though.'

She was staring at him, shocked that she was being compared to this awful teacher he was describing. 'He did?'

The lad nodded. 'Yeah, 'cos she was the only teacher that could get any work outta me. That it then, Missus, 'cos we wanna get off and spend some of this money we've made down the chip shop?'

'Yes . . . yes,' she murmured thoughtfully. 'And thank you.'

They both looked at each other as if to say they hadn't a clue what she was thanking them for, before they shot off down the stairs.

It was a very distracted Judith who returned to her bathroom to look at herself again in the mirror.

Those teenage boys had brought painfully home to her how she really came across to people. She had believed she was being business-like at work when in truth she wasn't, instead coming across as abrupt and nasty. She saw now that she carried that same manner over into her everyday life, and the awful thing was that she'd never realised it before. No wonder no one had ever shown any sign of wanting to get close to her. She had thought that was because she herself found it hard to converse on a friendly basis with others, but the truth was she put them off even trying by her attitude. She now understood why, despite the fact she would have had to decline due to her father's warning that she wasn't to become familiar with

149

any of the staff, she'd never been invited into their inner circle in any way. They hadn't just disliked her as their boss, they hadn't liked her as a person either. This knowledge hurt her a lot, but not so much as the mortification she felt for all the hurt she had caused others who had borne the blunt end of her manner towards them.

She felt tears of distress prick the back of her eyes as she suddenly realised she didn't want to spend the rest of her life friendless, have no one in the world to turn to for anything. She was not under her father's control any more and was free to act in any way she wished. She could either carry on as she was now and live in virtual solitude or she could do something to change herself into a person others would warm to and want to get to know better.

Deep in thought, she made her way back to the kitchen and sat down at the table, cupping her chin in her hands, staring blindly across the room. When you'd never had any friends, or in truth acquaintances, how did you make them? What did she need to do to make someone want to get to know her better? But after what the boys had so bluntly pointed out to her she knew that before she could expect anyone to want to get better acquainted with her, she needed to work on mellowing her attitude towards them. She thought long and hard as to how she could change her approach and came to the conclusion that she needed to think carefully about what she said before she said it and most importantly about the tone of her voice. It wasn't going to be easy changing the habits of a lifetime, but she was going to have to learn to take a deep breath before she responded to people and make herself smile. That's where she would start before she tackled anything else.

She rose to make herself another cup of tea, and as she filled the kettle an awful thought struck her. She was jobless. On top of the task of changing her personality, she had to find herself work.

Chapter Thirteen

Judith slept fitfully that night, the hurtful revelations about herself playing heavily on her mind. But regardless she woke the next morning determined to make profound changes within herself, and after attending to her ablutions again practised her smile in the mirror. It took several attempts for her to see looking back at her a woman who was smiling properly. What amazed her was that the woman smiling back at her looked so different from the one she was used to seeing, the one with the permanent frown. Her mouth now curved upwards, eyes sparkling. Her whole face seemed to be transformed, had a welcoming look to it. She could not believe that a simple facial expression could change her appearance so drastically. Now she knew how to smile, she had to remember to do it regularly. She needed to go out and get something for her evening meal, but most importantly the lunchtime edition of the *Leicester Mercury* to aid her in her search for a job. She would practise her smile on the shop assistants.

Colourfully dressed in a pretty sari, Mrs Chaudri was stacking shelves when Judith entered the corner shop. She

153

looked across as the doorbell jangled, smiled at her customer and in her broken English said, 'Mornin', lady. What please you want me get you?'

Judith lifted her head, brought her practised smile to her face, took a very deep breath and, hoping her tone was not showing the abruptness the teenage boys had told her it did, said, 'A quarter of Typhoo tea.'

Just then the doorbell clanged as another customer came in and approached the counter. 'Good morning, Mrs Chaudri. How are you today?'

Having fetched the packet of tea she put it before Judith and then turned to her other customer. 'I very vell, thank you, Missy Good. You 'usband, he is better today, yes?'

'Yes, he is, Mrs Chaudri, thank you. It's just a cold but you know what men are like. At the slightest sniffle they take to their beds. Your husband, he is well too?'

She flapped a hand. 'Phew, 'im. He say he gone wholesaler, but I know he round his cousin and they discussin' opening new shop.'

Mrs Good laughed. 'Men! They're all the same, ain't they? Mr Good tells me he's going to the allotment, he must think I'm daft not to know he's really popped down the pub for a swift half.'

Judith was listening to this exchange with deep interest as to how it had started and was progressing. She was beginning to understand how people became better acquainted with each other. She had been in this shop several times since she had moved into her flat but had never responded to Mrs Chaudri's polite questioning, thinking the woman was invading her privacy when in truth all Mrs Chaudri was doing was making an effort to show a friendly interest in her customer. Should Judith have responded in a similar fashion then it would now be herself and Mrs Chaudri who were having a conversation, possibly with Mrs Good joining in too. Judith now realised that a simple smile wasn't enough and that she had somehow to learn to drop her barrier and allow people in if she wanted to forge friendships for herself.

Mrs Chaudri had returned her attention to Judith. 'I get you anythin' else, please?'

Previously her response would have been short and to the point but this time, having put the smile back on her face, she said, 'I'd like some cheese.' And then quickly added, 'Please. A quarter should be sufficient.'

Mrs Chaudri smiled back at her. 'We have some nice in. You will like, yes.' It wasn't a question but a statement.

Mrs Good turned to look at Judith. 'Oh, I haven't seen you around here before. New are you?'

She looked at Mrs Good for several long moments before taking a deep breath and responding. 'I moved into a flat just down the road a couple of weeks ago.'

She sincerely hoped her reply had been suitable, her tone pleasant, and was gratified when Mrs Good asked, 'And settling in well, are you?'

'Yes, I am, thank you. I've . . . I've had a few mishaps but things seem to be going well now.'

Mrs Good laughed. 'Moving house is such a trying time. Me daughter moved last year – her furniture turned up at the wrong address and worse still in the wrong town. They all had to sleep on the floor, relying on neighbours to keep them supplied with hot drinks and food 'til their own stuff turned up. You wouldn't get me moving. Far too much trouble and one house is much the same as another in my book. It's the people that live in 'em what makes them a home. I've lived around here all me life. You'll like it, people are friendly enough. I wish you well, and good luck in your new home.'

This wasn't just empty words on the other woman's part, Judith knew she was sincere in her best wishes. 'Thank you,' she responded.

A warm feeling filled her. For the first time since she could remember she wasn't feeling awkward in a situation with strangers and wanting to get away as quickly as possible. Having paid her bill, she wished both ladies a polite good morning and made her way to the butcher's shop.

Remembering how Mrs Good had greeted Mrs Chaudri when she had first entered her shop she smiled at the large man behind the counter, wearing a bloodied apron. 'Good . . .' She faltered feeling her old reserve coming back but she couldn't let it. She was the new Judith now. One that people were going to like and want to get to know better. Taking a very deep breath she blurted, 'Good morning.'

He lifted his head and smiled at her. 'Good morning to you, Madam. And how are you today?'

Nobody usually got so far as the stage of enquiring after her health and she was quite taken aback. 'Oh, er . . . I'm . . . I'm very well, thank you.'

'And I'm glad to hear it. So what's yer fancy? I've a nice bit of pork or what about a bit of shin beef if yer making a stew? And I'm famed for me sausages. Make 'em fresh daily.'

She looked along the display counter at all the different cuts. 'A pork chop, please.'

He selected one from a row and, putting it on a piece of butcher's paper, placed it on the scales. 'That'll be two and sevenpence. Anything else?'

'I'll have half a pound of your beef sausages. I . . . er . . . must say they do look good.'

He seemed very pleased with her remark. Those weighed out, she paid over her money and as she collected her parcels he said, 'Good day, Madam. Look forward to seeing you again soon.'

She looked at him, stunned. No one had ever expressed such a thing to her before. She knew the butcher was just being polite, but then he needn't have said he was looking forward to her coming in again and she knew he wouldn't have if she had acted in her old sharp way towards him. She wished him good morning back and left.

Back at her flat she opened the outer door and almost fell into an elderly woman running a mop along the green, brown and white diamond-shaped mosaic floor.

'Oh, yer gave me a scare,' the old lady said, stopping her chore to look at Judith, shocked. 'Thought all the tenants was out at work. You must be the new lady moved into number three. Settled in all right, have yer?'

'Yes, I have, thank you.'

She held out a gnarled hand towards Judith. 'I'm Iris Day, come in once a week to give the corridors a mop over.' Judith felt herself shrinking away from the woman, her old habits taking over. This was a common working

157

woman and her father had always instructed her never to lower herself to the level of those types and always to remember her own position. But it suddenly struck Judith that her father had been wrong to heap such ignominy on them. He himself had been of working-class origin and so therefore was Judith herself, and in truth she was no better than this woman as they both worked for a living. As it was this woman at the moment *was* better than Judith. At least she had a job.

She grasped her hand and shook it firmly. 'I'm pleased to meet you, Mrs Day.'

The woman beamed happily at her. 'Anything I can do fer yer, me duck, don't you hesitate to ask and I'll do me best. I wish all the tenants were as nice as you. One or two pass me by as though I don't even exist. Stuck-up buggers they are. The rest are all right, though. Some even slip me a shilling when they've a mind to. Nice flats though, ain't they? Wish I could afford ter live in one. It used ter be one big house, yer know, 'til the old duck who lived in it passed on. It was sold and turned into flats. Oh, yer should have seen the mess the workers made.'

She gave a sudden grin. 'Here's me rattling on. Forgive an old woman but I don't get much chance for a gossip and I've took advantage of you. Did yer know you're the first lady tenant that's lived here? Oh, that reminds me. I was chatting to the milkman this morning and I told him we'd a new tenant moved in and he was wondering whether you was wanting him to deliver milk to you. So I shoved a note through yer door and left the complimentary bottle he asked me to give yer. If yer do want him to leave you a daily pint in future, leave a note under yer empty on the front doorstep when yer put it out.'

Judith smiled at her. 'Thank you.' Then she realised she ought to say something else to let the woman know she had appreciated her gesture. 'I'm very grateful to you for your thoughtfulness.'

Iris beamed in delight. 'Well, I do me best to keep the tenants happy, even though one or two don't appreciate what I do.'

'You will excuse me, won't you?' Judith said politely.

'Yes, of course, me duck. You get on. You young things are always busy, I know.'

Back in her flat Judith placed her shopping on the table along with her complimentary bottle of milk and took off her coat. She had set off this morning on a mission to begin to make changes in her attitude towards people and felt that her efforts had resulted in a good start. What surprised her was that once she had steeled herself to get started, it had become easier. She had been in this area for two weeks, gone out and about to do her shopping, and if she was honest during that time had encountered no one that she felt would want to cross paths with her again. But after an hour this morning she had met three, or four including Iris Day, who she felt would respond to her in a friendly fashion should they meet up, and it was all down to how she had interacted with them.

Judith felt inwardly proud of herself and even more determined to continue the process.

She spent the rest of the afternoon scanning the newspaper Job Vacancies and found ten companies that were seeking experienced clerical staff that were within easy distance of her. She wrote to all of them and posted the letters off, praying some of them, hopefully all, would earn her an interview.

It took several days for her to receive eight responses. Two companies rejected her out of hand but the other six requested an interview. Over the next couple of days she attended four of them and all turned her down, expressing their reservations about her taking a lower-graded job considering her previous managerial position. They felt she would become bored without the challenge of responsibility and leave, and were not willing to take the risk. Judith could not bring herself to explain her reasons for seeking a less responsible position and, despite knowing she would have given them her best, accepted their decision without argument.

It was looking very much to her as if no job using her office skills was going to be offered her but she had two more interviews to attend. Should she fail with these she would have to consider earning herself a living in a factory or suchlike. But at her age she worried that there'd be no employers willing to train her, and even if she was lucky enough to find a factory who would, the rate of pay while she trained would be low. She knew she couldn't live on it, even if she moved somewhere with a much-reduced rent. There was no telling she would be good at the work anyway and that they'd keep her on after her training.

She just had to hope that the last two interviews proved more fruitful than the rest. Making sure she looked her best, she set off again.

Judith didn't like the look of Bertram Archer the minute she set eyes on him. He was a short fat man with a bald head, purple-ended bulbous nose, thick rubbery lips which he kept constantly licking, and small piggy eyes. He was wearing a loud blue-checked suit and a red shirt. He kept glancing at her legs all the way through her interview, making her feel mortally uncomfortable. The job he outlined in his car saleroom sounded easy enough and as the only employee she'd be at liberty to carry out the work in any way she felt fit so long as it got done. The wage being offered was not as low as she had feared it would be, enough for her to manage on if she was careful, but she wasn't sure about having Bertram Archer for a boss. His last secretary had just left although he didn't give Judith her reasons for doing so.

He leaned across the desk and looked her full in the face. 'So when can yer start then?'

She stared at him blankly. He hadn't asked anything about her. 'Do you not want me to tell you about myself, Mr Archer?'

He gave a shrug. 'When yer've bin in the car business as long as I have, telling those that have the money to buy from those that are just wasting yer time, and have had as many flibbertigibbets come and go in this office, yer gets ter be a good judge of character. You looks an efficient woman to me. Yer can type, can't yer?'

'Yes.'

'File?'

'Yes.'

'So what more do I need ter know?' He heaved his bulk off his chair, walked around to the back of Judith's seat, placed one arm around her shoulder and leaned over to pat her knee. 'Yer a fine-looking woman, but I expect yer

161

know that. A Miss so yer've no husband at home looking after yer, if yer know what I mean. I know me and you will get along just fine.'

Judith's back stiffened, she firmly pushed his hand off her knee and stood up, glaring at him stonily. 'Maybe some other woman would jump at what you're offering, Mr Archer, but your judgement is way off if you think I would be one of them. Good day.'

As she strode out of the office she heard him call after her, 'Frigid bitch!'

As she made her way through the assortment of shabby-looking cars on his lot she might have been upset, thinking her effort to improve her outward persona had taken a major setback, but in this instance she didn't mind in the least being labelled what she had been by that sleazy character. Just because she was desperate for a job, didn't mean she had to lower herself to work for the likes of him. No wonder he'd had so many flibbertigibbets as he had called them come and go through his office, and now she fully understood why his last secretary had left. Nevertheless she was dismayed that yet again an interview had proved to be a failure and she wondered if it was even worth attending the final one from her current batch of applications or if that too would be a waste of time. But she had to get a job and she could not afford to leave any stone unturned. She must plough on, be prepared for more knockbacks. There had to be a job somewhere that had her name attached to it.

Neville James, a medium-built, pleasant-looking man in his early forties, rose to shake Judith's hand as she entered his cluttered office and indicated for her to sit down on a chair before his desk.

'Welcome to Fastway Transport, Mrs Chambers. Make yourself comfy. Would you like a cup of tea before we begin?'

From her first impressions as she had entered the building and by the way she had been treated up to now, Judith could tell that Fastway Transport was a decent company and the man about to interview her nothing like Bertram Archer. She knew even before her interview that she would like to work here. Neville James' own obvious attempt to put her at her ease helped her to relax. Instead of sitting with her knees together as usual, clutching her handbag close, she put her bag down on the floor to the side of her and settled back in her chair, crossing her shapely legs. 'No tea, thank you. And it's Miss, actually, Mr James,' she corrected him politely.

He looked at her, surprised. 'What, a pretty lady like you, unattached? Well, what is the world coming to?'

She realised his comment to be nothing more than a light-hearted compliment to an attractive woman and felt duly flattered by it. Regardless, her inexperience left her without a clue as to how to respond, and for fear she might say the wrong thing and humiliate herself, she declined to.

He relaxed back in his own chair and looked directly at her. 'Well, Miss Chambers, let me tell you a bit about the company. We've been operating for over ten years now and have a fleet of twenty lorries, ranging from artics down to seven-and-a-half tonners and a couple of transits. We deliver anything that customers want us to, anywhere in the British Isles. We've forty-five staff including the drivers. Our business has steadily increased over the last year and looks set to continue so what we're looking for is an all-rounder for our general office, someone who can turn their hand to almost anything, joining the other eight ladies. There'll be set duties for the new recruit but we're very flexible here and if someone is off for any reason we like to know that their workload can be spread around the rest of the clerical staff to keep it up to date until they get back.

'There's a subsidised canteen selling anything from bacon cobs to a full-blown lunch and the two ladies who run it will happily make up any special requests within reason. The tea and coffee trolley comes around twice a day when we all stop and have a fifteen-minute break. Two weeks' annual holiday, to be taken at your supervisor's discretion as we operate all year round and don't shut down like most other companies for the Leicester fortnight. Of course, there's the usual bank holidays on top. The pay we're offering for this position is nineteen pounds seventeen and six a week and there's a cost of living rise every April. There's also a personal increment each year for those who deserve it and it's usually the case that everyone gets something as we all pull together here. Those that don't, don't last long.' He paused and looked at her questioningly. 'Well, Miss Chambers, is the position of interest to you?'

The thought of working alongside eight other women in close proximity made Judith feel uneasy, but she knew this was something she had to get on with and which in turn could do much by way of helping her learn to act properly in other people's company. She knew that work-wise she could do everything expected of her and should she be fortunate enough to be offered the job, was determined to work hard to fit in and become accepted as one of the workforce here. If she was lucky some of the ladies she'd be working with might even want to become her friends. If all the staff were as nice as Neville James she felt sure she could be very happy here. 'It sounds very interesting to me, Mr James,' she said with conviction.

'I'm glad.' He looked down at her application letter. 'You wrote that your previous position was working for your family's firm which has now been sold. What exactly did you do?'

She took a deep breath. 'I supervised the staff.'

'You were the office manager?'

She swallowed hard. 'Yes, I was.' This is where Mr James tells me what the other firms did, she thought, and prepared herself to hear the worst.

She was very surprised by his response.

'Well, in that case you'll have no trouble turning your hand to anything that's asked of you.' He stared at her thoughtfully for a moment. 'Chambers Leather Goods? That name rings a bell.' He shook his head. 'I can't think why at the moment. Anyway, I'm not going to ask you to go into details as to why you want a less responsible job.' He looked at her knowingly. 'After years of all the worry attached to it, you've probably had enough and want something less demanding. I started this business by hocking myself up to my eyeballs and buying two second-hand lorries but, believe me, I sometimes wish I could go back to being a simple driver and having just my own load to worry about, instead of all that goes with owning a company.

'Anyway, all I'd like to know now, Miss Chambers, is if you think you'll have any problem being under supervision instead of supervising staff yourself?'

'None whatsoever,' she replied with conviction.

He smiled at her. 'Good. I see from your letter you type sixty words a minute. That's more than enough for our needs. Accurate, are you?'

'I pride myself on not making mistakes.'

'We all make mistakes, Miss Chambers. It's human nature. Can you operate a PBX switchboard?'

Her heart sank. 'No, I'm afraid not. We had a plug board at Chambers'.'

'Oh, well, no worries, even I can operate it so I've no doubt a woman of your capabilities will soon pick it up. Right, are there any questions you'd like to ask me?'

'No, I think you've covered everything.'

'Well, you're by far the best candidate I've interviewed for the job so I don't see the point in delaying matters further. I'd like to offer you the position, Miss Chambers.'

Her heart soared. She was being offered the job, she really was! She wanted to express her deep gratitude by thanking him profusely but quashed the urge. Her attempt to change her character still had a long way to go before she could allow herself to do anything so demonstrative.

He looked at her expectantly. 'So, do you accept or not?'

Smiling, she nodded. 'I accept, Mr James, and thank you very much.'

He held out his hand to her. 'Welcome to Fastway Transport, Miss Chambers. We'll look forward to seeing you on Monday morning at eight-thirty.'

She gladly accepted his hand and shook it firmly. 'I shall look forward to being here, Mr James.'

Judith was elated. She had a job and this time she wasn't going to lose it for any reason. The pay was enough to allow her to stay on in her flat as long as she was careful. Her vision of a happier future resurrected itself and it showed on her face.

On her way home a distinguished-looking man passed by, appraising her openly. 'Someone looks pleased with themselves,' he commented to her jocularly.

'I am,' she smiled back. 'Very pleased.'

And she was. But what pleased her most was that, without a thought, she had responded pleasantly to the man, without casting him a look of disdain for daring to invade her privacy. She was very much liking her new self and sincerely hoped her new work colleagues would too.

Chapter Fourteen

Determined that nothing was going to jeopardise her new start Judith took great pains over deciding what to wear for her first day, realising that should she wear her normal smart suit this could be seen as trying to outdress her as yet unknown supervisor and might result in getting off to a bad start with her. Judith had enough on her plate as it was already without that. She settled on a straight dark blue skirt, the hemline of which finished at her knee, and a white long-sleeved blouse with a high collar. Still smart, she felt, but in keeping with her new position.

Feeling a mixture of nervousness and determination to make great efforts to ingratiate herself with the rest of her colleagues and work to the best of her ability, she presented herself promptly in the Fastway reception area at eight-twenty-nine the following Monday morning.

The pretty young woman on reception had just arrived herself and was taking off her coat when Judith walked in and introduced herself.

'Oh, I was told to expect you by Mr James. You're our new office woman. You'll like it here, everyone's ever so nice and the drivers are funny. Well, most of them are.

One or two can be a right pain and moan worse than we women do. You'll also get the ones that think they're God's gift, but I'm sure you'll be able to handle them. You'll be relieving me sometimes on reception. Don't worry if you don't know how to work the switchboard, I'll show you and it's ever so easy. Right, I bet you're desperate to get started so I'll just get one of the girls down from the office to fetch you.'

Judith smiled warmly at her and waited patiently.

Shortly afterwards another young woman came trotting down the stairs. She was wearing a short blue-and-white-checked dress and chunky-heeled black shoes. Her blonde hair was cut in a fashionable chin-length bob, tapering up towards the nape of her neck. Long hooped earrings dangled from her ears. She came across to Judith, smiling broadly. 'Me name's Sally Draker and you'll be sitting at a desk near to mine.'

'Judith Chambers. I'm very pleased to meet you.'

'Oh, ain't you posh?' Sally chuckled. 'I'd love to speak like you – you can teach me. Come on, follow me up and I'll introduce yer to all the others. They're all dying ter meet yer.'

Judith followed Sally up a flight of open-plan stairs then along a corridor with several offices leading off it which she noted from the plaques on the doors housed the accounts, sales and transport planning departments. She hadn't been up to the second level on her interview as Neville James had his office through a door to the back of reception.

As they neared the bottom of the corridor, the clack of several typewriters reached Judith's ears. The door they walked through opened out into a large office with windows along the back. It was filled with desks and cabinets. Seated at most of the desks were women of varying ages, shapes and sizes, already working, who raised their heads to look at Judith as she walked through.

'Tek yer coat off and hang it on the coatstand,' Sally told her, and then followed up with: 'That'll be your desk,' pointing across the room towards an unoccupied desk at the end of a row of three. The two women at the other desks adjoining it smiled at her. 'First, though, Cherry wants to meet yer and give you a run through. She's our new supervisor. She ain't bin here long herself. Really nice though, she is. You'll like her.'

Judith's first impression of the office was that it was very cluttered, in complete contrast to the offices at Chambers' which had been almost sterile in appearance, and she wondered how they could possibly work in such seeming chaos, but they obviously did and very successfully. But what struck her most was the atmosphere. It was lively and had kind of a buzz to it, very different from the ambience that had filled the Chambers' building. And she suddenly realised now that that atmosphere had been depressing. She liked this one, it made her feel glad to be here. She had never felt glad to be at Chambers'. She was going to like it here, she suddenly knew without a doubt. All she had to do was make herself liked and accepted by the rest of the staff, and the way they seemed to be responding to her now gave her very high hopes of achieving that.

Having deposited her coat on the stand, she followed Sally across the room to an open door leading into an office. Sally tapped on it and addressed a woman sitting behind a desk whom Judith couldn't see as she was standing behind Sally.

'Cherry, I've brought Judith in to meet yer.'

Sally turned to her. 'I'll see yer later. Go in.'

Putting a smile on her face Judith stepped into the office, prepared to make her greeting. As her eyes fell on the face looking back at her she froze rigid, thinking she was seeing things. But the smug face definitely belonged to Cherry Campbell, the woman she had had to sack from her job at Chambers' on Father's orders.

'Well, well, well,' said Cherry, eyeing her mockingly, 'it really is *the* Judith Chambers, office manageress from hell.' Her mouth curled into a sardonic smile. 'When Neville told me he'd employed a new recruit for our office and gave me your name I thought, no, it can't be. But it is! I still keep in touch with a couple of the girls from my old job and they told me Chambers' had been sold. They're loving their jobs now, said I wouldn't recognise the place. They can laugh without getting told off, can yer believe, and the boss actually comes around and thanks them for a good job. If I wasn't so happy here I'd be applying fer me old job back.

'In all the time I worked for Chambers' I think I caught a glimpse of the old boy once and he looked at me like I was something he'd trod in. And I can never remember being thanked once by the hierarchy for anything. We were always being made ter feel like criminals, though.'

She glanced Judith up and down, finally bringing her eyes level with hers. 'So, the great Judith Chambers is having to make her own way in the world? Well, how the mighty have fallen. What's happened, done summat naughty and the family cut you off?' She gave a chuckle. 'Oh, but that can't be it, can it, the great Miss Chambers is perfect, ain't she? The gels back at Chambers' are gonna love it when I tell 'em Icy Lil's been toppled off her perch and is now having to slum it as a humble typist clerk.' Her eyes darkened and she looked at Judith warningly. 'Well, let me tell yer, *Miss Chambers*, if it was up to me I'd have you off these premises before yer could say Jack Robinson. Lucky for you I ain't got any jurisdiction when it comes to hiring and firing. But I'll warn yer now, I've Neville James' ear and as soon as I get summat remotely sackable on yer, you'll be out of here so quick yer feet won't touch the floor.

'As long as you work here I'm going to do my best to make sure you hate every minute of your working day. But then nothing I do to you as your supervisor could compare to what you put us through. I only stayed as long as I did because I was getting over the death of my husband and hadn't the will to seek other employment. And I liked the other girls – the ones that stayed long enough for me to get to know them, that is. Anyone in their right mind never stayed at Chambers' long, did they? That's if they weren't sacked first for some trivial matter that another company wouldn't even have batted an eyelid at.' She leaned across her desk and gave Judith a meaningful look. 'If you've got any sense, you'll walk out of here now.'

Judith would have liked to have done nothing more. As Cherry had been delivering her tirade all Judith's hopes

173

for what her new job would bring had rapidly disintegrated. In truth she couldn't blame Cherry for her deep grudge against Chambers', and particularly Judith herself as she was the one who'd had to carry out her father's orders. As she realised now the staff there had been treated appallingly, hardly better than slaves. Judith knew that if she stayed at Fastway Transport she was in for a very rough ride. But apart from her need of a job, and the fact that getting another could take time that she hadn't got, a huge part of her wanted to show Cherry Campbell that she was no longer the person she was previously, that she had changed and was prepared to put up with all Cherry might throw at her to prove that to her.

Judith looked her in her eyes and said resolutely but very mindful to keep her tone pleasant, 'I have been employed here to do a job, Mrs Campbell, and I'd really like to get on with it.'

It was very apparent that Cherry wasn't happy with her response. 'Huh,' she grunted. 'Well, it remains ter be seen how long yer can stick it out 'cos I meant what I said – I ain't gonna make it easy for yer. No, siree.' She rose from her desk and walked around to face Judith. 'Right then, let's introduce you to the rest of the gels.'

She walked out of the office and called out, 'Your attention, ladies.' When all the rest of the women had stopped what they were doing and were looking across at her, she announced loudly, 'Remember I told you my last job was for a firm called Chambers Leather Goods and how badly the staff were treated? Well, guess what, gels? Our new lady is none other than Hitler's office manager herself, Miss Chambers. She likes to be called Miss, gels,

174

'cos she thinks she's above everyone else. Obviously she's fell on hard times and has had to lower herself to get a new job. Let's see how she likes working on the other side of the fence. Now, I trust you'll give her the welcome she deserves and do your best to make sure her stay with us is as short as possible.'

They were all looking at Judith accusingly and one of the women piped up, 'Yer can count on us, Cherry.'

She beamed across. 'I knew I could. Right, in the circumstances I don't think it's a good idea *Miss Chambers* sits amongst you as I can assure you she ain't good company. The old desk in the far corner by the window, I think. Sally, want to take that piece of cardboard off the window pane, let the light in, so *Miss Chambers* can see what she's doing?'

Sally looked at her worriedly. 'But, Cherry . . .'

'Yes, I know, but just do it, please.'

'Okay,' she said, going off.

Cherry turned to Judith, her tone commanding. 'Go and clear the desk at the bottom of the office and then move the stuff off the desk that had been set out for yer on to yer new one. When yer've done that, report back to me. Come on, chop, chop,' she said, clapping her hands.

Cherry's introduction of her to the rest of the girls had Judith filled with humiliation but during it all her well-practised ability to mask her inner turmoil played its part and she held her head high and kept a smile fixed firmly on her face. She turned to Cherry now and said graciously, 'Yes, certainly, Mrs Campbell.'

For the next couple of hours she was kept busy clearing the mountain of discarded items piled on top of and around the isolated desk Cherry proposed to sit her at. Having stacked the boxes of archived paperwork neatly away from the desk, she then moved the typewriter and the other equipment that had been supplied for her to do her job over to the new desk. Not one of the other women offered to lift a finger to help her even when she knew they could see what a struggle she was having to heave some of the heavy boxes, and she had almost crumpled under the burden of the weighty typewriter. She was very conscious that as they worked away they were all glancing across at her periodically and whispering together, and didn't need to guess who was the topic of their gossip.

She had just finished her task when the outer office door shot open and a jolly-looking woman pushing a tea trolley bustled in. 'Tea's up, gels,' she called.

The women immediately stopped working and gathered around her then, armed with their cups of tea or coffee and Rich Tea biscuits, pulled their chairs into a circle in a space by a row of desks and started their break. Cherry came out of her office, collected her cup of coffee and joined them. No one looked in Judith's direction.

She was desperate for a drink and wasn't going to allow the others' behaviour to stop her. She made her way over to the trolley and smiled at the jolly woman. 'A cup of tea, please.'

She picked up the huge teapot and poured Judith one out. 'You must be the new lady,' she said. 'You'll like it here, everyone is really nice. I'm Maisie Todd and me and Florrie Short run the canteen. 'Ote yer want we don't have on regular, just give us plenty a warning and we'll do our best ter cook it for yer. Some of the gels ask us to

176

mek up special salads in summer, that sorta thing.'

'Thank you,' said Judith. 'It's very kind of you to offer.'

'Aim ter please, that's our motto. Help yerself ter biscuits, ducky, I can see you don't need ter watch yer weight. I'll be back in a bit to collect the tray of dirties,' she called out as she turned the trolley around and headed back out of the door.

Judith made her way over to her own desk, sat on her chair and proceeded to drink her tea. She became immediately aware of a stiff draught coming through the window frame she was positioned against, which had warped over the years. That was why a sheet of cardboard had been placed over it, she thought, to stop the draught coming in. Cherry Campbell had certainly told the truth when she had announced to Judith that she was going to make her life as uncomfortable as she could.

When morning break was finished Judith noticed the girls put all their used cups and saucers on a tray on top of a cabinet by the outer door ready for Maisie Todd to collect before they moved their chairs back behind their desks and resumed their work. Judith did likewise and as she had finished her task, she felt to the best of her ability, went over to Cherry's office and tapped on the door before she entered.

'I've done what you asked, Mrs Campbell,' she said to Cherry who was seated behind her desk.

She lifted her head from her task and looked at Judith icily. 'Properly?' she snapped.

'To the best of my ability,' she responded evenly.

She gave Judith a look of derision. 'I'd better come and check, just in case.'

She scraped back her chair and pushed past Judith and down the length of the office to where her desk was, Judith following behind her.

Cherry glanced slowly around. 'Mmm,' she mouthed. 'I thought you told me you'd done a proper job. Those boxes ain't perfectly in line with one another. See to it, *Miss Chambers*.'

With that she headed back to her office. En route she stopped by a line of desks and addressed the women in a quiet voice. They immediately looked over at Judith and started laughing.

She ignored them to get on with her task of straightening all the boxes to be as exactly in line with one other as she could get them, which in truth was what she had already done, but because the boxes were not all of the same size and pushed out of shape because of the way the paperwork inside had been rammed into them it was virtually impossible. Judith was very well aware that Cherry already knew that.

Just as she finished again the supervisor was at her side. In her arms she carried a huge mound of paperwork which she dumped unceremoniously on Judith's desk. A lot of it toppled off to scatter on the floor.

'This lot needs filing in the cabinets over there,' she said, nodding her head in the direction of a row of cabinets a few feet away from Judith. 'But before yer do that I want you to go through all the individual files in each cabinet and take out all the things that are older than two years. That's 1965, if you can't work it out,' she said nastily. 'Then all the stuff in each file needs to be put in alphabetical and date order. Then the stuff you've taken out needs to be archived in those boxes you've just straightened, again in date and alphabetical order. While yer at it yer might as well go through all the archive boxes and make sure everything in them is in order, 'case we need to dig anything out if we have queries on old deliveries et cetera.' She gave a smug grin. 'That should keep yer busy for a while, and be warned, I shall be checking at regular intervals that you're doing a proper job.' She pushed her face into Judith's. ''Course, yer could always leave.'

With that she turned and flounced off.

Judith fixed her eyes on the piles of overflowing boxes she had just stacked against the wall. There were at least thirty of them. The task Cherry had just given her was extremely laborious, mind-numbing and a mammoth undertaking which she suspected had been left to get in the state it had because no one else wanted to do it. But if that's what Cherry wanted her to do, then she would. She was being paid to do a job; whatever was asked of her she would do to the best of her ability, giving Cherry no excuse to report her to the boss and get rid of her. Maybe if her supervisor could see that Judith was here for the duration, smiling through whatever dire tasks were given her and however belligerent Cherry's and the others' attitude was towards her, she just might soften a little. Judith could live in hope anyway.

She arrived home that night with a dreadful headache from concentrating hard as she had begun her massive task of sorting the filing. Apart from the thirty or so archive boxes Cherry had told her to sort out, there were at least three hundred individual files, one for each customer Fastway Transport currently did deliveries for – some with a few pieces of paper inside, but the majority overflowing and all in a disorderly state which badly needed reorganising before she began on anything else. She had backache too from lifting the heavy loads she had moved that morning. Too tired to cook a meal for herself, she had decided on her way home to settle for a corned beef sandwich. She was then going to have a hot bath with a liberal amount of Radox bath salts poured in and was looking forward to curling up in her chair afterwards with the radio on low for background company, reading a book. She then remembered she had read all of her library books and the due date for their return was today. Judith issued a forlorn groan. The fine she would incur for each overdue book was not her principal concern so much as the fact that her delay in returning them would prevent the books giving someone else as much pleasure as they had given her.

Going into the lounge, she scooped up the books and as she opened the door to depart again, came face to face with her surly neighbour from opposite, his fist raised, about to knock on her door.

'Oh!' Judith exclaimed in surprise. Then she noticed the expression on his face. He didn't look at all happy, but on the several times she had encountered him previously he hadn't done then either. It crossed her mind that maybe she wasn't the only one who needed to take a look at themselves and address their attitude to others.

Before she could ask what he wanted her for he had lowered his arm and said stonily, 'You're on your way out but this won't take a moment, Miss Chambers. Your washing?'

She looked at him, bemused. 'My washing?'

'You've been hanging it out whenever you like.'

'Yes?'

'The tenants have a set day each.'

'Oh, do they? I didn't know that.'

'If you'd read your tenancy agreement properly, the hanging out of washing is clearly covered. Since the time you've been a tenant here you've disrupted several of the other tenants' washing day. We had nothing like this until you arrived. Please note, Miss Chambers, that your day for using the washing line is Tuesday.'

So her churlish neighbour was the spokesman for all the other tenants, was he? At that moment it felt to Judith like all her neighbours were ganging up on her, running to this man with their grievances for him then to come and give her a telling off as if she'd been a naughty child. She took a deep breath and looked him in the eye. 'I apologise for my laxness. But what if it's raining on a Tuesday?'

'Then that's unfortunate. You have heard of clothes horses, I trust?' he asked, looking at her as though she was stupid. 'And another thing, you've been helping yourself to my milk.'

In consideration of what she had done, albeit unwittingly, she felt she deserved to be put straight, but she felt mortally insulted at being accused of doing something she hadn't. 'I can assure you, I have *not* stolen your milk.'

'And I can assure you that you have. You've been taking the bottle with the gold top on. Not every day but on at least three occasions during the past two weeks. It's

181

Guernsey full cream and I have it delivered especially. It costs more too.'

In truth she hadn't noticed, just taken the first one that had come to hand out of whatever bottles remained on the doorstep when she had gone down to collect her milk. She had noticed that sometimes her milk tasted much creamier than others but hadn't given a thought as to why. She took a deep steadying breath. 'I apologise for my oversight. If you'll inform me of the difference in the price of the bottles, I will gladly refund it to you.'

'I'll let it pass this time.'

'Oh, no, I insist on paying. Is there anything else?'

'Not at the moment.'

Thank goodness for that, she thought. 'Then good evening, Mr . . . er . . .'

'Good evening,' he snapped.

As her neighbour disappeared inside his own flat she gave a sharp exhalation. This encounter was all she'd needed on top of everything else she had experienced today. So much for keeping out of his way, she thought. Pulling the door shut behind herself, she set off on her errand to the library, hoping she made it before they shut.

The young woman who had dealt with her previously was behind the counter when Judith arrived. When she looked up from her task to deal with her new reader her eyes settled on Judith and a smile lit her pretty face. 'Good evening, Miss Chambers. How nice to see you again.' She retrieved Judith's returned books to deal with and asked, 'What did you make of the Steinbeck?'

Judith was gratified that she had remembered her name as this library was very well patronised. 'I enjoyed it very much, thank you. The author certainly has the ability to stir the emotions. I enjoyed the Somerset Maugham too. But out of the three, I liked Laurie Lee the most. His description of himself as a child sitting in the middle of tall grasses was so vivid, I felt I was actually sitting beside him.' Judith was surprised at her own lengthy response. She had become conscious while she had been delivering it that the young woman seemed to be hanging on her every word and found her attention oddly unsettling. 'I'd better not keep you as I can see you're busy,' she added hastily.

'Oh, that's all right. I enjoy talking to you.' Then the librarian quickly added, 'To all our readers. I like to find out as much as I can about people's preferred reading matter so I can recommend new books to them should they ask my advice in the future.'

Judith felt it was good to see someone taking such a keen interest in their job. 'Then I shall not hesitate to ask you for recommendations in the future. Now I'd better hurry and make my choices as you'll be shutting soon.'

A while later Judith placed three books on the counter. 'Would you recommend these?' she asked the young librarian.

She glanced at each title. 'Oh, yes, I've read them all and they made very good reading.' She gave a laugh. 'My mother calls me a bookworm,' she said as she stamped Judith's books. 'I always had my nose in a book as a child, and neither of my parents was at all surprised when I informed them I wanted to work in a library.' She pushed Judith's books towards her and looked at her questioningly. 'Were you a great reader as a child, Miss Chambers?'

Judith stiffened as momentarily her old reserve flooded back. The feeling that her privacy was being invaded overwhelmed her. She gave herself a quick mental scolding. This young woman was only showing an interest in her, her question was not overly intimate merely a general enquiry, and Judith herself ought to recognise the difference and be glad that someone did want to know a little about her as a person. 'Yes, I was.' She picked up her books. 'Good evening.'

'Good evening, Miss Chambers.'

Judith felt lighter of heart as she made her way home. Her pleasant visit to the library had helped take the edge off her awful day. She was determined, though, that regardless of how badly she was treated at work, she wasn't going to be pushed out of her job.

Chapter Fifteen

Judith breathed a deep sigh of relief as she shut her flat door behind her. It was Thursday evening and there was only one more day to go before she had the weekend to look forward to, two whole days away from the oppression she was experiencing at work. She had been at Fastway Transport for over three months now and neither Cherry nor the other women had let up in the slightest in their hostility towards her. Any excuse to make her life uncomfortable was taken, and neither had Cherry's blatant manoeuvring to give Judith all the most mundane and laborious tasks she possibly could altered. Her hope of them mellowing towards her given time was beginning to fade. But despite all they had thrown at her, Judith had remained firm and stuck to her vow, politely smiling her way through their ill treatment. This was a good job that enabled her to live, she wasn't going to lose it lightly.

It had taken her several weeks of continuous effort to complete the huge task Cherry had set her in sorting out the filing and archive system, and Judith could tell that to her dismay her supervisor could find no fault whatsoever with the end result. Judith was also aware that her offer to keep the filing up-to-date in future, as well as fitting in everything else Cherry allocated her to do, had quite taken her superior aback. Although not actually expressing gratitude, she had clearly been relieved that this laborious task that no one had ever offered to do voluntarily was now being taken care of.

Judith had realised soon after her first day at Fastway Transport the true reason why the area at the bottom of the office had previously been turned over to storage space and why Cherry had chosen to ignore this and seen fit to move her down there. The piece of cardboard she had told Sally to remove had not only been put up in the first place by way of stopping the winter draughts from coming through the warped window frame, but also to prevent the sun from streaming in in its turn. The summer had turned into a stifling one, this month of August being the hottest, and according to the forecast there was no sign yet of a let up. As a consequence Judith had constantly to suffer her work area being flooded with heat for several hours during the afternoon and likened her ordeal to being in a desert in the middle of the dry season. She knew that all she had to do to relieve her suffering was put the piece of cardboard back in place, but pride prevented her. It was one thing striving all she could to show Cherry Campbell she was no longer the austere woman who used to rule her rigidly when she was under Judith's charge at Chambers'; another allowing her the satisfaction of seeing that her treatment was causing Judith such inward misery.

Her only consolation was that her wages covered her rent, gas and electricity and bought her nourishing food, but anything more costly she had to pass up. She wasn't unduly concerned about this state of affairs as regardless of what other people might have perceived as her privileged background, she had always had to save for anything costly so continuing this way was no hardship to her.

As to her conscious effort to improve her outward persona, Judith felt she was still making headway. Despite not yet having made any actual friends, she was now on speaking terms with several people in the area and was finding that she didn't have to work quite so hard at conversing with them, and whenever her old reserve did surface it was becoming easier to quash it.

One person she found to her delight that she did look forward to encountering was the young girl at the library whose name she now knew to be Kimberley. They shared a great interest in books and Judith much enjoyed their discussions on what they were both currently reading, or had read in the past, and what that particular book had brought to them. The length of these discussions depended on how busy the library was at the time and Judith found herself quite disappointed when other readers prevented Kimberley from spending a few minutes with her.

After taking off her coat that evening and hanging it up, she turned on the oven and while she waited for it to heat, went into the pantry and took a covered enamel dish from a shelf. She had set to and with the aid of her cookery book attempted to make herself a shepherd's pie the previous evening, and if she said it herself her finished effort did resemble that in the picture in the book. The proof was in the eating, though, and she was looking forward very much to sampling it.

The oven heated to the right temperature, she had just put the pie inside when the front door knocker went. Callers to her flat were rare and she wondered who it could be, praying it wasn't her surly neighbour. Thankfully since her last altercation with him over her hanging out of her washing and him accusing her of taking his milk, which had turned out, much to her embarrassment, to be justified, she had not spoken to him. She had put the money she owed him for her mistake in an envelope and posted it through his letterbox with a short note explaining what it was for. He had not responded. Since then their paths had only crossed on the rare occasion when they had either been leaving or entering the house at the same time. Their manner towards each other each time had been very formal, nothing more than a hurried stiff nod of acknowledgement.

Steeling herself for the possibility that it might be him with another complaint against something she had done, though what completely escaped her, she opened the door. The young woman who greeted her, Judith guessed, was aged in her late teens and looked very unkempt. Her mousy hair hung limp, her skin was dull and greasy-looking. The very short tight skirt and skimpy top she was wearing markedly emphasised her hefty build. She was a complete stranger to Judith and her immediate thought was to wonder what this woman could possibly want with her.

Before Judith could enquire, she blurted, 'You Judith Chambers?'

Judith eyed her curiously, wondering how the woman knew her name. 'I am she,' she responded warily.

The young woman gave a grin. 'So you're the one who dumped me. I've always wanted to see what me mam looked like.'

Judith gawped at her dumbfounded. Had this girl just said she was her mother? Surely she must be mistaken? 'I . . . I think you've made a . . .'

'Mistake?' she butted in, and shook her head positively. 'No, I ain't. You're my mother, all right. Yer gave birth ter me in the charity home on September the eighteenth 1945. That proof enough?' She gave a shrug. 'I can see my turning up has shocked yer. Forgot you ever had a baby, I expect. Well, I'm sorry ter disappoint yer but some mistakes don't go away forever. I wanted me son to meet his grandma.' For the first time Judith realised she had someone with her, a small boy of about five whom she pushed forward. 'Say hello to yer granny, Marty.'

Judith's eyes turned down to see a little boy at the side of her. He had a shock of bright red hair and a splattering of freckles over his cheeks and nose. He was wearing a pair of owl-shaped National Health glasses, one arm of which had obviously broken as it was held together by a piece of Elastoplast. He wasn't a particularly attractive-looking boy as his features seemed far too large for his small oval-shaped face. It was difficult to tell whether he was fat or skinny as the shabby blue duffel coat he was wearing was several sizes too big for him.

His mother pushed him again. 'Eh up, yer little bleeder, I said, say hello to yer gran.'

He lifted his head and looked at Judith sullenly. 'Hello,

Granny,' he muttered before hanging his head again.

Judith stared at him astounded for several long moments before she brought her eyes back to the young woman's. She couldn't take this in. It suddenly seemed to her that the years had rolled away and she was back in the home giving birth to a child she was never going to be allowed to set eyes on, let alone hold. That child, this stranger, was now standing before her and she had her own son with her – Judith's grandson.

'Well, ain't yer gonna ask us in then, Mam?'

Mam. The title felt so alien to her, Judith couldn't relate it to herself. 'Pardon? Oh, er . . .' Stupefied she stood aside and the woman, pulling the little boy along with her, walked past her and on into the lounge. Still reeling from the shock of it all, Judith automatically shut the door and followed them through. When she arrived in the lounge the little boy was sitting on the settee, his head drooping, sucking on a wooden toggle on his coat. The woman was standing with her back to the fireplace and looking around admiringly.

'Nice place yer've got here. Bit posher than we're used to, ain't it, son? Oi, I'm speaking ter you,' she shouted at him.

He raised his head and silently looked at her.

She grinned at Judith. 'Bit soft in the head I reckon my son is. Could be 'cos he was dropped on it when he was a tot. I'm only kidding! So, I can tell by yer face that we're a bit of a shock?'

A bit was putting it mildly. 'Er . . . yes. Yes, you are. How . . .'

'Did I know who you was and where ter find yer?' she

finished. 'Me adopted mam had yer details. Well, yer name and last known address, that's all she was given by the home, but she insisted she had it 'case I wanted to find yer when I was older. The woman where yer used ter live told me where yer was now. Don't worry, I told her I was yer niece and we'd lost touch.' She gave a sniff. 'Oh, summat smells good. We ain't eaten, have we, Marty? Both starvin', ain't we? Oi, yer dozy sod, I'm talking ter you,' she bellowed at him.

Having gone back to sucking on his toggle he lifted his head and muttered, 'Yes, Mam, I'm famished.'

'He only responds when yer shout at him. As well as being dozy, I reckon he's deaf as well. Any chance of summat ter eat then?' she asked hopefully.

Mind roaming haphazardly, Judith looked at her blankly. 'Er . . . yes. Er . . . I only have shepherd's pie.'

Her visitor gave a nonchalant shrug. 'If that's all yer got then that'll have ter do. Ter be honest, Mam, I'm that hungry I'd settle for rat stew. I ain't eaten for two days, see, 'cos his dad scarpered with all me money. Not that I had much for him ter scarper with but every last penny he took, the bastard. That's not me reason for coming here, I've bin wanting ter come for a long time, only it was plucking up the courage. But . . . well, we're here now, ain't we? You must have bin curious about me yerself? Wondered what I looked like?'

Judith stared at her blankly. How could she explain to this woman without hurting her that she hadn't allowed herself to be curious or even to think of her, except for a couple of times when her memories of the past had been beyond her control, because she couldn't bear to risk resurrecting the pain it would cause her. And besides she had been led to believe by the staff at the home that she would never see her child, that its adoption was final and thinking of it would only result in deep misery and regret about what might have been. This situation was one Judith had never expected to face and so she was unprepared, with no clue how to deal with it. At the moment all she wanted to do was escape from it.

'If you'd care to sit at the table, I'll get your food,' she murmured.

'Lovely,' the girl said, licking her lips. 'While yer getting it, I'll just nip to the lavvy.'

Acting mechanically, Judith went to the kitchen and got out two plates, took the pie out of the oven and divided it between the two of them. She then returned to the lounge and placed the plates before them. 'It's not much, I'm afraid, I wasn't expecting company.'

Pulling a face, the girl looked at her plate. 'It'll do fer now, help stave off me hunger pains.' She then proceeded to gobble it all down and when she'd finished looked longingly at her son's plate. 'You gonna eat all that?' she asked him.

He looked up at her and nodded. 'It's nice, Mam.'

She grunted and glanced at Judith who was hovering at the side of them. 'Any pudding?'

She shook her head. 'I'm afraid not.'

'Oh, well, I'll have ter mek do with that then.' She scraped back her chair, walked over to the armchair and retrieved her handbag from where she had placed it earlier. She removed a packet of cigarettes and a box of matches. Without asking Judith if she minded she took out a cigarette and lit it, blowing out a long stream of smoke. 'Want one?' she offered Judith, holding out the packet to her.

'I don't, thank you.'

'Suit yourself,' the girl said, putting the packet and matches back in her handbag. She looked at Judith searchingly. 'So am I the only one or are there others?'

Judith stared at her, stumped. 'I'm sorry?'

'Have I brothers or sisters?'

'Oh, no.'

She took a long draw from her cigarette and when ash from it fell on to the carpet, rubbed it away with her foot.

Judith stared at her, appalled. 'I've no ashtray but I'll get you a saucer.'

She disappeared off into the kitchen and moments later handed over a saucer.

The girl flicked her ash into it. 'So I was yer only bastard then, was I? What happened? Did me father dump yer when he found out yer was expecting me? I shouldn't worry, the same thing happened ter me when I was expecting him,' she said, inclining her head in the direction of her son who was still engrossed in eating his dinner.

Judith lowered her head, clasping her hands tightly in front of her. 'Yes, I'm afraid that's just how it was.'

'Wouldn't yer family stand by yer?'

She shook her head. 'I never got the chance to find out, but probably not.'

The woman glanced around her. 'But yer still seem to have done all right for yerself?'

'Looks can be deceiving,' Judith said quietly.

193

'Don't look deceptive ter me. This flat can't be cheap and yer clothes ain't exactly off the market, are they?' She gave a sudden grin. 'Can I expect an inheritance when yer kick the bucket? Lord knows, I could do with one.'

Judith stared at her. This woman was claiming to be her daughter, and how could she dispute that as she had information about Judith that only the baby she had given birth to in the home would have, but regardless Judith could see no resemblance to herself in this girl at all. A vision of Clive Lewis rose up before her suddenly and she could see nothing of him in his daughter either. But then twenty-three years had passed since Judith had last seen him and it could be that her memory of his features wasn't an accurate one after all this time.

But her daughter's unexpected arrival was not what was upsetting Judith the most, it was the fact that she felt nothing towards her, by way of any motherly emotions. She should feel a glimmer of something, shouldn't she, for the child she'd given birth to, even if that child had been taken from her without herself even so much as catching a glimpse of her face? There was something wrong with her, there had to be, because what she was feeling most was annoyance that this unwelcome guest seemed more interested in what Judith possessed than in anything else. But then, she reasoned with herself, maybe the girl was nervous and this was just her way. After all, this was a momentous occasion for both of them, and coming here, as she had said, had taken great courage. Maybe she herself would start to feel motherly towards her once she got to know her better. Trouble was, at the moment she didn't know whether she did want to get to know her better. She forced herself to smile.

'You haven't told me your name?'

Her back to Judith she had picked up the vase from the fire surround and was closely examining it. 'Didn't I? Well, it's Rachel.' She turned to face Judith. 'Nice name they gave me, in't it?'

All Judith was thinking of was she hoped the girl was careful with her vase and didn't drop it. 'Yes, it's very pretty.'

'Pretty vase too. Bet it cost a bit? Still, I expect you can afford it.'

Judith suddenly frowned at her, puzzled as something she had said earlier struck a chord. 'I thought you said your son's father recently ran off with all your money, yet you said before that that he had walked away from you when he found out you were pregnant?'

She turned away from Judith to replace the vase. 'Did I? Oh, yeah, I called me last feller Marty's dad, see, but he was just someone I was knocking round with.' She walked over to the armchair and sprawled in it, fixing her eyes directly on Judith's. 'As yer can see, Mam, I ain't fared all that well, and it's all your fault for abandoning me. Those people you let adopt me treated me rotten.'

Judith sank down into the armchair opposite. 'I didn't abandon you, I never had any choice in the matter.' She paused, deep in thought. Miss Hales had told her that her child's new parents were good people who'd look after her baby properly. Miss Hales had clearly lied to her. She looked at Rachel in concern. 'In what way did your adoptive parents treat you badly?'

She gave a shrug. 'Just did,' she said evasively. 'I left

home as soon as I could ter get away from them. Landed up with *him* 'cos I fell for the first bloke I thought loved me. Truth was he was only after one thing and soon as he'd had it he scarpered.'

Judith inwardly groaned. Three generations of women from the same family had suffered more or less the same fate. 'I'm so sorry,' she uttered remorsefully.

'So yer should be,' the girl snapped back aggressively. 'It's your fault I had such an awful life.' She stared at Judith for several long moments then glanced around before bringing her eyes back to rest on her face. 'Look, I ain't come here to have a go at yer, what's past is past and I ain't interested in that. As I said when I first arrived I wanted to meet the woman who gave birth ter me. I can't deny, though, that I was hoping yer might offer me some money to help me out. I'm in a right hole at the moment. It's for yer grandson, see. Now that bastard has scarpered with all me money, I can't feed Marty. I'm desperate . . . Oh, look, I'm sorry, I shouldn't have asked.' She jumped up from her chair. 'We'd better go.'

Judith rose also. She didn't know whether she felt guilty for . . . she couldn't think of this girl as her daughter, not yet . . . her visitor's plight, or angry that on their first meeting she was asking for money. Nevertheless she couldn't bring herself to send her away with nothing to feed her child when she herself did have the means. 'I can give you a few pounds to help you out.'

The girl's face broke into a broad smile. 'Yer can? Oh, I'm ever so grateful. I'll pay yer back.'

Judith flashed her a wan smile. 'Let's just call it a gift from me.'

196

She went over to the bookcase, took out a particular book and opened it. Inside was her savings: thirty pounds she had left over from the money her own mother had given her and ten pounds she had managed to add to it from her wages. There was so much she could have bought with it, things for herself, for her home, but she hadn't because having that money made her feel safe should a crisis arise. She counted out five single pound notes then on an afterthought counted out another five, closed the book, replaced it and walked towards Rachel, handing the notes to her. 'I hope this will help you get on your feet.'

She counted it out. 'Blimey, ten pounds! Can't remember ever having so much in me hand all in one go. I'll say it'll help. Ta, Mam.' She heaved a deep sigh. 'Well, I suppose we'd better go.' She looked across at her son who, having finished his meal, had got down from the table and was sitting on the settee staring at them both. 'Er . . . we couldn't stop the night, could we? It's a couple of bus rides back to where we live and Marty is fair tuckered out. When I went to the lavvy I noticed you had another bedroom. Marty can sleep in there and I can have the settee. Come on, Marty, get yer coat off, we're stopping with Granny fer the night. Ain't that nice? You go and get his bed made up, Mam, while I mek us all a nice cuppa tea.'

Judith stared at her, speechless. This woman might be her daughter but in truth she was a virtual stranger, as was her son, and Judith didn't like to admit it but the thought of them sleeping under her roof made her feel uneasy. But it appeared she had no choice in the matter as

Rachel was already taking off her son's clothes. Thank goodness the weather was warm, thought Judith, as she went into her bedroom and gathered her spare pair of sheets and a blanket from her bed bale, one of two which she had taken off her own bed as summer took hold. She picked up one of her pillows too before going into the spare room and making up the bed.

Just as she had finished Rachel was behind her. 'Come on then, Marty, in yer get.' The little boy, dressed in his shabby pants and vest, climbed under the sheets. His mother dumped the rest of his clothes at the bottom of the bed before she tucked him in. She leaned over and patted his head. 'Now you be a good boy for Granny. Night-night then.'

He cast a wary glance in Judith's direction before bringing his eyes back to his mother, then he turned over and closed them.

Back in the lounge an awkward silence ensued as they drank the tea that Rachel had made them while Judith had been making up the little boy's bed. She, feeling mortally uncomfortable, fought for something to say. 'Er . . . so where is it that you live?'

'Across town. In a flat. Well, a bed-sitter really, nothing like this. It's rough where we live.'

'Oh, well, maybe you could move to somewhere better in the future?'

'Yer've gotta be kidding, ain't yer? I find it a struggle ter pay the rent as it is.'

'Oh, I see. So . . . er . . . what do you do for a job?'

Rachel shrugged. 'This and that. It's hard working when yer've got a kid.' She looked at Judith closely. 'I

198

shoulda done what you did and had him adopted, then I mighta had a place like this and a good job ter go with it.'

Judith flinched, feeling as if she'd been slapped on the face. She didn't know what to say in response and another awkward silence engulfed them.

It was broken by Rachel giving a loud yawn. 'I'm bushed. Think I'll turn in.'

Judith jumped up. Despite its still being early she was glad that Rachel had suggested it so she could make her own escape. 'I'll get your bedding.'

Going into her bedroom, she retrieved her other pillow and last spare blanket. Returning to the lounge, she realised Rachel had disappeared into the bathroom. After making up the settee as comfortably as she could she waited for the girl to return. It was over fifteen minutes before she did.

'I'm sorry, I only have a spare blanket as I've used my spare sheets on your son's bed.'

'Your grandson,' Rachel corrected her. 'That's no bother. In my time I've slept with less. Good night then.'

'Er . . . yes, good night. I hope you sleep well. Oh, I have to leave at eight in the morning to get to work.'

'Don't worry, we'll be ready to leave too. I have ter get Marty ter school or I get in trouble with the authorities.'

Judith collected the dirty cups and saucers before she departed, closing the lounge door behind her. As she stepped into the kitchen she stared around in dismay at the debris Rachel had left behind her after making the tea. Tea leaves she had tipped out from the pot in order to mash a fresh brew were blocking the plug hole. Spilt milk on the kitchen table had not been wiped up, neither had the sugar that must have fallen off the spoon as she had heaped it into the cups.

After clearing it all up, Judith made her way into the bathroom and again stared around in dismay. Her bath towel lay sopping wet on the floor, the sink was still filled with dirty water, and Judith could tell that Rachel had opened up all her bottles of toiletries and sampled them. Her daughter certainly seemed to have no manners. Setting to, she cleared up the bathroom too before she had her own wash and retired to bed.

Sleeping without a pillow proved most uncomfortable but in any case Judith was far from sleep. Her mind tossed and turned, mulling over this unexpected turn of events. She didn't know what to do about it. After her first impressions tonight she didn't know whether she wanted to pursue a relationship with the young woman to whom she had given birth. She felt no bond with her whatsoever, nothing at all, nothing she could build on. Would that come, given time? Then she felt a sudden pang of guilt. It wasn't Rachel's fault that she had turned out like she had, it was that of the people who had raised her to act as she did. Judith knew she was far from perfect herself. If nothing else she owed it to Rachel to give her a chance and then maybe she could teach her some of the things it was very apparent her adoptive parents hadn't. Maybe in turn there were things that Rachel could teach her about life, things she'd never come across before.

Then a great worry rose within her. Rachel had said that she didn't want to know about the past, but what if she changed her mind and started asking probing questions about how she'd come into being? Did Judith tell her the truth, that she was the product of rape, or did she concoct a story to spare her feelings? Judith knew only too well how she herself had felt when her mother had told her about her own origins. Was Rachel strong enough to cope with such knowledge? From the way she had acted towards Judith she obviously bore her a grudge for being adopted at birth, but to learn the truth of her conception on top of that could have untold consequences.

She lay for a while pondering on the problem and decided it would be best to see how matters progressed between them and judge what best to do if and when the time came.

Her eyes drooped and the release of sleep overtook Judith.

Chapter Sixteen

At precisely seven o'clock the next morning the alarm shrilled loudly. Judith awoke with a start. It took her several moments to recall the events of the previous night and she lay for a moment, wondering if she had dreamt it all, but deep down she knew she hadn't. On the other side of the wall really was the baby she had given birth to twenty-three years ago, and with her, her own son. A situation Judith had never for a moment thought to find herself in.

Swinging her legs over the side of the bed, she sat for a moment deep in thought, wondering how best to proceed. Should she suggest to Rachel that she visit her again or wait until the girl suggested what she wanted to do next? She decided it would be best to wait for Rachel to decide for herself and take it from there.

Pulling on her dressing gown, Judith stood up and went across to open her bedroom door, standing listening for a moment. The flat was silent. Obviously they were both still asleep. As quietly as she could, she made her way into the bathroom, washed then returned to her bedroom to make her bed and dress for work.

Several minutes later she trod her way softly down the hallway towards the kitchen. There was still no other movement in the flat and Judith worried that time was wearing on and she really ought to rouse them both as she had to leave for work in half an hour. She decided to make a cup of tea and take it through to Rachel, hopefully hurry her on that way.

Cup of tea in hand, she tapped tentatively on the lounge door then slowly opened it, poking her head around, looking across towards the settee. The bedding she had provided Rachel with was piled in a heap on it and there seemed to be no sign of the girl herself. Frowning, she pushed the door further open and walked inside, looking all around. Rachel was definitely not present and there was no sign of her clothes. Then Judith noticed that her vase had gone from off the fire surround and for a moment she stared at the empty space, wondering where it had disappeared to. Then a sudden horrifying thought struck her and her eyes flew across to her bookcase. Books from one of the shelves lay scattered on the carpet. Rushing over to the coffee table, Judith put down the cup of tea and went across to the bookcase, staring down at one particular book, the one she had kept her savings inside. Heart hammering painfully, she bent to pick it up, opening it out. Her fear was confirmed. Her money was gone and she didn't need to guess what had happened to it. Rachel had stolen it. Her vase too. Then another awful thought struck. Her eyes flashed to the side of the armchair where she had left her handbag. It was open, her purse lying empty at the side of it. Rachel had taken the few shillings she had had in there as well.

Judith's shoulders sagged in despair. How could she do this? Was she that desperate that the ten pounds she had been given was not enough? If so why hadn't she said and given Judith the opportunity to give her more instead of just taking it? But had that been her purpose all along, to contact her natural mother in order to see what she could get out of her? After assuming Judith was affluent, had Rachel wormed her way into staying the night – just so she could help herself to what she felt was rightfully hers?

Judith felt sick. The child to whom she had given birth, the one she had hoped would be raised lovingly in a good home, turn into something worthwhile, was nothing more than a common thief. Should she report her to the police? But how could she report her own child, risk her being sent to prison? And what would become of Rachel's child during her incarceration should Judith do such a thing? She knew that she had no choice but to put this all down to experience. She doubted she would ever see Rachel again as the young woman had got what she had come for. The only saving grace was that it was pay day today. Thank goodness it hadn't been yesterday then Rachel would have taken that too.

Judith was so upset she hadn't the strength to tidy up. Feeling grief-stricken she hurriedly collected her empty handbag and set off for work.

In order not to antagonise the rest of the clerical staff, they thinking she was trying to make out she was more conscientious than them, Judith always timed her arrival to coincide with theirs, usually a couple of minutes before the working day started. Today her mind was too preoccupied for her to note she had arrived twenty minutes early, despite having to make her way on foot as Rachel had left her without the means even to pay her bus fare. Automatically she sat down in front of her typewriter and began to plough her way through a repetitive letter that was being sent to potential customers around the Midlands area. There were over three hundred of them, and Cherry, with her persistent vendetta against Judith, had seen fit to make her solely responsible for them instead of sharing such a mundane job around all of the typists, which would normally have been the case.

At eight-twenty-five, Judith felt a presence at her side and jerked her head up to find Cherry looking disdainfully down at her.

'Not trying to make the rest of us look like slackers, are yer, *Miss Chambers*?'

Mind still firmly on her personal matters, Judith frowned, nonplussed. 'I'm sorry?'

'Huh, don't give me that innocent act! I know your game. Hoping the boss would walk in and see you'd arrived early and were working away and then he'd think what a wonderful employee you are. Well, yer wasted yer time 'cos he's out all day on business.'

Without giving Judith the chance to respond, she turned and stalked off to her own office.

Judith let out a forlorn sigh. Would Cherry ever let up on her hostility towards her? But then Cherry herself was only venting her anger towards Judith for the way in which she had been treated at Chambers', and if Judith wanted to keep her job then she had no choice but to put up with what Cherry dished out to her, the same as the employees at Chambers' had had to do when Judith had been in charge. Sighing again, she immersed herself in her work.

Later that afternoon she lifted her head to notice that all the women, including Cherry, had gathered around Sally's desk and much camaraderie was taking place. It seemed it was Sally's birthday and a cake had been baked by one of the women and was being sliced up and handed around and presents were being given by each of them to Sally. Judith looked on, feeling loneliness steal over her. In the past she would have shied away from any such gathering, but now she would welcome an invitation to join in such an occasion. None was forthcoming. Cherry looked over at her, flashing Judith a triumphant smile. She lowered her head and carried on with her work.

Just before finishing time Cherry was at the side of her desk again, her face stony. Judith looked up at her, wondering what she was so obviously annoyed about. As far as she was aware she had done nothing to cause it.

'Well, the perfect *Miss Chambers* ain't so perfect after all,' she snapped. 'These letters you've done today that I've just checked through – and a good job it is that I *do* check everything you do – well, you've misquoted the reference. It should be CC for myself in capitals followed by slash and jc for yerself in *lower case*, not upper case as you have done. You're just a common typist, your initials are purely for our information, to let us know you're the one who typed this, and are of no other importance than that.' She slapped the pile of correspondence she was holding down on Judith's desk. 'Redo these.' She looked at Judith haughtily. 'And take this as your first warning.

207

Another lapse of such time-wasting magnitude and I'll report you to Neville James and have a good case against you for dismissal.'

She turned and stalked off.

Judith stared at the letters. She hadn't realised that the visit from Rachel had affected her so much. It was a revelation to her. Stalwart Judith Chambers, an expert at controlling her feelings, was turning into a human being after all. She felt she should be glad as it showed that her own hard work in changing her character, learning to express her feelings, was working, but in the circumstances she would have given a lot to have had this emotional breakthrough achieved in any other way.

She gave a deep sigh. There were at least forty letters and they had taken her nearly all day to do. In truth what she had typed was not usual office practice, but Cherry's reaction was taking it to the extremes as Judith doubted the recipients of the letters would have noticed anything amiss. If any of the other typists under Cherry's authority had done such a thing, Judith knew their lapse would have been overlooked. She couldn't blame Cherry, though, for seizing this chance for retribution. Her response was exactly how Judith herself, under her father's rules, would have acted should such a thing have happened at Chambers'. But that warning bothered her. It was no false warning, Judith was well aware of that. Cherry was determined to get rid of her. Very mindful of what it had taken to secure this job, and that should she be sacked from it, it would be much more difficult for her to get another, Judith gave herself a severe talking to. She must never again give Cherry the slightest reason to criticise her work or her conduct while at work.

Judith had never been so glad to see the end of a working day. Walking out at just after five-thirty into the warm sunshine of the late-September evening, she took a deep breath and with a tremendous sigh of relief began her journey home. The weekend stretched before her, two whole days to herself in which hopefully she could put the distressing events of the last day behind her and look to her future. Trouble was, though, that despite Rachel's appalling behaviour towards her, now Judith was aware of her, she doubted she could just forget about her. When all was said and done she had given birth to her, and if nothing else Judith did feel a certain responsibility towards her, worried for her welfare and that of her son. But there was nothing she could do to ease her conscience as apart from her Christian name, Judith knew nothing else about Rachel.

She was just about to enter Mrs Chaudri's corner shop when she heard her name being called and turned around to see Kimberley hurrying towards her.

The young librarian arrived level with Judith, smiling broadly. 'Oh, you do walk fast, Miss Chambers. I've been trying to catch up with you from the top of the road. How are you?'

Judith thought Kimberley looked very pretty in a short bright yellow shift dress, edged around the cutaway arm-holes and hem with a broad band of white material. Her thick long dark hair hung down past her shoulders and shone with health. 'I'm very well thank you, Kimberley. And yourself?'

'Oh, I'm very well too, thanks.'

Judith eyed her in concern. 'My library books, are they overdue?'

She looked back at Judith, bemused. 'They're due back next Tuesday. So no, they're not overdue. Why did you ask that?'

Judith was taken aback that Kimberley knew exactly when her books were due for return. 'Oh, I automatically thought that, since you were in such a tearing hurry to catch up with me.' She smiled at Kimberley warmly. 'You take a real interest in your borrowers from the library. Well, you must do to know without hesitation when my books are due for return.'

'Well . . . I have got a good memory and I do take my job seriously.' She took a deep breath. 'Miss Chambers, the reason why I wanted to speak to you was to tell you that I've moved into a little flat just down the road, not far from you in fact. I had quite a distance to travel back and forth to work so my move makes good sense. On the evenings I have to take my turn on the late shift I wasn't getting home until after eight. And, after all, I am twenty-three and thought it was about time I got myself from under my poor long-suffering parents' feet and started to become independent. Mind you, that's a bit of a joke because my mum has been around every night with a casserole or offering to clean, and my dad armed with his tool box tackling any odd job I can find for him.'

'They sound lovely people,' said Judith wistfully, wondering what it would have been like for herself to have had such parents instead of the ones she'd had.

Kimberley smiled tenderly. 'They are, the best parents I could ever have been blessed with. Anyway, I want to make new friends in the area so I was wondering . . .' She paused and looked at Judith hesitantly before asking, 'Well, I was wondering if you'd like to come around for a coffee sometime?'

Judith stared at her, astonished. Apart from the invitation from her fellow tenant, which hadn't appealed to her, in all her forty-three years she had never had an approach of such a nature and this one coming so out of the blue took her completely by surprise. 'I would love to,' she responded in genuine delight.

'You would? Oh, that's great. I shall really look forward to it. When? When would you like to come?'

Judging by her enthusiasm at Judith's acceptance, Kimberley really was keen to make new friends and Judith felt privileged that this young woman was considering her in that light. 'You tell me what time would suit you best?'

'Tomorrow afternoon? I'm working in the morning but the library shuts at two o'clock, so shall we say three?'

'I shall look forward to it.' Judith's mind whirled. What did people do in circumstances like this? She had overheard the women at work talking about visiting relatives and friends and how they'd made cakes to take with them. She didn't trust her baking as yet. The only attempt she had made at a Victoria sponge resembled a hard biscuit rather than the light cake the recipe had promised. It was going to take a lot more practice before her own efforts were worthy of passing around. She could buy a cake though. 'I'll bring a cake with me.'

Kimberley beamed at her. 'That would be lovely. I'll see you tomorrow then.'

Judith looked on as Kimberley stepped jauntily on her

211

way. Her own heart soared. She was making a friend at last and couldn't think of a better one than this lovely young girl. There were people in the world who actually liked her!

She spent a pleasant few minutes being served by Mrs Chaudri who was not a happy woman at the moment as her husband's mother and father had come over from Pakistan and were now living with them.

'She an interfering old woman,' Mrs Chaudri had told Judith in her broken English. 'She complain all the time I look after her son wrong. How does she think he still live after be married to me for twenty year, if I look after him wrong? My sons all four of them too. Now she's took over my house. I can't get in my kitchen for her cooking something or other and it's all Pakistani stuff. We're in England, I tell her, we eat English food now. She won't take notice of me. She say I blame for us losing our culture. My husband, he waste of time. He scared of his mother so won't stand up to her.' She had then ranted on in her own language as she had cut Judith a chunk of cheese, and it didn't take much to guess they were not polite words she was using.

She had just deposited her laden carrier on the kitchen table and was about to take off her coat when the door knocker was pounded. Her heart leapt. Had Rachel come back? She hesitated, not sure whether she was up to facing the girl or not. She hadn't a clue what to say to her or how to act towards her after what she had done, didn't know whether she wanted to see her or not. Maybe, though, Rachel had realised the error of her ways and come back to apologise, offer Judith her money back.

Although its return was not so important to Judith as her daughter being suitably ashamed of what she had done.

The knocker was hammered again. Heart thumping painfully in anticipation of what might be facing her, Judith went to open it, only for her spirits to sink rapidly as she stared straight into the eyes of her surly neighbour from opposite. Before she could enquire what he wanted of her, he said tartly, 'This is yours, I believe.'

Her eyes flew down to see his hands resting on the shoulders of the little boy in front of him. It was Marty.

Eyes wide in utter shock, she gazed down at him, speechless.

'I came home just before lunchtime today and found him sitting inside your doorway in a state of undress, clutching his clothes. I can't believe you went off to work and left him on his own,' Nathan said accusingly. 'Poor little mite was starving. It seems he'd had no breakfast, and almost choked gobbling down the sandwich and biscuits I gave him. You surprise me, Miss Chambers, a woman of your maturity and, I thought, intelligence, leaving a little boy of his age at home alone.'

She lifted her eyes to his and glared at him. 'I had no idea he was here. He's . . . He's the son of someone I know and must have come to visit me.'

He looked at her condescendingly. 'And he's got a key to your flat and, considering how tall the little fella is, reached up to the keyhole and let himself in? Then he proceeded to half-undress himself and sit in your doorway?' He fixed Judith with his eyes. 'He told me you're his grandmother, Miss Chambers.'

She stared at him, mortification flooding through her.

His whole face was questioning and she knew exactly what was going through his mind. She was a Miss yet this young boy had told him she was his grandmother. If he thought, though, that she was going to offer him an explanation then he was wrong. Her private business was nothing to do with him. She looked down at Marty. 'Go inside and wait for me in the lounge,' she instructed him. As the solemn-faced little boy walked past her and on down the hallway, Judith stared Nathan in the eye. 'Thank you for looking after him,' she said stiffly.

'Let's hope *you* do in future,' he said, flashing her a look of derision before he turned and walked back across the landing to disappear inside his own flat.

Judith shut her door and leaned against it, running one hand down the side of her face. Her mind whirled. The mortally embarrassing situation she had just found herself in was forgotten as a much more disturbing thought presented itself. After stealing what she could from Judith, Rachel must have sneaked out of the flat, leaving her son behind, which Judith hadn't noticed because she hadn't checked the spare bedroom, it not entering her mind that Rachel would have done such a thing as to abandon her own son with a woman who was virtually a stranger to him, and worse, a woman who had no idea how to look after a child. So where was Rachel? When would she come and collect her child?

Righting herself, she headed into the lounge. Marty was perched on the edge of the settee surrounded by the heaped bedding his mother had left, head drooping, twiddling with the rib on the bottom of his sleeveless pullover. Hands clasped in front of her, Judith stood before him. 'Marty, do you know where your mother has gone?'

He gave no response.

'Marty, your mother, do you know where she could be?'

He slowly lifted his head and looked at her blankly, pushed his glasses higher on his nose, gave a shrug, then returned to fiddling with the bottom of his pullover.

She sighed. He probably had no more idea where Rachel was than she did. Although his pullover had obviously seen much better days, Judith feared that what he was doing to it would ruin it further. 'Please stop doing that to your pullover, Marty, you will pull it out of shape.' She looked at him anxiously. What did she do with him? She ought to feed him, she supposed, and by the time she had done that his mother might have returned to collect him. 'I expect you're hungry. I'll tidy up then I'll get you some dinner. I hope you like pork chops? Marty, I'm talking to you. I asked if you liked pork chops?'

He lifted his head, gave a shrug, then hung it again and began pulling at a thread on his short trousers. As she folded the blanket Judith noticed what he was doing. 'Don't do that, Marty, or you'll make a hole in your trousers. Why don't you go and wash your hands in the bathroom ready for dinner?'

Without a word he rose and walked off to the bathroom.

Tidying done, Judith set about frying the pork chop, thinking she would give it to Marty and make do herself with potatoes and tinned peas, then she remembered she had a sausage left over from the half-pound she had bought from the butcher's on Wednesday evening, having

215

caught him still open on her way home from work. She popped the sausage into the pan next to the chop. The dinner was just about cooked when, cutlery in hand, she went into the lounge to set the table. Marty was sitting back on the settee, head hung low, picking his nails. 'Would you like to sit up at the table, Marty, I'm just going to serve up,' she called across to him.

Silently he rose, went to the table, climbed on to a chair and settled himself into it.

As Judith made her way back to the kitchen she stopped short, hearing the sound of running water which she realised was coming from the direction of the bathroom. Dashing in, she froze at the sight that met her. The hot tap was on full and water from the overflowing sink was pouring all over the floor. Quick as a flash she turned off the tap and pulled the plug in the sink, then dashing into the kitchen, she grabbed her mop and bucket and mopped up the floor. Judith knew by the amount spilled that the floorboards underneath the linoleum must be sodden and prayed no water had leaked through to the flat downstairs or she dreaded to think of the consequences.

Going back into the lounge, she stood before Marty and said crossly, 'You left the tap on and flooded the bathroom. That was very naughty. Don't do it again. Now I'm going to dish up the dinner, that's if it's not burned while I've been mopping up the mess you made. Sit there and don't move.'

With that she spun on her heel and strode back into the kitchen.

Judith was appalled as Marty stabbed his fork into the

pork chop then lunged his knife into it, using a sawing motion. The chop shot off his plate to land on the carpet.

'That is no way to use a knife and fork,' she scolded him. 'You don't hold them like that for a start.'

She rose, walked around the table and picked up the chop, then going into the kitchen she put it in the waste bin, annoyed at the waste of good food. Going back into the lounge she put the sausage from her own plate on to his then, standing at the side of him, took the knife and fork from him, replacing them in his hands properly. 'Now try cutting your sausage. No, not like that, like this.' She held her own hands over his to show him. 'There, that's how it's done. Now you'll know in future.'

By the time the meal was finished and Judith had cleared away it was nearly half-past seven. It didn't appear that Rachel was going to come and collect her son tonight. A bolt of sheer panic rushed through her. What was she going to do? Apart from having hardly any idea of a child's needs, she had no spare clothes for him. After drying her hands on the roller towel, Judith made her way into the lounge. Marty was sitting on the settee, tracing circles on his knee with one finger.

She stood before him. 'Do you know your address? Where you live? Marty, I'm talking to you.'

He lifted his head and looked at her blankly, giving a shrug.

She sighed. 'What's your surname, Marty? Your other name after Marty?'

He shrugged again.

'Surely you know your last name?' she said reproach- fully. 'You are five, aren't you?' He just stared at her and she inwardly groaned. This was getting her nowhere. She ought to put him to bed and just hope that Rachel turned up soon to collect him, otherwise she had no idea what she was going to do. It was very remiss of her daughter to do such a mindless thing and Judith would certainly tell her so when she finally turned up. She just thanked God it was Friday and she hadn't work in the morning.

'Come along, Marty. I'll run you a bath, then it's time for bed. I said, come along, Marty.' Though what she was going to put on him to sleep in she had no idea. One thing she did know was that his clothes badly needed washing. She would just have to hand wash them in the sink and hope they dried overnight on the clothes horse.

Having ran a couple of inches of warm water in the bath, she handed Marty a bar of soap and a flannel and gave him a warning not to touch anything, just to wash and dry himself and wrap the towel around himself when he came out. And not to be too long. She then went and looked through her own clothing for something she could give him to sleep in. The only thing remotely suitable was a short-sleeved white blouse. It would drown him but at least it would cover his modesty.

A while later she drew the bedroom curtains and walked back to the bed, watching as Marty climbed into it. Immediately he closed his eyes and turned away from her to face the wall. She looked down at the shock of red hair sticking up from the covers. This was her grandson, a child with her own blood in his veins. She suddenly felt terribly guilty for not feeling more grandmotherly towards him. What she was feeling instead was a great fear of not being able to cope with caring for him until his mother returned. 'Goodnight, Marty,' said Judith as, armed with his clothes for washing, she left the room, closing the door behind her.

A while later, his clothes washed and dripping over a towel on the clothes horse in the kitchen, she being thankful it was warm so there was a good possibility of them drying, she sank down in an armchair, nursing a cup of tea and staring into space. What if Rachel did not return to collect her son during the next two days? Judith herself had to go to work on Monday. And what was wrong with the child? Why wouldn't he talk to her? He'd obviously spoken to her neighbour, enough at least to inform him that Judith was his grandmother – and what her neighbour must be thinking of her now didn't bear thinking about. She gave a despondent sigh. How she wished she had someone to talk to about this, could ask their advice. Even if she had a friend close enough to confide something so personal in, questions about Marty were bound to be asked generally and how could she explain him away without having to tell her shameful secret? Her shoulders sagged despairingly. This situation was awful.

Rising, she absent-mindedly walked across to the window to stare out into the night and a thought struck her. Rachel was bound to be missing her son. She'd have to return for him. Hopefully very soon.

Despite its being early Judith decided to go to bed herself. It had not been a good day at work for her and the events of this evening had utterly drained her. Going into her bedroom she switched on the light and immediately saw someone standing by her window staring out into the street. It was Marty.

'Oh, my goodness,' she exclaimed. 'You did give me a scare.'

At her voice, the little boy jumped and spun round to face her, his little face filled with alarm.

'What are you doing in here?' she demanded.

He looked back at her blankly.

'I asked what you were doing in here, Marty? This is my private room.'

He continued to stare at her.

'Back to bed,' she ordered. 'And stay there this time.'

Like a bolt of lightning he shot past her and she heard the spare bedroom door slam shut. Sighing heavily, she prepared herself for bed.

220

Chapter Seventeen

As the weekend passed and there was still no sign of Rachel worry started building within Judith that she was not coming back. For fear she may miss her, she had only ventured out for less than half an hour on Saturday morning – taking Marty with her, hoping she bumped into no one she knew in case questions were asked – to buy a few provisions, leaving a note pinned on her door should Rachel call meantime, so Judith knew she hadn't been. The weekend had passed painfully slowly. Each time Judith had heard the slightest noise outside her flat she prayed Rachel had returned to reclaim her son. But as time passed her hopes faded. The only conclusion she could come to was that the girl must have met with some sort of accident and been unable to let her know. What other explanation could there be? But there was no way for Judith to check. She couldn't just call at the hospital and ask if a girl called Rachel had been brought in. They'd want more details than that. All she could do was wait for her to turn up, which Judith hoped would be soon.

Marty had still not spoken one word to her. At meal-times he gobbled down whatever food she placed before him, then spent the rest of the time looking out of the lounge window, out on to the street. Judith had been at a loss as to what to do with him. She had tried to remember back to when she had been his age, but the years had hazed those memories and all she could recall was spending most of her time in her room reading books. Not that she had any suitable reading matter to hand for a child but Marty appeared not to feel any interest in doing anything but staring out of the window. She was grateful for that as she had enough to worry about as it was without meeting the demands of a child which she wouldn't have known how to cope with anyway. What was paramount in her mind at the moment was that she had to go to work in a few hours' time and there was no one to watch him during her absence. What on earth was she doing to do?

She rose and walked across to the window to stare out in exactly the same way Marty had been doing until a short while ago when she had instructed him to wash himself and then get into bed. Her mind whirled. She felt it was no good hoping for a miracle. Rachel would hardly appear now so late in the evening.

Judith ran a hand over her face worriedly. She needed to find someone to look after Marty while she was at work, but how was she going to do that so late in the evening? And besides that she hadn't a clue how to go about seeking a child-minder and one who was willing to start from tomorrow. Her mind raced for several long moments then it suddenly struck her that people in the area advertised their services in shop windows. Would she be lucky enough to find a child-minder among them? She looked at the clock. It was a quarter to eight. Was it too late to call on someone at this time of the evening? She would just have to hope that if she did find an advertisement for a child-minder, they would not mind her calling so late as the only alternative left was to sort it out tomorrow and that meant being absent from work without permission, and she knew Cherry Campbell would not let *that* opportunity pass. Then Judith knew that she need not worry about a minder for Marty as she'd be at home to look after him herself.

She hurried through to check on him. He appeared to be sound asleep. Slipping out of the bedroom, she grabbed her bag and coat and opened the front door, then hesitated. She couldn't just leave him, even for a short while. What if there was a fire? Her eyes fell on the door opposite. She had no other choice.

Leaving her own door on the latch, she stepped across the landing, took a deep breath and knocked purposefully on the door of her obnoxious neighbour.

As soon as he opened it, he took one look at her and snapped, 'Oh, it's you. What do you want?'

Despite all her efforts to soften her attitude towards others, with this man she just couldn't, his ever-present rudeness towards her serving to resurrect her old icy manner. Face set, she said, 'I'm very sorry to disturb you . . .'

'So you should be,' he interjected sharply. 'What is it you want?'

She felt her hackles rising and fought to lower them. Whether she liked it or not, she needed this man's help.

'I have to pop out for a moment and . . .'

'And why would you need to tell me that?'

'If you would please do me the courtesy of allowing me to finish? Marty is in bed and . . .'

'You're asking *me* to baby-sit?' he exclaimed loudly.

Before she could stop herself she was saying, 'Believe me, I would not ask unless I was desperate. I would be grateful if you'd hear me out.' She just stopped herself from saying, 'But of course, if it's too much trouble, forget it.' She couldn't take the risk he would do that.

He stared at her for several long moments. 'Don't be long.'

It galled her to say it. 'Thank you.'

There were several plumbers, electricians, two builders, a couple of odd job men and a mobile hairdresser advertising their services in cards in Mrs Chaudri's shop window but no child-minders. Judith's heart sank. On her way here she had already studied the cards in the Post Office window and no child-minders were advertising their services there either.

Just then the gate at the side of the shop opened and Mrs Chaudri and her husband appeared. On this sticky Indian summer evening she looked fresh and cool in her white sari, long black hair hanging in a plait down her back almost to her waist; her husband too looked smart in a white shirt and blue trousers. The shop-keeper spotted Judith and beamed a welcome.

'Ahh, Missy Hambers. You well, yes?' she said, coming over to greet Judith.

'I am, thank you, Mrs Chaudri, and yourself?'

She pulled a face. 'Phew! I never be again while his parents still live. We just off to see Assam's brother. Peace,

224

no parents there. You wanted something from shop? We shut but I get it for you.'

'How kind of you, Mrs Chaudri, but no, I don't need any shopping. I was looking at your cards but I can't find what I need.' Then a thought struck her. 'Mrs Chaudri, do you happen to know any ladies around here who child-mind?'

The shop-keeper looked at her, puzzled. 'Child-mind? Oh, I don't mind the child. I got the four myself.'

She realised Mrs Chaudri didn't understand her. 'Someone who looks after children while their parents are at work?'

'Oh, stupid me.' She paused in thought. 'Ah, only lady I know, she live in number three around the corner,' she said, pointing at a road leading off the one they were on. 'She takes in the child. Missy . . . Missy 'ackett. That her name.' She frowned, bothered. 'But . . .'

'Oh, Mrs Chaudri, you're a life-saver,' Judith gratefully cut in. 'Thank you. Thank you so much. I hope you have a nice evening.'

With that she shot off in the direction Mrs Chaudri had pointed her in.

This street was not one of the nicest in the area, but intent on her urgent task of finding someone to care for Marty while she was at work, Judith was heedless of that when she knocked on the door of number three.

A young lad of about fifteen answered it. He was dressed in a pair of light blue denim jeans held up by a pair of red braces, and a white shirt, the sleeves of which were rolled up just past his elbows. His hair was close-cropped and on his feet were a pair of huge workmen's

225

boots. Framed in the doorway, he looked Judith up and down. 'Yeah?' he demanded.

'Does, Mrs Ack . . . Hackett live here?'

He looked at her warily. 'She might. Who wants her?'

'Miss Chambers. I've come to enquire about her child-minding services.'

'Who is it, Tyrone?' a loud female voice boomed out.

He turned his back to Judith and called down the passageway, 'Some woman asking about yer child-minding.'

'Oh, right, I'm just on me way.'

Immediately a woman appeared. She was large and jolly-looking, the motherly sort. She looked at the lad warningly. 'I thought you was going out?'

'I am,' he responded.

'Well, get going then.'

She watched her son as he swaggered off to be met a few yards down the street by a group of other young boys all dressed the same as him. The woman tutted. 'It was Teddy Boys a few years back, now they call 'emselves Bovver Boys. And then we've got them Mods and Rockers, and they all go round fighting each other. Still, long as they keep off my doorstep they can beat the hell out of each other for all I care.' She looked at the smart woman before her appraisingly. 'You're enquiring about me child-minding services, are yer, dearie? Lucky for you I have a vacancy.'

Judith was relieved that she seemed a nice woman, and even more relieved that she had a vacancy. 'My name is Miss Chambers and I do require your services but I'm sorry, I can't tell you for how long. I'm looking after a five-year-old boy called Marty whose mother's been called away urgently. It's happened very suddenly. In all honesty I've never had any need to call on a child-minder before so I'm not really conversant with such matters.'

The other woman glanced Judith up and down, stared at her thoughtfully for a moment, then her face broke into a wide smile. 'Oh, new to this game, are yer, dearie, you being a Miss? Well, nothing much to it really. You bring the child here in the morning and collect him in the evening, and I see to him in between. I do have me rules, though. You say you don't know how long yer want me services for? Well, if the child leaves me mid-week, yer still pay for the full week.'

'Oh, yes, well, that's fair enough.'

'He's five, yer say, so he'll be going to school. I don't do dinners, but he'll be having school dinners, won't he?'

School! With everything else on her mind Judith hadn't given it a thought. She looked at Mrs Hackett worriedly. 'As this has all happened so suddenly I haven't given his schooling a thought.'

'Oh, well, while he's with you he'll go to the local as a temporary,' Mrs Hackett said knowingly. 'You'll need ter enrol him in the morning.' She smiled at Judith kindly. 'But you'll need ter get yerself off ter work so I'll do it for yer, lovey. You leave everything ter me. 'Course I'll have ter charge yer extra for the time I'm enrolling him down at the school.'

Judith supposed that was fair. Then a worrying thought struck her. 'There's just one problem. With this being an emergency there are some details about the child I haven't got. His mother . . . er . . . well, she's a distant relative and

227

until yesterday when she came and asked for my help, I really hadn't had anything to do with her.' What she was saying wasn't exactly a lie so she didn't feel too bad about it.

'Oh, relatives, eh. Who'd have 'em? Mine are always crawling out of the woodwork when they want summat. Otherwise yer never see 'em from one decade ter the next. Don't yer worry yerself. I'll explain the circumstances to the school, and tell 'em we'll give 'em the rest of what details they want when we can.'

Judith smiled at her gratefully. 'You're very kind. I'll bring him in the morning just before eight and collect him about six, is that all right?'

'Fine with me, lovey. Just one stipulation. I insist on being paid up front. Had a couple of people welched on me in the past, see, and I ended up outta pocket. So you'll need to be giving me three pound fifteen shilling tomorrow morning. Three pounds for me payment for the week, ten bob for the little chap's school dinners and five bob for me time spent enrolling him at the school. Of course, me charges are more for school holidays.'

Judith hadn't thought how much this would cost but three pounds a week sounded rather a lot for a few hours a day looking after a child. It was as much as she paid for her weekly groceries. Then there was the additional ten shillings for Marty's dinners. Looking after a child was proving a costly business. She still had to find the money to buy him some clothes yet. Money was going to be tight while he was with her. She was going to have to find ways of cutting down on her expenses somehow. If this situation continued she may even have to consider finding somewhere cheaper to live. That thought did not appeal at all. She loved her flat, for the first time in her life felt completely at home in her surroundings, despite her neighbour opposite, and was slowly but surely making friends in the area. But she wouldn't think about that now. Rachel could return any time and then her monetary problems would be immediately resolved.

'I'll see you in the morning, Mrs Hackett, and I'll have your money for you then.'

'Look forward to it, dearie.'

Judith hurried home, feeling that at least one of her problems had been resolved, and as she arrived back in the passageway outside her flat noticed that the door to her neighbour's was shut. Great annoyance filled her. He had said he would listen out in case Marty woke up, and how could he do that with his door shut? This was the last time she would ask for his help, and although they were already on far from friendly terms she knew she'd have a job even to be civil to him when their paths crossed in the future.

Letting herself into her own flat, she stripped off her coat and hung it up, and made to go straight away into the bedroom where Marty was sleeping to check on him, when the sound of music reached her ears. Her radio was on and it hadn't been when she had gone out. Had Marty got out of bed and switched it on?

Tentatively she pushed open the lounge door and poked her head around. The sight that met her eyes was most unexpected. Sitting on the settee, engrossed in a concert on the radio, was her prickly neighbour.

Nathan suddenly sensed her presence and his head

jerked round. 'Oh, you're back,' he said brusquely, and stood up. 'Get your errand done satisfactorily?'

Judith slowly advanced into the room. 'Yes, thank you.' She didn't like the thought that this man had been inside her flat while she hadn't been here. 'What are you doing here?'

He looked at her, bemused. 'What you asked. I couldn't very well keep an eye on the lad from my own flat, could I?'

She shifted on her feet uncomfortably. 'Er . . . no, I suppose not. Has he been all right?'

'As soon as you'd left and I came in, I went to check on him and he was awake so I explained the situation, got him a drink of milk then settled him down. I haven't heard a peep from him since.' He cocked an eyebrow at her. 'You look surprised. If you didn't think I was capable of looking out for a child, why did you ask me to?'

She had asked him because she had had no other choice. But she was totally surprised to discover that this ogre of a man seemed to have a softer side to him, when all she had encountered of his nature so far was obnoxiousness and rudeness. Maybe, though, it was just Judith herself he didn't like? But that thought didn't bother her because she didn't like him either, not one iota.

She said, 'I expect you'll be wanting to get back to your own flat now.' And added, 'I very much appreciate your help but rest assured this will not become a habit.'

He looked at her for several long moments before responding tartly, 'Glad to hear it. Good night, Miss Chambers.'

She watched as he departed. What an infuriating man,

she thought, and suddenly wondered about him. What did he do all day? He seemed to come and go from his flat at odd times. The day he had found Marty outside her flat he had said he had come home just before lunchtime and it hadn't struck her before now but he had watched Marty all afternoon until she herself had come home from work, so he hadn't returned to work. Was he some sort of boss who worked hours to suit himself? Though she couldn't think of a job that would allow someone such flexibility.

She wasn't surprised he was living on his own, though. He might be good-looking and very presentable but she couldn't imagine any woman putting up with his abhorrent attitude. She felt the urge to go and tell him that she had once been like him and advise him that if he wasn't careful he'd end up old and lonely, like she had been in danger of doing until harsh lessons had shown her how others perceived her and she had taken a long hard look at herself and done something about it. But the urge to speak so openly soon vanished. She had no interest in the man, why would she concern herself about him?

Her mind settled on more pressing matters. In the morning she had to contend not only with getting herself up and ready for the off but with a little boy also, plus getting him around to the child-minder's before she caught her bus. She would need to get up at least half an hour earlier than normal to fit it all in if she didn't want to be late for work. That was the last thing she wanted, fearing the reprisals.

Back in his own flat Nathan switched on his radio, tuned it to the station he had been listening to in Judith

Chambers' flat, helped himself to a shot of malt whisky and sat down in his armchair, stretching out his long legs to rest them on the hearth. As he took a sip of his drink, his handsome face screwed up in annoyance. Until that woman living opposite had arrived on the scene his life had run exactly the way he had formulated it to over twenty-five years ago. He came into contact only with those of his own choosing and his privacy was respected. But she kept invading his privacy, disrupting his orderly life, despite his constantly informing her of his wish for her not to do so. Was she doing this on purpose just to rile him? In his experience women did that. They were conniving creatures who if he had his way would not exist to blight things for the male of the human species. A vision of Judith Chambers rose before him. Admittedly, she was a striking woman and smart of dress with it, but she was rude in her manner, outwardly icy, and he wasn't at all surprised that she was a spinster.

Then a question posed itself. The little boy? She had said he was the child of a friend, yet the child had told him that Judith Chambers was his grandmother. There was certainly a conflict of information there.

His thoughts settled then on the little boy. Nathan didn't like to admit it but the afternoon he had looked after him after finding him in Judith Chambers' doorway, and again tonight, had resurrected fatherly feelings in him that he had buried years ago, along with all his hopes for a family future. Tonight as he had sat on the bed while the little lad had been drinking his milk he couldn't stop himself from wondering what life would have been like for him if events hadn't soured him towards relationships.

Unwittingly he had found himself longing for what might have been.

Damn that woman, he thought. Her presence, and along with it that of the child, was turning his life upside down and he wasn't going to allow that. He had worked too hard at mending his shattered emotions to have them threatened again. Her tenancy came up for renewal in seven months' time and he was adamant that he'd make sure it was not renewed. In the meantime he would endeavour to steer clear of her.

Chapter Eighteen

'Marty, please get a move on, we need to leave. Oh, goodness me, you haven't tied your shoelaces.' Judith stared frantically at him. It was just after fifteen minutes to eight. She had to get him around to Mrs Hackett's then catch her bus which arrived at the stop anywhere between five to eight and five past. She hurriedly knelt down. 'I'll do them for you. Now watch what I do and you'll know in future.'

Shoelaces tied, she stood up then looked down to appraise him, standing before her as usual, his head hanging low. He looked clean and tidy but regardless his clothes were shabby, shoes badly worn, and he was desperately in need of a hair cut and his spectacles repairing too. She would have to work out her money tonight and see what she could spare towards sorting him out. Maybe, though, his mother might return with some of her stolen booty intact and Judith could tell her to keep it so she could rig out her son herself and then Judith's own life would return to normal, with only herself to worry about. That was more than enough for her without all this bother.

She realised he'd disappeared and looked around to see where he had gone to. He was tugging at the bottom of his duffel coat, trying to unhook it from the peg by the door. 'You don't need your coat, it's too warm for that,' she said, walking up to him, very conscious that time was wearing on. 'Now come along, we have to hurry.'

He shot her a look of such hatred that she gasped at its intensity. It left her in no doubt how much this child disliked her, but she couldn't understand why. She was caring for him, wasn't she? What more did he want from her? 'Look, whether you like it or not, we're stuck with each other until your mother comes back for you. Now come along,' she ordered, grabbing his hand. But still he clung to his coat, refusing to move. She sighed resignedly. She hadn't time for this. 'All right, if you insist.' She took his coat off the hook and helped him on with it. He clutched it around him, as though for protection, and as she opened the door for them to depart, she wondered why he was doing that.

He dragged his feet all the way to Mrs Hackett's, turning a five-minute walk into ten, and it was with great relief that Judith eventually handed him over. 'I'm in such a rush, Mrs Hackett, but here's your money,' she said, thrusting it at her. 'Including Marty's dinner money.' She looked down at him, standing sulkily beside her. 'Now be a good boy for Mrs Hackett.' She addressed the woman again. 'I'm so sorry, must dash.'

The child-minder smiled at her kindly. 'You get off, dear, and leave him ter me.' She took Marty's hand. 'Come on in, pet,' she said welcomingly. 'You're starting at a new school today and I bet yer really excited.'

Judith arrived breathlessly at the bus stop just in time to see it pull away. Oh, no, her mind screamed. This was all she needed. The next one wasn't due for another ten minutes and would get her there at twenty to nine. There was nothing for it, she would have to run to work.

She arrived, panting, at twenty-five minutes to nine. Cherry met her. 'I don't need to remind you, *Miss Chambers*, that we start work at half-past eight.'

'Yes, I know, but my bus . . .'

'Don't bother making excuses but be warned, this had better not happen again. I don't need to remind you that you've already got a black mark against yer for that shoddy work yer did last Friday. Now get to yer desk, and yer'd better mek the time up on yer lunch hour.'

With that she stalked off and Judith was very conscious all the other women were staring at her and sniggering.

Marty wouldn't even look at her as Mrs Hackett brought him to the door when Judith collected him that evening, and she couldn't for the life of her think what grudge he was nursing against her. 'Has he behaved himself?' she asked Mrs Hackett.

'Oh, yes. He knows who's boss, don't yer, Marty?' she said, looking at him meaningfully, then brought her attention back to Judith. 'That's the secret of handling kids. Let 'em know who's boss then yer get no nonsense from 'em. Marty has settled in well at school. Teacher understood when I explained why I couldn't give her all his details, just said to let her have them when yer could. They get a lot of this sorta thing. Kids going to stay with a relative for a while. Main thing they were concerned about was that the lad was going to school.'

Judith smiled warmly at the woman. 'Thank you, I appreciate your help.'

'Oh, er, afore I forget. School informed me ter tell yer that Marty needs a PE kit. Now as it happens I've a new one just his size, and plimsolls too. Me being in the child-minding line, I get things come my way. Now I'm prepared ter sell 'em yer for what I got 'em for. Ten bob the lot, and that includes a string bag to carry it in.'

'Oh, thank you.' Judith opened her handbag and pulled out her purse. Her wages were rapidly running out and she had been hoping at least to buy him some new underwear, but if Marty needed a PE kit then she had no choice but to get it for him and she was grateful to Mrs Hackett for saving her some money, dreading to think what a new PE kit cost if this one was cheap at ten shillings. She had been going to call into Mrs Chaudri's tonight to buy something for her evening meal but as it was she had better make do with what she still had in her pantry. Thank goodness Marty had had a hot meal already so a sandwich would suffice him.

Matters settled, she said goodnight to Mrs Hackett and, walking beside a very sullen child, made her way home. As they passed the secondhand shop on the corner opposite Mrs Chaudri's shop, a box by the door caught her eye. It was full of used children's books all priced at tuppence. She stopped and gazed down at them and then picked one up. It was called *Bom the Little Drummer Boy*. Maybe Marty would like to read this. It would give him something to do other than staring out of the window. She could barely spare the pennies but regardless went in to buy it.

Back at her flat, she took his coat from him and handed him the book. 'I thought you'd like to read this while I get your tea.'

He looked at the book, then snatched it from her hand and threw it to the ground, stamping his foot hard on it, then ran off to the lounge. Completely bewildered by his actions, she picked the book up and followed him through. He was standing by the window staring out. She gave a sigh, at a complete loss as to what to do with him. Putting the book on the coffee table, she went to make his tea.

She stared appalled at him as he scoffed it down as if he'd not eaten for weeks. Then, as soon as he was finished, he scrambled down from the table and by the time she had followed him through to his bedroom had wrenched off his clothes, which were piled on the floor in a heap, and despite its being early was climbing into bed. Framed in the doorway, she stared across at him, again totally bemused by his bewildering behaviour. Going over to the bed, she bent and picked up his clothes to fold them up, extracting his shabby underwear so she could wash it fresh for the morning, very mindful that should he still be with her come next pay day then somehow she was going to have to find the money to start to rig him out. What was wrong with the child? she thought. Why was he so hostile towards her? She gave another sigh and said good night to him before leaving the room.

By Thursday morning Judith was almost at her wit's end. As the days passed Marty's behaviour was worsening. He still hadn't said a word to her; each morning he dawdled

239

getting himself ready, despite Judith's constant urging of him to hurry himself along, and she had to drag him around to Mrs Hackett's, only just managing to catch her bus. Every evening he'd not even lift his head to acknowledge her when she called to collect him. They walked home in silence, Marty with his head hanging so low it was almost touching his chest. He then practically choked himself in his urgency to get his tea down him and then immediately took himself off to bed. He still hadn't to her knowledge so much as glanced at the book she had bought him. Today looked like it was going to be no different.

'Marty, please can we get a move on?' she scolded more severely than she'd meant to. 'I cannot miss the bus today.' The thought of running to work she just could not face. Having the care of this child was mentally and physically affecting her, she was feeling drained. He was tugging at the bottom of his coat again, trying to pull it off the peg. 'Why you want that coat is beyond me,' she said, getting it down for him and handing it over. 'It's a wonder you aren't boiling in it.' She watched in bewilderment as he put it on then clutched it around him.

He reluctantly dragged his feet all the way down the road towards Mrs Hackett's and then on the corner of her street, suddenly and without warning, abruptly turned and, before Judith could stop him, bolted back down the street towards the flat. So surprised was she by his sudden action, Judith stared after him, stunned. 'Marty, come back!' she shouted after him. 'Marty, do as you're told. Come back now,' she commanded. But he kept on running.

Her hand slapped her forehead in dismay. This was the last thing she needed right now. Kicking up her heels, she chased after him. She was too old for this, she thought, as she dodged between other pedestrians, knowing they were looking at her bemused, wondering why a middle-aged woman was racing down the street after a little boy who seemed hell-bent on getting away from her, but she didn't care what they thought. She needed to catch him, get him to Mrs Hackett's, then get to the stop before she missed her bus.

She finally caught up with him just before the gate to her house. She leaned down, grabbed his arm and pulled him around to face her. 'What on earth is the matter with you? I have to get to work and you to school. Now stop this nonsense this minute.' Taking a firm grip of his hand, she straightened up and ran him all the way back to Mrs Hackett's.

The woman met her at the door. 'Bit late this morning, ain't yer?'

'Er . . . yes,' she replied breathlessly, looking at the sullen child beside her. 'Now be a good boy for Mrs Hackett.'

The minder took his hand. 'Oh, he'll be a little angel for me, won't yer, pet?' she said, looking down at him.

He continued to stare at the ground.

Why was it Marty behaved well for others and not for her? Judith thought. 'I must rush, Mrs Hackett. See you tonight.'

Although she already greatly feared she had missed her bus, nevertheless she ran all the way to the stop. There were no people waiting and no sign of the bus so she

241

knew she'd missed it by minutes. Already she was very fatigued and didn't know if she could summon the energy to run all the way to work. Even if she did she would still be late as, glancing at her watch, she saw to her horror that it was approaching eight-fifteen. Several people were starting to arrive at the bus stop and she knew the next one was imminent so she might as well wait for it, though what faced her at work didn't bear thinking about. She could only hope that Cherry would excuse her for her lateness, though she gravely doubted it after her reception the previous Monday.

It was five minutes to nine when she finally arrived at Fastway Transport. Filled with trepidation, Judith opened the general office door to find Cherry ready to pounce on her.

'Come through to my office,' she commanded, walking into it.

Filled with dread, and conscious that all the other women were watching her, Judith followed her and shut the door behind her.

Seated behind her desk, Cherry glared up at her. 'What time do you call this, *Miss Chambers*?'

She took a deep breath, fixing Cherry with her eyes pleadingly. 'I'm so sorry, Mrs Campbell, but . . .'

'I don't want to hear excuses,' she barked, cutting Judith short.

A great dread filled her. If her supervisor wasn't even going to listen to her excuse then there was only one outcome to this interview. Judith couldn't just give up, though. 'It won't happen again, I can assure you it won't, Mrs Campbell.'

'No, you're right, it won't – because you won't be here. It's not just your lateness twice in one week, you produced all that shoddy work too.' She sat back in her chair and gave Judith a smile of smug satisfaction. 'I've been waiting for this opportunity to see the great Judith Chambers sacked for misconduct, and I can't tell yer what pleasure it gives me. Now you'll know what it feels like. But then, it won't bother you, will it, 'cos frosty Judith Chambers ain't got any feelings, 'as she?'

Judith gulped. 'Please, Mrs Campbell. I know you've good reason to dislike me, and I appreciate why, but please, I beg you, give me another chance.'

'Like yer gave me, yer mean? Well, you can sod off! I wouldn't give you another chance if yer paid me a million pounds. You don't fit in here. Nobody likes you. Now wait here while I go and see Neville James and, believe me, by the time I've finished telling him about you, you'll be off these premises so quick yer feet won't touch the floor. And don't think yer'll get a glowing reference either, 'cos yer won't.'

Judith's mind raced frantically. At this moment what anyone thought of her was not important. She couldn't lose this job, she just couldn't! 'Please, please, Mrs Campbell . . . I *need* this job. I . . . I . . .' Suddenly it all became too much for her; everything she was trying to cope with single-handed pressed down on her, and before she could stop herself a rush of distraught tears welled in her eyes to gush down her face. 'You don't understand,' she sobbed. 'I had no choice but to be like I was. I didn't even realise how horrible I was until recently and I've worked so hard at changing myself. But I need this job . . . the

243

little boy . . . I can't look after him if I haven't got a job. And his behaviour towards me is . . . well, he won't speak to me, he hates me, I know he does. I don't know what to do to make him like me. But if I can't look after him, he'll have to go in a home. I don't know where his mother is. Oh, please, please, Mrs Campbell, I implore you to reconsider your decision.'

Cherry was staring at her astounded. The formidable Judith Chambers, who she hadn't thought possessed a caring bone in her body, was sobbing hysterically before her, pleading for her job. She'd never thought to live to see the day. She couldn't believe this was happening, neither could she believe she had heard what had just spewed from Judith's mouth. She had expected the usual icy cool as she accepted her fate with her accustomed stiff detachment, but this totally unexpected tirade had taken the wind from Cherry's sails and she didn't know how to respond. After several long moments she rose from her chair, walked past Judith and opened the door.

'Sally,' she called out, 'go and fetch me a cuppa from the canteen, would yer, please? Put plenty of sugar in it. In fact, mek it two. I think I need one as well.' She shut the door and walked back behind her desk to sit down again, bewildered eyes still fixed on the distraught woman weeping uncontrollably. 'Look . . . er . . . sit yerself down. I've asked Sally to get you a cuppa and she'll be here with it in a minute.'

Judith raised her head and through tear-blurred eyes looked at Cherry, shocked by this show of unexpected compassion. Nevertheless she felt mortally ashamed of her own emotional outburst and fought to control herself.

244

Opening her handbag, she pulled out a handkerchief and wiped her eyes, then blew her nose. 'I'm very sorry, Mrs Campbell, this is so remiss of me. I shouldn't be burdening you with my troubles. I deserve to be dismissed. I'll clear my desk . . .'

'Oh, fer God's sake, sit yerself down, will yer? While yer at Fastway Transport I'm in charge of yer, and I'll be the one to tell yer when yer can go and clear yer desk.' She looked at Judith searchingly. 'Look, I have ter say, you've shocked me. You was always so . . . well, so . . . I wasn't on me own in thinking you'd a heart made of stone. Seeing yer like this . . . well . . .' It had shocked Cherry to realise she felt sorry for Judith. She looked so vulnerable. If ever she had witnessed a woman crying out for help, that woman was sitting before her now. Her bad feelings towards her ex-boss were suddenly replaced by the urge to help another woman, regardless of who she was. 'What did yer mean by saying yer had no choice but to be like you was?'

Judith stared at her. Cherry's question was a very personal and probing one, an invasion into Judith's privacy. That invisible protective barrier automatically clamped itself around her. 'I . . . I don't find it easy to talk to people about my personal business.'

'Then it's about time yer learned, Miss Chambers. I'd never have come through some of the things I've faced without talking to someone, particularly the women, and especially when my husband died. Now it's very obvious ter me that you're a woman with a lot on her plate, and I'm offering to help yer. It's your choice whether you accept my help or not.'

Judith knew Cherry was right. She had spent her life keeping everything bottled up within herself, and where had it got her? It suddenly struck her that the process of changing herself included allowing other people an insight into her. Cherry Campbell was convinced Judith was a callous woman without a shred of human compassion, someone who derived great pleasure from upsetting those around her. In the past she had acted like that through her own naïvety but she knew better now and that person Cherry thought she was no longer existed. This offer was an opportunity for Judith to prove that to her. If she let this pass she might not get another. There was no doubt in Judith's mind that Cherry was going to get her dismissed but this way at least Cherry might not feel so vengeful towards her after she had gone.

Judith took a deep shuddering breath, sinking down on the chair before Cherry's desk. 'I was acting as I'd been told to by my father. I didn't know any better. I'd only ever worked for him so I thought all firms had the same rules as Chambers' and all bosses acted towards their workers like my father instructed me to. It's only recently I've realised exactly how awful it must have been for anyone employed there, and I'm not surprised now that no one stayed any longer than they could help. I knew everyone hated me and I don't blame them, I don't blame them at all, but my father constantly reminded me that I wasn't there to be liked, that I was there to make sure the workers followed his rules to the letter or it wasn't just them that risked losing their jobs, I was under threat too.'

Cherry stared at her in astonishment. 'We all thought you enjoyed treating us all rotten.'

'Enjoyed? I thought I was doing my job, Mrs Campbell. Look, I'm not trying to excuse my behaviour. I was . . . I was just doing as I was told, like all good children do, obeying their parents. Call me naïve, I didn't realise I was being led by such bad example. When my father died, as you already know, my mother sold the business. Well, she also sold our house and went to live in Italy, leaving me for the first time in my life to fend for myself. Rather laughable that situation, isn't it, Mrs Campbell? A forty-three-year-old woman with no idea how to cook a meal for herself or wash her own clothes. Thankfully my mother did see fit to give me a token bequest. I was left with just a few pounds after I'd secured myself somewhere to live, so my only means of income is what I earn myself.

'I've already lost one job through my misguided ideas on how an officer manager should act and it was very humiliating for me, but in its way it was a mixed blessing. It made me start to look at myself, to see myself as others saw me. I didn't like what I saw. You have to believe that I'm really trying to make amends, to be the kind of person that other people will like. I've tried so hard to fit in here but no one would give me a chance. I really want to make friends with people. I'm not the old Judith Chambers any more, really I'm not. I just want to be allowed to prove it.'

Just then there was a tap on the door and Sally entered, carrying a tray with two cups of tea on it. She walked across to Cherry's desk and placed them on it. She looked at Judith, noted the state she was in, then back at Cherry questioningly. 'Everything all right, Cherry?'

'Eh? Oh, yeah, yeah, it's fine. Just . . . er . . . shut me door on yer way out and tell the others I don't want disturbing unless there's a real emergency. Thanks for the tea.'

'No probs, Cherry.'

After the girl had left Cherry pushed a cup before Judith. 'Drink this, it'll do yer good.'

'Thank you,' she said, picking it up.

Cherry sighed heavily. 'I feel so bad now.'

Putting down her cup on the desk, Judith wiped her still-watering eyes and blew her nose again, then looked at Cherry quizzically. 'Why on earth should you feel bad?'

'Because I always thought you had the life of Riley, living in yer big house with yer well-off parents, getting a great deal of pleasure out of making all of us that worked for yer miserable.'

'You couldn't have been more wrong.'

Cherry was beginning to realise this. 'I owe you an apology.'

'*You* owe *me* an apology? Whatever for?'

'Just 'cos you treated me badly, I never had to do the same to you. I couldn't help meself, though. It was like I couldn't stop. I couldn't believe it when I found out you was our new employee. I enjoyed watching you suffer 'cos for me it was like payback for what you'd done to me, and the friends I made at Chambers', and all the other staff that have come and gone there over the years.'

'I don't blame you. As I said, I understand.'

'Yeah, but if I'm honest, deep down I didn't like what I was doing and I'm not proud of meself. It's not really in my nature to treat people badly, no matter how badly they

248

treat me. In a way I was cutting off me own nose to spite me face. You've bin a great worker and if I'd had me way and got rid of you then you'd have bin hard to replace.'

Judith looked at her, shocked. 'Do you mean that?'

'Bloody right I do! You get through more work, properly done, than all the rest of the gels here put together, and they're all good at what they do.' Cherry gave a sudden grin. 'Well, apart from the slight mishap yer made on Friday, and if you've been dealing with personal problems I can understand now why yer mind wasn't fully on yer job.' Her face clouded over. 'It's my place to notice these things and offer help, and if it'd been any other of me gels I would've. I should never have asked yer to do them letters all again for such a petty mistake that no one would have noticed but I . . . well, I've already explained meself.' She paused, took a sip of her tea, then cradling her cup, looked at Judith quizzically. 'What's this about you looking after a little boy?'

Judith gasped, her face filling with horror. 'Little boy?' she exclaimed.

Cherry nodded. 'I'm sure you said that if yer lost yer job you wouldn't be able to care for him. You said he didn't like you and you didn't know what to do about him.'

'Did I?'

'I'm positive you did. In fact, I know it.'

Judith stared at her wildly, her already pale face draining ashen. Had she really blurted out that? Oh, God, her mind screamed. How did she explain about her relationship with Marty and what had brought about his being with her? It was all so sordid, so humiliating, and her

249

secret had never been divulged to anyone.

Cherry could tell by the look on Judith's face that her question had struck a raw nerve somewhere. The woman looked to be on the verge of fainting. 'Just who is the boy you're looking after, Miss Chambers?' she probed again.

She stared at Cherry mutely, her mouth opening and closing. 'He's . . . he's . . .' She suddenly clamped her mouth tight shut. Whether she liked it or not Marty was her grandson and it wasn't right of her to deny that fact, to lie about his connection to her in order to cover up her own shameful secret. She'd already divulged to Cherry things about her life that she'd never told anyone. In a strange way she felt better for it, as if a burden had lifted. Clasping her hands tight, she lowered her head and whispered, 'He's my grandson.'

Cherry's face filled with shock. 'Your grandson!'

Judith lifted her head and looked her in the eye. 'Yes.'

'But . . . but . . . you're a . . .'

'Miss? Yes, I am.' Judith took a deep breath. 'I had a child when I was very young. A daughter. The boy is her son. Until last week I never knew he existed. In fact, I never knew my own child was a girl until she turned up unexpectedly last Thursday night.'

'You never? But how . . .'

'The baby was taken from me unseen at birth. I never had any choice in the matter.'

'But your parents . . . They wouldn't help you then?'

'They never knew. No one did. You're the first person I've told. The whole experience was so traumatic for me that I locked it away and pretended to myself it never happened. That's how I coped with it all.'

'What about the father? Did he not know either?'

'Oh, he knew but he didn't want to know.'

'Oh, I see,' Cherry said knowingly. 'But what about your friends? Didn't they offer some help?'

Judith swallowed hard. 'I've never had any. My parents weren't the type to encourage that. I was very shy as a child, and consequently grew up without the ability to make them. I never really was any use in social situations.'

Cherry was looking at her, speechless. She couldn't comprehend anyone not having the know-how to make friends, and couldn't for the life of her understand how this woman had gone through her life without any. 'Oh, Miss Chambers, I don't know what to say.'

Judith flashed her a wan smile. 'The perfect Judith Chambers isn't so perfect after all, is she? She's a woman with a dirty little secret, and a lonely woman too.'

'No, I never meant that at all,' said Cherry with conviction. 'I've children of me own. I can't begin to imagine how I would've felt if any of them had been taken from me at any time, let alone just after I'd given birth to them. It must have been terrible for you, having no one to share any of this with. I wouldn't have come through some of the things that have happened to me without my friends to help me, especially when my husband died. As for a dirty secret – you're not the first to have a child and not be married, and you certainly won't be the last. If it's any consolation I know women who've had kids and don't even know who the father is. At least you knew that. And . . . er . . . well, being's we're being honest with each other, I was expecting me first before I married. I was lucky with Brian.' She took a deep breath and asked, 'So

251

how come your grandson is with you now? You said you don't know where his mother is?'

A flood of fresh tears welled up in Judith's eyes. 'I don't. I haven't a clue.' She wiped her eyes and took a shuddering breath. 'Rachel arrived last Thursday night and, after telling me who she was, said she just wanted to meet me and introduce her son to his grandmother. I can't tell you how shocked I was but I invited her in. Well, the truth of it is she invited herself in, and to stay the night. When I got up in the morning I found she'd already left and taken all my money with her. And not only that, she'd left her son behind with only the clothes he was wearing.'

Cherry gasped, appalled. 'She'd what? How could she steal off yer? And that poor little boy. He must have been terrified.'

Judith frowned at her, perplexed. 'Terrified?'

'Yeah, 'cause he would be. His mother disappearing off like that and you being a stranger to him. How old is he?'

'Five.'

'How did you explain to him what had happened? Well, whatever you said I expect he didn't understand anyway, him being so young. All he knows is that somehow his mother's disappeared and he's living in a strange house with a strange woman.'

'But he knows I'm his grandmother.'

'Oh, goodness me, you really don't have any idea how kids' minds work, do you, Miss Chambers? Your grandson met you for the first time a few days ago and up 'til then he never knew what a grandmother was. He still won't. It's just a name to him. You did say he won't speak to you? That's why. He's probably got it into his head that you're responsible for his mother going away.'

'Oh!' Judith exclaimed, mortified. She hadn't even given Marty's feelings on the matter a thought, so consumed by her own fear of being left with him to care for. She suddenly felt guilt for the fact that all she had done was scold him when he'd done something she didn't think was right. No wonder he wouldn't speak to her. No wonder he'd looked at her with such hatred. He saw her as a monster. 'I haven't told him anything. I never even gave it a thought. It was all such a shock to me, and I was so obsessed by trying to cope with him, I couldn't think of much else. Oh, I've been so selfish, I haven't considered what he must be going through at all, just what a mess I was in myself. I've never had the responsibility of a child in any way before. I've no idea what to do. I'm doing my best, though. I make sure he's clean and fed and he's going to school. I have a child-minder to care for him while I'm not there. As soon as I can find the money, I'm going to buy him some clothes.'

'But a child needs more than that, Miss Chambers. They need to be made to feel safe and loved. Your grandson won't be feeling none of that and you need to make him feel it.'

She ran a weary hand over her forehead. 'How do you deal with a child who won't talk to you and spends most of his time looking out of the window, staring out on to the street? And it's been so hot but he insists on wearing his duffel coat. I'm at a loss to know why he's acting so strangely.'

Cherry looked at her meaningfully. 'Can't yer remember back to when you was a child and how yer parents loved and cared for you? What it felt like to have a kiss and cuddle from them, how it made yer feel?' She saw the look on Judith's face and uttered, shocked, 'Are you telling me that your own parents never did anything like that with you?'

'No,' she confessed. 'No, they didn't. They weren't the type to show their feelings.'

'Oh, my God, you poor woman. No wonder yer turned out like yer did. You do need help, don't yer? A lot of it. Look, I ain't no expert on kids, just what I've learned from being a mother, but it seems to me that your grandson is one hell of a confused little boy. When my husband died my youngest lad took to wearing his dad's slippers and we couldn't get them off him. I was trying to cope with the loss of Brian, and this on top was driving me crazy. It was my mother that finally got out of him why he was doing it. My youngest didn't understand about death. He thought his father had just gone away to work for a while and my son was keeping them warm for him until he came home.

'Seems ter me that your grandson stands by the window 'cos he's looking out for his own mother, waiting for her to come and collect him. As for insisting on wearing his duffel . . . well, you said yourself his mother left him with you with only the clothes he stood up in. That coat is about the only thing he's got that his mother bought him. He's frightened that if he's not in sight of it all the time that'll disappear too and he'll have nothing of her left then. It's his only connection to her.'

Judith was staring at her, open-mouthed. 'All of this

never entered my head. I thought he was just being awkward.'

'Well, no disrespect, Miss Chambers, but if yer never received any loving as a child, then it's hard to know how to give it, ain't it? And, if yer've never had any dealings with children, then yer won't know all their needs, will yer? I think yer to be commended. You could have handed the lad over to the authorities ter look after.'

'Oh, I couldn't do that. Risk him going into a home. And how would I explain to his mother what I had done with her son when she comes back for him?'

'Well, then, you have got a heart after all.'

Judith looked at Cherry gratefully. 'Thank you so much for allowing me to talk to you. I feel so much better. I will try and talk to Marty tonight. Try to help him understand what's going on.'

'Don't bombard him with questions. He'll clam up if yer do. He'll tell yer things when he's ready to tell yer. Ask him to do things for yer. Kids love to help, it makes them feel wanted. And if he gets things wrong, don't scold him. That's the worst thing you can do. If he'll let yer, sit him on your knee and cuddle him. But whatever yer do, don't expect too much of him. He needs to learn to trust you before anything else.'

'Yes, I realise that now. I can't begin to imagine what's been going through his mind. How awful of me not to have realised! I value your advice, it's very helpful to me.' She wrung her hands. 'I'm worried about his mother, though. I can only think that she's met with an accident. I can't even check as I know nothing about her, only her Christian name.'

255

Cherry gave a shrug. 'Then until she turns up there ain't n'ote yer can do. I'm not sure I have any sympathy with her, though, going off like that after robbing you and leaving her son behind. Even you, Miss Chambers, don't deserve that, and neither does her son. But then, I shouldn't make a judgement on yer daughter. I don't know her or her circumstances. I suppose she'll have her own good reason for doing what she did. Let's hope she turns up soon and puts your mind at rest. And her son's.'

She paused and stared at Judith thoughtfully. She couldn't believe that the woman before her was the same Judith Chambers who used to be so formidable that behind her back she was nicknamed Icy Lil. Judith had told her she had worked hard at changing herself from an unlikable person into one who was more personable. It was Cherry's opinion that she had done a good job on herself. The transformation in her was incredible. Cherry had not liked the old Judith Chambers one little bit, but this one . . . well, this one had great possibilities.

'Look, why don't yer bring the little chap over to my house on Sat'day af'noon?'

Judith looked back at her in astonishment. 'You're inviting me to visit your house?'

'You'll have ter take me as yer find me. Me house ain't posh. Far from it. And it ain't easy working full-time and being a mother of two lively kids. Me own mother helps out as much as she can but she's getting on and can only do so much, bless her. Might do your grandson good to play with my boys, though. If yer not offended, I've got some clothes that my two have grown out of that might help you out 'til yer can afford ter rig him out yerself.' She reached for a piece of paper and a pen, scribbled something on it then pushed it across to Judith. 'Here's me address. Arrive what time yer like.'

Judith accepted the paper and stared down at it, then lifted eyes filled with gratitude to Cherry. 'I'd be honoured to come,' she said with great sincerity.

'That remains to be seen,' Cherry said with a laugh. 'My kids are enough to drive anyone daft, but they're good kids for all that.' She looked at Judith thoughtfully again. 'Look . . . er . . . why don't yer go down to the canteen and get yerself another cuppa? Tek a few minutes to yerself.'

Judith looked at her worriedly. 'What about my job?'

'What about it? Yer do like working here, don't yer?'

'Oh, yes.'

'Well, then.'

Judith looked at her hopefully. 'Does this mean you aren't going to speak to Mr James about dismissing me?'

Cherry smiled. 'Not today, Miss Chambers. We're all late now and again, as you know yerself. Even I've been known to be late.'

The look of relief that flooded Judith's face was unmistakable. 'Oh, thank you, Mrs Campbell. Thank you so much. I'll make up the time I lost this morning at lunchtime.'

'Forget it this time. And, for goodness' sake, do me a favour. Call me Cherry, everyone else does.' She looked at Judith meaningfully, eyes twinkling warmly. 'And from now on, no more of this Miss Chambers nonsense. You're Judith . . . no, Judith reminds me of the old Miss Chambers, the one I used to know and hate . . . Judy, that's better. Far more friendly-sounding. What do you think?'

Judith was far too overwhelmed with all that had transpired even to think about anything else. She had come into Cherry's office expecting to be dismissed and was leaving with her job still intact and a new sense of belonging here – but even more important than that an insight into the reasons for her grandson's behaviour. She hoped that maybe they would get on better now until his mother came back for him.

'At this moment, Mrs . . . Cherry . . . I'd be happy for you to call me anything you like.' And she meant it too.

By the time she had made her way down to the canteen, drunk her tea and returned to the general office again, twenty minutes had passed. As Judith had sat sipping her tea, she'd marvelled at this surprising turn of events. When she had risen this morning, if anyone had prophesied that in less than a couple of hours she would be spilling her innermost secrets and listening to profound advice, Judith would have scoffed, never believing such a thing would ever take place.

She arrived back in the office. As she prepared to make her way past the other women's desks towards her own, tucked away down at the bottom of the room, she heard her name being called out and looked across to see Sally beckoning her. 'You're next ter me now, Judy.' The girl grinned at her cheekily. 'And get a move on 'cos we've a mountain of work to do.'

The others looked over at her then, all smiling. 'Yeah, come on,' called out Mary who was sitting across from Sally. 'We're a team here, yer know, and you're part of it.'

Judith felt a lump rise in her throat as she saw that her

old desk had been cleared of all her equipment and papers and everything had been moved from it to the original desk she had been going to have when she had first started. Before Cherry had realised who she was.

The supervisor came out of her office then and gave her a big wink. 'I hope you've got a good excuse fer not being at yer desk working, Judy?'

She was too overcome to reply but smiled broadly back at her. Cherry had obviously got her out of the way so she could talk to the rest of the girls. What she had said to them Judith had no idea, but she didn't care. She had no secrets any more. For the first time in her life she was being accepted by others in their inner circle and the feeling this gave her was indescribable.

Chapter Nineteen

Judith had never enjoyed a day's work so much in all her working life. As they had worked away the other women had chatted and joked and she had been included. As the day had worn on she had found to her surprise that now all her barriers were down, responding to her colleagues' quips and joining in their conversations was becoming much easier for her. On leaving that evening they had all wished her goodnight, saying they were looking forward to seeing her in the morning, and she had responded in kind. For the first time in her working life she was actually looking forward to her next day's work. She was, though, eager to get home. She was still feeling very guilty for the way she had badly mishandled her grandson's arrival in her life and urgently wanted to start putting that right. Marty's grandmother was mortally sorry for her own lack of understanding of his needs, and just hoped that any damage she may have done wasn't permanent. She hoped he would be more receptive towards her now she had an idea how to handle him.

A while later she looked at Mrs Hackett in bewilderment. 'What do you mean, Marty isn't here, Mrs Hackett?'

'Well, he ran off after I smacked him.'

'You smacked him? Whatever for?'

'For breaking me back winder. He threw a stone at it in temper after I told him off for laying in ter Billy Watson next door. Billy wouldn't give him his football so Marty took it off him. Ten bob that winder's gonna cost me ter get repaired. Luckily me neighbour up the road works for a glazing firm and he'll do it cheap for me. I'll need the money now,' she said, holding out her hand expectantly.

Blindly Judith delved into her handbag and took out her purse. Taking out ten shillings, leaving her with just enough for her bus fare in the morning, she thanked God it was payday tomorrow and handed it over to Mrs Hackett who thrust it straight into her pinafore pocket. 'I do apologise for Marty's behaviour, Mrs Hackett. I'll speak to him about it.'

'Well, kids will be kids. I do wish you'd have warned me about him, though, so I coulda bin prepared.'

'Warned you about what?'

'Well, apart from his temper, what a little liar he is. I saw him break the winder with me own eyes yet he looked me straight in me face and told me it were Billy what done it. And so convincing he was that if I hadn't seen him do it meself, I would have believed him. But don't you worry, Miss Chambers. I've handled as bad in me time so Marty's no bother to me.'

Judith's mind was racing. From what she knew of Marty he was a quiet little boy. He'd not spoken a word to her at all and she found it hard to believe that not only was he seemingly causing mayhem while he was with Mrs Hackett but was also vocal enough to lie. But then, he had snatched that book from her hand and stamped his foot on it; had left her tap running and flooded her bathroom; was blatantly unwilling to ready himself in the morning when he knew she was in a rush. Had they been signs of his true nature, and in her inexperience she hadn't realised? She was overwhelmingly thankful that Mrs Hackett was still willing to look after him.

'Oh, by the way, Miss Chambers. That new PE kit yer bought off me for Marty. Well, he came home without it tonight and when I questioned him he reckons he's lost it so you'll have to get him another 'cos the school insist all the kids have one. I might be able to get me hands on another for yer. Cost yer the same, though.'

Judith stared at her, deeply distracted. 'Oh, yes, I'd be very grateful if you could get me another.'

'I'll need the money now.'

'Oh, but I haven't got it until I get paid tomorrow.'

'Oh, well, termorrer will have ter do then. You remember too that yer need to pay me as well for next week's child-minding?'

'Oh, yes, I haven't forgotten, Mrs Hackett. I'll have it all for you when I arrive to pick Marty up tomorrow evening. I can only apologise again and hope he causes you no more bother.' Meanwhile concern was building within her as to where he could possibly be. 'Now I must go and look for Marty. Have you any idea where I should start?'

'Try home first. He's probably starving by now and it's my experience all kids find their way home when their stomachs call. Now you get off, ducky, and remember my advice: don't be taken in by that little 'un's lies and give him a firm hand. It's what he needs and what he'll understand. Yer'll be making a rod fer yer own back if yer don't.'

'I appreciate your help. Good evening, Mrs Hackett.'

As she hurried towards home, Judith's mind was filled with worry. Handling Marty's trauma over the disappearance of his mother and trying to build a trusting relationship with him was one thing; dealing with his delinquency was something else. She still couldn't believe that the quiet little boy she knew was capable of doing all Mrs Hackett told her he had.

Arriving in the passageway outside her flat door she was dismayed to find him not waiting for her and her mind raced, wondering where else he could be. Knowing he was in trouble, maybe he was hiding in the back garden. She was just about to turn and go to look when the door to the flat opposite opened and her surly neighbour appeared imposingly in the doorway.

He looked at her disdainfully. 'I expect you're wondering where Marty is.' His tone was icy. 'Well, he's in here with me. I found him in a very distressed state outside your flat a couple of hours ago. I should inform you that I am going to the authorities over the way you treat him. You should be ashamed of yourself.' He held up a crumpled brown paper bag. 'Is this the best you could give him for his lunch?'

She looked at the bag, bewildered. 'I'm sorry?'

'And so you should be. A thin round of bread and lard is hardly sufficient to feed a growing boy, and the bread is stale at that.'

Before she could respond suitably a woman arrived at

the top of the stairs, panting breathlessly. 'Ah, Miss Chambers, I need to talk to you.'

Judith looked across at her, surprised. It was Mrs Williams with whom she was acquainted from her visits to Mrs Chaudri's shop.

'I'm sorry if this is inconvenient,' she said, coming up to Judith, 'but since Mrs Chaudri told me what was happening, I've been so worried about it all and it's my Christian duty to tell you what I know. It's not something we can discuss out here so shall we go inside?' She looked at Nathan and Judith could tell she was wondering who he was, considering Judith was a Miss. 'Good evening,' Mrs Williams said to him, and walked past him into his flat where she obviously assumed Judith lived too.

Nathan looked at Judith, raised his eyebrows at her, then held his arm wide. 'After you.'

Wondering what Mrs Williams could possibly want with her and very aware she had another pressing matter to deal with, Judith followed her inside and found her waiting in Nathan's living room. Despite all that was on her mind Judith did note that the flat was very nicely finished and clean and tidy. Nathan arrived behind her. 'Please take a seat,' he invited Mrs Williams.

'Thank you,' she responded, perching on the edge of an armchair, knees together, clutching her handbag on her lap.

'Miss Chambers,' he said to Judith, indicating the chair opposite.

Sitting down in it, she looked up at Nathan enquiringly. 'Marty . . . ?'

'He's in the kitchen drawing pictures on some paper I gave him.'

Judith looked across at Mrs Williams. 'What is so urgent, Mrs Williams?'

Her visitor was a thin woman, wearing a very staid Crimplene belted dress in cream and beige and sporting a short, tightly wound perm. She was what some in the area called a pillar of the community. She reminded Judith of a sparrow, perched as she was on the edge of the chair as if ready to jump up and peck any crumb that was dropped before any other bird got it.

She gave a discreet cough. 'It's regarding Mrs Hackett. I believe you use her as a child-minder for the little boy you're caring for? Let me assure you, Miss Chambers, that Mrs Chaudri is no gossip but this situation worried her. She did try to tell you at the time but you never gave her the chance. So she told me about it, asked my advice as to what she should do. You being new to the area, you wouldn't know. I told her she must tell you but it appears you haven't been in her shop all week. I saw you on your way home tonight and so I've taken it upon myself to do the deed as I feel you ought to be made aware before it goes on any longer.'

A great fear was building within Judith as to what this woman had to tell her.

'There are some people in this world, Miss Chambers, who are only out for themselves with no thought to the suffering they cause others. Mrs Hackett, I'm afraid, is one of that kind. The authorities banned her from child-minding a long while ago. Regardless, she still does it when she can get away with it. Forgive me for saying so,

Miss Chambers, but for want of a better expression, she saw you coming. She would have been aware that it was only a matter of time before you found her out but it's my guess that in the meantime she's fleeced you for all she can get out of you, and what she's put the child through is anyone's guess. She's very plausible, is Mrs Hackett. Fobbed off the authorities for quite a few years before the complaints against her were far too many for them to ignore.'

Judith gasped, mortified. 'She mistreats the children.'

'Oh, yes. One child who threatened to tell his parents about her was thrashed so hard she broke his arm. Of course, she said he fell in her yard. It was the child's word against hers. She comes across as being so kind and motherly that it takes a while for the parents to realise that their children are not liars, not causing the trouble she says they are while in her care, but she's making out they are in order that her word will always count for more. In the meantime she pockets her extortionate charges and whatever else she can get away with because the parents badly need a minder so they can go to work. With more women choosing to work now, those willing to child-mind are not so readily available as they used to be.

'Mrs Hackett's husband is serving a long sentence for robbery and grievous body harm. Her two sons both belong to a group who abuse any people they don't believe conform to their own racist standards, especially coloured people arriving in the area. Mrs Chaudri has had the windows of her shop broken twice. They go inside to steal what they can and taunt her. The police are aware of them, though, and are keeping their eye on them. It's only a matter of time before they land up where their father is.'

'I can't believe all this,' Judith uttered, deeply distressed.

'I wouldn't lie to you, Miss Chambers.'

'Oh, no, I never meant to accuse you of that. I just can't believe all this of Mrs Hackett . . . as you say, she comes across as being so genuine.' She frowned and spoke her thoughts aloud. 'As the days have passed I've had more and more of a job to get Marty around to her house in the morning. I thought he was just being awkward, but he wasn't. She's been treating him badly and he didn't tell me.' She wrung her hands. 'Tonight Mrs Hackett told me that Marty had caused bother and she'd had to punish him. Asked me if I knew what a liar he was.'

Mrs Williams looked at her meaningfully. 'She was preparing the ground. Must have had a good idea that your little boy was going to start to rebel against her.' She stood up. 'I expect you'll be wanting to get your dinner, having just arrived home from work, and I need to get off to my WI meeting. If you'll take my advice, you'll stop using Mrs Hackett immediately, but of course it is your choice. I hope you'll appreciate that I've told you all this from the best of intentions. Good evening, Miss Chambers.' She glanced at Nathan. 'Good evening, Mr . . . er . . . Good evening. I'll see myself out.'

A very distressed Judith rose too. 'I need to get Marty home and talk to him,' she said to Nathan. 'Er . . . thank you for taking him in.' Her chin up, she added: 'And that lunch you accused me of giving him? Well, I didn't. I had given Mrs Hackett money for his school dinners and was under the impression that he was having them. Obviously she didn't give the money to Marty and it went into her pocket instead. It was her who gave him that sandwich.'

He looked uncomfortable. 'I owe you an apology, Miss Chambers. It was wrong of me to jump to conclusions without ascertaining the facts. I'd . . . er . . . better take you to Marty.'

She followed him through to his kitchen. As they entered the child glanced up, took one look at Judith and cried out: 'I hate you! I'm ain't coming with yer, I'm staying here.'

Judith flinched at his tone. But then thought that though it might not have been the reaction she would have liked, at least he had spoken to her. Remembering all Cherry had advised her, she smiled kindly at him as she walked across to the table, pulled a chair out next to his and sat down. It didn't escape her notice that he leaned as far away as he could from her. When she spoke her voice was soft. 'Marty, I know you don't like me much at the moment and I understand why. You and I hardly got off to a good start, did we?'

Pushing his spectacles on to his nose, he screwed up his face accusingly. 'You keep telling me off.'

Judith swallowed hard. 'Yes, I know, and I'm very sorry for that. You see, I've never looked after a little boy before. It's all new to me.'

'But you sent me mam away,' he blurted out.

'No, I didn't, Marty. She . . . she left you with me because she had some important things to do and wanted to know you were safe meantime. I know you're missing your mother and I'm sure she'll be back to fetch you soon, but until she does you've got me.'

'Don't want you!' he shouted. 'I want to stay with Misterank 'til me mam comes back.'

She looked at him, perplexed. 'Who?'

'I think that'll be me,' piped up Nathan, who was standing behind her, listening to these proceedings with great surprise. Miss Chambers, it seemed, had a softer side to her that he hadn't for a minute envisaged. Maybe it was just him she was off-hand with. When she turned her head and looked at him he said, 'We've never properly been introduced. I'm Nathan Banks.'

Ignoring his gesture, and before she could stop herself, she replied curtly, 'I wish I could say it was a pleasure but I can't and I know that the feeling is mutual.' She returned her attention to Marty. 'You can't stay here, you have to come home with me.'

He shook his head vehemently. 'No. You make me go to that lady's. She smacked me. I didn't do nuffink! I was just sitting on the chair, waiting for you to come and get me. She smacked me hard around me head and said if I told you I wasn't having school dinners and she was giving me a sandwich, she would tell you I was a fibber and then smack me again and it would hurt more next time. She said I broke her winder, but I din't break no winder, and she told me to tell yer that I lost me gym kit that she give me but she never give me one, 'onest. I don't like her. She's 'orrible.'

Judith's shoulders sagged, mortified for what Mrs Hackett had put this innocent little boy through to feed her own greed. 'Please believe me, I didn't know she wasn't a nice lady, Marty. But I do now. You aren't going back to her, I promise you.'

Adjusting his glasses, he eyed her warily. 'I ain't?'

'No. Definitely not. I promise to find a very nice lady to look after you while I'm at work.'

'But you're not a nice lady neiver. You tell me off and I din't do nuffink!'

'Oh, Marty, I didn't mean to be cross with you. I didn't understand about little boys, you see. Will you help me to understand?'

His face screwed quizzically. 'Whatja mean?'

'Well . . . I just mean . . .' Her mind raced frantically for a way to put what she meant into words he would understand. 'Well, you know what little boys like to do and you could tell me. And when I ask you to do something and you don't know how to do it, you could tell me and then I can show you.'

'I never left yer tap on. I never meant the water to go all over yer bathroom. I couldn't turn it off, it was too stiff.'

Her heart sank. That thought had never entered her head. How could she not have realised that such a simple thing to her was a huge task for a little boy? 'I'm so sorry, Marty. I won't make that mistake again.' She looked at him closely. 'Do you think you and I can start again? I'd like that very much.'

He still looked at her warily. 'I really don't have ter go to that 'orrible lady no more?'

'No, you don't. You have my promise, Marty. Oh!' she suddenly exclaimed as a dreadful thought struck her and she said aloud, 'I need to go to work tomorrow and I'll have to find someone urgently to look after you. I should have asked Mrs Williams if she could recommend anyone.' She turned her head and looked at Nathan. 'Do you

271

happen to know Mrs Williams' address?'

He shook his head. 'I don't. The lady in the corner shop who alerted her to your situation will know, I expect. But I remember Mrs Williams saying she was going to a meeting straight from here.'

'Oh.' Judith gnawed her bottom lip anxiously. What on earth was she to do? Her mind raced. Would Cherry be understanding if she telephoned in tomorrow morning and asked for the day off so she could seek out a proper child-minder for Marty? But then she had only just ingratiated herself with her supervisor and her other work colleagues and they could think she was taking advantage by asking for time off so soon which might undo some of the good that had been done today. What a dilemma she was in.

'Seems you have a problem, Miss Chambers,' Nathan said.

She looked at him sharply. 'I'm well aware of that.'

'Misterank could look after me?'

They both looked at Marty, stunned.

'Oh, no, Marty, that's not possible, I'm afraid,' Judith told him.

'Why not?' he said, looking at them both questioningly. 'I like Misterank. And you like me, don't yer, Misterank?'

'Well . . . er . . . yes,' he said awkwardly.

'Well, I can stop with you then.'

Nathan Banks' face was a picture. 'I suppose . . .'

Before he could finish Marty beamed in delight, clapping his hands, obviously of the opinion his request had been granted.

Judith shook her head at him. 'No, Marty, I'm sorry,

Mr Banks can't possibly look after you.'

Nathan looked at her sharply, his back bristling, and before he could stop himself, asked her, 'And why not?'

She looked at him, taken aback. 'Well, you're a man for a start.'

Which meant he was automatically incapable of caring for a little boy? Well, he'd show her. Before he could stop to think of the consequences, Nathan blurted, 'There's no law saying it's only women who can child-mind, is there? I work from home as I have my own business, and when I do have to go out I can fit it in during Marty's school hours.'

She considered Nathan quizzically. 'But have you ever looked after a child?'

'No, I've none of my own. But then, from what I can gather, neither had you until Marty arrived on the scene.' And there was much that still intrigued Nathan regarding that state of affairs. Was Miss Chambers indeed Marty's grandmother? Maybe he called her Grandma as a courtesy title, though Nathan couldn't think why. To his knowledge spinster ladies, if not addressed by their title of Miss whatever, were courteously called Aunt not Grandma. He surveyed her haughtily. 'Besides, I've looked after him twice now and no harm has come to him, has it? In fact, just the opposite.' Then the significance of his offer, one made only because this woman's attitude towards him had annoyed him so much, registered full force and he suddenly hoped it would be refused.

But Marty had other ideas. 'Please, Gran'ma,' he pleaded. 'Please let Misterank look after me? I'll be good, promise.'

She rose from her chair and looked at Nathan thoughtfully. This unexpected turn of events was like a godsend to her. It would be so convenient, him only living across the landing. 'Are you sure about this, Mr Banks?'

No, he wasn't, but he couldn't back out now. He wasn't worried about upsetting her, but he didn't like the thought of disappointing the boy. 'Well, it's not like it's for long, is it? Only for as long as it takes for Marty's mother to return for him.'

'Please, Gran'ma,' the child begged again.

She wasn't sure about this but as matters stood she really wasn't in any position to refuse Nathan Banks' offer. The one to consider was Marty and if he was happy with Nathan Banks looking after him while she was at work then it just might help her own relationship with the child.

'We could give it a try,' she said, hoping she was not going to live to regret her decision. 'See if it works out on both sides.'

'That's fair enough,' said Nathan.

'Goody,' said Marty. 'Can I play with yer cars again, Misterank?'

'If you promise to look after them, I don't see why not.'

'Oh, I do,' he cried eagerly.

'I've a garage somewhere too,' Nathan said to him.

'A garage?' Marty cried in awe. 'If yer let me play with it, I'll look after it, promise.'

Judith's guilt returned. While Marty had been with her he had had no toys to play with. She had given him a tuppenny secondhand book and expected him to occupy himself with that as she had done when she was a child.

'What will your fees be?' she asked Nathan.

He stared at her. 'Fees?'

'Your child-minding charges?'

He eyed her sharply. 'Please don't insult me, Miss Chambers. Being paid for looking after Marty never entered my head.'

She was shocked by his generosity and couldn't deny that the money she'd save on minding charges would greatly ease her strained financial situation, give her the means to start buying all the things that Marty needed. Regardless, her pride would not let her accept his offer without her own stipulation. 'I must reimburse any expenses you incur during the hours you have him.'

He cocked an eyebrow at her. 'I'll keep a tally.'

She turned her attention to Marty. 'We really ought to go and leave Mr Banks in peace. I expect you're very hungry?'

'Misterank gave me a chunky and soldiers but I'm famished again.'

At the look on her face Nathan explained, 'A boiled egg and strips of bread and butter. It's a child's name for it.'

She hadn't known that. All in all it seemed to Judith that Nathan Banks was far better equipped to look after Marty than she was. 'Yes, of course it is,' she said to cover her own ignorance. She suddenly became very conscious that she was conversing with a man who until a few minutes ago she had only ever had altercations with. Suddenly being on civil terms with him, even for the sake of Marty, was going to take some getting used to. 'Shall we go home, Marty?'

His little face puckered up and Judith worried for a moment that he was still going to refuse to come with her. 'Okay,' he said, much to her relief, scrambling down from his chair.

As he saw them out of his front door, Judith said to Nathan, 'We'll see you in the morning about ten minutes to eight? Will that suit you, Mr Banks?'

'Fine with me,' he said stiffly.

As he closed the door after them and made his way back into the kitchen to prepare his evening meal, he sighed heavily, having difficulty believing he had just allowed himself to offer what he had. It wasn't just the child he was caring for, this arrangement meant daily contact with Judith Chambers – a woman – something he'd avoided as much as possible for the last twenty-five years after making a vow to himself never to allow himself to be at a woman's mercy again. But then he reasoned with himself, as he had told Judith Chambers, this arrangement was only short-term, probably only for a matter of days, and then his life would immediately revert to the way it had been. He might seem like a recluse to some people, but it suited him and he meant to keep it that way.

A while later in the flat opposite Judith was looking with concern at Marty, sitting at the dining table opposite her. Due to the amount of money Mrs Hackett had wangled out of her, she'd decided to make a meal from the store cupboard. Until she received her wages the next day the pantry held little more than enough breakfast cereal for Marty in the morning, several potatoes, a small piece of butter and a chunk of cheese. She worried that he required a nourishing meal now she was aware he hadn't been having one at school each day, and wondered what she could make for him with what she had to hand and her own somewhat limited skills. Scouring her cookery book, she had come across a recipe for cheese and potato pie which she had set to and made, following the instructions exactly, and which he was now tucking into.

'Are you enjoying your meal, Marty?' she tentatively asked him.

Filled fork poised mid-air, he looked back at her and nodded before resuming his eating.

Great relief filled her. 'I'm so glad.' And at least he had responded to her favourably instead of with his previous blank shrug.

As she busied herself clearing away after the meal she noted with dismay that he had gone across to the window and was staring out again. Washing the dishes, she worried how long he would keep this up for. When she went back to the lounge to inform him it was time to get ready for bed she was surprised to see that he was sitting on the settee, looking through the book she had bought him. He was so engrossed he was unaware she was watching him. She felt an urge to ask if he'd like her to read the story to him, but remembered the advice that Cherry had given her, to let him be the one to come to her when he was ready to. Marty looking at the book was a small step forward and she wanted to do nothing to reverse matters.

A while later she watched as he climbed into bed, shutting his eyes and turning to face the wall. 'Good night, Marty,' she said, and her face filled with surprise, thinking she was imagining things, when he responded, 'Good night, Gran'ma.' A rush of hope filled her. Another step forward, just a small one, but a step forward all the same.

Chapter Twenty

Cherry gawped at Judith, astounded. 'I can't believe it! You're seriously telling me, Judy, that your new child-minder is a man?'

'It wasn't my idea, it was all Marty's. And after the way Mrs Hackett treated him, I hadn't the heart to refuse.'

Cherry ruefully shook her head. 'I'm not a violent person but if he had been my child and I'd found out what Mrs Hackett had done to him, I'd have took a knife to her. The cow!' she spat. 'People like her shouldn't be allowed to walk the streets.'

'Then it's lucky for her it was me and not you who's responsible for Marty. For once I'm glad I'm well-practised at keeping my emotions in check. What good would it do for me to confront Mrs Hackett? I could end up in jail for assault and then where would Marty be? I'm just so relieved that Mrs Williams did tell me about it and this situation didn't go on any longer. Anyway, Mr Banks certainly seems to have Marty's vote. He went happily yesterday morning, and when I picked him up last night they had just come in from playing football in the garden. Marty looked so happy. And, very surprisingly, Mr Banks

279

is being civil to me now, which of course is all for Marty's sake but it's something, I suppose.' A thought struck her. 'There's no reason why Mr Banks shouldn't look after him, is there? I mean, him being a man.'

'Not that I know of. As long as Marty's being looked after properly what difference does it make?' Cherry looked at her keenly. 'So tell me more about the mysterious Mr Banks?'

'Not much I can tell you, really. I don't know much about him except that he likes to keep himself to himself. Well, so far as I'm concerned, it seems.'

'What about the other women tenants? Does he keep his distance from them too?'

'There aren't any. I'm the only female. Apparently I'm the first there's ever been for some reason since the house was converted into flats a few years ago.'

'Oh, really? What a great situation to be in. The only woman among several men,' Cherry said, winking at her suggestively. 'So what are the others like then?'

'Well, I've only actually spoken to one. A rather overbearing man who lives in the attic flat upstairs – when I encountered him I made a rapid escape. The two young men downstairs I've only ever caught glimpses of as I've been coming and going. Both seem to have their fair share of female admirers, judging by the different girls I've seen them each with.'

'Oh, I see. None of them likely prospects then?'

'Not that I'm an expert on such matters but I don't think you'd be interested, Cherry.'

'I wasn't thinking of me. So, you were telling me about Mr Banks. What does he do for a living?'

'He told me he has his own business, working from home, but I've no idea what he does. I must admit though that every time we crossed paths when I first moved into my flat, he caught me in embarrassing situations. I just wish it had been anyone but him.'

'And just what were these situations?' Cherry asked eagerly.

'Well, as I said, they're embarrassing,' said Judith evasively.

'All the more reason I want to hear?'

Judith knew she wouldn't get any peace until she had divulged all.

Several minutes later Cherry was giggling hysterically. 'Oh, my God, as if not knowing yer had to put money in the meters wasn't bad enough, seeing you sprawled over a dustbin must have been some sight.' Eyes twinkling wickedly, she asked, 'So yer don't think there's any chance of a romance between you two then?'

'A romance with any man is not on my agenda, Cherry, and I think you appreciate the reason why. But even so, a romance between myself and Mr Banks . . . well, you have more chance of becoming Queen.'

Cherry looked at her searchingly. 'Yeah, well, maybe not with Mr Banks but some other chap. Yer can't let what happened over twenty years ago rule yer life forever. Yer a good-looking woman for yer age, with a better figure than some women half that. Now yer've sorted out yer problem with getting on with people, I reckon yer going to have queues of eligible men knocking on your door.'

Judith blushed at her compliment. 'It's very nice of you

281

to say so but I prefer to keep things as they are. I'm too old and set in my ways now.'

Cherry grinned at her. 'My mam always says yer never too old, and I don't agree that yer that set in yer ways 'cos look how yer've taken to looking after a kiddy, how quickly yer've adapted to that.'

Judith stared at her thoughtfully. Yes, she supposed she had. 'Looking after a child isn't the same as having a relationship with a man, though.'

'No, not quite, I agree, but you're just frightened of getting involved with someone 'cos of what happened before. Don't be. There's some nice men out there, Judy, if yer'd just allow yerself to find them.' An idea began to form in her mind. Neville James was a widower and Christmas wasn't far away. The firm had a Christmas do and whether Judith liked it or not, Cherry was going to make sure she went. She smiled to herself, liking the thought of playing Cupid. 'More tea?' she asked Judith. 'And help yerself to another biscuit 'cos as soon as the kids come back in they'll all be demolished before yer can say Jack Robinson.' She picked up the teapot and refilled Judith's cup and her own then settled back in her chair. 'So how are things with you and Marty? Any improvements?'

'A little better, I'm glad to say. I've taken your advice and I'm being patient, letting him come to me. He does respond to me more. Instead of giving me a look and a shrug, he answers when I ask if he's enjoyed his dinner and such like and he's said good night to me for the last two nights. He hasn't looked out of the window so much either.'

'It's a start.' Cherry looked at her shrewdly. 'You're growing very fond of that little boy, I can tell you are.'

Judith stared at her. Marty's well-being was important to her. He needed her. For the first time in her life she was finding out what it felt like to be needed by someone and she rather liked the feeling. Did that mean she was fond of him? She had never felt close enough to anyone before to know what it felt like.

'He seems a nice little boy ter me, Judy,' Cherry was saying. 'Missed out a bit in the looks department, but then I went to school with one of the ugliest kids yer could imagine and he grew up into a stunner. I really regretted being the one who instigated the nickname of Frankenstein.' Cherry quickly realised what she'd said and added, 'Not that I'm saying Marty's ugly, Judy, far from it. He's just . . . well . . . he wouldn't win first prize in a looks competition.' She really felt it was time she changed the subject. 'I've sorted out a bag of clothes for him. All good stuff that my two have grown out of. There's some shirts and trousers, a couple of jumpers and pairs of pyjamas. I got the kids to sort through their toys as they've far too much to play with and there's a bag of games and a couple of puzzles too. I hope yer not offended?'

'Not at all, Cherry, I'm very grateful. I did rig Marty out when we went shopping this morning with new underwear and socks, and I got his spectacles repaired at the optician and had his hair cut, but my money this week won't stretch to anything else after how much I had to pay out to Mrs Hackett last week. It was a toss up whether Marty got a new pair of trousers, or they waited until next week and I replenished my larder so I can feed him properly. You must let me give you something towards all that?'

'Not on yer Nelly. I used to give all me old stuff to the charity shop 'til I found out the workers there got best pickings and it was only what they weren't interested in that went on sale to the needy. I can't think of a better home for my stuff than giving it to you.'

Just then Cherry's youngest child, Douglas, aged six, rushed in dragging Marty along with him. 'Mam, our Richie called Marty Four Eyes.'

'Oh, did he?' said Cherry sternly. 'And you're a little snitch. Come here, Marty,' she said to him. When he was standing before her she placed her hands gently on his arms and looked at him kindly. 'My Richie is a silly boy, ain't he, Marty? Because everyone knows that four eyes are better than two.' She ran her fingers through his shock of red hair. 'You know, when I was little, I used to wish so much I had hair your colour. It's like permanent sunshine. You're a lucky boy 'cos not many people are fortunate enough to have hair the colour yours is. Now off yer go and play. Douglas, tell our Richie he's not getting an ice cream when the van comes round 'til his manners improve.'

'Eh up, our Mam,' wailed Richard, entering. 'I called Marty Four Eyes 'cos he called me a little bleeder when I kicked him by accident as I was climbing on to the shed roof.'

Judith gasped, mortified. 'Did you say such a thing to Richard, Marty?'

He looked at her innocently and nodded. 'That's what me mam calls me.'

Yes, she did, Judith thought. She had heard Rachel call him that. She could see Cherry was having trouble controlling an eruption of mirth. 'Er . . . Marty, sometimes older people say words that aren't fit for little boys to repeat and . . . er . . . bleeder is one of them. Now I'm not cross with you but you won't say it again, will you?' He shook his head and she smiled warmly at him. 'Good boy.'

'And you shouldn't have bin climbing on the shed roof,' Cherry scolded her eldest son. 'If I catch you doing it again it's bed for you for the rest of the day. Now go on, skedaddle the lot of yer, and give me and Marty's grandma some peace.'

After the children had rushed out again, not before taking a biscuit each, Cherry looked at Judith, impressed. 'You handled that great, Judy.'

'Did I? Really?'

'I couldn't have done better meself. You're learning. Sorry for laughing but I thought it was so funny. Mind you, it's not really if his mam does call him a little bleeder, is it?'

Judith didn't want to continue this line of conversation as she felt utterly ashamed that her own flesh and blood could speak to her son in such a way. She looked at Cherry enquiringly. 'Did you really wish for red hair when you were young?'

'No, but it don't do any harm to let kids think they've got something you hanker after. Meks 'em feel special. Nothing does kids more good than praising 'em for something even if they've made a bad job of it.'

Judith stored that advice away for future use.

285

Cherry picked up a chocolate digestive and bit into it, staring thoughtfully at Judith. 'Can I ask what it was like for yer, coming face to face with yer daughter for the first time? You must have wondered sometimes over the years what she looked like and what she'd turned into, 'cos it's only natural, ain't it?'

Judith sighed heavily. 'Well, as I told you previously, I had locked it all away and didn't allow myself to think of it much, but a couple of times over the years even I couldn't stem the memories. So, yes, I did wonder. When the home took my baby from me I was led to believe that I would never see it again so it was some shock when she arrived so unexpectedly. This stranger was standing before me, telling me she was my daughter and presenting me with a grandson. I couldn't see anything of myself in her. My memory of her father is hazy but I can only assume she takes after his side.' Judith's eyes glazed over. 'I feel terribly guilty because surely I should feel something for her yet I feel no connection whatsoever.' She looked at Cherry questioningly. 'I should love her, shouldn't I? Or if not love at the moment, I should feel something for her. But I just don't.'

'Yeah, well, she robbed yer, didn't she, and went off leaving her son with yer.'

'Yes, I admit, I did feel angry with her for taking all my money. I just wish she had asked me and given me the opportunity to give it to her. And I was panic-stricken at being left with Marty to care for. I feel terrible for the fact that the people who raised Rachel weren't the type the home led me to believe they would be, and I don't think she's had a good life with them. But . . . well . . . it's how I feel about Rachel herself that I feel most guilty for. I didn't like her as a person and I feel terrible when she's my own daughter.'

Cherry looked at Judith sadly, thinking it must be awful for someone not only to lose their own child but to meet up with that child years later and find they didn't like them. 'Well, things take time, don't they? Maybe something will grow inside yer for her once yer get the chance to know her better.'

'I hope you're right. I also hope she comes back soon for the sake of her son. Just letting us know she's all right would be better than not knowing.'

'Once your money runs out it's my betting she will turn up.'

'You don't think she's had an accident then?'

'You really are naïve, Judy. I don't think that for a minute. Raising kids is hard, especially when yer on yer own. She had Marty when she was very young and from your description of her adoptive parents it doesn't sound like she got much help from them. I think she's off enjoying herself on what she got outta you. She knows Marty is safe with you. Mind you, that's only my opinion. She could have had summat happen to her, but yer won't know 'til she comes back. Still, look on the bright side, some good has come out of all this.'

Judith looked at her, taken aback. 'Has it?'

'Yeah. Marty has certainly changed your life in the week that you've had him. If you hadn't had him to care for yer might not have pleaded with me for yer job. And then we wouldn't be sitting here now getting to know each other, and I might still have been under the impression

287

you was that horrible woman and not the nice one I'm finding out you are. I still have trouble believing you were once that awful Judith Chambers. You really should congratulate yerself on how yer've changed yerself around.'

Judith smiled at the compliment. Several months ago she had been living for the most part a reclusive life, unaware of what had brought about her own existence and embittered her parents, especially her mother, towards her. Oblivious also of the way others really saw her. Yes, she had worked hard to bring about the changes in herself, and it hadn't been easy either. It wasn't over yet as there were still parts of herself she knew needed working on. And now she was learning to care for someone else apart from herself.

She suddenly realised that her panic regarding her ability to look after Marty was gone, replaced by an unquenchable desire to make him happy and content while he was with her. In turn she really had much to thank him for as Cherry was right: without him to care for she would not have lost her pride and pleaded for her job, and by doing that gained all that had come with it.

She looked at Cherry's wall clock hanging above the fireplace. It was approaching five. 'I ought to be getting Marty home,' she said, collecting her handbag from the side of her chair. 'Cherry, I want to thank you so much. Not just for the clothes and toys you've given me for Marty but for the lovely afternoon I've had too. I know Marty has enjoyed himself. It's been very gratifying for me to hear him laughing with your boys. And you're right, they are lovely boys.'

'I think so,' said Cherry, beaming. 'Bring him again. I'm always in Sat'day af'noons.'

'I'd like that. Er . . . maybe you would like to come over to my flat sometime?'

'Yeah, I would. Tell yer what, I'll bring my boys over to you next Sat'day, how about that?'

'It's a date.'

Later that evening, just as she was drying her hands after tackling the dishes, Judith felt a tug on her apron and looked down to see Marty at the side of her, holding out the book she had bought him. 'Will yer read this to me, Gran'ma?' he asked.

She stared at him for a moment in complete surprise then her face broke into a big smile. 'Yes, of course I will.' She took his hand and led him into the lounge. She sat down on the settee and he clambered up and sat close beside her. She opened the book and began to read. When she had finished she closed it and looked down at him. 'Did you like that story, Marty?'

He nodded and Judith was surprised again when he confided in her: 'I had a drum like Bom the Lical Drummer Boy had. Mine was red. The lady next door give it ter me but Mammy took it off me 'cos she said I made too much noise and gave her a headache. When's me mam coming ter fetch me?'

She swallowed hard. 'Soon, Marty, I'm sure.'

'Have you got a mammy?'

'Yes, I have, but she lives a very long way away.'

'Misterank's mammy's in heaven.'

'Is she?'

He nodded. 'I asked him where 'is mammy was and

289

that's what he told me. I like Misterank. I want to go to bed now, Gran'ma, I'm tired.'

'Oh, yes, all right. As well as the toys that Richard and Douglas's mummy gave me for you she also gave me some clothes, including pyjamas. Wasn't that nice of her?'

He nodded. 'I like going there. Richie and Duggie are me friends. Can we go again?'

'Yes, we can. They're coming to see us next Saturday afternoon.'

His little face lit up. 'Oh, goody. Will Misterank play football with us in the garden?'

'Er . . . well . . . I think Mr Banks has lots to do on a Saturday.'

'Why?'

'Well . . . grown-ups do. Grandma has lots to do, doesn't she?'

'Well, you could do Misterank's lots to dos, Gran'ma, and then he can play football with us. Can I wear me new jamas ter bed tonight?'

'Yes, of course. I'll fetch them for you. We ought to get you bathed first, though, as you've been playing in the garden all afternoon.'

He looked at her anxiously. 'Will you bath me, Gran'ma? I can't do it meself 'cos the soap keeps slipping out me hands, and I can't dry meself properly neiver.'

At his words tears suddenly stung her eyes. Of course Marty couldn't bath himself, he was only five. How could she have expected him to wash and dry himself? She stood up. 'Come along then,' she said, holding out her hand towards him.

A while later Marty took his glasses off and put them

on the floor by the side of his bed then snuggled down under the covers, turned towards the wall and closed his eyes. Judith gazed down at him. 'Goodnight, Marty.'

'Good night, Gran'ma.' He suddenly opened his eyes and turned his head to face her. 'I didn't like the other gran'mas, and I didn't like you, but I do now.' Then he turned back over and closed his eyes.

Open-mouthed, she stared down at him. Her grandson had told her he liked her and she couldn't describe the feeling it gave her. It was like the sun had suddenly come out from behind a dark cloud and was bathing her in warmth. 'Oh, Marty, I like you too,' she murmured. She suddenly knew what being fond of someone felt like. Cherry was right, she was fond of Marty, very fond. She felt a great urge to bend over and kiss him, but fought it. He might not welcome that from her yet but she hoped he would soon.

She padded softly out of the bedroom and shut the door. Then something he had said struck her. What had he meant by saying he hadn't liked the *other* grandmas? She must have heard him wrongly. He had meant that he hadn't liked his other grandmother, who was Rachel's adoptive mother, surely? Had the woman mistreated him? Judith worried. But then Marty liked her and at this moment that was all she cared about.

Chapter Twenty-One

It was the following Saturday afternoon and Cherry had just arrived with her sons. 'Nice flat yer've got, Judy,' she said, looking round appraisingly. 'Very nice. Could do with a couple more pictures on the walls and a few more ornaments dotted around. A nice vase on yer fire surround would look a treat. A blue one.'

It had done, Judith thought. 'Yes, it would,' she agreed quietly.

'But even without ornaments and pictures it still feels homely, don't it?'

Judith smiled broadly. 'Yes, I think so. Shall I take your coat?'

Cherry's face suddenly clouded over with embarrassment as she stripped it off and handed it to Judith. 'Oh, Judy, me and me big mouth. I expect yer've far more important things to do with yer money just now than wasting it on dust collectors, as me mam calls 'em.'

'Well, children cost far more than I ever realised.'

'I don't know where my money goes ter be honest. If one's not wanting shoes then the other is.'

'Yes, I'm finding that out more and more. But I have it

easy compared to you as I only have the one. I took Marty to the shoe shop this morning and had him measured. The shoes I bought him cost just under two pounds.'

Cherry gawped at her. 'What did yer buy him, gold-plated ones? Yer could have got them cheaper than that and just as good. Tell me the next time yer need 'ote for him and I can tell yer the best places to shop.'

'I appreciate that. If Marty is going to be with me for much longer then I will seriously have to consider cutting my overheads somehow, like moving to a place with a cheaper rent.'

'Won't be as nice as this one,' said Cherry.

'No, but then I will have more money at my disposal to look after Marty better.'

'Seems to be thriving all right to me. Two weeks yer've had him now and you ain't killed him yet,' Cherry said, grinning at Judith mischievously.

She laughed. 'Thank you,' she said sincerely. Two weeks. Was that all it was since the day she had come home to find Rachel had left her son behind? It seemed so much longer than that.

Cherry looked at her enquiringly. 'I tek it yer ain't heard n'ote from his mother or you'd have said?'

She shook her head. 'No.'

Cherry patted her arm in an affectionate gesture. 'Ah, well, I'm sure she'll turn up soon.'

Judith smiled wanly at her. 'I hope so for Marty's sake.' But what about her own sake? Suddenly it struck her that when Marty did leave her, she would miss him. 'I'll . . . er . . . just hang your coat up and fetch through the tea.

Sit down and make yourself comfortable, Cherry. The children seem to have made themselves at home. I can hear them all giggling in Marty's bedroom.'

A few moments later Judith put a laden tray on the table and poured them both a cup of tea. This was the first time she had ever entertained a guest and she was enjoying the whole process. 'I've juice and biscuits for the children,' she said, handing Cherry her cup. 'I'm sure they'll let us know when they're ready for them.'

'Sod the kids,' laughed Cherry. 'What goodies have you got for us? I hope yer've made a cake in honour of me coming?'

Much to Cherry's surprise Judith said, 'Well, actually, I have. I was going to buy a Lyon's sponge but they aren't very big, are they? I don't know what my effort is going to taste like. The other attempt I made at baking a cake — well, it went straight in the dustbin. The girls at work were talking of baking a few days ago and Mary mentioned she always used the Be-Ro cookery book for her cakes and they always turn out well so I asked her for the recipe. She had a spare Be-Ro book and brought it in for me. Wasn't that nice of her? I set to and made it last night. Marty helped me. Well, he had a stir of the mixture and licked out the bowl. It looks all right.'

'Let's hope it tastes all right,' said Cherry. 'Go and fetch it then.'

'Not bad,' she said a few minutes later. 'Better than mine.'

'Really?'

'Mine all sink in the middle. Me mam says I'm too heavy-handed and I never get the temperature in the oven just right. Give us another slice before the kids come through.'

A warm glow filled Judith as she happily cut another slice and put it on Cherry's plate. She was so pleased that her effort was being well received.

'So how's the baby-sitting service going?' Cherry asked her.

'It seems to be going very well. Marty is very happy. Mr Banks hasn't said anything to the contrary so I assume everything is fine with him too.'

'But are you two getting on?'

'Depends on what you mean by that. I drop Marty over in the morning and we say good morning to each other. I collect him in the evening, ask if Marty has been a good boy, Mr Banks tells me he has and that's about it really.'

Just then there was a knock on the door.

'Expecting more company?' Cherry asked.

Judith shook her head. 'No. Please excuse me, won't you? I won't be a moment.'

On opening the door Judith was taken aback to find Kimberley on her doorstep. 'Hello, how nice to see you,' she said in genuine delight.

The young woman looked at her in concern. 'You are all right then, Miss Chambers?'

She looked back, perplexed. 'Yes, very well, thank you. Any reason I wouldn't be?'

'Well, I thought you must be sick or something when you never turned up at my flat that Saturday afternoon. We made an arrangement, don't you remember?'

Judith's face filled with horror. 'Oh, Kimberley, I'm so sorry, I completely forgot about it. Oh, what must you think of me? It's just that . . . Well, a situation arose that took my mind off it completely.'

'Oh, I see. Nothing serious, I hope?'

'Er . . . well . . . Look, would you like to come in?' she asked, standing aside.

'I'm not inconveniencing you, am I?'

'No, not at all, it's lovely to see you. I have a friend here with her children. That's the noise you can hear coming from the bedroom.

'Cherry, this is Kimberley,' she said, introducing the young woman when they arrived in the lounge. 'Cherry's my sup—'

'Friend,' cut in Cherry, holding out her hand in greeting to Kimberley. 'Pleased ter meet yer, Kim.'

'Please sit down, Kimberley,' Judith invited. 'I'll go and fetch another cup.' She disappeared off into the kitchen. As she returned seconds later Cherry asked her, 'So how do you two know each other, Judy?'

'Oh, Kimberley works in the library and is very helpful, advising me on what she thinks I would enjoy reading, and I have to say she's always been right,' Judith replied as she poured out tea. 'She's just moved into the area and invited me round to her flat a while ago but, well, it slipped my mind.' She looked at Kimberley apologetically as she passed over her cup of tea. 'I hope you will forgive me for my lapse? Would you like a slice of cake?'

'I can highly recommend it,' said Cherry, taking a large bite of her second slice.

Kimberley nodded. 'It does look good. Yes, I would love a slice, thank you.'

Just then the children bounded in. 'Can we go and play

297

football in the garden, Gran'ma?' Marty yelled, rushing over to her to jump up and down excitedly before her. 'Richie brought his ball with him.'

'Yeah, can we, Mam?' shouted Douglas and Richie.

'No need ter shout, we ain't deaf. All right with you?' Cherry asked, looking at Judith.

'Yes, of course. Just be careful where you kick the ball, though. It's not very warm outside so you might need your coats.'

'No, we won't,' they all sang in unison.

They all noticed the cake then and looked at it longingly.

'Can we tek a slice with us?' asked Richard expectantly.

'I helped Gran'ma make it,' said Marty proudly.

Judith laughed. 'I'll cut you all a slice. I should have made two cakes, shouldn't I?' Cake cut and a slice each handed to the boys, she rose to her feet. 'I'll leave the door on the latch for you. Come back in when you're ready.'

After doing this, as she sat back down again and picked up her cup she noticed a worried expression on Kimberley's face and asked, 'Are you all right, Kimberley? It's not my cake, is it? If it's not to your liking, I won't be offended.'

'Pardon? Oh, no, the cake's fine, it's just that . . .' Her face clouded in confusion. 'Well, the little boy with the red hair, I thought I heard him call you Grandma?'

Cherry noticed Judith's face pale and piped up, 'Yes, that's right. Judith is his grandma and that's why he called her that.'

'Oh!' she exclaimed, looking at Judith, shocked.

Cherry noticed Judith's discomfort. 'Tell Kim the truth, Judy, yer've n'ote ter be ashamed of.'

For a moment she stared at her friend frozen-faced, then she smiled at her gratefully. 'No, I haven't, have I?' Taking a deep breath, she raised her head proudly and fixed Kimberley with her eyes. 'I had a child when I was very young, a girl. I didn't even know that at the time as unfortunately I wasn't in a position to raise a child myself and so she was adopted at birth. I never saw my own baby. Three weeks ago, out of the blue, Rachel, that's her name, called on me unexpectedly to introduce herself and her son to me. And . . . well . . . she . . .'

'Had a few problems, and while she's dealing with 'em Judy offered to look after her grandson,' Cherry finished for her. 'Great kid he is an' all. Brought Judy a lot of joy, ain't he, Judy?'

'Yes, he has,' she said with conviction.

'Oh, I see,' said Kimberley. A look of compassion filled her face. 'Life never runs as smoothly as some of those romance novels would have us believe. I'm sorry you've had such an awful time of it in the past and I'm so glad that it seems to be coming right. It must have been a difficult decision for your daughter to go in search of you, not knowing what she might find. It could have been disastrous, couldn't it? And, of course, she must have her adoptive parents to consider. I'm really so pleased it's all working out for you.'

Judith looked at her gratefully. 'Thank you. I hope this revelation won't spoil our friendship.'

'Why should it?' said Cherry.

'Why, indeed,' announced Kimberley. 'I'm lucky

enough to have wonderful parents, who dote on me and have no skeletons in their cupboard, but I haven't been so closeted by them that I'm unaware that not all lives are as straightforward as mine.'

Just then a commotion infiltrated from outside. 'What on earth is that noise?' Cherry crossed to the window and looked out. 'Well, it's not coming from the front so it must be from the back garden. Oh, the kids!' she cried in alarm. 'Sounds ter me like they're causing mayhem.' She rushed off to the kitchen to check out of the window overlooking the garden.

Judith and Kimberley jumped up and rushed after her. 'Well, would yer just look at this.'

Judith's jaw dropped at the sight that met her at the window. Along with the three boys were three grown men and all of them were running around, chasing after the ball. It arrived level with one of the men. Swinging his leg back, he kicked it hard and it rose high in the air to land in the shrubbery edging the lawn. Jumping up and down, arms outstretched, the man shouted, 'Goal!'

'Well, they're obviously enjoying themselves,' Kimberley laughed.

'Yer can say that again,' Cherry giggled. 'Look at Marty. He's having a whale of a time. Which one is your Mr Banks?' she asked Judith.

'He's not my Mr Banks, Cherry. He's the one going into the shrubbery to fetch the ball. The other two are the young tenants I was telling you about who live in the flats downstairs. Oh, Mr Banks has fallen over. Look, Marty has gone to help him. He's all right, look, he's getting up. Oh, goodness, he's covered in mud.'

'He's not the only one,' said Cherry. 'Just look at the kids.'

'I'm so sorry, Cherry,' Judith exclaimed, mortified.

'Why should you be sorry? The kids are enjoying themselves. Ain't yer heard the expression: a happy kid is a mucky kid?'

'No, I can't say I have.'

'Well, you have now and it's true. Those people who always have clean kids ain't letting them be kids.'

'And you're both going to have your work cut out cleaning them up,' said Kimberley. She smiled warmly at Judith. 'I'd better be off as I'm going out with friends tonight. When you come into the library next time we can arrange a date for you to have a coffee at my flat, if you'd like to.'

'I would, very much so,' said Judith.

'And I'll make sure I have some biscuits in for your grandson.' Kimberley smiled at Cherry. 'Nice to have met you and I hope we meet again. I'll see myself out,' she said to Judith.

'She seems a nice gel,' Cherry said, but before Judith could respond, Cherry cried, 'Oh, look, they're coming in.'

The noise the boys were making as they climbed the stairs arrived ahead of them.

It was Richie who appeared first. 'Hiya, Mam.' He beamed happily across at her. 'We ain't half had a great game of footie. I scored two goals.'

'Yeah, I can see yer've had a good time,' she said, looking him up and down. 'Could grow a ton of spuds in the amount of mud you have on you.'

Nathan arrived at the top of the stairs then, and as he walked towards Cherry and Judith looked at them both sheepishly. 'We . . . er . . . got a little carried away, I'm afraid.'

Cherry grinned at him. 'Well, yer all seemed to enjoy yerselves and that's the main thing. Mr Banks, I presume? I'm Cherry, Richie and Douglas's mother and Judith's friend.'

'Pleased to meet you,' he said stiffly. 'If you'll excuse me, I'd better get these dirty clothes off myself and have a wash.'

Just as he was letting himself into his flat, Marty arrived. 'Thanks, Misterank.'

Nathan paused, turned and smiled warmly at him. 'My pleasure, Marty. Thank you for calling for me and asking me to play with you.'

Judith gasped, 'Oh, I'm so sorry he disturbed you, Mr Banks. Marty . . .'

'It's quite all right, Miss Chambers. If I hadn't wanted to join the boys then I would have told them so. Good afternoon,' he said, disappearing inside his flat.

'Well, that told you,' said Cherry, grinning wickedly. 'Nice-looking man for his age that is but I see what yer mean about him being gruff. Come on, lads, and you Duggie,' she called to her youngest son who had just arrived at the top of the stairs. 'Let's get you all scrubbed up.'

Later that evening Judith handed a glass of milk to Marty who was sitting on the settee dressed ready for bed. 'Did you enjoy yourself today?' she asked, sitting down beside him.

302

He took the glass of milk from her and nodded. 'I want ter be a footballer when I grow up.'

She smiled at him tenderly. 'And I'm sure you'll be the best. I'll come along to your matches and cheer you on.'

His eyes lit up and he looked at her excitedly. 'Will yer, Gran'ma?'

'Yes, of course I will.'

'Me mam too?'

She took a deep breath. 'I'm sure your mother wouldn't miss a single match.'

'Misterank said he wanted to be a footballer when he was lical but he couldn't 'cos when he growed up he'd got two left feet.' He eyed her worriedly. 'I won't have two left feet when I grow up, will I, Gran'ma?'

Judith suppressed a smile. 'No, I don't think so.' So, she thought, Nathan Banks had got a sense of humour. It totally surprised her as she hadn't thought him to possess one at all. She watched Marty drain his milk then took the glass from him as he gave a loud yawn. 'I'll take this into the kitchen then I'll come and tuck you into bed.'

Chapter Twenty-Two

Several evenings later, Judith fondly looked across at Marty, as he lay on Kimberley's rug in front of her electric fire. He was engrossed in a picture book the young girl had given him. 'Time to go, Marty. I need to get you to bed as you've school in the morning.' She turned her attention to Kimberley who was sitting in the chair beside her. Despite their difference in age, the more they got to know each other, the more they discovered they had in common, far more than their shared love of reading.

On first entering Kimberley's living room Judith had been taken aback to see, sitting on a shelf above the fire, an identical vase to the one she herself had fallen in love with, later to be stolen by Rachel. Kimberley had explained that on spotting the vase in Gadsby's shop window she had become so taken by it that she had lost all sense and, using money meant for kitchen equipment, had purchased it before she had time to check herself.

'I've had a lovely time and, obviously, Marty has too, thank you,' Judith said now.

Kimberley beamed. 'Do you know, my mum and dad,

especially my mum, weren't exactly happy when I told them I'd be leaving home. They both fretted I wouldn't cope but now they see how well I've settled in and hear how many friends I'm making and they've come round to the idea. I'd like to introduce you to my mum some day. You two would get on famously, I know you would.'

A warm glow filled Judith at Kimberley's compliment. 'I'd like that.'

Ready for the off, Judith and Marty headed for the door. Pulling it open to see them out, Kimberley was surprised to see a woman standing on the other side, hand poised about to knock. 'Mum,' she exclaimed in delight. 'Well, isn't this a coincidence, you calling just as I was talking about you and, before you ask, yes, all good things. This is Judith Chambers and her grandson, Marty. She's a friend I met at the library. I was just saying how well you two would get on.'

Kimberley noticed a look of absolute horror flash across her mother's face. 'Is something wrong, Mum?'

'Oh, no, no, nothing.' Rosalyn Hardy held out a hand to Judith. 'Pleased to meet you,' she said stiffly.

By her reaction it was clear that Kimberley's mother was not pleased that her daughter had chosen to befriend someone so much older than herself. Judith sincerely hoped that it would not put an end to their relationship but she did not wish to come between mother and daughter. 'Yes, you too,' she responded firmly. She then took Marty's hand. 'Thank you, again, for a lovely evening.'

'We'll do it again soon,' Kimberley replied.

Judith hoped so.

On Friday evening two weeks later, Nathan opened his door to Judith and a very excited Marty greeted her.

'Gran'ma, the fair's come and Misterank said he'd take me tonight if you say he can. I can go, can't I?'

'Oh, er . . .'

'Please, Gran'ma, please! I ain't never bin ter the fair before.'

'I'm sorry about this, Miss Chambers,' Nathan said, looking at her apologetically. 'It's just that obviously all the children are talking of nothing else at school, and when Marty told me about it, asking if he could go, well, he was so full of it I'd agreed before I realised.'

She was embarrassed that Marty had made him feel obliged to offer. Judith had never been to a fair before herself and how the subject had ever come up she could not recall but as a child she remembered her father describing them as cheap thrills for commoners, hives for criminals, not places where decent people would consider being seen. She knew now her father's views were twisted but whether his idea about fairs was or not she wasn't sure. Judith could not ask Mr Banks his opinion, not wanting him to know she was so ignorant of such things. She would ask Cherry on Monday. If her opinion was favourable then Judith would take Marty herself, and if not then she would make him understand why.

'Well, I'm sure Marty will understand that he can't just expect you to do things like this for him. I'll explain to him, Mr Banks, that he mustn't put you in such a position in future. Come along, Marty,' she said, holding out her hand to him. 'We're having sausages tonight for dinner.'

He pulled a face at her. 'I don't want dinner, I wanna go

307

to the fair. Misterank said he'd tek me. Why won't yer let him, Gran'ma?'

'It's not that I won't let him, Marty, but you gave Mr Banks no choice, did you? That's why he agreed to take you in the first place.' She looked at Nathan, embarrassed. 'I'm sorry about this, Mr Banks.'

'But he don't mind, do you, Misterank?' Marty cried, looking up at him expectantly.

'No, I don't, not at all.' Surprisingly, he'd found himself elated at the prospect when Marty had excitedly told him that the fair had arrived, seeing taking the child as an excuse to visit a place he hadn't been since he was young himself and his parents had taken him.

'See, he don't mind teking me, Gran'ma,' Marty cried eagerly. 'So can I go?'

'Just for an hour,' Nathan said. 'Before the adults take over. I really don't mind, Miss Chambers.'

It didn't look as though she had any choice but to agree. Surely someone like Mr Banks would not be considering taking Marty if fairs were as bad as her father had said? She smiled down at Marty. 'Just for an hour then.'

He let out a whoop of glee and grabbed Nathan's hand. 'Come on then, let's go, Misterank. You too, Gran'ma, come on,' he said, grabbing her hand also.

'Oh, but I can't come . . .'

Marty looked at her questioningly. 'But I want you to, Gran'ma.' He looked at Nathan. 'You want Gran'ma ter come, don't yer, Misterank?'

No, he certainly did not, but how could he explain himself if he refused? 'Er . . . yes. Yes, of course she must come. Shall we go then, Miss Chambers?'

With Marty skipping happily ahead they walked in awkward silence together and as they did so it struck Judith in a moment of pure horror that the direction they were taking must surely mean the fair was taking place in Victoria Park, the very place she had purposely avoided setting foot in since that fateful night when Clive Lewis had taken advantage of her twenty-four years ago. She felt old ghosts returning to haunt her and an urge to turn and run almost swamped her. But she knew she couldn't because how could she explain away her actions if she did? She had no choice but to get on with this. It was ironic, though, that her grandson should unwittingly return her to the place where his own mother had so traumatically come into being.

As they rounded a corner bringing the fair into view loud music greeted them and Marty jumped up and down excitedly. 'Oh, look! Look!' he cried in awe, eyes drinking it all in. 'Come on, come on!' He urged them both to hurry and get there, as if afraid it was all going to disappear.

The fair was already teeming and the lively atmosphere rapidly enveloped them. Marty soon spotted a carousel of vibrantly coloured kiddies' cars and begged to go on it. Judith and Nathan stood in silence as they watched him going round and round, his face reflecting how much he was enjoying it. As soon as he got off he spotted the candy floss stall and looked expectantly at them. Nathan glanced at Judith. 'Is it all right if I get him one?' She hadn't the heart to refuse and nodded. As Marty ate the sugar confection, which stuck all around his face, they strolled in silence through the various stalls, stopping now and again as he went off to investigate something that caught his eye.

Nathan watched in amusement as Marty stood before a row of mirrors, each distorting his image into different shapes. 'He's certainly enjoying himself,' he said aloud. And so am I, he thought.

Yes, Marty was, thought Judith. And, surprisingly, so was she. Dubious characters might well frequent such places as fairs but so clearly did law-abiding, decent folks who seemed to be in the majority here.

Egged on by Marty, Nathan had a go on the rifle range and much to his own surprise won a small furry bear which he gave to the boy. Then, spurred on by Marty, Judith hooked a winning duck and was presented with a plastic spider which Marty took great delight in trying to scare her with. Finally they came upon the big wheel and he gazed up at it in wonder. 'Can I go on that, please, Gran'ma?'

Judith was terrified of heights. 'Oh, I don't think . . .'

'But Misterank'll take me on, won't yer, Misterank?'

Nathan too was terrified of heights. He felt hot under the collar. 'Well . . . er . . .'

'Oh, please, Misterank?'

He gulped. Male pride would not let him voice his fear. He would just have to shut his eyes and hope no one noticed. 'Come on then,' he sighed.

Once they were seated in the cradle, the attendant was just about to flap the security bar over them when Marty shouted across to Judith, 'Come on, Gran'ma.'

'Me!' she exclaimed. 'Oh, but . . .'

'Hurry, Missus, we're waiting to start the ride,' urged the attendant.

How she landed in the seat jammed right next to Nathan she had no idea but next thing she knew the security bar was slammed down across them and they were all going up. Both Nathan and Judith squeezed their eyes shut as sheer panic gripped them, both of them clinging on to the security bar for dear life, both aware of Marty's whoops of delight as the air rushed past. Round and round they seemed to go for an eternity until thankfully they felt the wheel slowing down, finally coming to a stop. Both heaved a sigh of relief as they opened their eyes, and both were mortified to find that it wasn't the security bar they were clinging on to but each other. Simultaneously they sprang apart, murmuring apologies, and scrambled out of the seat as quickly as they could.

'It were great, weren't it?' enthused Marty to them both.

'Yes,' they lied to save face. 'It was great.'

'Can we go on again then?'

They both shook their heads. 'Another time, Marty.'

'It's about time we went home,' said Judith.

'Oh, do we have to?' he wailed.

''Fraid, so. It's past your bedtime and you haven't had your dinner yet. Have you enjoyed yourself?'

He nodded vigorously. 'Have you, Gran'ma?'

Apart from the terrifying ride on the big wheel she had, which surprised her considering who she had been with. Once the atmosphere had taken hold of him Mr Banks had proved a most congenial companion. 'Very much so,' she said truthfully.

311

'You too, Misterank?' Marty asked him.

He smiled down. 'Yes, I have, Marty, thank you.' In fact Nathan couldn't believe how much he had enjoyed himself. The fairground atmosphere and the child's exuberance had somehow made him forget himself. Most surprising of all Judith Chambers had proved distinctly amiable company. The last hour had been memorable – apart that was from his hellish ride on the big wheel.

As Judith prepared him a quick meal and readied him for bed Marty chattered non-stop about his visit to the fair. He couldn't wait to tell his mates at school. In the kitchen she was just about to hand him his glass of bedtime milk when suddenly there was a tinkling sound and the light overhead went out, plunging the room into darkness, the only light coming from the hallway. The bulb had blown.

'You stay there, Marty, while I change it,' she told him. Judith had never had to change a light bulb before but couldn't imagine it was a difficult task. You just took the old one out and put a new one in. The landlord had thoughtfully provided two spare bulbs which she'd found in the pantry when she had moved in. Having fetched one, she pulled a kitchen chair underneath the light, climbed on to it and reached up to take out the bulb. It was still hot so she took off her apron to use it for protection. It then took her a moment to work out that she had to push the bulb up and twist it so it slipped out of its moorings. That done, she leaned over and put the spent bulb on the kitchen table along with her apron, then picked up the new one. She stood on tiptoe and as she grabbed hold of the socket so she could insert the new bulb, a shock of electricity shot up her arm and the next thing she knew she was lying on the floor in a dazed heap. In the distance she could hear Marty shouting at her. She tried to answer but couldn't. The next thing she knew Nathan Banks was bending over her, looking at her in concern.

'Take it easy, Miss Chambers.'

She gazed up at him, fighting to focus her blurred vision. 'What . . . How . . . Where am I?' she said, struggling to sit up.

He put his arm around her, helping her upright to sit on a kitchen chair.

'Do you feel dizzy? Anything hurt?' he asked her.

'Just a bit dazed, that's all. What happened?'

'I think you must have given yourself an electrical shock. You were changing the bulb and didn't turn off the switch. I can only think that when you took hold of the socket to put the new bulb in somehow one of your fingers went inside it and that's how you got the shock. You fell off the chair and must have passed out.'

'But how did you . . .'

'Marty fetched me. He pulled a kitchen chair over to the front door and stood on it to open it. Clever lad, aren't you, Marty?' he said, looking down at the boy, impressed.

'You ain't gonna go to heaven like Misterank's mam, are yer, Gran'ma?' Marty blurted, his bottom lip quivering.

She could see tears glistening in his eyes and felt a lump constrict her own throat. 'No, Marty, no,' she assured him. 'I've just been a silly woman, that's all. I didn't think about what I was doing. It's lucky for me you were here to

313

look after me.' And then she added as an afterthought, 'Mr Banks too.'

Marty was looking at her so worriedly, his deep concern for her very apparent, that suddenly a great rush of emotion swept through her. Her heart began to feel as if it had swelled big enough to burst and she knew without a doubt what she was feeling. This was love, pure and unmistakable. She loved her grandson with every ounce of her being. Cherry was wrong. He would come first in any competition because her grandson was the handsomest, most wonderful boy in the world. Judith held her arms wide.

'Come here, Marty,' she urged him. Without hesitation he went into her arms and she hugged him so tightly he could hardly breathe. 'I love you,' she whispered emotionally. 'I love you so much.' She then gently released him and looked up at Nathan, her face bathed in grateful smiles. 'Thank you, Mr Banks.'

Nathan was staring at them both mesmerised. As he had witnessed the touching scene between grandmother and grandson – if indeed she actually was Marty's grandmother as the true facts still eluded him – something had happened within him, something that had pierced his reserve so quickly he hadn't been able to stop it from happening. He had wanted Marty to be hugging him, showing worry for his welfare, arms encircling him in love. Nathan suddenly realised how much his life had changed since this child's arrival in it. Somehow this little boy had unlocked emotions within him he had forgotten existed. He suddenly knew he didn't want to go home to his empty flat, his own solitude, he wanted to stay here with them. Them? Both of them, not just Marty. He didn't want Marty alone to be hugging him, he also wanted this woman's love.

The realisation shook him so badly he stepped backwards. No, no, this could not be happening to him, his mind screamed. A woman had wrecked his life once and he wasn't going to allow it to happen again. They had all gone to the fair tonight like one happy family. Next he'd be asked for dinner . . . This was women's cunning, weaving their webs, snaring men before they knew what was happening to them. He had to put a stop to this here and now before he risked landing in the same situation he had before.

Judith was wondering why he had been looking at her and Marty with that strange expression on his face. A kind of longing. This man suddenly seemed vulnerable to her and it was with a sense of shock that she realised she had a sudden urge to put her arms around him too and give him a comforting hug. She mentally scolded herself. The shock she had received had affected her more than she had realised. 'I expect you'll be wanting to get home, Mr Banks.'

'Pardon? Oh, yes. Yes, I do. Look . . . er . . . my looking after Marty. It's gone on for much longer than I thought. The arrangement isn't suiting me any more. Best you find someone else as soon as possible. Good night.'

With that he spun on his heel and strode out.

Judith stood staring after him, stunned.

'Don't Misterank like me any more, Gran'ma? Why don't he like me?'

Judith couldn't answer Marty. She had no idea why

315

Nathan Banks had suddenly announced what he had. He had seemed to enjoy looking after Marty. She realised her grandson was crying then and anger exploded within her. How dare he upset Marty for seemingly no reason? 'Don't cry, sweetheart,' she said, grabbing her apron to wipe his eyes gently. 'I'm sure Mr Banks didn't mean to upset you. Get your milk and sit and drink it. Grandma won't be a minute.'

Putting her own door on the latch, she stepped across the landing and knocked loudly on the door opposite. As soon as Nathan opened it to her she blurted, 'You agreed to look after Marty, Mr Banks. If you don't want that arrangement to continue then surely you could have thought of a better way to end it? You have devastated Marty. He thinks you don't like him. He doesn't deserve this treatment. Now I have to find some way of putting things right so I hope you're proud of yourself?' She glared at him stonily. 'Mr Banks, my impressions of you are not favourable. You've always treated me in a way I find offensive and as far as I'm aware, I did nothing to warrant that. But since you've been taking care of Marty I had started to think you were mellowing, especially after that game of football the other Saturday and again at the fair tonight. I was clearly wrong to think that. You're not a nice man.'

She took a deep breath, on a roll now. She couldn't seem to stop until she had said it all. 'I used to be like you, Mr Banks, surly and offensive though I wasn't aware of it. But, thank goodness, I was made to take a long hard look at myself. I didn't like what I saw and didn't like what I knew would happen to me if I carried on the way I was. I've worked hard at changing myself. Now I'll tell you something else. My grandson, a little boy, taught me how to love – something I think might benefit you too. I don't know what made you like you are, or if you've always been like it, but I suggest you do what I did and take a long hard look at yourself. Do something about it before you find it's too late and you end up a lonely old man with no one at all to give a damn what happens to you. Marty cared very much for you and if I'm honest I was starting to as well. Be assured, neither I nor Marty will be bothering you again. Goodnight, Mr Banks.'

With that she abruptly turned and strode across the landing to disappear inside her flat, leaving Nathan staring after her, stunned.

Judith's heart was hammering painfully when she went to seek Marty. She couldn't believe all she had said to Nathan Banks, never having lost her temper before with such ferocity, but his appalling behaviour towards Marty had pushed her to it and as far as she was concerned Nathan Banks deserved every word she had said. She had no regrets. She found Marty sitting on the settee in the lounge, finishing off his milk. 'Ah, there you are,' she said, smiled tenderly at him and sat down beside him.

He drained his glass and handed it to her. 'Where did yer go, Gran'ma?'

'Oh, I just had an errand to do. I promised I wouldn't be long and I wasn't, was I?'

He shook his head. 'Is Misterank still going ter be looking after me?'

'No, Marty. Mr Banks was only helping us out while Grandma found someone else.'

His face filled with confusion. 'But I liked Misterank, Gran'ma.'

'Yes, I know you did.'

She saw his face pucker with worry. 'I won't be going back to that 'orrible lady, will I, Gran'ma?'

'Oh, no, definitely not,' she said with conviction. Thank goodness it was Saturday tomorrow, she thought, leaving her free to seek a new child-minder, something she wished she had done immediately after discovering what she had about Mrs Hackett. She now deeply regretted her decision to allow Nathan Banks to look after him. 'I'll find out where Mrs Williams lives tomorrow and I'm sure she'll be able to tell me about a very nice lady.'

Suddenly she realised that she didn't want to live in this flat any more, risk bumping into the man across the way all the time, the man who had caused her grandson so much hurt. She took Marty's hand and squeezed it tenderly. 'How would you like it if Grandma tried to find us a little house, maybe with a yard so you wouldn't have to go all the way downstairs to play in the garden? Somewhere close enough, though, so you'd still be at the same school and wouldn't lose your friends. We'll make sure your mother knows where to find us when she's finished her business and comes back to fetch you.'

He seemed to be mulling the prospect over for several long moments before finally nodding. 'I'd like that, Gran'ma.'

'Then that's settled. Grandma will get straight on to organising it. Come on,' she said, standing up and holding out her hand for him to take. 'Let's get you to bed.'

After drawing the curtains, she went across and gazed

fondly down at Marty. She was surprised to see that although his eyes were closed he wasn't facing the wall. She couldn't help herself but bent down to kiss his forehead gently. 'Good night, Marty,' she whispered as she straightened up.

'Good night, Gran'ma.' He opened his eyes and looked at her. 'Gran'ma?'

'Yes, Marty?'

'I love you.'

His unexpected admission took the breath from her body and the burst of emotion she had experienced a short while ago returned with a vengeance. Dropping down at the side of his bed, she took him in her arms and cradled him tight. 'I love you too, Marty, so much it hurts.'

After closing the door on Judith, Nathan immediately went into his lounge and poured himself out a large malt whisky. Dragging a chair over to the window, he pulled aside the curtains and sat down to stare out into the night. He took a large gulp of his drink, swallowed it down, then let out a loud anguished sigh. Judith Chambers' tirade had shocked him. It had been entirely unexpected but, regardless, she had spoken the truth. He was well aware his manner was offensive but that was to deter people from wanting closer contact with him. He thought he'd been so clever, shielding himself from possible further heartbreak, but all he'd done was to allow one woman's actions to ostracise him from everyone else. And that's how he had wanted it. He'd worked hard at keeping it that way.

Until Marty had come along.

Without Nathan himself realising it, somehow that little boy had started to turn him back into the man he had once been, before Natalie had destroyed him and he'd been consumed by mistrust. With Marty, he had somehow dropped his façade, enjoying every aspect of minding the child. The walks to and from school; the chats they had shared; playing childish games with him, and the ones of football involving the tenants downstairs, two men he'd hardly said good morning to previously and who he was now on speaking terms with. Then tonight the highly enjoyable visit to the fair – all brought about by Marty. Now those pleasurable times, and others he might have had, were over thanks to his own stupid fear of having his emotional wounds reopened. As a result he'd turned two lovely people away from him.

He suddenly felt an overwhelming sense of loss for what might have been. He gave a desolate sigh. But it was too late. He could never expect either of them to forgive him. He'd done what he'd done, there was no going back. But he suddenly realised he didn't want to be on his own, reach old age with no one to care whether he lived or died as Judith Chambers had prophesied would happen to him. He knew he'd done too much damage to save his relationship with the two people across the landing but maybe he could try to forge himself some new ones in the future. He suddenly realised he very much wanted to.

Chapter Twenty-Three

Judith looked at Cherry in concern. 'You really don't mind me and Marty coming this afternoon, only this is the fourth week in a row we've spent Saturday afternoon together? I wouldn't wish to abuse your hospitality, Cherry.'

'Stop whittling yerself, Judy. Look, I know we see each other every day at work but we don't get time for a proper chat, especially as we've been so busy just lately. Besides, if yer want the truth of it, well, now I know the real Judy Chambers I just feel sad for all the lost time we could have been friends but never got the chance to be.'

Judith smiled warmly at her. 'So do I.'

'Right, that's settled then, so give us yer coat, sit yerself down and tell me what goss yer've got while the kids are playing upstairs. Because as sure as my name is Cherry Campbell it won't be long before mayhem breaks out. Yer know what kids are like when they get together . . . narking, snitching, punching and kicking . . . and in between doing all that they're as thick as thieves doing something they shouldn't. Kettle's on the boil, it won't be long.'

Judith related to her what had transpired the previous evening while Cherry sat listening to her, riveted.

'So yer really leaving yer flat?' she asked after Judith had finished.

'Yes, and I hope the agents find us somewhere quick. I feel it's best I get Marty away from there as fast as possible so he's not constantly reminded of how Mr Banks treated him. And in all honesty I don't feel comfortable there myself any more. It's not just what has transpired between me and Mr Banks; I think my friendship with Kimberley might be over. Her mother didn't seem very happy when she saw how much older I am than her daughter, and I haven't seen Kimberley since.'

'Well, that's her loss,' said Cherry tightly.

'Mine, too, Cherry, as I really liked her. Anyway, I had a hard job getting the agents to let me out of my tenancy, still having some months to run on it, but I eventually persuaded them, saying that my circumstances had changed and I was having difficulty finding the rent at what they deem to be the better end of the market. It's true, I am finding it hard now I haven't just myself to provide for. They only have a skeleton staff in on Saturday morning and said they'd inform their rentals people of my situation first thing Monday morning, get them to let me know if they have anything suitable. I told them I could go to about five or six pounds a week at most, and of course I hope it will be furnished as I haven't the means to buy any of my own yet.'

Cherry pulled a face and before she could stop herself spat, 'No, 'cos that little bugger stole what yer had, didn't she?' She looked remorseful then. 'Sorry, Judy, I shouldn't speak about your own flesh and blood like that even if it is the truth. Well, I hope yer get something decent as it's a nice flat yer've got and you did like living there before that miserable sod opposite soured it for yer. Oh, boy, wouldn't I have loved to have been there when yer gave that awful man a rocket. I bet he was shocked?'

'I didn't wait around long enough to find out. After I'd said my piece I wanted to be away from him as fast as I could.' She stared at her friend thoughtfully. 'To be honest, Cherry, I felt sorry for Mr Banks.'

'Felt sorry for him?'

'Yes. I see in him what I used to be like, and part of me wanted to help him become a nicer person. He was good with Marty, Cherry, when all's said and done, and someone who is good with children can't be all bad, can they? What made him suddenly say he didn't want to take care of Marty any more I still can't fathom. We'd had a lovely night at the fair. I'd never been before and . . . well, I found it all quite exciting. The atmosphere kind of takes you over, doesn't it? And I'd been made to believe they were highly dubious places. Mr Banks was just so different, so unlike his normal self. It was like he'd forgotten himself, if that makes sense. I would say he enjoyed himself as much as Marty did. Still, we did agree when this situation first arose that we'd see how it went on both sides. It was working out fine on our side but apparently not on his. I just wish he'd have taken me aside and told me instead of the way he did it in front of Marty.'

Cherry was miles away in thought. 'I met my Brian at the fair,' she said, sighing wistfully. 'It was just before me fifteenth birthday and I was dressed up to the eyeballs in

323

me best friend's rock and roll skirt and top and me little white socks, me hair scraped up in a pony tail. I'd gone up there with me mates behind me mam and dad's back, and thank God they never found out 'cos they would have pasted the living daylights outta me. I first set eyes on Brian standing with a bunch of his mates by the waltzers. He looked like Marlon Brando in *On The Waterfront* and I fell in love instantly. We had a wonderful time . . . well, before I was sick from going on too many rides and having one too many hot dogs. When he walked me back to me friend's house he asked me to go to the flicks with him the following Friday night, and that was that. We were inseparable.' She gave a deep sigh. 'I'd like to think I'll meet someone else in time but I'll never love anyone as much as I loved my Brian. He was a great husband to me and such a good father to his kids, loved us all so much.' She gave another sigh then shook herself. 'Anyway, you were talking about Mr Banks acting like a kid at the fair?'

Judith had been listening to her friend reminisce about her first meeting with her husband, filled with sadness for her. It didn't seem fair that such a happy family had been so cruelly smashed apart through a freak accident, especially as at the time Brian had been trying to earn extra money to take them away on holiday. Judith most sincerely hoped Cherry met another man to equal her first love. 'Oh, let's not talk about Mr Banks, the man isn't worth discussion. I'm just bothered that my grandson is getting used to having people suddenly disappear from his life. First his mother, now Nathan Banks.'

'Kids are very resilient, Judy. My two lost the dad they idolised. I'm not saying they'll ever stop missing him but they're okay, they're getting on with life, like your Marty will. It wasn't like Mr Banks was his dad, just someone who looked after him for a couple of weeks. Anyway, I don't think Marty's mam's completely disappeared off the scene. She'll be back soon as your money runs out, you mark my words. Just you make sure she ain't expecting no more from yer.'

'I haven't got any to give her.'

'Well, you didn't exactly give it her before, did yer?'

'No.' She suddenly paused and looked at Cherry worriedly, wringing her hands. 'I have to be honest, I'm dreading Rachel coming back and taking Marty away. When she first left him with me I never thought to hear myself say that. But I've grown to love him so very much and I'm so used to having him around to look after. He makes me feel needed. My flat would seem empty without him.' She looked at Cherry searchingly. 'I was thinking about something and I'd like your opinion.'

She jumped up from her seat. 'Save it for a minute while I mash the tea, then I'm all ears.'

She came through carrying a laden tray. Having poured out the tea and offered Judith a choice between a slice of buttered shop-bought malt loaf or ginger cake her own mother had made, Cherry sat back in her chair and said, 'So what's this something you'd like my opinion on?'

Judith placed her cup down on the coffee table and clasped her hands. 'I thought I could ask Rachel to stay with me and let me help her raise Marty. She did tell me how hard she was finding it and that she wasn't getting any help from her adoptive parents, or Marty's father either.'

Cherry gawped at her. 'Are you serious? But you said you didn't like her?'

'I judged her on one meeting, Cherry, and it wasn't exactly a social event for either of us. Maybe my feelings for her will grow once I get to know her better. I want to do something for her, Cherry. This is my chance to make up for the fact I couldn't raise her myself. I do feel responsible for the fact that she hasn't had a good life as I was led to believe my child would.'

Cherry looked at her, uncertain. 'This ain't summat you should do without thinking lots about it, Judy. Anyway, she might not accept yer offer.'

'Then that's her decision but at least I'll have made it. But I can only hope she'll allow me regular contact with them both.'

'But what if she says yes to living with yer? You could be taking on more than you can handle. I mean, it ain't so long back that you hadn't a clue how ter look after yerself, let alone anyone else. You've come on leaps and bounds since yer've had Marty. I think you do a great job with him. Well, yer ain't killed him yet, have yer?' she said, laughing, before her face once again took on a serious expression. 'Having another woman about the place – and remember, she's Marty's mother and what she says about how he's raised goes – well, your ideas and hers might clash and you might find that hard ter deal with.'

She leaned forward in her chair and eyed Judith. 'Look, is this all because yer can't bear the thought of losing Marty? I can understand if it is. But you could visit, have him for weekends, take him on holiday, keep an eye on him that way. Yer don't have to resort to having yer

326

daughter live with yer, a woman you hardly know. Listen, I'm struggling to raise my two on me own now but me mam ain't asked me to go and live with her 'cos she ain't that daft. She knows we'd end up coming to blows very quickly over summat trivial 'cos she's got her way of doing things and I've got mine.'

'You're saying I'm mad even to be thinking of such a thing?'

'I think yer more than mad, I think yer've completely lost yer marbles! Look, Judy, all I'm really saying is, don't do anything rash. Why not wait until Rachel does show her face, suss things out first, then decide whether yer think it's a good idea to ask her to move in with you or not?'

Judith stared thoughtfully at her and then nodded. 'You're right, Cherry, that's what I'll do.' She smiled, eyes twinkling. 'You're very wise, aren't you?'

Cherry laughed. 'I don't know about wise exactly but I've got me uses.'

An eruption of childish squabbling rent the air and she jumped up, going over to the door leading to the hallway. At the bottom of the stairs she shouted, 'Oi, you lot, if yer gonna kill each other then go outside and do it 'cos I cleaned up this morning and I'm not in the mood for wiping up blood and guts after you tear the limbs from each other. And keep the noise down! Mr Evans next door will be having his afternoon kip and yer know what he's like if he gets woken. Now be warned, 'cos I won't tell yer again.' She came back and retook her seat, grinning broadly and shaking her head. 'Kids, who'd bleddy have 'em?' She took a sip of her tea, popped the last of a slice of ginger cake into her mouth and looked at Judith questioningly. 'What yer going to do about another minder for Marty?'

'I got one for him this morning.'

Cherry looked at her, impressed. 'God, gel, you have been busy.'

'Marty and I set off early into town so I could arrive at the agents as soon as they opened for business. Then we caught the bus straight back and while I was doing the shopping I asked Mrs Chaudri if she knew Mrs Williams' address. Luckily she did. Marty and I called on her and she was relieved to hear that I had stopped using Mrs Hackett and did know of a minder she highly recommended called Mrs Liversage. She just happens to live around the corner from me. We went to see Mrs Liversage and luckily she was at home too. Cherry, she's a really lovely young woman in her early thirties who's got two children of around Marty's age and minds a couple of others. She has room for another child as one has just left her, the family having moved away from the area. Luckily she hadn't got anyone else yet to fill the place.

'She invited us in for a cup of tea. Marty took to her children immediately and they seemed to like him. Mrs Liversage has all sorts of toys for the children to play with and in her garden there's a swing and a climbing frame. Marty was in his element. Mrs Liversage thought him a lovely boy and happily agreed to mind him even though I told her it would only be for a short while as we'll either be moving ourselves or Marty will be going back to live with his mother. She gave me the names of current people who use her and past ones should I want to check she's kosher. Her charges are two pounds a week, which is a pound a week less than Mrs Hackett charged me, and she didn't want paying a week in hand unlike Mrs Hackett. Now of course I know the reason why she insisted I do that.'

'Yes, the thieving cow,' Cherry hissed. 'If it weren't bad enough fleecing you, what she did to Marty and the other kids she's had charge of don't bear thinking about. One day she'll pick on the wrong parents and end up in hospital. I'm surprised it ain't happened before.'

'Well, she's not exactly the shy retiring sort herself and her sons seem to belong to a nasty group. Maybe most people find that a deterrent. I'm just glad I got Marty away from her and only sorry I accepted her services in the first place. I saw Mrs Hackett this morning. She pretended she hadn't seen me, although I knew she had, and I was rather glad about that as I didn't want a confrontation with her. I just want to forget it all happened, Marty too. But anyway, I'm really pleased I've secured Mrs Liversage's services and Marty is very happy about the arrangement too. Although . . . .'

'Although what?' asked Cherry.

'Well, he was very quiet first thing this morning. I just worry that despite me assuring him that it was nothing to do with him, he still feels that he did something to turn Mr Banks away from him. And deep down I think he's worrying about his mother too.' She gave a deep sigh. 'You see children playing and getting on with things and you never quite know what's going on in their little minds, do you? Whether they actually understand what you're telling them.' Her eyes became distant. 'My own parents never explained anything to me. Anything that eluded me I had to work out for myself if I hadn't read about it in my books. As a child, because my world was so restricted, I was often confused about things. Still am to this day about some matters when I wouldn't be if they'd been the kind of parents who'd talked to me. I don't want that for Marty.'

'Well, he's lucky he's got you then, ain't he? And I'm sorry to say this, but from what you've told me your own parents didn't sound the type who really wanted kids.'

Judith avoided Cherry's eyes. Her mother, she knew without a doubt, had certainly not wanted her and she had no idea if her father had or not. Regardless he certainly hadn't acted towards her in any fatherly way.

Cherry suspected she had touched a raw nerve when Judith didn't reply to her. She smiled at her encouragingly. 'Well, if you want to know 'ote about anything you can ask me, gel. I'll put yer straight as best I can.'

Judith smiled at her gratefully. 'You've put me straight on so many things already.'

'Nice ter know I'm useful.' She picked up another slice of her mother's home-made cake and took a bite. 'So, have you given any thoughts to what yer gonna wear to the staff Christmas do?'

Since Monday Judith's working companions had talked of nothing else. Notice of the venue had been posted on the staff bulletin board by Neville James' personal secretary.

'With all this going on, I haven't had time to think of much else. But I . . . we . . . I think I'll leave the firm's do

330

for you young ones to enjoy yourself at,' Judith said dismissively.

'It's a staff do, Judy. That means *all* the staff, young, middle-aged and old, including you.'

'Oh, but Christmas is a few weeks away yet.'

'Christmas maybe is but the firm's do is purposely organised for a couple of weeks before so it doesn't clash with any of the employees' other festive plans. You must have seen the notice, Judy? It's on the twelfth. Every company I've worked for, except Chambers' of course, has a Christmas knees up. It's the social event of the year for us workers. We have to start planning early so we look our best on the night. What yer got in yer wardrobe?'

'Nothing suitable, and I can't really afford anything new.'

'This ain't yer ball gown and tiara type of do, yer know, Judy. It's a disco in the function room of the working men's club around the corner from Fastway Transport. Sally will be wearing the shortest outfit she can find, and it'll be tight too 'cos she's after that young new driver that's just started; Mabel in accounts will have summat last worn by anyone else in the 1940s 'cos everything else she wears is from that period; Cynthia in sales I'm safely betting will wear a skirt and twinset 'cos I've never seen her in anything else since I've been working at Fastway; me, well, I'm wearing a black midi-skirt and white mutton-sleeved blouse. And you . . .' She looked at Judith appraisingly. 'Summat simple but classy. I think a fitted black sleeveless dress with a boat neckline to show off yer great figure which I'm sure you'll pick up in somewhere like C&A for no more than a couple of quid, three at the most, and to finish the outfit off a pair of black patent court shoes. You must have a pair of court shoes even if they ain't patent? If yer can't afford to buy a dress, Mary at work I know for a fact will be happy to run one up for you on her sewing machine if you get her the material. She's a cracking dressmaker, yer know, so she'll do yer proud. I'll have a word with her on Monday for yer. You needn't worry about a babysitter either 'cos me mam's coming here to sit with my kids and Marty can come too and sleep over.'

Judith looked at her uncomfortably. 'That's very kind of you, Cherry, but . . .'

'But what now?' She eyed her shrewdly. 'Come on, what other excuse are yer gonna throw at me for not going? 'Cos that's what yer doing, ain't it?'

'Well . . . I shall feel awkward. I've . . . well, I've never been to a dance before. I can't dance.'

Cherry gawped at her, stupefied. 'You've never been to a dance? You're having me on?'

'No, I'm not.'

'Bloody hell, Judy, you never cease to amaze me. The more you divulge about yerself, the more I realise what a miserable life you must have led. Well, that kinda life is over for you, Judy. You said goodbye to it when yer dad died and yer mam moved away. Yer might have been scared shitless at the time but yer got yer freedom and that means having some enjoyment too. I don't think you've had much before and it's about time you did.'

She leaned forward in her chair, wagging a warning finger at Judith. 'Now you listen ter me. You're going to that dance if I have ter drag yer there kicking and screaming. Be good for yer to let yer hair down. And yer never know,' she said, looking at her meaningfully, 'this might be your lucky night, the one when yer meet the man of your dreams.'

The look on Judith's face did not escape her. It was Cherry's opinion that Judith was wrong to have let what happened to her in the past sour her towards men. Since she had worked hard at changing herself a very kind, caring, thoughtful woman had emerged, a woman some man would be proud to have by his side. Judith could bring a lot of joy to someone and receive it in return. And Cherry knew just the man: Neville James. He and Judith would make a lovely couple. Neville was a childless widower who in his grief at losing his beloved wife had thrown himself into his business. It was about time he learned to live again and Cherry felt Judith was the woman to make him do it. They both needed a little nudge towards each other which Cherry herself would do her best to make sure they got.

'You look as though you're plotting something?' Judith said, looking at her searchingly.

She smiled teasingly. 'Maybe I am. Have another piece of cake.'

Chapter Twenty-Four

The following Wednesday morning Cherry approached Judith. 'Judy, how's yer workload?'

'I've just this second finished typing a pile of invoices and was going to ask the others if they wanted me to help them with anything they have.'

'Well, I need yer to do something for me as I'm snowed under at the moment with one thing and another. Can yer type these letters, please, 'cos I need to get them out urgently. They're Neville's private letters, he asked me to do them 'cos his secretary's gone home not well.' She leaned over and whispered in Judith's ear, 'He won't mind me giving them to you as I've told him how competent and trustworthy you are.'

Judith smiled at the compliment as she took the pile of correspondence to copy type. 'Of course I will. I'll have them done for you as fast as I can.'

'Thanks, Judy.' Cherry made to head back to her office then stopped. 'Oh, heard 'ote from the estate agents yet about yer move?'

She shook her head. 'No, nothing yet. I was hoping I might hear something by now but there was no letter

335

waiting for me last night when I got home. Maybe there will be today. Or maybe they haven't got anything suitable for me on their books at the moment, which I hope is not the case as I really want to get Marty away from living opposite Mr Banks as soon as I can.'

'Well, they should let yer know if they ain't 'cos there's other agents you can try. Bleddy solicitors, estate agents and their like never contact yer when they say they will. Why don't yer give them a call?'

'Yes, I suppose I could. I'll go to the telephone box during my lunch hour.'

'Yeah, and they'll be on their lunch hour too. Come through to the office and use my telephone. Neville won't mind in the circumstances.'

As Judith took a seat at her desk and picked up the telephone, Cherry said to her, 'I'll leave yer in peace to make your call and pop to the lavvy meantime.'

Several minutes later Judith was putting the phone down as Cherry returned to her office.

'What did they say?' she asked.

Judith looked at her, perplexed. 'There's a letter in the post to me apparently which should be waiting for me when I get home, but they did tell me what was in it. It seems that on revising their records of the tenancy of my flat after I said I wished to leave they found that a mistake had been made.'

'Oh? What sort of mistake?'

'That the rent should have been five pounds a week and not the eight that I have been paying for it.'

'How did they make a mistake like that?'

'I don't know, they didn't elaborate. But it seems I'll get

336

my overpayments refunded and they asked me if I wanted to reconsider my decision to leave. They also said that if I still decided I wanted to give up the tenancy, then if I was prepared to wait a short while a furnished property they felt sure would suit me is coming on to their books soon and I would get first refusal on it before they showed anyone else around.'

Cherry frowned at her, bemused. 'I pay five pound a week for my house but it ain't half as nice as your flat and you live in a much better area than I do. My house ain't furnished either. Sure you heard right, Judy?'

'I'm positive I did.'

'Bloody hell, that's a turn up for the books. Nice little bonus coming your way so unexpectedly. Should add up to quite a few quid 'cos yer've bin in the flat six months or thereabouts now, ain't yer? Just in time for Christmas too.'

She nodded. 'I have so many uses for the money. I can buy some decent presents for Marty, and something nice for your boys and you, and still have plenty left over.'

'And don't forget a dress for yerself for the firm's Christmas do.'

Judith was still working out a way she could evade that. 'Yes,' she said hurriedly.

'So are yer staying put or waiting 'til the new property comes on the agents' books?'

'I told them I'd go for the new property. Despite the flat being far more affordable for me now, I still have my reasons for leaving. I shall just have to hope that the new property is available sooner rather than later.'

'Where is this property?'

'They couldn't tell me that.'

'Why not if they know it's coming up?'

'I don't know. They couldn't tell me anything about it at all.' Judith stood up and walked around Cherry's desk. 'I'd better make a start on those letters you want doing urgently. Thank you for letting me use the telephone.'

That evening Marty chattered away on their way home after Judith had collected him from Mrs Liversage's. He had bounded up to her when she arrived and she had knelt down so they could hug each other. Looking on, Mrs Liversage had commented that it was obvious how much they loved each other and Judith herself marvelled at the way such a strong feeling could develop in the short time they'd had together. But then, according to books she had read, people had been known to fall in love instantly so maybe a few short weeks was enough to bring about the depth of feeling she and Marty shared.

'Rodney showed me how ter play Snakes and Ladders, Gran'ma,' he told her, trotting happily beside her. 'You have ter shake the dice in an egg cup and move yer counter along the board. It's ever so good. I didn't win, though, I kept going down the snakes. If you got a game of Snakes and Ladders me and you could play, Gran'ma, couldn't we?'

'Yes, we could.' That was an idea for her, she could get him some board games for Christmas. 'Let's see what Santa brings you. It isn't long now before he comes.'

Judith's mind drifted back to past Christmases spent in her parents' home. They had been very sombre, no tree or decorations, hardly any different from any other day except that she would find a present by her place at the table when she arrived down for breakfast. It had always been a book. When she had been earning she herself would hand her parents whatever she had bought them, usually toiletries. Now she knew why no celebrations had taken place in their house. Her parents had had no regard for each other so had nothing to celebrate. They never even contemplated making an effort for the sake of their child, whether she had been wanted or not.

This year was going to be different, though. This would be her first real Christmas and she could celebrate it exactly how she wanted. More importantly, Judith was going to make a great effort for Marty, doing everything for her grandson that her parents had denied her. For Rachel too if she had returned by then. Judith hurriedly quashed the hope that she wouldn't return, feeling guilty. She was after all Marty's mother and Judith's own daughter.

'Will Santa find me at your house, Gran'ma?'

She smiled down at Marty warmly. 'Don't you worry, I'll let him know.'

As they walked along he chatted away happily. 'I got a colouring book from Santa last Christmas and some pencils.'

'Oh, that's a lovely present.' It wasn't much of one by some standards, Judith thought, but at least Rachel had made the effort to buy her child something and for the first time since their meeting Judith felt kindly towards her daughter. 'Did you find it under your tree on Christmas morning?' she asked him.

'No. It was on the table. I woke Mammy up climbing out of bed and she was cross.'

Judith saw the opportunity to question him gently on his life with his mother. Maybe she could discover more about them. 'Did you sleep with Mummy on Christmas Eve then as a treat?'

He looked up at her, puzzled. 'I always slept with Mammy on the mattress on the floor, not in a bed like I got now at your house.'

'Oh, I see. What's your house like where you live with Mummy?'

'Up the stairs it is.'

'Oh, you live in a flat like Grandma has?'

He shook his head. 'No. You got lots of rooms. I got me own bedroom, ain't I, at your house, Gran'ma? We only got one room at Mammy's. Only lical it is. The paper keeps coming off the walls and Mammy has ter stick it back up with sticky stuff. The people in the other rooms made lots of noise and sometimes I couldn't get to sleep, Gran'ma. I didn't like the man downstairs. He shouted at Mammy 'cos I was crying once 'cos I'd got bellyache.'

Her heart sank. From Marty's description Rachel and he lived in a squalid bed-sitter. Her mind was made up. She would do her utmost to get Rachel to move in with her. Would do her best to make sure they got on, pander to Rachel's whims if necessary. She couldn't bear the thought of Marty returning to such a way of life when she could do something to avoid that. If she could somehow get the address where this bed-sitter was then maybe one of the other tenants would know where Rachel was or what had happened to her.

'Marty, do you know your address?' she asked him.

'I don't wear no dress, Gran'ma,' he said indignantly.

'Why d'you ask me that? I'm a boy, I am. Gels wear dresses.'

'Oh, no, sweetheart, I didn't mean that. I meant, do you know the place where you live with Mummy? It's called your address.'

'Oh.' He nodded his head. 'Down there,' he said, pointing in the direction of the town.

'Do you know where down there, Marty?'

He nodded. 'On the bus. We got two buses to come and see you, Gran'ma. Mammy let me give the pennies to the 'ductor.'

She sighed. He obviously had no idea of his actual address but then he was only five. She decided to try and find out something else. 'Marty, do you know your other name, the one that comes after Marty?'

He nodded.

'Are you going to tell Grandma what it is then, Marty?'

He nodded. 'Batty. Teacher asked me and I told her too. She said I was a good boy for telling her.'

Judith felt she was finally getting somewhere. 'You *are* a good boy, Marty. So your name is Marty Batty and Mummy's is Rachel Batty?'

He looked up at her, frowning quizzically. 'Not my mammy, Gran'ma. My mammy's name is Paula.'

She stopped abruptly, looking down at him in confusion. 'Your mummy's not called Rachel?' She stared at him, puzzled. 'Marty, that *was* your mummy that brought you to Grandma's house, wasn't it?'

He nodded.

She sighed in relief. For an instant she'd feared it hadn't been. They began walking again. Why had her daughter

341

given her a false Christian name? Had she meant to leave Marty all along and given a false name so she could not easily be traced? Was Batty the name she was going under now? Judith sighed. She would only ever find out the truth if and when Rachel or rather Paula came back for Marty. She felt she had questioned him enough for now. 'Shall we get a Christmas tree to put in the lounge, Marty? A big one. You can help me choose it.'

'Oh, really, Gran'ma?' he cried. 'Can I help yer put the pretty things on too and a fairy?'

'Yes, of course. After Santa has been on Christmas Day we'll have a big chicken for dinner. And so it's ready you and I will have a go at making a Christmas pudding this weekend.'

'Oh, goody, Gran'ma! Can I lick out the bowl?'

'Yes, of course you can.'

'Can I buy me mammy a present, Gran'ma?'

She looked down at him tenderly, wondering if he would get the opportunity to give it to her, feeling terrible for the fact that deep down she really hoped he didn't. 'I'll take you to the shops and you can buy something special then we'll wrap it up nicely and send it off to Santa ready for Mummy to open on Christmas Day.'

'Will Mammy be back soon, Gran'ma, 'cos I want to tell her about the tree and Santa and the presents?'

'I don't know, sweetheart, we can only hope she is.' Judith thought it about time this line of conversation changed or she risked getting him upset. 'Would you like a chucky egg for your tea?'

He nodded. 'And soldiers, Gran'ma?'

'Yes, and soldiers.'

They turned into their gate and after Judith had let them in through the main front door Marty ran ahead of her and up the stairs. She climbed the stairs herself, hearing voices, and as the landing came into view saw Marty talking to Mr Banks. Annoyance immediately rose in her. What audacity the man had, even looking at Marty let alone talking to him after the way he had so thoughtlessly upset him. Children it seemed had very short memories and were very forgiving. Not herself, though, not after what that man had done to her grandson.

Nathan sensed her arrival and looked over at her awkwardly. 'I was just on my way to put my rubbish in the dustbin.'

She wondered why he felt she would be interested in anything he was doing.

'Marty was . . . er . . . just telling me about the lady who looks after him now. He seems to like her very much.'

She stared at him stonily. 'He very much liked the person who looked after him before her, but at least I know Mrs Liversage won't suddenly announce without any apparent reason that she doesn't want him any more. Now if you'll excuse me, Mr Banks, I have a little boy's tea to get. Come along, Marty,' she said, turning from Nathan to open her door. Once they were both inside she immediately shut it. As she helped Marty off with his coat she wondered if she was mistaken or had she seen deep regret in Nathan Banks' eyes as she had delivered her stinging reply?

Chapter Twenty-Five

Judith wandered around the house dumbstruck. It was detached, three-bedroomed, its large lounge with French windows leading out on to a well-maintained garden. There was a separate dining room and good-sized kitchen, the house was decorated throughout to a very high standard and the furniture was all of good quality and obviously new. The smallest bedroom, which was double the size of Marty's room back at her flat, was even decorated for a young boy. It was as if the house had been custom-built for them.

She met up with Cherry in the main bedroom. 'What do you think?'

'What I think is that we're in the wrong house! Well, we've got to be, Judy.'

'That's what I was thinking. Let's go and find the agent.'

They made their way down the stairs and found Mr Braithwaite waiting for them in the lounge. 'Is it suitable for you, Madam?' he asked Judith, smiling at her encouragingly.

He reminded Judith of a retired sergeant major with his

345

large handle-bar moustache. 'It's very suitable, but there must be some mistake surely? You haven't by any chance shown me around the wrong house, Mr Braithwaite?'

He puffed out his chest indignantly. 'Madam, I can assure you, J. Jarrom and Sons, estate agents of excellent reputation, do not make mistakes.'

'Yes, they do,' piped up Cherry. 'You found you were charging Judy too much rent on her flat and knocked it down to what it should have been and gave her a rebate.'

He shuffled his feet uncomfortably. 'Yes, well, maybe one mistake,' he admitted gruffly. 'I can assure you this isn't one, though.'

Judith looked at him, mystified. 'But I can't understand it. I'm no expert as far as rental properties are concerned but the rent on this house must surely be much more than five pounds a week?'

'I pay five pound for mine and it's a dump compared to this palace. I'll move in if you don't want it, Judy,' said Cherry.

Mr Braithwaite looked at her condescendingly. 'The negotiations for this particular property are between Miss Chambers and J. Jarrom and Sons. Should you wish to apply for any property we have to let on our books then you'd need to go through the proper channels.'

Judith wondered what he meant by 'proper channels' as all she'd done when she had acquired her flat was call into the office and state her requirements; she was shown round several before she'd made her choice and been taken back to Jarrom's offices to sign the tenancy agreement and pay over her deposit. But before she could say anything he asked her, 'Would you like to look around again, Miss Chambers, before you make your decision? We can hold it for you if you'd like to take more time to decide?'

She looked at him, surprised. She hadn't received such courtesy from the assistant who had shown her around her flat. By him she had been urged to make her mind up there and then or risk losing it. 'Is there a reason why the rent is so obviously low?' Judith asked him.

'We act on behalf of the landlord, Miss Chambers, and it isn't really for us to query their instructions. The landlord instructed us to find a suitable tenant and charge five pounds a week for this property.' He could see neither Judith nor Cherry was at all happy with his answer and looked at them both for a moment before saying, 'Ladies, I maybe shouldn't divulge this information but I can see that you think that something untoward is going on. The last thing I would wish is for J. Jarrom and Sons' reputation to be tarnished.

'To the best of my knowledge the landlord bought this house for himself, his wife and young son to move into and had just had it all done out to their specifications when his employers suddenly moved him abroad for a number of years. We were instructed that it was more important to find a certain standard of tenant who would appreciate the house in exchange for a nominal rent than the sort who could afford a high rent but wouldn't care so much for the property. We immediately thought of yourself, Miss Chambers, as you've been an excellent tenant. As it so happens just when we learned this property was coming on our books, you requested a move to a house here in the same area.'

'Oh, I see,' said Judith.

'Well, that answers that then,' said Cherry. 'So, yer gonna take it?' she asked.

'Most certainly. I've no doubt Marty will love it here. He'll be so excited when I tell him. It's not far from Mrs Liversage's or his school.' And, she thought to herself, should Marty's mother decide to accept her offer to move in, then this house would provide plenty of room for the three of them.

Cherry grinned. 'Well, yer'd have been a fool to turn it down. Now I hate ter rush yer but we have to get back to work before lunchtime is over, and that waiting taxi must be costing a fortune. And remember, Judy, we want to leave sharpish tonight as we've a do on. I'll have a wander around again while you sort the business side out with Mr Braithwaite.

'Talk about lucky,' said Cherry again, looking at Judith as they rode back to work in the taxi. 'It's one of those things yer dream of happening, like suddenly finding out yer've got a large inheritance from a distant relative yer knew n'ote about just when the bailiff comes knocking.'

'I'm still having trouble believing it myself,' Judith replied.

'Well, believe it. You've signed the contract, ain't yer?'

'Yes, Mr Braithwaite had it with him. He said there was nothing else to do as they'll just transfer my bond money from the flat to the house and I will continue to pay my rent as normal. It was all so easy. And another thing, Mr Braithwaite said that there was a gardener who comes in twice a week and his money is included in the rent!'

Cherry affectionately patted her arm. 'It's about time

348

summat good happened for you, Judy. I'm pleased for yer, gel, I really am.'

'You and your boys are welcome any time,' Judith said earnestly.

'I should bleddy think so, I'm yer friend, ain't I?'

Judith smiled at her. 'Yes, you most definitely are.'

'So when are yer moving?'

'Next weekend.'

'So near Christmas? Yer must be mad.'

'Well, it's not like I've much to move, only my own and Marty's clothes, bedding, towels and a few bits and pieces. No heavy furniture to shift. I suppose it was rather presumptuous of me, but I thought as I have some holiday due to me that maybe you wouldn't mind if I took a couple of days to get Marty all settled in time for Christmas Day?'

''Course yer can have a couple of days' holiday. And yer right, what's the point in waiting? If it was my house I'd be desperate to move into it. I'll be on hand to help yer too.'

'Will you? Oh, thank you, Cherry.'

'I know a man who's got a transit van who'll do the move for yer for a couple of quid.'

'You do? Oh, Cherry, that would be just marvellous.'

'And I'll see if me mam will have the boys, including Marty, for the day which I'm sure she will, so we won't have them getting under our feet.'

'I appreciate your offer, Cherry, but the boys can't miss all the fun.'

'Moving house ain't fun, Judy.'

'Oh, this move will be. My first move into the flat was a rather frightening experience for me, but this one feels so very different. I feel . . .' She paused for thought for a moment, then her eyes shone brightly. 'Oh, Cherry, for the first time I know what excitement feels like! We are going to be very happy in our new house, I just know we are.'

Cherry looked at her. The old Judith Chambers hardly existed any more and if Cherry got her way, the new Judy Chambers was in for another kind of excitement tonight. 'So, all ready for tonight?'

Judith paled. She didn't know whether she was looking forward or not to the firm's Christmas party. She didn't know what to expect or what would be expected of her. She had no choice but to go, though, as Cherry, despite all the excuses Judith had put forward, would accept none of them.

Cherry sensed what she was feeling and patted her hand reassuringly. 'Don't you be fretting 'cos you'll be with me. Once I've got a few bevvies down yer neck you'll soon relax and get into the swing of things. We'll have yer on that dance floor kicking yer legs higher than the rest of them.'

Judith stared at her. 'Oh, but . . .'

'I'm joking, Judy.' Cherry giggled at the look her friend was giving her. 'Take that horrified expression off yer face and calm down. We're having a night out, that's all, so stop worrying. Oh, here we are. Pay the man quick and let's get cracking 'cos if we've all our work done Neville might let us off early. In fact, I know he'll let us off even if we haven't finished our work, 'cos he's a bloody good boss is our Nev. Eh,' she said, giving Judith a nudge in her ribs, 'he's a really nice man, yer know. Mek someone a lovely husband.'

Chapter Twenty-Six

At seven-thirty that evening Judith appraised herself in her wardrobe mirror. Staring back at her was a very attractive woman who in early January would turn forty-four. She was wearing a black sleeveless scooped-neck dress, black stockings and low-heeled black court shoes. A single row of inexpensive imitation pearls hung around her neck. Her face, which was only just beginning to show signs of ageing, wore a light application of tastefully applied makeup and her dark brown chin-length hair was sleek and smooth. The overall effect quite took Judith aback. She was used to seeing a more businesslike reflection; this one looked softer and more feminine. She felt very vain to be thinking it, but she really did look nice.

Having resigned herself to the fact that she was not going to be allowed to dodge the dance, and having far more important uses for the windfall on the rental of her flat than buying dresses ready-made, she had not stopped Cherry approaching Mary on her behalf to make her a dress. Mary had done her proud and for the small amount the material had cost, plus a zip and bias binding, had produced a garment worthy of sale in a high-class ladies' outfitters. Neither would she accept any payment for her labour. She did things willingly for friends and wouldn't dream of charging them. Judith was very touched, not just by her generosity but more by her inclusion of Judith amongst those friends. Despite her reluctance to attend the do, Judith did know for certain that her presence would be welcomed by all the other partygoers and the reassurance this gave her meant so much to her. She already knew what it felt like to be a social outcast; now she knew the joy that the total opposite brought and without a doubt which she preferred.

It was time for her to leave. She had ordered a taxi to take her to the venue and it would be arriving any minute now to pick her up. It struck Judith that this was the second taxi she had taken today and despite both being necessary this method of transport must not become a habit or she'd not have the means to fund the kind of Christmas she intended for Marty or their move to the new house. Closing the wardrobe door, she gathered up her handbag and walked into the hall to collect her coat.

She suddenly stood stock still. The flat seemed strangely quiet and empty without Marty there. She felt a lump form in her throat at the thought that as he was over at Cherry's house being looked after by her mother, Judith herself would not be able to tuck him into bed tonight or kiss him goodnight. She suddenly missed him dreadfully; tomorrow morning when she'd journey over to collect him seemed so far away. She mentally scolded herself. She was being selfish. Marty would be having fun with his friends Richie and Duggie and this little adventure, spending the night away from home, would be good for him.

Checking she had her keys in her handbag, she opened the door and let herself out. Just as she shut it, the door to the flat opposite opened and Nathan Banks emerged carrying a milk bottle.

They looked at one another, startled for a moment, before Nathan said, 'Er . . . good evening, Miss Chambers.'

His tone of voice was pleasant and this took her by surprise. Nevertheless she responded coolly, 'Mr Banks.' She didn't wish him good evening because she didn't care whether he had a good one or not.

Nathan flashed a hurried look at her. As he did so his face clouded over in an expression Judith couldn't quite decipher. He brought his eyes back to meet hers. 'You're . . . er . . . going out.'

She didn't know whether this was a question or a statement but the memory of his recent upsetting of her grandson was still very fresh inside Judith, she was still deeply wounded on Marty's behalf, and could not help but respond sharply. 'Is going out against my tenancy agreement, Mr Banks?'

'No, of course not. I just . . .'

'Oh, I see,' she interjected. 'You think I've left Marty inside the flat to fend for himself while I go off socialising and now you're going to tell me you'll report me to the authorities. Well, let me save you the bother, Mr Banks. He's over at a friend's house being more than adequately cared for.' Just then a car horn sounded. 'That's my taxi. I

353

expect you'll be pleased to excuse me.' She made to walk off then paused and turned back to face him. 'I have some good news for you, Mr Banks. Marty and I will be vacating our flat a week tomorrow. I do hope for your sake that the next tenant who moves in will meet your high expectations. Good evening.'

With that she walked off, leaving him staring after her.

The Fastway Transport Christmas party was in full swing when Judith arrived. Despite her work colleagues and Cherry herself talking of little else for the last few weeks, Judith still hadn't quite known what to expect from the picture they had painted between them. She certainly hadn't realised the jovial atmosphere would engulf her as soon as she hesitantly pushed open one of the doors leading into the function room. Pop music from the discotheque over in the far corner was blaring out too, and it all overwhelmed her. She was about to make a hasty retreat when Mary spotted her and came over to greet her, slipping her arm through Judith's and looking at her admiringly.

'My God, gel, don't you look the business in my creation? If I say it meself, I've missed me calling. We've saved you a seat at our table and I'm dying for me husband to meet you. Mind you, on second thoughts, I've changed me mind now I see what yer look like tonight. My old man might want to run off with yer,' she said, laughing.

Mary looked lovely herself in a straight black skirt and sleeveless gold lamé top and when Judith sincerely reciprocated her compliment she beamed in delight. They made their way through the throng, acknowledging greetings from others as they proceeded to their table which apart from a couple of spare chairs was crowded out with staff from the general office plus several accompanying husbands and boyfriends.

Cherry's face lit up and she waved wildly at Judith, patting the vacant seat beside her. 'Over here, Judy,' she shouted above the noise. 'You look . . . well, just lovely,' she commented as her friend inched her way around to occupy the seat. 'Just like one of them models in the *Vogue* magazine I look through in the doctor's waiting room. I never asked what you drink so I took it upon meself to get you a vodka and lime same as me. Knock it back, gel, 'cos we're just about to go to the bar for another.'

Judith looked doubtfully at it. Then, after telling Cherry she looked very fetching in her outfit, which she most certainly did, asked her: 'Was Marty all right when you left?'

'He was fine. All the kids were causing me mam a headache, running her ragged. Only joking . . . she was reading them a story. Anyway, forget about kids tonight, we're having a well-deserved night out. Oh, cooeee, Mr James,' she said, suddenly spotting him and beckoning him over. 'Hotch up, gels, and let the boss sit down.'

'Good evening, ladies and gentlemen,' he said, glancing around at them all. 'Has everyone got a drink?'

'We ain't if the boss is treating us,' piped up Cherry, at which they all laughed.

He summoned over a waitress. 'Take everyone's order, please,' he instructed her. 'And give me the bill. Oh, and

I'll have a pint of best bitter.' He sat down in between Mary's husband and Sally, and after a quick comment to the girl turned his attention to Mary's husband and got into conversation with him.

'He's a nice man, yer know, Judy,' Cherry whispered to her. 'A few here I know would snap him up given the nod from him, but I reckon he's saving himself for someone special.'

'Like who?' asked Judith.

Cherry gave her a secretive wink. 'Well, I'm not sure he knows himself yet – but if I have my way he will before the night's out, and so will she.'

Judith looked at her, puzzled, wondering what she meant but before she could probe Cherry clapped her hands in delight as a record started playing. 'Oh, it's the Stones, "Brown Sugar", one of me favourites. Let's dance, Judy,' she said, jumping up from her seat.

'Oh, I . . . er . . . think I'll sit this one out.' When Cherry seemed to be about to argue she insisted, 'I've only just arrived, let me at least catch my breath.'

'I'll dance with yer, Cherry,' said Sally, noticing the new driver she had her eye on standing with a group of others, supping on their pints at the edge of the dance floor, watching the dancers.

Cherry glanced her up and down. 'Yeah, well, pull yer skirt down first 'cos I ain't being seen dead with you on the dance floor showing yer knickers.'

Sally flashed her a look of derision. 'No, I ain't showing me knickers. You're just jealous, Cherry Campbell, 'cos you ain't got such good legs as me,' she said cockily, standing up to show them off.

All the table laughed.

Cherry laughed too. 'Wait 'til you've had a couple of kids then you'll have varicose veins too. Come on then, let's go if we're going else the record will be over.'

Several other women rose to join them too.

Neville, seeing Judith had been left on her own, excused himself from Mary's husband and moved over to sit next to her. 'Not dancing with the others, Judy?' he said loudly over the din.

She shook her head. 'I'm not much of a dancer, I'm afraid, Mr James.'

'Oh, I'm Neville tonight, Judy, we're not in the office now. I don't mind the slow dances myself but I leave all this jigging about to the youngsters.' His attention was caught by the arrival of the waitress with their tray of drinks. After helping her sort out whose was whose he paid the bill then turned his attention back to Judith. 'You've proved yourself a very welcome addition to our workforce, Judy. I have to say, I wasn't sure at first that you would. Whenever I enquired of Cherry how you were getting on during the first few months after you arrived she was very non-committal and I had the feeling that things weren't right, but now she positively sings your praises. I do realise, though, that it takes some employees longer to settle in than others. You are happy with us, aren't you, Judy?'

'Oh, very much so . . . Neville.'

'Good, I'm glad to hear it. I like to know that the people who work for me enjoy their jobs.'

'It's made all the more enjoyable because Cherry is a first-class supervisor.'

He looked at her searchingly. 'Of course, I've realised now why your name was familiar when I first met you. It must have been rather a surprise on your first day at Fastway, discovering your supervisor was an ex-employee you'd previously supervised yourself?'

'Yes, it was rather,' she said evasively, remembering back to the first day and Cherry's reception of her, and marvelling at the way their relationship had changed so drastically in the intervening weeks. 'But our reversal of roles didn't pose any problem, I'm glad to say.'

'Obviously not as I understand from Cherry that you've both become good friends. You know, Judy, you might not see much of me around the office – too busy keeping the company afloat, taking care of our customers and bringing in new business – but I still find time to take an interest in what goes on through talking to my senior staff.'

She thought that very commendable in him, thinking it was a pity her own father hadn't had the foresight to get to know his staff and then maybe his distorted view of life might have changed significantly.

'Yes, Cherry and I are good friends. Her presence in my life has greatly enhanced it, Neville. I don't think she's even aware how wise and compassionate she is. In fact, she's just an all-round lovely lady and I am very honoured she sees fit to include me in her circle of friends.'

He looked at Judith for several long moments, seeming to be digesting what she had just said, then turned his attention to the group of dancers, Cherry amongst them. By the look on his face it appeared to Judith that Neville James was seeing his general office supervisor for the very first time. After what seemed an age he seemed to give himself a mental shake and bring his attention back to Judith. 'You . . . er . . . haven't touched your drinks,' he commented, looking at the two short tumblers of untouched vodka and lime on the table before her.

She looked down at them. 'No.' She picked one up tentatively and took a hesitant sip, pulling a face as the sharp sting from the spirit hit the back of her throat.

He smiled. 'Not quite to your taste, I take it? Let me get you something else. Rum and black, schooner of sherry, barley wine? What's your fancy, Judy?'

'Would you mind if I had a glass of cordial?'

'Judy, it's a Christmas party. You can have whatever you want and it will be my pleasure to get it for you.' He rose to his feet. 'I'll instruct the waitress to bring it across for you. And you will excuse me, won't you, but I'd better mingle with the other staff.'

She smiled warmly at him. Cherry was right, Neville James really was a very nice man. She felt it was a real pity that his wife had died so young and left him alone.

Just then Cherry, accompanied by several of the other women, came back. She resumed her seat next to Judith and picked up her drink. Taking a gulp of it, she looked at Judith enquiringly. 'You and Neville seemed cosy. Getting on well, were you?'

'We had a chat, Cherry, I'd hardly class that as getting cosy.'

'Ah, well, the night is still young.' She looked bemused as the waitress arrived with Judith's glass of orange cordial and gave it to her. 'And what the bleddy hell is that yer drinking?'

'Please don't be offended, Cherry, but vodka and lime really isn't to my taste.'

'Oh, well, it is mine. I'll have 'em,' she said, moving the glasses in front of her.

The next couple of hours passed very pleasantly for Judith who delighted in the good-humoured banter passing between the occupants of the table and took great pleasure in watching the dancers enjoy themselves. She felt no inclination to get up on the dance floor herself, grateful she was managing to fob Cherry off with constant excuses to sit them out. Dancing was not for her, she preferred to listen to the music. In their individual ways a good time was being had by all, Judith included.

Towards the end of the evening the pace of the music slowed to what Cherry termed 'the smoochies' and she danced to a couple with male employees who asked her. She arrived back at the table, flushed with drink and pure enjoyment of the evening. 'Phew! I need a seat, 'cos me feet are killing me.' She looked at Judith as she rested one leg across her other knee, taking off her shoe and rubbing her foot. 'You sure yer having a good time? Only you ain't danced at all and neither have yer had a proper drink.'

'I'm having a wonderful time, Cherry, thank you,' Judith said sincerely. 'I'm what you would call a natural observer rather than a participant.'

Cherry looked at her meaningfully. 'Well, that might be the case but I intend for you to have at least one dance before the end of the evening.' She turned and scanned her eyes through the crowd, spotted the man she was looking for, put her shoe back on and stood up. 'Don't go away,' she ordered.

360

Wondering what she was up to, Judith watched her weave her way through the crowds and approach Neville James. Cherry stood and chatted to him for a moment then hooked her arm through his and guided him back over to their table. 'Come on, Judy,' she ordered. 'Nev wants the pleasure of this dance, but he's too shy to ask yer himself, ain't yer, Nev?'

He smiled at Judith and nodded. 'Be a great pleasure, Judy, if you'd have this dance with me?'

Embarrassment flooded through her. It was very apparent to her that Cherry had cajoled Neville into asking her to dance. But then she noticed something else. He was no longer looking at her but at Cherry, and to Judith, albeit she was very inexperienced in such matters, it was readily apparent who Neville would sooner be dancing with. But that glaring fact had obviously escaped Cherry herself. Well, who was Judith to monopolise the company of a man who wished to be with someone else?

She did no more than grab her handbag and stand up. As she inched her way around the table to join them, she said, 'Please don't be offended, Neville, I'm very honoured by your offer but I've developed such a terrible headache that I'm going to make my way home. I'm sure Cherry won't mind taking my place on the dance floor with you.' Before her friend could respond Judith turned and addressed her friends sitting around the table. 'I've had a lovely evening, thank you all so much. Please say goodbye for me to all those up dancing, at the bar or wherever. I'll see you all at work on Monday.' She turned her attention back to Cherry and smiled warmly at her.

'I'll see you in the morning when I come to collect Marty. Goodnight to you too, Neville.'

For a mid-December evening it was quite mild. As Judith stepped into the street she immediately decided to walk back to her flat. The person who had turned it into a home was not there. Had he been, she would have felt an overwhelming desire to rush back to be with him, but as things stood she was in no hurry to return. She couldn't wait for the morning when she would have Marty back with her. This short time away from him had shown her just how much he had come to mean to her. She was unable now to visualise her life without him in it and marvelled how it was possible to love a child so completely when she hadn't actually given birth to him herself. In order to secure Marty what she felt positive would be a better way of life she had grown used to the idea that she must somehow forge a relationship with his mother, and wondered now if feelings of such a nature would develop in her for her daughter should Rachel ever give her the chance. She hoped so. She knew she owed it to her daughter at least to try her best. Her adoptive parents had obviously failed her badly and this was Judith's chance to make it up to her in the best way she knew how. She felt positive that Rachel would be receptive to her offer, knowing now how much of a struggle to raise Marty she'd actually had. At least her daughter had not had her son adopted at birth, had tried to raise him. Judith felt she had to give her credit for that, feeling sure that despite their own bad start there must be depths to Rachel she had yet to discover.

Arriving outside her door, she was just inserting the key in the lock when she heard the door opposite open and automatically turned around and saw Nathan coming out. He looked awkwardly at her, then brought her attention to the milk bottle in his hand by holding it up. 'I'm . . . er . . . just putting my bottle out.'

But hadn't he been doing that earlier when she had been leaving her flat? He had either drunk a lot of milk or it was the same bottle.

'You got back safely then?' he said to her. 'Have a nice night, did you?'

Whatever her night had been like it was none of his business. She couldn't understand why he was suddenly so interested in what she did. 'Yes, thank you,' she responded dismissively. She pushed open her door and walked into the flat, wondering why he was looking at her so strangely.

'Er . . . Miss Chambers?'

She stared back at him blankly.

'Er . . . it's nothing. Good night.' He about turned and disappeared inside his own flat.

She closed her door, wondering what it was he could possibly have wanted to speak to her about. As far as Judith was concerned they had nothing to say to each other. Then it struck her. She had obviously done something in violation of her tenancy agreement. What it was she couldn't think, but it was obviously something big enough for Mr Banks to feel he needed to bring it to her attention. Though why he had suddenly changed his mind was a mystery. She pitied the poor tenant who was moving in after her and thanked goodness that within a week she would be rid of her surly neighbour once and for all.

Chapter Twenty-Seven

Judith was up early the next morning, unable to sleep any longer, desperate to have Marty back beside her. At nine o'clock precisely she knocked on the back door of Cherry's house. Her dishevelled-looking friend, still dressed in her night clothes, opened it to her. 'Good God, Judy, I didn't expect yer this early. What's up, couldn't you sleep or something, or are yer that desperate to get yer grandson back?' she said, giving a yawn and standing aside to allow Judith entry.

'Well, actually I have missed him,' she said, walking inside. 'I'm sorry if I've called too early . . .'

'Oh, stop whittling, Judy. Just put the kettle on and mash me a cuppa. And for God's sake, don't let Marty know yer here yet or they'll all be down demanding. Me head feels like a bulldozer is rampaging through it and me mouth's like Skegness beach. I can't face any kids 'til I've had a cuppa.'

Judith looked at her in concern. 'Oh, I see, a hangover, have you?'

'No, alcohol had nothing to do with why I spent half the night down here drinking tea, and the rest tossing and turning.'

'Oh, the children . . .'

'The children were fine, all of them. They were snoring their heads off when I got in and so was me mother on the settee. She was a right crabby old bugger when I woke her up to send her home.'

'And that's what upset you?'

'No.'

'Did any of the children wake up in the night and cause you bother then?'

'No. They woke about half an hour ago and they're still in bed playing some game or other. I've told 'em to stay there 'til I get me head sorted. If yer wanna know what's bothering me, it was summat you did.'

'Me?' she said aghast, mind racing, trying to think what it could possibly be. 'Whatever it is, I'm so sorry, Cherry. Please believe me, I am.'

Cherry grinned at her. 'Well, I ain't.' She grinned even more broadly at the confused look Judith gave her. 'Just put the kettle on, mash me that cuppa and I'll tell you what you've been the cause of,' she said, rubbing her aching head.

Judith had never willed a kettle to boil so fast in all her life. Finally the tea was made and she sat down opposite Cherry at the kitchen table and looked expectantly at her. 'I'll pour out your tea as soon as it's mashed. Now will you please put me out of my misery?'

Cherry took a deep breath, leaned her arms on the table and looked at Judith intently. 'You made a quick exit when Neville asked yer to dance with him and you also talked about me to him, didn't you?'

Judith looked at her guiltily. 'Yes, I did both of those

things. I felt you'd somehow pushed Neville into dancing with me and was embarrassed for him. I really was ready to go home, though, I wasn't making that up. And, yes, I did say to him that I thought you were a lovely lady with special qualities. But I was just being honest and paying you a compliment. Why? Has what I did or said to Neville caused you a problem? I can't see how it possibly could have.'

'Well, I couldn't leave the bloke standing there looking like an idiot after you'd turned him down in front of all the staff so I offered ter dance with him meself. Well, one dance led to another, then he asked if I'd like a drink, and we sat chatting about this and that to start. Then I found I was telling him all about meself and the kids, and he was telling me all about himself and his wife, and we both understood exactly how it felt to have someone you love so much die and leave you feeling like yer life has ended. By this time quite a few people had followed your lead and gone home and the place wasn't so rowdy. Next thing I knew the staff were kicking us both out as we were the last ones there and neither of us had noticed! But it was strange 'cos I found I was really disappointed. I didn't want the night to end. I'd never talked to Nev personally before, only stuff to do with work, and suddenly I started to see him as a man and not as me boss.

'I've always thought him lovely, though not in that way 'cos you know how much I loved my Brian. I never thought another bloke would interest me, let alone me boss and a man who's a few years older than me, so I was quite shocked by what I was feeling. To be honest it was my intention to try and get you two together last night, I never thought for a minute me plan would backfire and I'd end up with him. It's all your fault 'cos if you'd have just had that dance with him maybe us getting together would never have happened. And if you hadn't said to him what you did about me, he might not have started looking at me in a different light, seen more to me than just one of his employees. Then he might not have asked me to have a drink and a chat with him after we'd stopped dancing.

'Judy, this might sound stupid to you . . . after all, we only spent a few hours together last night . . . but yer know when you realise something special is happening? Well, that's how it was between me and Nev, and I know he felt it too 'cos he told me so.' She smiled warmly at her friend. 'Me and Nev have such a lot to thank you for, Judy, whether yer realised what you were doing or not. That's why I couldn't sleep last night, I'd all this on me mind.'

Judith was staring at her, stunned. 'I'm not surprised you couldn't! Oh, Cherry, I'm so happy for you. I can't tell you how much. I'm just so glad I never accepted that dance and that I told Neville my feelings about you.'

'Yeah, I am too.'

'So what happens now?'

Cherry's face lit up excitedly. 'I'm seeing him tonight. He's taking me for a meal. I want to keep this quiet for the time being, though, Judy, you're the only one I'm going to tell. Neville and I both agreed it's best to let our relationship get off the ground before we allow the gossips to have a field day. When I asked me mam to baby-sit again tonight I told her I was coming over to you for a girlie night. I hope you don't mind? If I'd told her the truth she'd be planning the wedding already. I know I fibbed but it's best for now, believe me.'

'No, I don't mind at all. Covering for you is the least I can do in the circumstances. Oh, I know I'm repeating myself but I *am* so happy for you, Cherry.'

'Yeah, well, it's made me realise that sometimes yer just don't know what's staring yer in the face. I only wish you could meet someone, Judy. Someone who makes yer feel just like Neville does me. You would make someone so happy, I know yer would.' She suddenly stared at her thoughtfully. 'You know, it's not just you that I need to thank for all this, it's Marty too. In fact, he's really the one responsible for this happy outcome. If you hadn't pleaded for yer job 'cos you needed it to look after him, then we wouldn't have become friends. And if that hadn't happened I wouldn't have tried to get you and Neville together which ended up like it did.'

Just then a face appeared around the doorway. It lit up on spotting Judith. 'Gran'ma!' Marty shouted in glee, rushing over to her to jump on her knee and give her a hug.

'Hello, sweetie. Oh, how I've missed you,' she said, hugging him back tightly and kissing his cheek.

'I've missed you too, Gran'ma. But I did enjoy meself here, so can I come again?'

Judith's arms tightened around him. She knew without doubt she did make someone happy, this little man in her arms. No one else could ever make her feel so loved and needed as Marty did. Cherry was right: he was responsible for so much. She couldn't believe now how much she had resented him when she had first been left with him to care for.

''Course yer can come again, darlin',' Cherry said to him. 'You've bin an absolute treasure.'

Judith lifted him off her knee and stood him on the floor. 'Right, let's get you home because we've some packing to start doing ready for moving to our new home, haven't we, and I can't manage it all without you to help me.'

He grabbed her hand, pulling her towards the back door. 'Come on then, Gran'ma, let's go.'

'I think you'd better get dressed first, Marty,' she said, laughing.

Chapter Twenty-Eight

A harassed-looking Helen Liversage stared at Judith when she opened the door to her the following Monday evening. 'Oh, Miss Chambers. Marty isn't with you then? I was so hoping he was . . .'

'But of course he isn't with me, Mrs Liversage, I've just come from work to collect him.' To Judith's horror she saw Helen Liversage's face turn ashen, and panic flooded through her. 'Where is Marty, Mrs Liversage?' she demanded.

She looked at Judith helplessly. 'If he's not with you, Miss Chambers, then I don't know. He never came home with the others from school. They all met at the school gates like they always do to walk home together. They know how strict I am about them doing that, I remind them every morning before they leave and today was no exception. But Marty didn't show up tonight. The others waited a while but when he still didn't show, thought he'd come home ahead of them. When they all trooped in and I realised Marty wasn't with them I immediately ran down to the school to look for him, thinking he was still there for some reason. By the time I got there all the teachers had gone home and the caretaker told me they always check that all the children have gone before they themselves leave. So I ran home again, thinking that maybe he had lagged behind at school and missed the other children and was at home with them by now. I was frantic to find he wasn't.'

'But where could he be, Mrs Liversage?' Judith asked, panic in her voice. 'Has he any friends he might have gone to play with?'

'We've checked all around the ones he might have gone with and none of them has seen Marty since leaving school. Peter Bain said he saw him walking out of the cloakroom with Geoffrey Plant.'

'And what did Geoffrey say?'

'He's the only one we haven't been able to check with yet. I know the Plant family very well, they only live a couple of doors down. I know Geoffrey's mother was collecting him from school today as she was taking him straight over to visit his grandmother. It's her birthday today. I've been watching out for her to come back, which should be any time now as her husband will be home from work shortly and he'll be wanting his dinner.'

Judith's heart was pumping painfully. Where could Marty possibly be?

'It's just a thought, Miss Chambers, but do you think he might have gone home for some reason?' Helen asked her.

She shook her head. 'As you said yourself, Marty knows to come straight here with the other children.' A memory of what had happened once at Mrs Hackett's struck her. 'Unless he was upset?'

372

'Not that I know of. He was his usual happy self when I sent him off to school this morning. In fact, he was chatting to me excitedly about your move to your new house and telling me about the Christmas tree he was going to help decorate. I said we could make some gingerbread men to hang on it when he came home from school and he was looking forward to helping me. Look, Miss Chambers, why don't you go and check to see if for some reason he has gone straight home? Maybe Marty was just over-excited about your move or maybe something happened at school that upset him. Either way, he could have lost himself in his own little world like children often do and now he's there waiting for you. I just feel bad I never thought to check before.'

Judith looked at her hopefully. 'Oh, I do so hope he is. I'll go now, and come straight back and let you know he's safe.'

'The more I think about it, the more I think that's what's happened. But I'll still keep an eye out for Mrs Plant just on the outside chance he's not waiting for you there and Geoffrey knows where he's gone.'

Judith kicked up her heels and ran as fast as she could all the way home, her mind so filled with finding Marty that she did not realise she narrowly missed being hit by a car as she blindly raced across a busy road. Arriving at the house, she hurriedly let herself in at the front door and bounded up the stairs, calling out Marty's name as she did so. Arriving at the top of the stairs she rushed towards her flat but knew before she arrived that Marty was not waiting for her. There was no sign of him. Her hands flew up to her face, her mind screaming silently:

Marty, Marty, where are you? Her eyes fell on the door opposite and she stared at it wildly. Was he with Mr Banks? Had he come straight home from school like Helen Liversage had suggested and Nathan Banks had found him and taken him inside until Judith came home as he had done before?

Without another thought she hammered loudly on the door. It took seconds for it to be opened, seconds which to Judith seemed like hours.

Nathan was most surprised to see who was summoning him. 'Miss Chambers . . .'

'Marty! Is he with you?' she demanded frenziedly.

He shook his head. 'No. Why do you think he would be?'

'He's . . . you were my last hope. Oh, God, he's gone missing.'

'What do you mean, gone missing?'

'He never turned up at the child-minder's after school this afternoon and no one knows where he is.'

'Look, calm down, Miss Chambers. I'm sure . . .'

'Don't tell me to calm down!' she cried, staring at him as though he was stupid. 'My grandson is out there somewhere and I don't know where he is. Anything could have happened to him.'

Nathan immediately disappeared inside his flat and unhooked his coat from the stand just inside the door. 'He must be somewhere,' he said, coming back out to join her, pulling on his coat. 'I'll come and help you look.'

Just then the sound of the front door opening and feet pounding up the stairs reached their ears and they both turned to see Helen Liversage arriving on the landing, panting heavily. 'Oh, Miss Chambers,' she said breathlessly, 'just after you left, Mrs Plant came back with Geoffrey.'

A surge of hope flooded through Judith. 'And they have news of Marty's whereabouts?' she cried.

'Well . . . news of sorts. It seems that Marty went to the school gates with Geoffrey, for him to meet his mother and for Marty to wait for the others to walk home with them. Geoffrey was excited about going to his granny's and Marty couldn't wait to get home to help me make the gingerbread men so they were both among the first to come out. As the boys split up at the gate, Marty to wait for the others and Geoffrey to go and join his mother, Mrs Plant says she noticed a woman approaching Marty. They seemed to talk for a second or two, then she took his hand and they walked off together. Mrs Plant said she didn't think anything of it because Marty seemed to know the woman. She said as she was making her way to her mother's she saw the woman and Marty standing at the bus stop.'

'A woman! He went off with a woman?' Judith cried. Then the awful truth struck, her face paled alarmingly and she visibly shook. 'Mrs Liversage, did Mrs Plant describe this woman?' she demanded, hoping vehemently it wasn't who she thought it was.

She gave a shrug. 'Only that she was a young, hefty-looking woman who didn't look very wholesome, to use Mrs Plant's expression. Do you know her, Miss Chambers, or should we get the police?'

Judith thought she was going to faint. 'I know her,' she uttered. 'It's all right, Mrs Liversage. I know who Marty is with.'

She sighed with relief. 'Oh, thank goodness. For a minute I thought the little lad had been kidnapped. Thank God your mind's been put at rest. I must get back to my children, I've left them in the care of Mrs Plant. I'll see you in the morning. Good night, Miss Chambers,' she said, spinning on her heel and rushing off.

As Nathan turned his attention back to Judith it was very apparent to him that the news Mrs Liversage had delivered had greatly added to her distress. He took her arm. 'I'm not sure what's going on here, Miss Chambers, but it's obvious you've had a terrible shock.' Her face was like death and she was physically shaking. 'Please come inside and sit down for a minute. I'll get you a drink.'

She fought with all her might to pull herself together. 'I'm fine,' she said, just a little too brightly for his liking. 'I need to get home.'

'You're not fine,' he said firmly. 'Now you'll do as you are told. Come inside and let me get you that drink.'

Judith's world had come crashing down around her. Rachel, Paula, or whatever she called herself, had taken her son away without telling Judith, letting her know where they were going or even giving her a chance to put her proposal. Never had it crossed her mind that Marty's mother would do something like this. Where she had been and what she had been doing since she had abandoned her son wasn't a factor, but worry that Judith would never see her beloved grandson again was. Consumed by grief at the suddenness of it all, she had no further energy to protest. The next she knew she was sitting on Nathan's settee and he was thrusting a tumbler into her hand, ordering her to drink whatever was in it which she did without thinking, coughing and spluttering as the sharp, bitter-tasting liquid hit the back of her throat.

He took the glass from her, refreshed it and handed it back to her then sat down beside her. 'Do you feel any better?' he asked in concern.

Judith looked at him wildly. 'Better?' And before she could stop herself she blurted out hysterically, 'My grandson has just been taken away from me! I don't know if I'll ever see him again, and you ask if I feel better?'

He stared at her, startled. Something was going on here that he could not fathom. 'But this woman Mrs Liversage said her neighbour saw Marty with will surely bring him back? You said you knew her. She must have had your consent?'

Judith's hands shook so hard he saw she was in danger of spilling her drink. He took the tumbler from her and put it on the coffee table. 'If she didn't have your consent then she had no right . . .'

'She had every right,' Judith exploded. 'She's Marty's mother.'

'His mother? But then, I don't understand. Why are you so worried? I mean, if he's with his mother, you'll know he's safe and that you can go and see them. You did say you were only looking after him for a short time until his mother came back for him.'

A great well of tears suddenly overflowed to gush down her face. 'But I don't know where they live!' she sobbed. 'I don't know anything about them.'

Nathan scratched his head, this situation completely confusing him. 'But how come? She's his mother, he's your grandson, therefore she must be your daughter . . .'

Judith was too distraught to realise what she was saying or to whom. 'A daughter I knew nothing about from the minute she was taken from me just after she was born until the night she appeared on my doorstep twenty-three years later, announcing who she was and introducing my grandson to me. She asked if they could stay the night. I got up the next morning to find she had gone, leaving no word of where she was going or for how long, but not before she had stolen all my money from me and left her son behind. I can't tell you how I felt, not just about her stealing from me but because I'd never looked after a child before. I didn't know the child, he didn't know me.' Her voice suddenly faltered and a fresh flood of tears cascaded down her face. 'But I grew to love him so much. I feel he's part of me, and he loves me too. I can't bear the thought . . .'

Judith suddenly realised where she was and just who she was talking to. Pulling a handkerchief out of her coat pocket, she hurriedly wiped her face. 'Well, now you know I was an unmarried mother, Mr Banks, and I don't care what you think of me. Anyway, I already know what you think of me and Marty. You've made it very plain you dislike both of us intensely.'

She made to jump up, feeling an overwhelming desire to get away from him, but he grabbed her arm, his face wreathed in annoyance. 'Don't assume you know what I think of you and Marty, Miss Chambers. If I'd disliked you both that much I would never have done what I did to make sure you stayed put in the flat or else moved to a comfortable house, so either way I at least knew where you both were.'

She looked at him, stunned. 'What do you mean?'

He looked back at her, horrified, realising what he'd just revealed. 'I . . . I didn't mean anything by it.'

'Yes, you did. Explain yourself, Mr Banks?' Momentarily all thoughts of her distress over Marty were forgotten, overtaken by confusion that this man was involved somehow with the house she and Marty had been planning to move into. But why would he be? In what way could he be?

He was staring at her stupefied, then suddenly an all-consuming need for her to know his feelings for her and her grandson filled him. He had nothing more to lose anyway, he'd lost them both already, but at least she would know the truth and this might be the only opportunity he'd ever have of telling her.

'You've both come to mean so much to me, Miss Chambers.' He looked at her intently and said without hesitation, 'I love you. It hit me like a bolt from the blue on the night of the fair and your accident. I was terrified witless by the strong feelings I had for you. I can see by your face that I've greatly shocked you. I've always acted so stiffly towards you, and the way I treated Marty was unforgivable. But, you see, the character I presented to you, to everyone in fact, was not the real me, just someone I'd created to put people off wanting to get close to me. I was terrified of getting hurt. I couldn't face going through such pain ever again so I did everything I could to prevent that from happening. I thought I was happy with the way things were, I was protecting myself and meant to keep it that way, but I'd bargained without you and Marty coming along.'

379

He wasn't conscious that Judith was staring at him speechless, he was only conscious of his own overwhelming need to unburden himself of things he'd never told a living soul before. Judith was the only person he could tell it all to because of how he felt about her and of his need for her to understand him completely.

'I was married once and was so very happy. I thought I had everything. A nice home, a beautiful wife who I loved more than life itself, a good business that was doing well supplying machine parts to factories all over Britain. I'd plenty of good friends, one in particular who I'd known since school days and who I trusted above anyone. I was looking forward to Natalie and myself starting a family. I was convinced she would be a wonderful mother. She gave me every reason to think she would be and I wanted us to be the kind of parents mine had been to me before they both died: loving, caring, the best parents a man could wish for. Then by accident I found out that all I held sacred was just a lie. My wife it seemed was having an affair with my closest friend, the man I'd have trusted with my life. He was married himself but they'd been seeing each other even before Natalie and I had married, and I'd suspected nothing.

'We had been married for two years when I returned home early from closing a business deal. It was bigger than I'd ever secured before and I was in the mood to celebrate. I couldn't wait to tell Natalie. She wasn't expecting me until later that evening. I thought I'd surprise her with a huge bouquet of flowers I had bought her, and over dinner that night at the table I had booked in our favourite restaurant I would tell her my good news.

'It was Natalie who was to surprise me. When I quietly let myself in and walked into the lounge, I got the shock of my life to see her and Harry in each other's arms. I just stood there frozen, staring at them, not believing what I was seeing. They were so engrossed in each other they didn't even know I was there. I heard clearly what he said to her, every word. "Natalie, this can't go on. It's driving me mad. You love me, I love you. I'll leave Margaret. We'll go away together. I don't know why you married him in the first place."

'If hearing this didn't shock me to the core then what Natalie replied sent my blood cold. "Now stop being silly, Harry," she scolded him. "You know why I wouldn't let you leave Margaret and why I married Nathan. He can give me what you can't. I know what it's like to be worried over money, fearing the bailiff's knock on the door. When I met Nathan I saw a chance to end all that and I've no intention of being in that situation ever again. I don't love him, never have, it's you I love, Harry. But your salary wouldn't pay for this lovely house or the clothes allowance I get or the nice meals out and everything else Nathan gives me. Should your financial situation improve then I might reconsider, but until such time I have no intention of changing my life. Now stop being silly and take me to bed. Nathan will be home soon and Margaret will be expecting you home, so we haven't much time."

'They must have realised I was present then because they suddenly sprang apart as if they'd suffered an electric shock. Natalie tried to act as if I'd heard nothing, just caught them in a friendly embrace, saying how pleased she was to see me home early, asking if I'd like a drink.

381

Harry too was telling me he'd just popped in as he'd been passing this way to say Margaret wanted to know if we'd both like to go over for dinner the next week. They were both so convincing that for a moment I questioned whether I had dreamt what I'd seen and heard. But I knew I hadn't. I told them both to get out, that I never wanted to see either of them again, and left them in no doubt that I meant every word. There was no going back.

'To say I was devastated would be putting it mildly. What they had done had broken me. What made matters worse if that was possible was that I found out that all my friends knew what was going on behind my back, as did Margaret, Harry's wife, and no one had said a word to me.

'For days I wandered around the house, not going out, not washing, shaving, hardly eating, certainly not sleeping. When friends called I wouldn't answer the door to them. They weren't my real friends. If they had been they would have told me about this. I knew the business was suffering but I didn't care. I didn't care about anything any more. But although at times like that you feel your life has ended, it hasn't. Eventually you have to eat because your body makes you, and you have to wash because even you get to the stage when you can't stand your own stench any more. I'd also reached the stage where I knew I couldn't stay in the house any longer as everything in it was a constant reminder of Natalie and the perfect life I thought we'd had together. I just wanted rid of it. I wanted rid of the business too because I'd built it up to provide for the family I'd longed to have with her.

'I didn't know what to do, though. How to avoid this

ever happening again, because I knew I couldn't go through it a second time. Then it came to me. It was people who hurt you, people who betrayed your trust. I would cut myself off from them as much as possible. I would make myself into a person no one would want to get close to. I would earn my living in a way that gave me as little contact with others as possible. My life would be for the most part solitary but at least then no one could hurt me. I put the house and business on the market and sold both for a reasonable price. I could have got more for them but I just wanted shot. I bought a small detached house for myself, and with the rest of the money I had left over I bought three terraced houses, putting them into the estate agent's hands to handle on my behalf so I didn't need to have unnecessary contact with anyone. I lived off the rental money and over the last twenty-five years, since I found out about Natalie and Harry, I have built up my properties to over thirty. During all that time I've kept myself strictly to myself.

'I was quite happy living in my new house, couples to either side with whom I had little or nothing to do. Then five years ago one side sold up to retire to the coast and an attractive widow moved in. She made it very clear from the first day she moved in when she knocked on my door to introduce herself that she didn't intend being single for much longer and she had her eye on me. I set about moving straight away. This place had just come on the market as the old lady who had owned it had died. It was badly in need of renovation, but I immediately saw it as a great opportunity. Once and for all I could secure my own position. I bought the house and turned it into flats, taking one for myself and putting the rest in the hands of the letting agents with strict instructions that all the tenants were to be male.

'That was always the case until the estate agent's assistant made a mistake and let the flat to you. I was most upset when I was informed but there was nothing I could do because the tenancy agreement had already been signed and executed. I comforted myself with the thought that you were a middle-aged spinster not a divorcee or a widow and therefore not the sort of woman to pose a threat to me. And after all, your tenancy was only for a year and when it came up for renewal I would simply instruct the agents not to do so. I was determined not to like you, give you no impression that we were in any way going to become acquainted, and I think I was relieved when at first I found you, although very attractive, a rather impersonal sort of woman as it made things so much easier.' He paused for a moment and drew a deep breath. 'Then Marty came into my life.'

A hint of a smile touched his lips. 'That little boy gradually uncovered feelings within me that I had buried so long ago I'd forgotten they existed. Your remark that I hadn't the ability to care for him after that terrible experience with the child-minder riled me and I have to say I rose to the bait to prove you wrong. But right from the start I found myself looking forward to Marty coming, more and more so as the days passed. When I was in his company I seemed to come alive. I laughed for the first time in years, enjoyed myself . . . something I had forgotten how to do. I didn't realise it until later, when I looked back over that time, but I think that's when I noticed a change starting to come over you, too. I began to see the real woman who lay beneath that icy surface and despite myself I found myself thinking of you when I least expected to. As time passed it became harder and harder for me to push those thoughts of you away.

'That night after coming back with you both after our enjoyable excursion to the fair, and then Marty fetching me after you'd had your accident, I saw you and Marty clinging together so lovingly and it hit me like a thunderbolt then just how much I felt for you both – especially you, Miss Chambers. I knew I loved you, loved you both, and wanted so much to be part of what you were sharing together, to be included in it. But, believe me, the realisation shook me rigid. I panicked, fearing I was in grave danger of having my life destroyed again. That's why I acted as I did. After I returned home I was fully of the opinion that I had done the best thing for me but when you came over and delivered your opinion of me, told me some home truths, I realised too late what an utter fool I had been.

'All that wasted time spent thinking I was protecting myself from hurt when in truth all I had achieved was a miserable lonely existence for myself, nobody caring whether I lived or died. Losing you and Marty caused me far more pain than ever I suffered through my loss of Natalie because this time the loss was my own fault. But I knew it was too late to try and put things right with you. I had hurt you so badly, I didn't deserve your forgiveness or to be given another chance. But I vowed to change myself, turn myself back into the man I had been before my vow of solitude. Make the rest of my life mean something. At least die with someone mourning me instead of no one at all.

'When the agents told me you were leaving I knew it was really because you wanted to get away from me – get Marty away from me. But I couldn't bear the thought of not knowing where you both were or how you were faring and so I wanted to do something for you both, in my own way, to make up for what I had done to you. I instructed the agents to reduce your rent and, if you still insisted on leaving, to tell you that a house was coming up for rental that they felt would suit you and be in your price range. If you questioned them regarding it I told them what story to tell you. They did this for me because I'd been such a long-standing client of theirs and brought them in a substantial amount of revenue over the years. When Albert Braithwaite informed me of your decision to take a house, I bought the one you are moving into and had it decorated and furnished with you both in mind. I wanted you to be happy there, but I wish you would believe me when I say how much I longed to be moving in with you both.'

He stopped short, took a deep breath and turned to look at her, searching her face intently. 'Now you know it all, Miss Chambers . . . Judith. I daren't think what you feel about me. I can only hope that you can find it within yourself to forgive me for how I've treated you. You were quite right to tell me you didn't deserve it. You were just responding to the way I was with you, and I can't blame you for that. Please be assured I am not that bitter man any more. He's gone and he's not coming back. What you see now is the real Nathan Banks. I know my timing telling you all this is most inappropriate when you're worried for Marty, but I couldn't help myself. I needed you to know and I might not have been given another chance. I would do anything, Judith, to hear you say that you feel the same for me as I do for you, if not now then maybe at some future time. I know, though, that this is all very sudden. All I'm asking for right now is that you will allow me to be your friend? Let me help you find Marty at least?'

Her thoughts were racing wildly. His story had shocked her and her heart went out to him for what he must have suffered over his wife and best friend's betrayal, for all the wasted years he had spent in virtual isolation for fear of ever being hurt again. She sympathised with that very much, fully understanding why he had chosen to do as he had. Hadn't she cut herself off from ever experiencing such hurt and pain again after what Clive Lewis had done to her? But what shocked her more was his declaration of love for her, for Marty too, and what he had done for them by way of trying to heal the hurt he had caused them both – something she might never have discovered if Marty's mother had not done what she had today. To have acted as he had Nathan Banks must really be kind, caring, thoughtful, and most importantly sincere.

She studied his face and suddenly felt she was seeing him for the very first time. If she had had any doubts about his feelings for her, she had none now. The depth of his love for her was shown all over his face. She suddenly knew that Nathan would never let her down, wouldn't ever betray her, that she was safe with him. Without warning a sudden rush of emotion ran through her, so overwhelming it took her breath away. It was so like the feeling she had had for Marty but different from the protective and caring love of an adult for a child; this had a hunger and a deep passion attached to it and was so strong it made her shake with its intensity.

Nathan saw the look on Judith's face and knew he had the answer he had hoped for. His arms enveloped her and he pulled her close. 'Oh, Judith, Judith, you love me, I know you do. I won't let you down, I promise. I will make you so happy.'

She pulled away and looked at him tenderly. 'I know you will,' she said with conviction. 'You have to know, though, Nathan, that I intend to find Marty, and when I do I mean to ask his mother to move in with me and let me help her raise him. I'll do whatever it takes to try and make that happen. Won't rest until I find him and know he's safe.'

'That's the least I'd expect you to do, my darling. I'll help you. Whatever happens, from now on we are in it together. I won't rest either until we find him. Marty is responsible for bringing us together and I want to thank him personally for that. Besides, I love the little chap as if he was my own and I'd do anything for him. We'll start looking first thing tomorrow.'

'But we have so little information and even what I have I can't rely on.'

'We'll find them, Judith, you have my promise on that. We will leave no stone unturned. Now, please may I kiss you?'

Without waiting for her response he pulled her to him and pressed his lips against hers. His kiss was tender yet full of passion. For the first time in her life Judith knew what it felt like to be loved and wanted by a man whose feelings she returned, and the joy this brought her was immeasurable. She had never expected to experience such emotions, and now she had she never wanted to lose them. All she needed to do was find Marty and then her life would be complete.

Chapter Twenty-Nine

Cherry was looking at Judith, thunderstruck. 'Good God, you and Nathan Banks? Well, I don't believe it.'

Judith smiled shyly. 'I'm still reeling from it all myself, Cherry. This turn of events is ... well ... you wouldn't believe it if you read it in a book. You'd throw it down, fully of the opinion that things like that don't happen in real life. I mean, to absolutely detest a man one day and the next be so head over heels in love with him you can't think straight! But then, look at you and Neville.'

'I know. Who'd have put me and him together, eh? Just goes to show though, don't it? Yer never know what life's got in store for yer.' She smiled at her friend warmly, leaned over and patted her hand. 'I'm so pleased for yer, though, Judy. I wished for someone to sweep you off yer feet, 'cos you above anyone I know deserve some happiness, and I got me wish, didn't I?'

'Yes, you certainly did. As you know my experience of men, apart from my terrible one with the father of my child, is non-existent but I believe without a shadow of a doubt that Nathan and I will be extremely happy together. All my instincts tell me that. But I can't think

391

about planning our future yet, Cherry, I need to find Marty first. I can't concentrate on anything else until I find him. I can't imagine just what's going through his little mind. I've no idea what his mother would have told him when she collected him without warning.'

'It's what *you're* feeling, Judy, that I can't imagine. What possessed his mother just to take him like that without even telling you? Well . . . she can't have no feelings, that's all I can say. Look, whatever I can do to help yer, Judy, you've got it, yer know that.'

'Thank you, Cherry, I can't tell you how much I appreciate that. I need to take some time off work to look for Marty.'

'You've got it, gel. Take as long as yer need and yer job will be waiting for yer. This is a family crisis. Nev will back me fully on this one, so don't you worry. The gels will cover your work meantime, I know they will, they all think the world of yer.' Her face screwed up questioningly. 'But how are yer gonna start looking, 'cos you don't even know if the name you have for Marty's mother is her proper one or not?'

'Not her Christian name certainly but I feel what he told me about his surname must be right. He said it without any hesitation.'

'Yeah, I see what yer mean. Kids have a habit of letting yer down when you ask 'em to tell a fib for yer. "Well, Mummy told me to say . . ." So, hopefully Batty is her real surname. It's summat to go on but it still ain't much, is it?'

'No. Nathan has some ideas, though. He's going to ask the agents he knows to use their influence in the business to check around, see if anyone they know has a Rachel or Paula Batty who rents accommodation from them.'

'What if she rents from a private landlord, like I do?'

'That possibility had occurred to us. Nathan said if our first option doesn't bear fruit we could scour the *Leicester Mercury* for letting advertisements and telephone them to enquire if she's already renting one of their properties or bed-sitters – presuming, of course, they will divulge this information. We can only hope they will. Then, if we still haven't discovered their whereabouts, it's a case of walking the streets knocking on doors until we do.'

'That could take forever.'

'I don't care how long it takes, I need to find them and won't rest until I do.'

'I'll do me weekly shopping on Friday night straight from work, I'll get me mam to watch the kids, and I know without asking Nev too will come out with me on Sat'day, and every Sat'day after 'til we find 'em.'

'I couldn't expect you to do that, Cherry. Neville neither.'

'I'm yer friend, we're both yer friends, and friends do what they can for each other. Besides, I wanna know Marty is okay too. I kinda like him. Anyway, what yer doing about yer move?'

'It's on hold. Being on such friendly terms with the landlord helps in situations like this,' said Judith jocularly, despite her worried expression. 'I can't move. What if they come back and think I've just packed up and left, despite me leaving a forwarding address? What if Marty needs me and somehow does find his way to me and I'm not there?' Tears glinted in her eyes. 'It's Christmas Day in just over a week's time, my first real Christmas, and I wanted to make it so special for him. He was so excited over our plans. I can't bear the thought of dragging through every day, not knowing if he's all right. We made a Christmas pudding together and had such fun. I can't believe that it seems to have turned out all right, but I couldn't eat it, not without Marty sharing it.' She took a deep breath. 'Nathan is quite happy that I'm staying put in the flat because as he says this way he has me close to him. But we have both decided that we will eventually all move into that house together because when we find Marty, and hopefully I persuade my daughter to move in with us too, that's when Nathan and I will marry.'

'Blimey, you did discuss everything tonight.'

'We covered a lot of ground. Once I'd got over the shock of his declaration of his feelings, and I'd realised mine for him, it was so easy to talk to him. I told him everything about myself, things I've never told anyone before . . . no disrespect but not even you, Cherry . . . and Nathan filled in gaps he hadn't told me previously. We know as much about each other now as it takes some couples years to learn. I would still be talking to him only I broke off because I needed to inform Mrs Liversage that for the time being I won't be requiring her services, and I so needed to talk to you, not only to ask for your help with my search for Marty but also to tell you about Nathan and me.'

'And that coming from a woman who never opened up to anyone only a few months ago! My, how you've changed, Judy Chambers. For the better, most definitely,' Cherry told her approvingly.

A thought suddenly struck Judith. 'Oh, forgive me, Cherry. With all this on my mind I haven't asked how your meal with Neville went on Saturday night? I felt it improper to ask you today at work just in case we were overheard. Needless to say I was desperate to.'

Cherry smiled broadly. 'It was just perfect. I must admit I was very nervous before he came to call for me. Well, it's two years since Brian died and I'd not looked in any man's direction meantime. I kept thinking Nev would regret Friday night, that he was probably drunk or something, but he turned up early with a great big bunch of flowers for me, sweets for the kids and a box of chocolates for me mam to thank her for baby-sitting so he could take me out. We never stopped talking and he was so attentive. When it came to saying goodnight I didn't want to leave him, and he didn't me. He came over yesterday afternoon and played with the kids, had his tea, and it was like we'd always been a family. Sounds stupid, doesn't it, but it was all so natural and comfortable. He even helped me dry the dishes. I had to chuck him out at gone twelve 'cos he seemed to forget we had jobs to go to this morning.

'How the hell we're going to keep this under wraps at work until we're ready to let everyone know, I ain't got a clue. It was hard today, acting boss and employee with him, and I know it was as hard for him too. I keep pinching meself, Judy, I can't believe that twice in me life I've found the perfect man for meself, despite 'em being so completely different from each other. But when yer think, some women ain't lucky enough to find even one love, are they?'

Judith nodded her understanding. 'I never gave finding

love a thought, I was fully of the opinion that I was on my own for life. Now, with just these few hours of knowing how Nathan and I feel about each other, it's as if I've always known him. It's like you say, it all feels so natural and so right. I expect, like you, I'll keep pinching myself until it finally sinks in.' She picked up her handbag. 'I must go, Cherry. Not only is it very late, and I do apologise for that as I know I caught you about to go to bed, but Nathan is waiting for me outside in his car. He understood why I didn't ask him to come in with me. Apart from what I had to tell you about Marty, he knew I also wanted to break the news about him and me. I never realised he had a car, though. It shocked me when he insisted he should drive me here. It seems he keeps it in a garage around the corner, uses it purely to travel to inspect his properties. He never went anywhere else in it, but he says now he can't wait to take me and Marty for rides . . .' She stopped short. 'I need to find him first.'

She rose, stepped around the table and kissed her friend affectionately on the cheek. 'Thank you for everything, Cherry.'

Then she made her way back to the man waiting patiently for her, missing her every moment she'd been inside Cherry's house, as she had missed him.

Chapter Thirty

Four nights later Judith sighed despondently and looked at Nathan, downcast. 'I was wrong to build up my hopes of finding Marty and his mother quickly, wasn't I, Nathan?'

He took her hand and gently squeezed it. 'We will find them, darling, you have my word. We won't give up until we do. Maybe it's just going to take a little longer than we hoped, that's all. All right, so nothing came of our enquiries around the agents, but now we'll start going through the newspaper and telephoning private landlords who are advertising. One of them might well be renting to Marty's mother. That could take a while, of course, because landlords only advertise when they have a vacancy. We'll also start going around areas of Leicester where I know properties are let out and we won't stop until we've visited every conceivable place we know of or find out about. During the week it's just us two but on Saturdays we'll have Cherry and Neville on board and then we can really cover some ground between us. Have patience, darling. We'll find him, trust me.'

She looked at him thoughtfully, then smiled lovingly. 'I

don't know how I ever managed without you beside me.
I'd be lost without you now.'

He looked deep into her eyes. 'Good, because that's
how I want you to feel, for ever.' He leaned across the
table and picked up the newspaper he'd been out to fetch
earlier, opening it before them at the Properties to Let
page. 'Right, I'll read the contact telephone numbers or
addresses out and you write them down.'

Just then there was a knock on the door.

'Expecting anyone?' he asked her.

She shook her head. 'You make a start, I won't be a
minute.'

She was surprised to see two women on her doorstep.
'Kimberley! Mrs Hardy! How lovely to see you both.'

Rosalyn Hardy looked uncomfortable. 'I hope we
haven't called at an inconvenient moment but there is a
matter we'd like to discuss with you.'

Suffering from the mental anguish of Marty's abduc-
tion, Judith really didn't feel up to a confrontation with
Kimberley's mother. However, she stood aside, saying,
'Please come in and make your way through to the
lounge.'

Nathan stood up in gentlemanly fashion as they
entered.

'Nathan, this is Kimberley with whom I've become
friendly through my visits to the library,' Judith introduced her. 'This is Kimberley's mother, Mrs Hardy. This
is Nathan Banks, my—'

'Fiancé,' Nathan cut in, flashing a smile at Judith.

'Your fiancé, Miss Chambers?' queried Kimberley,
surprised.

She blushed. 'Yes, I've got engaged since I last saw you. Please, both sit down and make yourselves comfortable. And call me Judith or Judy, all my friends do.'

'I'll make tea,' said Nathan to Judith, disappearing into the kitchen.

After they had settled themselves on the sofa, Judith sat down in an armchair and looked at Rosalyn expectantly. 'You said you had a matter to discuss with me?'

Mother and daughter looked at each other, then back at Judith.

'This isn't easy,' began Rosalyn.

Judith took a deep breath. 'I understand if you'd prefer Kimberley to make friends with people her own age.'

Rosalyn looked at her blankly. 'I'm sorry? Who Kimberley's friends are is entirely her own business. No, the matter we need to discuss is regarding your daughter.'

'My daughter!' Judith exclaimed. 'You know where she is? You have news of where she and Marty are?'

They looked confused.

'I'm afraid we know nothing about that,' said Rosalyn. 'What you must know, though, is that the woman claiming to be your daughter most certainly is not.'

Judith looked at her as though she was stupid. 'Pardon? But of course she is. She had information to prove it that only the child I gave birth to could have known.'

'She might have had information, and how she got it is worth investigating, but she's definitely not your daughter,' said Rosalyn resolutely.

'You know this for a fact?' Judith demanded.

Rosalyn nodded solemnly. Taking a very deep breath she said, 'Because Kimberley is your daughter.'

The breath left Judith's body and for several long moments she stared at them wild-eyed. Finally she uttered, 'But you must be mistaken.'

Rosalyn shook her head. 'What I am saying is true because I was in the room next to yours while you were giving birth to Kimberley at the home. Miss Hales handed your daughter to me when she was barely a minute old and Miss Brewster took care of all the paperwork.'

Judith was hardly conscious of Nathan entering the room and putting a tray of tea things on the coffee table until she felt his hand grip hers tightly. She looked up blindly to see him perched on the arm of her chair. She flashed a quick grateful smile at him for his moral support and then brought bewildered eyes back to the two women facing her. 'You're sure you're not mistaken?'

Rosalyn gravely shook her head. 'Apart from the details I insisted I had on my adopted baby's natural mother, in case she decided to find her when she was old enough, I actually saw you once. You were pointed out to me as the woman whose baby I was adopting. You didn't see me. You happened to walk through the reception area carrying a pile of laundry when I was being taken into the office for a progress report, which took place every two months or thereabouts. The young woman who was escorting me, who I believe helped out in the office, momentarily forgot herself. After she had carelessly pointed you out to me, she realised her error and swore me to secrecy in fear for her job. Now I'm meeting you again, of course you're older, but you're definitely the same woman I saw pointed out as the one carrying the baby I'd adopt.

'My husband and I couldn't have children, you see, Judith. It was heartbreaking for us but we knew we would make good parents. We desperately wanted to be, and felt we could offer a needy child a good and loving home – a far better future for it than being raised in an orphanage. We decided to approach the charity organisation as we felt the babies born there were most in need of people like us.'

She looked at Judith meaningfully. 'I want you to know that I appreciate very much what you must have gone through in giving up your child, but if it's any consolation at all Kimberley has brought me and my husband great joy.'

Kimberley took Rosalyn's hand, squeezed it affectionately and smiled at her lovingly. 'You've been the best mother to me, Mum. Dad, the best father. I love you both so much, you know that.'

'Yes, I do,' she said softly. 'But we made a mistake in not telling you that you were adopted. Then it wouldn't have come as such a shock now.'

She looked at Judith shamefully. 'We never meant to keep it from Kimberley, it just never came up. We had always intended telling her when she was old enough to understand, but as time passed the truth just faded away because I loved her as much as if I had given birth to her myself.'

Kimberley spoke up. 'I couldn't understand Mum's frosty reception towards you when you met each other at my flat. It was so unlike her that I questioned her.'

'Please accept my apologies,' Rosalyn said to Judith. 'I was completely unprepared for coming face to face with the natural mother of my daughter. My first instinct was to fob off Kimberley with an excuse for my behaviour but then it struck me that she deserved to know the truth of her origins.'

'I have to admit when Mum told me she wasn't my natural mother, it was such a shock,' said Kimberley. 'I was so unprepared. To be told that all I'd ever believed was no longer true, and, if that wasn't enough, then to be told that the woman I was befriending was my real mother, well . . .' She gave a deep sigh. 'I'm ashamed to admit that I was hateful to you, Mum. I practically threw you out of my flat and then I wouldn't answer the door to anyone. I was so angry. Angry against you and Dad for keeping such a secret from me. Angry at you too, Judith, for giving me away in the first place. I so desperately wanted my old life back without having to deal with any of this. Finally, thank goodness, I began to see sense. You must have had a good reason for giving me away and also I realised how lucky I was to have been adopted by such wonderful people as Mum and Dad. You did have no other choice than to have me adopted, didn't you, Judith?'

Still reeling from the shock of all this, Judith's voice faltered. 'I was in no position whatsoever to raise a child myself, had no means at all to provide for one, and the whole matter was taken out of my hands by the people at the home.' May God forgive me, she thought, for what she was about to say next, but there was no way Judith could tell this lovely young girl, who'd had enough shocks as it was, that she was in fact the product of a rape. 'Your father, you see, was accidentally killed before I knew I was pregnant and my own parents were not the type who would have supported me.'

'Oh, I see,' said Kimberley. 'It must have been a dreadful time for you.'

Judith smiled bleakly. 'I comforted myself with the knowledge that my baby was being raised by good people who'd cherish it.'

'Then your wish was granted,' said Rosalyn.

'Yes, it most certainly was,' said Kimberley.

'I can see that,' Judith said softly. 'I might have given birth to you, Kimberley, but your true mother is Rosalyn, the woman who's been there for you through sickness and in health, raised you to be the lovely woman that you are.'

'Thank you,' Rosalyn said graciously. 'Kimberley has assured me that whatever happens between you two in the future, I will always be her mother. Our real dilemma now is, this other woman claiming to be your daughter, her son your grandson.' She paused, looking with deep sympathy at the stricken woman before her. 'I can see this is all a terrible shock for you. We ought to leave you now,' she said, rising and motioning Kimberley to do likewise. 'After all this upset we feel we need time together as a family, so my husband and Kimberley have managed to get leave from their jobs and we're going away tomorrow on a trip around Europe and won't be back until after the New Year.' She looked at her daughter, then back at Judith. 'Kimberley has told me she would dearly like to build a relationship with you, if that's agreeable to you, and I have no objection. Maybe . . . well, maybe, come time, we could all become friends.'

'I would like that very much,' Judith whispered.

403

'Then you don't mind if I contact you when I return?' Kimberley asked eagerly.

'No, I don't mind at all. I'll look forward to it very much.'

Nathan gently squeezed Judith's hand. 'I'll see them out.'

Moments later he returned to perch back on the edge of Judith's chair and taking her hand, looked with deep concern into the stricken face of the woman he had come to love so deeply. 'Judith, how are you?' he asked softly.

She slowly turned her head and looked up at him, the pain in her eyes unmistakable. 'That lovely young girl is my daughter,' she uttered. 'I can't believe it, Nathan, I really can't. I thought Rachel was my daughter and now I find she isn't. Why did she say she was, Nathan? What possessed her to pass herself off as my daughter? How did she get the information she had about me? Oh, God, now I know she really isn't my daughter it makes more sense to me. I felt nothing maternal for her, you see, nothing whatsoever. I thought something was wrong with me. But there was nothing to connect us, no natural feelings to draw upon.

'But Kimberley . . . Oh, Nathan, I liked her from the moment I met her. And, now, to find out she's the child I gave away . . . I'm too stunned to explain how I feel. It's a mixture of utter shock and utter joy, if that makes sense. I do want to get to know her better and I'm so glad she wants that too. How big-hearted of Rosalyn not to intervene. I would never try to come between them. I owe Rosalyn and her husband far too much gratitude for what they have done for Kimberley.'

404

'What about Marty,' Nathan gently probed.

'Marty? Oh, nothing has changed regarding him, Nathan. I love him. Just because I've found out he's not my natural grandson, I can't just switch my feelings for him off, they go far too deep. As far as I'm concerned I am his grandmother, and to him I am his grandmother. My need to find him is just as strong.'

'What about his mother, Judith?'

'His mother?' She stared at him thoughtfully. 'The poor girl obviously believes I'm her natural mother. Her own adoptive mother must have been given the wrong information when she collected her baby from the home when she was born, being given my details instead of those she should have been given. There's obviously been a mix up. Marty's mother needs help, though, doesn't she, Nathan? She turned to me thinking I was her mother because she had no one else. She must have been desperate. She told me how hard raising Marty was proving to be and that she got no help from anyone. I can't turn my back on her. I must help her if she will let me.'

He leaned over and tenderly kissed her lips, looking at her knowingly. 'I expected no less. We'd better find them then, hadn't we?'

Chapter Thirty-One

Judith kissed her friend's cheek warmly as she let her in early one Saturday morning in late January, nearly five weeks after Marty's mother had taken him without warning.

'Bloody hell, it's freezing out there,' Cherry moaned as she followed Judith through into the kitchen. 'Cuppa, I think, before we make our start,' she said, stripping off her thick gloves and rubbing her hands.

Judith turned the electric plate on underneath the kettle then faced her with a worried expression. 'It's not really the weather today for traipsing the streets, Cherry. Why don't you go home and I'll manage by myself?'

'Of course I'm coming with you. I ain't letting you wander the streets by yerself. Nathan wouldn't be very pleased with me if I did that either.'

Judith knew that in fact he would have been most annoyed if he had found out she had gone out alone knocking on doors in what he deemed to be the rougher areas of the city as he was very protective of her. It was just one of so many qualities in him she was constantly discovering, and why, as their relationship deepened, she found herself loving him more and more. 'I appreciate that, Cherry, but this has been going on for weeks now, you giving up your Saturdays to help us find Marty when you have children of your own to be with. And there's your mother to think about, using her own Saturdays sitting for you. Nathan warned me this could take a while but I really thought we would have found them by now.'

'Not giving up, are yer?'

'No, never,' said Judith resolutely. 'I'll never give up, Cherry.'

'I don't know why I asked that 'cos I already knew the answer you'd give me,' she said, unbuttoning her coat and sitting down at the table, waiting expectantly for her much-needed cup of tea. She giggled. 'Me mother might moan and grumble about having her grandkids, but she knows I know she loves having them, and they love being with her 'cos they have her wrapped around their little fingers and get away with far more with her than they do with me. Anyway, I've told yer this so many times I'm getting sick of telling yer. Me and Nev are in this with you and Nathan 'til we turn up trumps. And before yer ask it, which I know yer about to, yer job is safe. Nev's told yer that himself and the gels and I are covering your work just fine.'

'I don't know how to thank you, Cherry. Especially Neville insisting on still paying my wages.'

'Yeah, well, that ain't common knowledge 'cos the gels might be a bit disgruntled to find out that and then all of them would want time off to search for long-lost relatives they ain't even got! Best keep that to yerself. It's Nev's way of helping you, Judy, as my friend and his now, so don't insult him by refusing. Yer can't afford that. Now get me that bloody cuppa, will yer, 'cos otherwise by the time we get out the day will have gone.'

Judith knew without doubt she really was a lucky woman to have friends like she had, willing to do anything for her. She just hoped she was worthy of them. Handing Cherry her cup, she sat down opposite with her own.

'I can't try and guess the number of houses, flats and bed-sitters we've enquired at now between the four of us, Cherry. The number of times we've persuaded occupiers or landlords to pass on requests for a Rachel or Paula Batty to contact us should they come across her. You'd have thought something would have borne fruit by now, wouldn't you?'

'We've covered a lot of ground since we first began, Judy, but we've still a way to go before we exhaust all the possibilities of where she could be living. I didn't realise there were so many streets with little hidden courtyards off them in Leicester, had no idea that so many people let out all sorts of accommodation, 'til we started all this. It's just got to happen though that one day we'll knock on a door and either Marty's mam'll answer it, or someone who knows her will, or else she'll contact yer through someone we've left your number with coming across her and asking her to get in touch.'

'But what if she turns up at one of the places we've already been to and is given our number but decides not to get in touch? That's what worries me, Cherry?'

'Don't be daft, Judy. The woman will be curious if nothing else to know what you want with her. Yer never

told those yer gave yer telephone number to yer name or
the reason why you wanted her to contact you, just that
you needed to find her because you had something to tell
her that would interest her. Nathan was very clever to
think of doing that. She's bound to think the telephone
number is that of a solicitor and she's in for an inheritance or summat. Well, that's what I would think if I was
in her shoes, so she'll contact you if she's given the
message, believe me she will.'

'I so hope you're right. Yes, of course she will make
contact, out of curiosity if nothing else.' Judith's face was
aggrieved. 'I do worry about Marty forgetting me as time
passes, though.' Her thoughts flashed back to Christmas
Day, a day she'd promised would be so special for him
and one she had been so looking forward to herself. Every
day without word of him had been difficult for her to get
through, even though on the surface she was carrying on
as normal. She was slowly building her relationship with
Nathan. They spent a lot of time on their search for
Marty and his mother, but in between these expeditions
they took care to share what normal couples in love did,
such as having meals out or cooking for each other at
home, or just sitting talking or quietly reading. But
Christmas Day had been especially hard on Judith, and
on Nathan too because his feelings for Marty almost
matched her own.

She had been relieved when it had finally come to an
end and they could get on with their search again.
Presents they had bought for him were wrapped and
ready, sitting on the bed in his room, waiting for him to
open them. More and more she worried as their search

proved fruitless that years' worth of presents would build before he ever did.

'Marty, forget yer?' Cherry scoffed now. 'How could that little lad ever forget yer, Judy? No child forgets someone who's made it plain how much they love 'em. I know how safe and secure he felt with you, and in all honesty, from what I can gather about his mother, the time Marty spent with you was the most stable he's ever had. Now don't let me hear you say anything like that again. Oh, by the way, have yer heard any more news from yer real daughter?'

Judith smiled. 'Yes, I have. In fact, another card arrived this morning. They were in Italy when Kimberley wrote it. Having a marvellous time by the sound of it, but she did add at the bottom of the card that she was looking forward to seeing me when she got back, which will be next week.'

Cherry smiled. 'Things look very promising on that front.'

'I daren't build up my hopes too much but I have to say, I agree.'

Cherry drained her cup. 'Right, we'd better get out there or the men will be coming back asking us how we got on today and we'll have n'ote to tell 'em. When Nev came over last night he told me that Nathan had called him to ask him to meet up over the other side of town. There's a house he wants to have a quick look at as a possible rental investment and he thought it'd be a good idea to make some enquiries over that way at the same time. Apparently there's lots of rental properties around there and it's somewhere we ain't made our way over to

411

yet. I don't know that side of town meself as I've never had any need to go over that way. Nev dropped me off here this morning and I should imagine met up with Nathan a while ago.'

'Yes, the estate agent called him yesterday afternoon. He suggests, though, that you and I should carry on finishing off the area we've half-covered already. We need to be thorough or it's all wasted effort. Searching for someone takes some planning, doesn't it, and such a time to do.'

'But when yer find Marty it'll have been worth it. And when you do his mother's gonna get quite a shock to find out that the information she's been given is wrong and you ain't her real mother, especially having to face yer after robbing yer blind. But even if you do fail to convince her that you bear no grudge against her and just wanna help her, it's got to be some callous woman who won't let you have contact with her little boy, 'cos she must know from Marty what yer felt for each other. He might be back with his mother but I know that little lad will be missing you like hell.'

Judith hoped so.

Just then they both jumped as they heard the front door opening and looked up in surprise to see Nathan charging in. 'Quick, both of you,' he blurted. 'We've seen Marty with someone I assume is his mother.'

A great surge of excitement raced through Judith. 'You have? Oh, Nathan . . . where . . . what . . . How was he?'

Nathan couldn't bear to tell Judith that the shabby, miserable-looking little boy so badly in need of a hair cut had looked nothing like the happy, chatty, well-kept one

412

she had brought about through her love and care for him while he'd been with her. 'Just hurry up and I'll tell you on the way over in the car. I've left Neville keeping watch.

'It was when I was just leaving the house I'd been to view and was waiting for Neville to arrive,' Nathan told them both as he drove. 'As I was just saying my goodbyes to the estate agent, telling him I'd let him know my decision on Monday, raised voices coming from the house next door caught my attention and I looked over to see two women having words. But it was the mop of red hair on the child with them that caught my eye, then the fact I could just see he was wearing glasses. So I took a proper look and it was Marty, definitely. I just stopped myself from shouting across to him because I realised something was going on between the women. I couldn't quite hear what was being said because there was a lot of traffic passing on the street.

'The older woman, who obviously lived in the house, was looking very angry and wagging her finger at Marty's mother. Then she suddenly disappeared inside and returned moments later, opening her purse. She took money out and shoved it at the young woman. Marty's mother took it and put it in her pocket. I did hear what the other woman said then because she raised her voice.

' "Now that's all you're getting off me so don't come back thinking there's more because there's not. My husband would kill me if he found out about you, and especially that little 'un yer've got too. Now just go, the pair of you, and heed my warning – don't come back." The woman went back inside her house then, slamming the door, and Marty's mother ushered him down the path into the street where they hurried off together down the road.

'I made to follow them, hoping Neville would forgive me for not being there to meet him as we'd arranged. Luckily he pulled up then so I quickly told him what had happened and we made plans to follow them, Neville in his car and me in mine. We caught them up at the bus stop just down the road as they were getting on a bus and followed it a little distance behind until they got off near the bottom of King Richard's Road. Then we saw the young woman go down a side street, knock on a door and be let in. Neville and I parked our cars and conferred on what to do. It was decided that he would stay and keep watch and I would fetch you both, hoping you hadn't already left, then we could all decide what to do next. If Neville's gone when we get there then we know Marty and his mother have left the house and he has followed them. All we can do then is go back home and wait for him to return with news of what happened.'

'What do yer think was going on between Marty's mam and that angry woman?' Cherry asked him. 'Why do you think she was giving her money and telling her not to come back?'

'I don't know. Maybe the woman owed it to her for some reason and Marty's mother was having a job to get it out of her. Though that doesn't really make sense of those parting words, does it?'

Cherry mused, 'Mmm. No, it don't, does it? I can't think what all that would have bin about.'

'Look, our aim was to find Marty and his mother and

persuade her to let us help her, or at the very least let Judith keep in touch with him,' said Nathan. 'I think she should be the one to go and knock on the door and ask if Marty and his mother live there. If they don't, ask whoever they are visiting if Judith can speak to them.'

Cherry turned to address Judith, sitting on the back seat beside her. She noticed immediately that her friend looked very pensive. 'What yer thinking, Judy?'

'Pardon? Oh, nothing.'

'Yer thinking about summat, you were miles away.'

'Yes, I was. But I don't like what I'm thinking, Cherry.'

'I don't care whether yer like what yer was thinking or not, just tell me?'

Judith took a deep breath. 'When Nathan told us about what happened on the doorstep between Marty's mother and the other woman, what was said and the fact that money was handed over and a warning given, for some reason it triggered a memory of something Marty said to me once. He said, "I didn't like the other grandmas but I like you, Grandma." '

'And?' queried Cherry, wondering where this was leading to.

'Yes, just what is your line of thought, darling?' Nathan urged.

'Well, it is only a thought but you'll see why I don't like it. Could it be that Marty's mother has known all along I am not her real mother because she has somehow found out about women who have had babies in the past and now she is visiting them all and maybe demanding money from them in some way? Probably she hopes they'll give it her quickly to get rid of her, for fear of their families who probably have no idea about the past finding out and not taking the news very kindly.

'When she turned up at my door that night she very soon made it apparent that she needed help, but I had no family to find out my secret. That's why I asked her in in the first place, or should I say she invited herself in? But say she had done that with the woman you saw her with this morning, and her husband or other family members were inside the house or due to come home, how could she introduce Marty and his mother to them out of the blue like that? It's not the sort of news that's taken happily, is it, finding out such a dark secret about your wife twenty odd years later? I feel most women in such a situation would panic and give in to any demands to make trouble go away.' Judith took a deep breath, gnawing her bottom lip anxiously. 'Now I've voiced my thoughts, the whole thing sounds over-elaborate. Far too complicated a plan for someone of Marty's mother's background to have come up with and execute.'

Cherry was gawping at her. 'Bloody hell . . . but say she somehow did? It's some scam is that. But then yer right, Judy, how would she get hold of the sort of information she needed about all those women who had babies secretly in the first place? What do you think, Nathan?'

'We're here,' he said abruptly. 'Neville's still waiting so that means they're still inside.'

As they all hastily got out of the car, Neville came up to join them. 'There's a young girl left but it wasn't a woman with a red-headed child. She came out as soon as you went off to fetch the ladies, Nathan, and I was close enough to hear what the woman who let her out said to her.'

'What was that?' Cherry demanded.

'Patience, my sweet,' he said, smiling at her fondly. 'She said, "Remember, get as much money as you can out of them, because the more you do, the bigger your share will be. And don't try any tricks, thinking you can fool us about how much that is, because if we ever find out you're cheating on us you'll be damned sorry, believe me. See you next Saturday, same time." She went back inside then and the young woman went off.

'Well, that got me intrigued, especially after what Nathan had told me about the scene he witnessed this morning. I decided to see if I could make my way round the back of the house and have a look through the window. I didn't know what I expected to see, if anything, but it was better than doing nothing.'

'You could have been caught,' snapped Cherry.

'Well, I wasn't,' he said, leaning over and pecking her cheek.

'Did you manage to see anything?' asked Nathan.

He nodded. 'It was only a quick look as I didn't want to be spotted, but I saw two older women and two young ones sitting around a table. One of the older women had a bulky folder in front of her and I saw her pass a piece of paper from it to one of the girls. I think I saw a cash box on the table too. I decided it was best to leave then and I've been out here ever since.' He grinned at Cherry. 'I felt like Dick Tracy.'

'This is no time for jokes,' she scolded him.

'Did you see Marty, Neville?' Judith asked him hopefully.

He shook his head. 'No.'

Nathan looked gravely at Judith, then at Cherry and Neville. 'It does seem to me from what we've learned today that the young girls are working for the older women in some way. Maybe what you guessed, Judy, was on the right track, but you hadn't got all the information. It's obvious to me that the older woman Neville saw inside is in charge. But whatever is going on, it doesn't sound all that good to me.'

'What did Judy come up with?' asked Neville.

Nathan quickly told him.

'Oh, bugger, no!' he exclaimed, shocked. 'If those women somehow have information on lots of others who've secretly had babies then getting hush money out of them . . . well, that's damned criminal! How do we find out if what we suspect is true?'

'Only one way to,' replied Nathan. 'Ask.'

'We can't just barge in and ask,' Judith protested. 'What if we're wrong?'

'Then we apologise. Judy darling, I hate to remind you of this but we already know that Marty's mother is a thief because she stole money from you. If we're right we could be saving other innocent women from suffering as you have.'

'Yes, I agree, if this is the case then we have a moral duty to stop it, but what about Marty?' she insisted. 'If we do find out what we suspect is true that means his mother is involved in . . . oh, I just hate to think . . . but what will he think of us, being responsible for putting her in jail?'

'I am thinking of him, Judy. What damage is being done to him if his own mother is presenting him to all these women as their grandson, and telling him to call them Grandma just so she can get money out of them? If this really is the case then at the moment all he thinks is that he's got lots of grandmas, most of them probably like the one today who treat him angrily and shout at his mother. But he's a bright boy, Judy. Before long he'll twig what's going on and, knowing no different, could turn criminal himself when he grows up.'

Judith fought with her conscience but her love for Marty was far stronger than her scruples. 'Yes, I agree. But what if we're wrong when we accuse his mother of extorting money? She could turn against us and then I'll never see him again or get the chance to help her.'

'Judy's right, Nathan,' Neville said. 'Must be some other way we can approach this without so much risk of you losing contact with Marty for good.'

Nathan stared at them thoughtfully. 'I've an idea . . . We need to get inside and quickly suss out what's going on then we'll play it by ear. Follow me.'

With that he strode up to the front door of the house and with the others behind him, all confused as to what he had in mind, rapped purposefully on the door.

It was quickly opened by a young woman who looked surprised to see a tall distinguished man greeting her. She was obviously expecting someone else.

Before she could utter a word Nathan announced, 'Landlord. I've come to do an inspection of my property. These are my staff.' He gestured to the others gathered behind him. Without waiting for her response, he barged past, pulling Judith along with him, Cherry and Neville following immediately behind. Nathan headed straight for the back room and as they approached a deep female voice was heard to say, 'That you, Lorraine? And about time. You're late so I hope you've got good news for us on the money front. Oh,' a woman mouthed, spotting Nathan framed inside the doorway. 'Who the hell are you?'

'Landlord. Come to do an inspection,' he said authoritatively.

Two women were sitting around a table, one young, one middle-aged. Another thin, sharp-featured middle-aged woman was standing close by, about to put a heavy iron kettle on top of an old-fashioned range. They were all staring at Nathan.

The young woman who had let them in pushed by to sit back down at the table.

'They just barged in,' she blurted. 'I couldn't stop 'em.'

The severe matronly woman sitting at the table, a bulky folder open before her, cash box to the side of it, frowned at Nathan questioningly. 'You ain't the landlord,' she accused him.

'I am now. Property changed hands last week. These are my staff,' he repeated, walking inside the room, taking Judith with him, Cherry and Neville close behind.

As Nathan and Judith came into view of all the occupants of the room a voice exclaimed: 'Gran'ma! Misterank!' And from a chair in the corner Marty shot to his feet and leaped at Judith, throwing himself on her. 'Oh, Gran'ma, I've missed yer!'

She scooped him up and hugged him fiercely. 'I've missed you too,' she whispered, burying her face in his neck.

At Marty's action and Judith's response the woman

holding the kettle blurted out: 'You're no landlord and his staff. Just who the hell are you?' Suddenly she gazed knowingly at Judith, still fiercely hugging Marty. 'She's one of the mothers.' She spun to face one of the young women sitting at the table. 'She's one of yours, Paula. Must be if your son is calling her Grandma. You dozy cow, you've led her here!' Without warning she swung back the kettle, bringing it round again to land hard against the side of Paula Batty's head.

She shrieked out in pain from the blow, clapping her hand to her head. 'No, I didn't! Honest I didn't! I don't know what they're doing here. Yer godda believe me . . . Oh, me flipping head!'

Cherry rushed across to Paula. 'Are you all right?' she demanded, looking down at her worriedly.

'That lady hit my mammy,' Marty cried, pointing an accusing finger at the woman who had just attacked Paula.

'And you can shut up, you little tyke!' the woman shouted back at him.

Judith flashed a murderous glance at her then froze as recognition struck. She slowly turned her head and looked at the other woman now holding on to the cash box. 'I know who you both are. You're Miss Brewster and Miss Hales from the home where I had my baby.'

Marjory Brewster smiled sardonically. 'Well, well, well, if it isn't Chambers. I remember you, all right. The posh one who thought she was better than anyone else.' Scowling fiercely, she glanced at Paula and before she could check herself, blurted, 'I sent you to her, just before you were laid up with 'flu for over a month . . . You said

421

things didn't work out there. She'd left the address I had
for her and the neighbours didn't know her forwarding
address. But if your son calls her Grandma then you *must*
have met up. How much did you get out of her and never
told us, you thieving little bugger?' she demanded harshly,
making to rise out of her chair.

Nathan and Neville dashed over to stop her. Neville
pushed her back down in her chair and, before she could
prevent him, Nathan had grabbed the bulky folder and
was scanning it.

'You were right, Judith. This dossier contains the
names of all the women who've had babies in that home,
back to when it first started in 1912 up to the time it
closed. It's got all their last known addresses, dates of
birth, and also the dates of birth of their babies and
details of the adoptive parents. Nice little scam you've got
going, Madam. Both of you, in fact, as I assume you're in
this together?' He looked harshly at both Marjory Brewster and Eunice Hales.

Miss Brewster's face turned thunderous. 'And why
shouldn't we make a living out of those we'd served well
when we had ours taken from us? The charity decided
they could no longer fund the home after Eunice and
myself had given over thirty years of our lives to their
rotten cause! Gave us a month's notice that they were
closing the place with no golden handshake for us. Nothing, in fact. We hadn't even anywhere to live because that
place had been our home, too, as well as providing us
with a living, such as it was. Who's going to employ us at
our age? Cleaning was about the only job open to us. As if
either of us would stoop so low!'

'But you'd stoop low enough to extort whatever money you could out of innocent women, frightened that their secret was about to come out and they risked losing everything they had built up since,' snapped Judith. 'It's not even as if the girls you used were their real daughters. How could you do it to them? And you dragged these girls here and whoever else you have working for you into your terrible racket too.'

'All the girls we have working for us do it willingly. They need the money as much as we do,' Marjory Brewster shot back. 'So now you know how we make our living, what do you think you can do about it? None of our girls will come clean publicly and the women who've already paid up aren't going to admit to anything. They were all told they'd had daughters, by the way, because as you well know, Miss Chambers, the mothers in the home weren't allowed to know the sex of their child.'

Judith was so appalled by all this she was speechless.

'The money in that cash box is the last you'll earn this way,' Nathan hissed angrily. 'We might not be able to get you convicted for what you've done but we can stop you fleecing any more women in future. I'll keep this folder, which I assume you stole before you left the home for good. I'll make sure it's handed to the proper authorities so that in future any children born in the home you presided over can find out who their natural mothers are through official channels. You disgust me,' he said, looking at the two hard-faced women. Then he turned to the worried young girls sitting at the table. 'I'd advise you to find yourselves proper jobs before you land in jail. Come on, Judith, let's get out of here. The air is vile, don't you think?'

Heedless that the two older women were glaring at her with hatred, Judith hurriedly handed Marty over to Nathan then rushed over to Paula, putting her arm around her shoulders and looking at her in concern. 'Come on, Paula, you're coming with us.'

Still in a daze from the attack, she looked blankly at Judith. 'But I ain't yer real daughter, and I stole from yer.'

'I know all that. I just want to help you, believe me. Come home with me and we'll talk. But do you need medical attention for your head first?'

'No, I'm fine, honest. Just a bad headache.'

'Come along then, let's go,' Judith urged.

424

Chapter Thirty-Two

Sitting on Judith's settee in front of the blazing gas fire, Paula accepted a cup of tea gratefully. As Judith sat down beside her, Paula asked, 'Where's Marty?'

'Oh, he's found the Christmas presents we bought him. He's with Nathan, opening them all in his bedroom. Cherry and Nev have gone home to see to their own family but you'll meet them again.'

Paula took a sip of her tea. 'You love my son, don't yer?'

Judith smiled wanly. 'Yes, I do, very much.'

'I didn't mean to leave him with yer when I first came.'

'Why did you then, Paula?'

'Well, you weren't like the other women I've bin to. Most of them were terrified when I tried to get inside their house and quickly gave me money to go away. The ones we did get inside . . . well, they'd not got much so I wheedled what I could and made me escape. Only . . . well, you've got money, ain't yer? When you gave me that ten quid I couldn't believe me luck. I saw yer take it from its hiding place and I could see there was more where that came from. That's why I persuaded you to let me stop the night. As soon as I knew you was sleeping I meant to lay me hands on everything I could then get Marty and we'd scarper and you'd never see us again.' She paused for a moment and winced. 'Those tablets you gave me ain't done n'ote ter shift this headache.'

'I could call a doctor to see you?'

'No, I'll be all right. I've never had a headache as bad as this, though . . . The tablets will work soon, I s'pose. Anyway, as I lay on your settee waiting for a suitable time ter pass so you'd be asleep, I'd already got the rest of the money from yer hiding place and what was in yer purse. Over forty quid! I ain't never had so much money in all me life. Marty needed lots of things and so did I. We'd never had a holiday. I thought I could tek him to the seaside for a couple of days.

'I had him when I was fifteen. Soon as me mam knew I was pregnant she chucked me out only I wasn't bothered 'cos she'd never been what yer could call a good mother to me. One of her blokes beat me up once and she never did nothing about it. I thought I'd be all right 'cos Marty's dad would look after me and the baby. What a prat I was to think that! We'd been seeing each other since we were fourteen and I thought he loved me but as soon as I told him about the baby he ran off and joined the Merchant Navy. I never heard a word from him again. His family wouldn't have n'ote to do with me neither.

'I ended up in the charity home. Miss Hales delivered Marty. I was relieved he was being adopted 'cos I couldn't care for him, could I? Well, the adoptive parents refused to take him when they saw him 'cos he had red hair and his eyes were a bit wonky. Poor little sod, he weren't the prettiest of babies. They couldn't find no one else willing to tek him so they made me keep him and gave me five quid to help me on my way when it was time for me to leave. Five quid! A lot of money to some but it don't go far when yer got nowhere ter live and a baby to look after. But I'd grown to love Marty by then and I wanted to look after him proper. I tried, really I did.

'When the home chucked me out I managed to get a room in a house with an old lady who liked kids. Most places where I tried to get lodgings people didn't want babies so I was lucky. The house was awful, falling down practically, and it smelt. But it was better than n'ote and the old lady was glad of the bit I paid her. She watched Marty for me while I went to work doing any jobs I could get, cleaning and waitressing, that sorta thing. No money to speak of and to say we scraped through is putting it mildly. I was so hungry once I searched the old lady's dustbin for any food she'd thrown out. I found a carcass of a chicken with a bit of meat left on it. I was sick after scraping it clean and eating it. Marty was fed proper, though, I made sure of that.

'I did approach me mam for help one time but she shut the door in me face. I'd got nobody else to turn to, grans, or aunties or uncles, cousins or anything, 'cos me mam hadn't spoken to 'em for years. She was the sort who argued with everyone and they more than likely got fed up with her and wouldn't have n'ote to do with her. I didn't know where me dad was as he'd left when I was only ten and he never contacted me at all since he walked out.

'Anyway about a year ago I was in British Home Stores. I was stealing a blouse so I could sell it on when I came face to face with Miss Brewster. She remembered me from

427

the home and had seen what I was doing. She told me to put the blouse back, she knew of a better way I could make money if I was interested. 'Course I was. She took me for a coffee and told me about what they were up to. Said if I was game they'd tell me exactly how to act with the women, and any money I got out of them we would split. They said they'd give me at least three names and addresses a week to visit, and when I handed over the money and got me share they'd give me another three for the following week and so on.

'It was easy money really. Yer just changed yer age around to suit the date the woman had her baby and I didn't really see the harm in it. It wasn't like I was telling these women's secrets to their families, was it, and causing trouble that way – although that's what I was told by Miss Brewster to threaten to do as a last resort if they wouldn't pay up for me and Marty to go away.'

She stopped talking again and clapped her hand to her head, giving a groan of pain.

'Are you sure you don't want a doctor?' urged Judith worriedly.

'I'll be all right in a minute.'

'Well, maybe you should have a sleep and we can talk later.'

'No, I wanna tell yer everything. You're nice, you are. Not many people have been nice to me. Hardly any, in fact. Marty thinks the world of yer. He loves yer. I was jealous of his feelings for yer when I fetched him back, I don't mind telling yer. He never stopped talking about yer, asking when he was gonna see yer.'

Paula took another sip of her tea before she resumed

her story. It pained Judith greatly to hear how this girl had struggled to raise her child, doing anything it took.

'The money I earned working for Miss Brewster and Miss Hales didn't amount to that much but it meant me and Marty could move to somewhere better than the room at the old lady's. She was sorry to see us go but I couldn't live there no longer. We'd been there four years as it was and Marty had suffered constantly with colds from the damp. Anyway, I got us a bed-sitter. Weren't much to speak of, we had to sleep on a mattress on the floor but there was an old gas cooker for me to cook on. The paper was coming off the walls and the neighbours were bloody awful. But at least it wasn't damp. I was still finding things a struggle, though, as the thirty bob on average I made working the scam didn't go far when I still had to pay people to watch Marty while I did me other jobs. And the landlord put the bloody rent up five bob a week just after we moved in! Marty was growing fast and always needing clothes and things. I couldn't tek him on holiday, buy him toys, none of the things what other mothers do for their kids. I had no life either 'cos I couldn't afford to go out.

'Then I landed in your house. I'd never been inside such a nice place before. As I lay waiting to leave your flat when I thought you'd be asleep, as well as thinking what I could do with the money I'd got from yer, it hit me that when it had gone I'd probably never get as much again and then we'd be back to struggling. It struck me how much you could give Marty that I couldn't. That night he was sleeping in a warm comfortable bed for the first time in his life. Until he was old enough to earn a wage for himself that might be the last time he did that. I realised you could give him a proper life, all the things he needed, be a proper mam to him. Leaving him with you was the right thing to do, I knew it was. I hurried to get dressed as fast as I could before I changed me mind but I did go in and kiss him before I left, even though he was sound asleep, telling him I was sorry and that I just wanted him to be happy.

'When I left your flat I went to the station and spent the rest of the night in the waiting room, then I caught the first train to Mablethorpe. I had a wonderful three weeks there just enjoying meself. I got drunk, met a couple of lads, just had fun. Don't think I didn't miss Marty 'cos I did, but I knew he was best off where he was. Then me money started running out and I tried to get a job but the season had finished so there was nothing going that I could do. I had no option but to come home, with what money I had left, settle up the rent I owed and get meself a job. The bed-sitter seemed empty without Marty but I convinced meself he was happy and managed to get a job waitressing in a café, but the money was terrible and didn't leave me much over once I'd settled me bills. At least now there was only meself to worry about.

'I was coming home from me shift one afternoon, passing through the market, when I bumped slap-bang into Miss Brewster. 'Course she wanted to know where the hell I'd been 'cos the last I'd seen of her was several Saturdays before when we'd settled up the money and she'd given me three more names and addresses to go to next week, the top name on the list being yours. I quickly spun her a cock and bull, saying that I'd got n'ote out of you 'cos the address she'd given me, you'd moved from and no neighbours knew where you'd gone to. I just prayed she believed me and then I told her that I'd been really sick with the 'flu and hadn't managed to visit the other two on the list she'd given me so I hadn't any money for her.

'I was just so relieved that she believed me, but then she said she hoped I was well enough to start working for her again now. I told her I wasn't going to do it any more. She turned nasty then, said she would tell me when I wasn't working for them. She said I was her best earner 'cos I took Marty with me. The women paid up a bit more to get rid as it was bad enough suddenly having to explain away a daughter that no one knew about, let alone a grandson. Miss Brewster threatened she'd report me to the police on some trumped up charge which'd put me away for years if I didn't do as I was told. She terrified me. I had no choice but to start working for her again.

'That's why I came and got Marty back. I knew it wasn't right of me just to take him off like I did without telling yer but I couldn't face yer, I just couldn't. I watched yer that morning tek him to that lady's and then him going to school with those other kids. I hung around 'til school came out. He was so pleased ter see me but he thought I was just collecting him from school and we were coming back here. I managed to get him on the bus and then I told him that he was coming back to live with me and he'd see you soon. I was hoping he'd forget about yer but he never. All the time he kept asking when he was going to see his gran'ma.'

She paused again, rubbing her head, and Judith noticed how pale she had grown.

'I'm going to call the doctor.'

'No, honest . . .'

'I insist. I can see you're in terrible pain. He can give you something stronger than I have to take your headache away. I shan't be a moment, I need to use the telephone in Mr Banks' flat.'

She popped her head around Marty's bedroom door. He and Nathan were engrossed in playing with a train set Judith had bought as one of his presents. She caught Nathan's attention and silently summoned him over.

'How's it going?' he whispered to her.

'Oh, Nathan, Paula has just told me the most heart-breaking, terrible story but she isn't well from that blow on her head. She's got a terrible headache that the aspirin I gave her hasn't taken away at all. I'm going to call the doctor in to give her something stronger to ease it. Could I use your telephone, please?'

'Oh, Judith, you don't need to ask. What's mine is yours. You have a key to my flat, help yourself. Do you need me for anything?'

'You just keep Marty occupied, darling,' she said, kissing his cheek.

Several minutes later she returned to the lounge and knelt before Paula. 'The doctor is on his way. He only lives around the corner so he should be here any minute. I've left the door on the latch so he can let himself in.'

'Thank you,' she said quietly.

Judith smiled reassuringly at her. 'We'll soon have you right as rain. Listen, Paula, I want to do something for you and Marty. Both Mr Banks and I do. We're moving into a big house and there's plenty of room for you both.

432

Come and live with us, Paula. You can raise Marty with our help. Maybe I could become like a mother to you, if you'd let me?'

Hand cradling the side of her head, she looked at Judith, astounded. 'You would do that for me and Marty? Why? I know you love him, but me . . . well, I've done such terrible things to you.'

'That's all past and forgotten, Paula. I know after hearing your story how hard life has been for you. With my help and Mr Banks' too it would be far easier for you. You and Marty would both be the family we've never had. I've found my true daughter, Paula. You and she could get to know each other as I am doing her. You might even become like sisters in time. Oh, here's the doctor. We'll talk more after he's seen you.'

'Miss Chambers,' Paula called as Judith made to greet the doctor who had just walked in.

She turned back to face her. 'Yes, Paula?'

'Thank you. I'd like to come and live with you. I really would. I know I'd be happy with you, like you've made Marty.'

Her face filled with genuine delight and she smiled warmly at Paula before turning back to address the doctor. 'Dr Franklin, this is Paula Batty. I've called you in as she has had a nasty blow to the side of her head. She has the most terrible headache which the aspirins I've given her an hour ago haven't helped at all. I wondered if you would take a look at her and give her something stronger?'

'Yes, of course I will.'

'I'll leave you to it. Please call me if you need me, I'll be in the kitchen.'

433

Several minutes later the doctor joined her. 'I want to get Miss Batty X-rayed at the hospital. It's just a precaution on my part in respect of the severity of her headache. She may have concussion. Have you a telephone I can use to call an ambulance?'

'Yes, of course.'

She led the doctor into Nathan's flat and while he was dealing with the matter she slipped back and quietly summoned Nathan into the hallway. 'The doctor is sending Paula to hospital just to have her checked over as he thinks she may be concussed.'

The doctor returned. 'The ambulance is on its way and should be here in less than five minutes. I've explained the situation to the staff and she'll be in good hands. I have to go now as I have another patient to see.'

'Thank you, Doctor,' she said, seeing him out.

'Right, I'll go with her,' said Nathan to Judith. 'You stay here and look after Marty. He's starting to complain he's hungry, bless him.'

'Should we tell him about his mother, Nathan?'

'Yes, we should.' He re-entered the bedroom with Judith and gathered Marty to him. 'Your mummy's not feeling too well and she's going to the hospital to be made better. Are you going to kiss her before she goes? Then Grandma is going to stay here with you until I come back with Mummy all better again.'

'I'll kiss her now,' he said. 'Then can I have me dinner, Gran'ma? I'm starving.'

She couldn't help but smile. 'Yes, of course.'

He ran from the room and Judith and Nathan followed him, watching tenderly as he kissed his mother and gave her a hug, telling her his grandma was going to make him dinner while she was away getting better in the hodpiddle.

The ambulance arrived then.

Judith busied herself getting Marty's dinner, then bathing and changing him for bed ready to welcome his mother back home. The joy within her at having him back again was immeasurable, marred only by concern for his mother's health. She prayed though that strong medication would soon put her right. She felt positive that Paula's acceptance of her help was going to work out just fine for them all and then they could live happily together. Judith would work hard to make it a success.

It was approaching eight o'clock when she heard the front door open and close. Judith had just been reading Marty his second story and was wondering how much longer she could keep him up. He was getting really sleepy but she felt that she ought to take a back seat and let his mother put him to bed. She knew it was going to be hard for her to stand back in future but Paula was his mother, she only his adoptive grandmother when all was said and done. Judith wanted to do nothing that would compromise Paula's position with her son.

She lifted Marty off her lap and settled him comfortably on the settee then went into the hallway to greet Nathan and Paula. She was shocked to find only a very grave-looking Nathan, no Paula.

'Oh, they've kept her in overnight for observation, have they?'

His face grew even graver as he placed both hands gently on her arms to look deep into her eyes. When he spoke his voice was low and husky, emotionally charged

435

with the severity of the situation. 'I'm so sorry, my darling, but you need to prepare yourself for the worst.'

This news was so unexpected that Judith was unable to comprehend it. 'The worst? What do you mean, the worst?'

'Paula is very sick. By the time we arrived at the hospital she was unconscious. The blow to the side of her head caused a haemorrhage and they don't know the extent of the damage until they start to operate on her. It's a very delicate procedure; so the surgeon told me. Paula's in theatre now. They . . . well, they don't hold out much hope.'

Eyes wide, mouth gaping, Judith uttered, 'Surely you can't mean . . . ? No, Nathan, please don't tell me Paula might not pull through? Oh, but she's so young with so much to live for. And Marty? He can't lose his mother. I must go to the hospital. She needs me.'

He looked at her in understanding. They both knew what it was like to be alone in the world and, except for her son, Paula had no one to look out for her. He unhooked her coat and helped her on with it. 'Don't worry about Marty, he'll be fine with me. I'll explain to him as gently as I can what's happening. If you need anything, anything at all, telephone and I'll be down straight away.'

She gave him a wan smile. 'Just pray, Nathan, that we can pull Paula through this.'

He declined to comment. He knew it would take more than prayers.

Chapter Thirty-Three

Judith gazed down tenderly at the newborn baby that had been placed in her arms. After a while she raised her head and looked up at the baby's father, a look of pure joy all over her face.

Her grandson, now a handsome young man of thirty, smiled back at her, the deep love he held for her readily apparent. 'So how does it feel to be a great-grandmother?' Marty sat down beside her and laid his hand gently on her arm. 'I don't need you to tell me. I can see by the look on your face.'

'She's as thrilled to be a great-granny as I am to be a granny,' piped up the woman sitting in the chair on the other side of the hospital bed, her own face bathed in rapturous delight. 'Isn't that right, Judy?'

Judith looked across at Marty's mother and suddenly the last time Judith was in this hospital with her, twenty-five years ago, came flooding back. It had been dreadful. Judith, knowing Marty would be safe and well-cared for by Nathan, had refused to move from Paula's bedside while her life hung in the balance. Despite the surgeon giving her little hope that Paula would survive after the operation, Judith had refused to give up. For five solid days with hardly any food or sleep, she had sat by Paula's bed holding her hand, constantly talking to her of the bright future she would have with Marty under her and Nathan's care. She had prayed that her words, so sincerely said, would somehow be heard and give Paula the inner strength to fight for her life. Miraculously, Paula had eventually opened her eyes and given Judith the briefest of smiles.

Though a long period of rehabilitation stretched in front of Paula, the day Nathan, Judith and Marty took her home was a joyous one.

It hadn't all been plain sailing as the four of them had settled into family life together. Marty took it all in his stride. For him, he had his mother, gran'ma and grandpa doting on him. And he was a joy to them all. Paula, though, found it difficult adjusting to the fact for the first time in her life she had parental guidance to cope with, and her rebellious side proved very testing for Judith and Nathan. They were, meanwhile, adjusting to their own newly married life having a family to care for, and getting to know Judith's natural daughter Kimberley.

Paula and Kimberley were such opposites and, in their own way, were trying to be top in Judith's affections. But an unwavering desire on Judith and Nathan's part to make all this work eventually won through. Kimberley became as much a part of their family as any daughter could be without causing a rift between her adoptive parents and herself and, slowly but surely, Paula blossomed into a lovely woman. Encouraged by Nathan and Judith, she enrolled in college, attaining grades she never dreamed she could achieve, and she forged a career as a social worker helping young girls in similar situations to the one she had been in, but without Judith and Nathan to come to their rescue.

Marty, now a strapping six foot, with flaming red hair and trendy spectacles, had gone through university and graduated with honours. He now ran a successful business of his own, initially funded with help from his beloved grandpa.

'Gran'ma. Mum,' he now announced looking at them both proudly. 'We're going to call our son Paul Julian Nathan. It was Tracey's idea.'

The extremely pretty new mother lying in the bed next to them, surrounded by a sea of flowers, smiled brightly. 'It's our way of showing you all how much you mean to us. I'm lucky enough to already have the best parents a girl could wish for but having you all on top now Marty and I are married, well, how lucky can a girl get!'

Paula was too choked to speak.

Judith, wiping a tear from her eye, looked down at the baby again, drinking in his tiny perfect features and the shock of red hair he was sprouting. 'Well, hello, Paul Julian Nathan. You are going to be one spoilt little boy with all these people around you who love you so much.'

'Oh, and here's the proud great-gran'pa,' Marty announced, standing up to greet Nathan with a bear hug.

'What a job I had to park the car. Now, give me that baby,' he ordered Judith, sitting down beside her and lifting his great-grandchild gently out of her arms. He looked up at Marty. 'Your Aunt Kimberley and Uncle Gerald are waiting very impatiently outside, and Aunt

Kimberley has the biggest teddy bear for her great-nephew that I've ever seen. Cherry and Neville are there too, and all of them are champing at the bit to see the new addition to the family.'

'And who can blame them because isn't he just the most beautiful baby you ever saw?' Marty said proudly as he headed off towards the door to bring them in, ignoring the fact that hospital rules only allowed three visitors around the bed at one time.

Paula stood up also. 'I'll go and see if I can rustle up some tea,' she said following her son out.

'We're all going out to wet the baby's head tonight,' Nathan told Judith. 'Neville's booked a table for the seven of us. You and me, Paula, Cherry, Kimberley and Gerald. At the Grand Hotel. He said it's his treat.'

'That's very generous of him,' Judith said sincerely. 'We have such wonderful friends, don't we, darling?'

Cuddling his great-grandson, Nathan looked lovingly at the still attractive, smartly dressed woman sitting beside him. 'Who'd have thought, all those years ago when you first moved into the flat opposite mine, that we'd end up like this? Happily married grandparents. Great-grandparents now.'

Who indeed? she thought. Least of all herself. For a moment her mind flashed back to the time when she had first arrived in the flat. She had just been told so cruelly by her own mother what Winifred truly felt for her daughter, and the awful story of why she harboured such hatred for her. Judith had had no friends to her name, her only skill being her ability to alienate people from her with her own surly manner. She gave a shudder, as if someone had walked over her grave, and for a second feared that the last twenty-five years had just been a dream and she was still that lonely, friendless person.

Then she felt her beloved husband's hand on her arm and mentally shook herself as she smiled into his still handsome face despite the approach of his seventieth year. She had no fear of her old self ever being resurrected. There were far too many people who loved and cared for Judith now for that ever to happen. The woman she had been was gone forever and there was no going back.

Now you can buy any of these other bestselling
books by **Lynda Page** from your bookshop
or *direct from her publisher*.

FREE P&P AND UK DELIVERY
(Overseas and Ireland £3.50 per book)

Out With The Old	£6.99
A Cut Above	£5.99
All Or Nothing	£5.99
In For A Penny	£5.99
Now Or Never	£6.99
Any Old Iron	£6.99
At The Toss Of A Sixpence	£6.99
Just By Chance	£6.99
And One For Luck	£6.99
Peggie	£6.99
Josie	£6.99
Annie	£6.99
Evie	£6.99

TO ORDER SIMPLY CALL THIS NUMBER

01235 400 414

or visit our website: www.madaboutbooks.com

Prices and availability subject to change without notice.